21世纪英语专业系列教材

莎士比亚戏剧欣赏
Appreciating Shakespearean Plays

王磊 编著

北京大学出版社
PEKING UNIVERSITY PRESS

图书在版编目(CIP)数据

莎士比亚戏剧欣赏/王磊编著. —北京：北京大学出版社，2015.8
（21世纪英语专业系列教材）
ISBN 978-7-301-26070-8

Ⅰ.①莎…　Ⅱ.①王…　Ⅲ.①莎士比亚，W.（1564～1616）–戏剧文学–文学欣赏
Ⅳ.①I561.073

中国版本图书馆CIP数据核字（2015）第163039号

书　　名	莎士比亚戏剧欣赏
著作责任者	王　磊　编著
责任编辑	朱丽娜
标准书号	ISBN 978-7-301-26070-8
出版发行	北京大学出版社
地　　址	北京市海淀区成府路205号　100871
网　　址	http://www.pup.cn　　新浪微博：@北京大学出版社
电子信箱	zpup@pup.cn
电　　话	邮购部62752015　发行部62750672　编辑部62754382
印刷者	三河市博文印刷有限公司
经销者	新华书店
	787毫米×1092毫米　16开本　13.25印张　450千字
	2015年8月第1版　2015年8月第1次印刷
定　　价	38.00元

未经许可，不得以任何方式复制或抄袭本书之部分或全部内容。
版权所有，侵权必究
举报电话：010-62752024　电子信箱：fd@pup.pku.edu.cn
图书如有印装质量问题，请与出版部联系，电话：010-62756370

Preface

  2014年——威廉·莎士比亚诞生450周年,世界各地纷纷通过举办"莎士比亚周"、排演或重新诠释莎剧、召开学术研讨会和书友会等丰富多彩的活动,向这位跨越时空和国界的伟大剧作家致敬。以举办热点问题辩论著称的组织 Intelligence Squared 也不甘落后顺势推出了 Shakespeare vs Milton: The Kings of English Literature Debate 辩论。① 中国北京的国家大剧院也隆重推出长达数月的"致敬!莎士比亚"系列演出,不同国家、不同语言、不同表现形式的几台大戏竞相登场,展现了莎士比亚戏剧的独特魅力。

  莎士比亚这个名字可谓妇孺皆知,其人其事都已成为人们经久不息的谈论话题。英语中有句谚语: Many talk of Robin Hood who never shot with his bow, 翻译成汉语大致为:人人侈谈罗宾汉,几人试过其弯弓? 同样,又有多少人曾读过莎翁的原作,并体会到其爬罗剔抉的戏剧构思、精妙绝伦的语言魅力以及鞭辟入里的人生哲思呢? 毕竟,莎士比亚的那个时代离我们已很遥远,讲述的方式也因语言和文化的变迁显得晦涩难懂。然而,你可曾知道这样一些事实:众多莎剧仍在世界各地上演,且被反复地改编成电影、电视剧;人们在英语中仍大量地使用着莎翁所创造的语汇,尽管自己浑然不知;无处不在、无时不有的媒体、广告也在时不时地"糟蹋"(murder)着大文豪的名言警句,如 Two beer or not two beer 之类。作为英语学习者和使用者、立志做世界人的我们是否应该进一步了解莎士比亚,并原汁原味地阅读他的一些作品呢?

  莎士比亚于1564年4月26日出生于英国南部的一个小镇 —— 埃文河畔的斯特拉特福(Stratford-upon-Avon)。他的童年是在镇上的文法学校(grammar school)度过的。18岁时,他与大自己八岁的安妮·哈瑟维(Anne Hathway)②结为夫妻,可谓奉子成婚(shotgun marriage)的先行者。在生下两男一女之后,莎士比亚的人生中出现了长达十年(1585—1592)的空白期("lost years"),其行踪令坊间莎翁学者颇费周章。其中一种推测认为莎士比亚为躲避因偷猎当地乡绅 Thomas Lucy 庄园的鹿而可能招致的牢狱之灾逃往伦敦,从此开始了演艺和戏剧创作生涯,至1592年已成为令人瞩目的剧作家。③ 他一生创作了大量的作品,包括

---

 ① http://www.intelligencesquared.com/events/shakespeare-vs-milton.
 ② 英国文人兼音乐家 Charles Dibdin (1748—1814)巧用姓氏写就的诗歌对这桩当时罕见的姐弟婚恋做出了比较合理的解释:But were it to my fancy given/To rate her charms, I'd call them heaven;/For though a mortal made of clay,/Angels must love Anne Hathaway;//She hath a way so to control,/To rapture the imprisoned soul,/And sweetest heaven on earth display,/That to be heaven Anne hath a way;//She hath a way,/Anne Hathaway, - /To be heaven's self Anne hath a way.
 ③ 同城对手 Robert Greene (1558 — 1592)在其忏悔录 Groats-Worth of Wit 中对声誉日隆的莎士比亚的攻讦成了无心之佐证:… there is an upstart Crow, beautified with our feathers, that with his Tigers heart wrapped in a Players hide, supposes he is as well able to bombast out a blank verse as the best of you: and being an absolute *Johannes factotum*, is in his own conceit the only Shake-scene in a country.

37个剧本、6首长诗、154首十四行诗（sonnets）。莎士比亚的戏剧创作大致可以分为三个时期。1594年之前为第一时期。其间的作品多为喜剧，如《错误的喜剧》《驯悍记》《爱的徒劳》等，另外还有几部历史剧，如《亨利六世》《理查三世》等。喜剧多以有情人历经磨难终成眷属为主题。历史剧则着力刻画你死我活的权利斗争中人物的性格。17世纪最初几年为莎士比亚第二个创作时期，也即他的艺术生涯的巅峰期。在这一时期，他写出了最著名的四大悲剧《哈姆雷特》《奥赛罗》《李尔王》和《麦克白》。这些悲剧都以细致的笔触剖析了人性弱点是如何导致了戏剧人物的毁灭，可谓研究人类心理学的百科全书，也是引用率极高的剧本，其中尤以《哈姆雷特》为最。1608年之后为莎士比亚最后的创作时期，作品多为实验性质，融合了喜剧、悲剧等多种元素，被后人称为"传奇剧"（the romances），如《辛白林》《冬天的故事》《暴风雨》等。这些"传奇剧"与莎翁早期的戏剧有所不同，戏剧冲突都是通过悔罪、宽恕来解决的，弥漫着浓重的宗教色彩。1610年左右，如《暴风雨》中普洛斯彼罗所暗示的那样①，莎士比亚告别了伦敦的舞台回归故乡小镇，与妻儿老小过起了恬静的乡村生活。1616年4月26日（一说4月23日），这位"不属于某个时期，而属于所有时代"（He was not of an age, but for all time. — Ben Jonson：1572—1637）的大文豪在家人的关爱中安然辞世，身后留下颇具争议的馈赠妻子"次好卧榻"（second best bed）的遗嘱以及令盗墓毛贼望而却步的墓志铭。②

莎士比亚离世至今已逾400年。其间，各种阴谋论（conspiracy theory）甚嚣尘上，认为就其平庸的教育背景、文学修养和有限的人生阅历而言，莎士比亚是创作不出如此朗朗上口的散文和诗歌，多样而丰满的人物以及引人入胜的情节的，更加够格的应另有其人，如哲学家兼散文家弗朗西斯·培根、剧作家克里斯托弗·马洛、笃爱戏剧创作的贵族爱德华·德·维③等，或者那些旷世之作的作者并非一个人。更有甚者，有些人（甚至包括世界文坛巨擘）对莎士比亚所享受的尊荣不以为然，认为他是个"被英人包装成神牛似圣物的浮夸、自大的大家伙"（亨利·米勒），其作品"每六行就有一处败笔"（塞缪尔·约翰逊）、"虽被世人奉为天才之作，但我从中得不到愉悦，反而心生厌恶之感"（列夫·托尔斯泰）。④尽管如此，莎士比亚作为西方经典核心的地位业已确立，⑤那些伟大的作品便是其高贵遗骨的纪念碑。⑥

---

① … I'll break my staff,/Bury it certain fathoms in the earth,/And deeper than did ever plummet sound/I'll drown my book. (*The Tempest*, 5.1:59—62. 注：本书引用莎剧原文所使用的行数标记均依 *The RSC Shakespeare*: *William Shakespeare Complete Works*, 2007。)

② Good friend for Jesus sake forbear/To dig the dust enclosed here!/Blest be the man that spares these stones,/And curst be he that moves my bones.

③ 于2011年公映的德英两国合拍的 *Anonymous* 便是以该牛津伯爵为原型、颠覆莎翁形象的历史题材政治惊悚电影。

④ Esptein, 1990：250—251.

⑤ Bloom, 1994：45—75.

⑥ 参见约翰·弥尔顿的诗作"论莎士比亚"（On Shakespeare. 1630）：What needs my Shakespeare for his honour'd Bones,/The labour of an age in piled Stones,/Or that his hallow'd reliques should be hid/Under a Star-pointing Pyramid? /Dear son of memory, great heir of Fame,/What need'st thou such weak witnes of thy name? /Thou in our wonder and astonishment/Hast built thy self a live-long Monument./For whilst to th' shame of slow-endeavouring art,/Thy easie numbers flow, and that each heart/Hath from the leaves of thy unvalu'd Book,/Those Delphick lines with deep impression took,/Then thou our fancy of it self bereaving,/Dost make us Marble with too much conceaving;/And so Sepulcher'd in such pomp dost lie,/That Kings for such a Tomb would wish to die.

现代读者初次接触莎翁的剧作自然有佶屈聱牙之感,因为莎士比亚时代的英语正处在变动不居的状态中,其文法、词汇乃至拼写均与当今英语有很大的不同。再加上莎士比亚自己的创造性的恣意运用,词汇的原有之意也悄然发生了奇特的变化。了解这些可大大有助于莎剧的理解和欣赏。首先,同现代英语的 S(主) V(谓) O(宾) 语序不同,莎士比亚多采用 SOV、甚至完全倒装的语序,它反映了英语所受到的日耳曼语言语序以及意大利和法语押韵诗歌的影响。同时,莎士比亚通过倒装语序的运用可灵活处理韵律重音,使得语句间的过渡更为自然、顺畅;在韵律诗中使用异于口语中 SVO 语序的倒装语序可使主语得到突显,从而增加语言的诗歌韵味。实际上,莎士比亚戏剧作品约有四分之三的篇幅使用的是诗歌或韵律体裁,也即所谓的"五步抑扬格"(iambic pentametre)。该体裁的诗行多由含有十个音节单词,即五对轻重读交替出现的音步组成。由于"五步抑扬格"比较接近人们正常说话的节奏,可以表现说话者悠然自得、从容不迫的态度,如:Care **keeps** his **watch** in e**very** old **man's eye**,/And **where** care **lod**ges, **sleep** will **ne**ver **lie**. (*Romeo and Juliet*, 2.2.36-37)①。它也用来突显紧张、躁动的心绪,如:To**mor**row, and to**mor**row, and to**mor**row,/Creeps **in** this **pet**ty **pace** from **day** to **day** …(*Macbeth*, 5.5.19-20)"五步抑扬格"不仅能够反映戏剧人物的性情和心态的变化,它还常常通过与无韵散文的交替使用体现戏剧人物不同的社会地位以及场景的切换。比如,《亨利五世》中的哈里王子随着活动场所在王宫和依斯特溪泊野猪头酒店之间的转换及交往对象的改变,他也便在两种语体之间进行着自如的"语码转换",折射出该王子八面玲珑的性格特点。

本·琼生谓莎士比亚"拉丁语稀松、希腊语更是了了"("small Latin and less Greek")②,一方面证实了诗人所受的相当初级的教育,但另一方面也佐证了荷马(Homer)、奥维德(Ovid)、维吉尔(Virgil)、塞内加(Seneca)、普鲁塔克(Plutarch)③等希腊、罗马作家的神话故事对莎翁剧作的影响;而其中影响最巨者当属奥维德的神话。但莎士比亚在运用源自这些作家作品的典故时是有分别的:在需用优雅词藻来描写美妙意象时多使用神话典故,而在对人生的种种不解之谜苦思冥想时则用的很少。④ 例如,《仲夏夜之梦》戏中戏为出自奥维德的《变形记》中"皮拉摩斯与提斯柏"(Pyramus and Thisbe)的神话故事,大大渲染了该剧的喜剧色彩。又如,尽管《威尼斯商人》神话典故俯拾皆是,但在第四幕那场肃穆、紧张的法庭较量戏中却难觅踪影。对莎士比亚戏剧创作产生巨大影响还有英文《圣经》。据统计,他在剧中共引用和提及了《圣经》中的 42 卷。⑤ 不管莎翁的《圣经》知识是经由日常生活中的耳濡目染轻易获得而显得只鳞片爪,还是通过苦心研读修炼而成令人啧啧称奇,他对该典籍的利用大大丰富了戏剧语言,也使人物更为丰满、多样。鉴于以上两者对莎翁戏剧的影响,读者也应有希腊罗马神话及《圣经》方面的知识储备,以更好地读懂和鉴赏这些作品。

英语文学爱好者大多怀揣着赏读莎士比亚戏剧原作的宏愿,但面对陌生的五步抑扬格

---

① 本书莎剧原文引用标号(幕. 场. 行)均根据 Bate, J., etc. (eds.) (2008). *William Shakespeare Couplete Works*. Beijing: Foreign Lauguage Teaching and Research Press.
② "To the memory of my beloved, The AUTHOR Mr. WILLIAM SHAKESPEARE, and what he hath left us",1623.
③ 这些作家对莎士比亚戏剧创作产生影响的作品包括:《荷马史诗》、奥维德的《变形记》(*Metamorphesis*)、维吉尔的《埃涅阿斯纪》(*Aeneid*)、塞内加的悲剧、普鲁塔克的《希腊罗马名人传》(the *Lives of the Noble Greeks and Romans*)。
④ Root, 1965:8.
⑤ Noble, 1935:20.

韵律,暗设机巧的一语双关,与现代英语迥异的文法等障碍时常常望而却步,即便踌躇满志一心向读,但也多半途而废、掩卷叹息。故阅读莎剧应循序渐进,幻想着一日、一月或一年便可轻松赏读都是不现实的。笔者认为对莎剧先行做一概览,了解各个剧情,并对其中最为精粹片段进行研读,不失为一项很好的入门功课。然后,随着对莎剧了解的逐渐加深,阅读信心的不断增强,便可选择自己最感兴趣者细细把玩体味直至卒读。这样,再拿起第二部、第三部剧本时便有举一反三、茅塞顿开之感。另外,在阅读莎剧原文时,了解莎剧特征和与主题相关的背景知识,并结合莎剧题材的艺术、音乐和影视、广播剧等直观素材,可对莎剧有立体和深刻的理解和欣赏。与此同时,了解莎剧在英语文学和现代英语中的灵活运用可大大地提高我们的鉴赏水平和文化敏感度。

以上便是编写《莎剧欣赏》的出发点和目标。本书围绕莎士比亚戏剧中最具代表性的17个剧作,设计 I. Introduction(导读:介绍剧作的背景、主题及相关的话题)、II. Plot Summary(剧情梗概:以流畅的现代英语并适当嵌入剧中精彩语句介绍剧作的主要情节)、III. Selected Readings(剧作选读:提供剧中最著名的选段或完整场景,并结合详细的注解和理解思考问题,帮助读者体味莎剧的魅力)、IV. Shakespearean Relevance(莎剧关联:设计"日常英语中的莎剧""文学中的莎剧""音乐、艺术和银幕中的莎剧"三个栏目,帮助读者了解莎剧的影响)、V. Shakespeare Quotes(莎剧名言:选取剧作中妙语和警句以供赏读和引用)。本教材还配有与莎剧相关的艺术作品图片以直观呈现莎剧情节并提高审美志趣。每章还设计了一个剧作相关知识的 Beyond the Play(莎剧之外)链接。为了帮助读者更好地了解和阅读莎剧,书后还编辑了附录 A Partial List of Phrases and Sayings Attributed to William Shakespeare(莎士比亚所创造的部分英语词汇、警句及例释)。

本书行将付梓之际,追忆、怀旧情绪不免涌上心头。上个世纪八十年代末,作者的岳丈李国云先生从羞涩的工资中挤出可观的款项为我购置了一套人民文学出版社1978年版、朱生豪主译的《莎士比亚全集》,从此为我打开了一扇通向五彩斑斓的莎翁世界的大门。该版本我珍藏至今,成为与原著比照阅读的案头书。在不时地惊叹于莎翁的天才创作和朱生豪的精妙译笔的同时,我也常常感念于父辈对后生的殷殷期待。嗣后,随着人生际遇的不断变化,我经历了上个世纪九十年代在九省通衢武汉的华中师范大学英语专业课上与学生们品味莎剧片段,本世纪元年在即将完成研究生学业之际于申城勾勒出该书的雏形,以及五年前在上海外国语大学英语学院人文教育春风的吹拂下开设了同名课程,再到如今承蒙享誉海内外的北京大学出版社的提携而出版该书。可以说,正是那些写尽世间百态、洞察人生堂奥的莎翁戏剧才让我能在纷纷扰扰的喧嚣中保持一份平静和执着。衷心希望读者也能经由此书体味到赏读莎剧的乐趣并有所启迪。囿于学识,书中舛误颇多,故恳请不吝赐教,以便适时更正。

王磊

上海外国语大学英语学院

2014年12月

Table of Contents

Comedies 喜剧
1. A Midsummer Night's Dream 仲夏夜之梦 / **1**
2. The Merchant of Venice 威尼斯商人 / **9**
3. As You Like It 皆大欢喜 / **19**
4. The Taming of the Shrew 驯悍记 / **28**
5. Twelfth Night, or "What You Will" 第十二夜（又名：各遂所愿）/ **38**
6. The Tempest 暴风雨 / **47**

Histories 历史剧
7. Henry Ⅳ, Part 1 亨利四世·上篇 / **58**
8. Henry Ⅳ, Part 2 亨利四世·下篇 / **67**
9. Henry Ⅴ 亨利五世 / **74**
10. Richard Ⅲ 理查三世 / **84**

Tragedies 悲剧
11. The Tragedy of Romeo and Juliet 罗密欧与朱丽叶 / **94**
12. The Tragedy of Julius Caesar 裘力斯·凯撒 / **103**
13. The Tragedy of Macbeth 麦克白 / **115**
14. The Tragedy of Hamlet, Prince of Denmark 哈姆雷特 / **126**
15. The Tragedy of King Lear 李尔王 / **137**
16. The Tragedy of Othello, the Moor of Venice 奥赛罗 / **146**
17. The Tragedy of Antony and Cleopatra 安东尼与克莉奥佩特拉 / **159**

Bibliography / **169**

Appendices
A List of Works of William Shakespeare / **170**
A List of Works of Art and *Beyond the Play* Topics in this Book / **172**
A Partial List of Phrases and Sayings Attributed to William Shakespeare / **175**

Comedies 喜剧

1. A Midsummer Night's Dream
仲夏夜之梦

I INTRODUCTION

在希腊神话英雄 Theseus 公爵治下的雅典城,各色人等出于各自的原因于仲夏之夜齐聚郊外森林,他们有追求婚姻自由的贵族千金小姐 Hermia 和青年 Lysander,痴情不移的 Helena 和移情别恋的 Demetrius,为公爵大婚赶排节目的粗鲁手艺人(rude mechanicals)。此时的森林为仙王 Oberon 和仙后 Titania 及其他仙人和精灵出没之地。于是便上演了一出城市与森林、上流与下层、黑夜、现实与梦幻、俗语与雅言盘根错节、交相呼应的喜剧。复杂的恋爱关系、仙王仙后的争强好胜、令人捧腹的戏中戏以及诗歌语言和抒情告白使得该剧成为最受欢迎的莎剧之一。由刚刚辞世的美国巨星罗宾·威廉姆斯主演的励志电影《死亡诗社》(*Dead Poets Society*, 1989)中预科生 Neil 不顾父母的反对坚持参演该剧便是其明证。它更是文人雅士乐于赏读的案头之作,无怪乎被英国著名莎剧学者 William Hazlitt (1778—1830) 称为适合阅读的"书斋剧"(closet drama)。在原作选读部分,第一个选段为 Helena 对负心郎 Demetrius 的抱怨,其中冰雹的比喻生动有趣;第二个选段是以上那对欢喜冤家的对话,奥维德《变形记》中"阿波罗和达芙妮"故事的引用表达两性在追求爱情方面的不平等,对当下的婚恋仍具现实意义;在第三个选段中,公爵夫妇对疯子、情人和诗人纷乱的思想和幻觉进行了一番有趣的探讨。

II PLOT SUMMARY

In a mythical Athens, **Theseus**,[1] the reigning Duke, has conquered **the Amazons**[2] and fallen in love with their beautiful queen, **Hippolyta**.[3] As the play opens, he observes to the Amazon queen that "I wooed thee **with my sword**,[4]/And won thy love doing thee **injuries**"[5] (1.1.17-18) and proclaims that their wedding is to take place in five days.

At this point, **Egeus**,[6] a wealthy Athenian, brings his daughter **Hermia**[7] before the Duke. Having fallen in love with **Lysander**,[8] a young man of whom her father disapproves, Hermia has refused to marry **Demetrius**,[9] who is her father's choice. Demetrius had been in love with Hermia's friend, **Helena**,[10] but had abandoned her for Hermia.

Angered by Hermia's disobedience to his will, Egeus demands judgment on his daughter.

---

1 **Theseus** (/ˈθiːsiəs, ˈθisjuːs/ 忒修斯), a mythical character noted for his six labours accomplished during his land journey as well as the slaughter of Minotaur in the Cretan labyrinth and conquest over the Amazons 2 **the Amazons** A race of female warriors in Greek mythology 3 **Hippolyta** /hɪˈpɒlɪtə/ 希波吕忒 4 **with my sword** Hippolyta was captured during Theseus' campaign against the Amazons 5 **injuries** wrongs 6 **Egeus** /iˈdʒiəs/ 伊吉斯 7 **Hermia** /ˈhɜːmjə/ 赫米娅 8 **Lysander** /laɪˈsændə/ 拉山德 9 **Demetrius** /dɪˈmiːtrɪəs/ 狄米特律斯 10 **Helena** /ˈhelɪnə/ 海丽娜

Regretfully, the Duke tells Hermia that according to Athenian law, she must yield to her father's choice by marrying Demetrius. Otherwise, she will have to "Either to **die the death**[11] or to **abjure**/[12] Forever the **society**[13] of men" (1.1.67-68) by living a life of chastity as a virgin priestess. She has until the Duke's wedding day to decide.

After the others leave, Hermia and Lysander stay behind to fret about their predicament. Lysander reassures Hermia that "The course of true love never did run smooth" (1.1.136) and both determine to meet in a wood near the city the following night. Then they plan to leave the city and go to a place where the harsh Athenian law cannot pursue them. Helena promises to help the lovers, and they leave. When Demetrius returns, Helena, who is hopelessly in love with him, tries to win his favor by telling him of Hermia's plan to elope. She is bitterly disappointed when Demetrius hurries away to stop the elopement, but she follows him.

The Quarrel of Oberon and Titania, 1850, Joseph Noel Paton

In another part of Athens, a group of common laboring men, led by Peter Quince, a carpenter, are preparing a play to be given at the wedding feast of Theseus and Hippolyta. The "star" of the group, Nick Bottom, a weaver, struts and boasts of his ability to play any and all parts and is finally cast as the hero in a "most lamentable comedy and most cruel death of **Pyramus and Thisby**."[14] All the parts are assigned and the rehearsal is set to take place the next night in the wood outside of Athens—the same wood in which Hermia and Lysander are to meet.

The night in question is Midsummer's Eve, a time of great rejoicing and mischief among the fairies who live in the wood. **Oberon**,[15] their King, and **Titania**,[16] their Queen, have quarreled over possession of "A lovely boy, stolen from an Indian king;/She never had so sweet a **changeling**."[17] (2.1.22-23) To resolve the quarrel, humble his proud Queen, and gain the boy for his own group of followers, Oberon enlists the aid of Puck (Robin Goodfellow) to use a herb on the Queen and "The juice of it on sleeping eyelids laid/Will make or man or woman madly dote/Upon the next live creature that it sees." (2.1.173-175) But when Oberon orders him to sprinkle "love juice" in the eyes of an Athenian man, he mistakes Lysander for Demetrius, the intended recipient. As a result, Lysander, once passionate about Hermia, is now deeply in love with Helena, retorting that "Who will not change a raven for a dove?/The **will**[18] of man is by his reason swayed,/And reason says you are the worthier maid." (2.2.114-116) Into this confusion come Bottom and his amateurish acting troupe. Puck turns Bottom's head into the head of an ass, and at the first sight of the "translated" Bottom, all his friends run away. Bottom then comes upon Titania, the Queen of the Fairies, and awakens her from her sleep. Her eyes, like those of Lysander, have been anointed with the magic nectar, and she falls in love with the first creature she sees—the ass-headed Bottom, tickling him with "Thou art as wise as thou art beautiful." (3.1.108)

---

11 **die the death** be executed   12 **abjure** /əbˈdʒuə/ renounce upon oath   13 **society** company   14 **Pyramus and Thisby** (/ˈpirəməs/皮拉摩斯, /ˈθizbi/ 提斯柏), a story told by Ovid in his *Metamorphoses* (变形记). Pyramus and Thisby are next-door neighbours in Babylon who are in love with each other but whose parents forbid them to marry. They are able to talk to each other through a hole in the wall that divides their houses. Eventually they arrange to meet outside the city. Thisby, arriving first, sees a lion fresh from the kill and flees, dropping her cloak. When Pyramus arrives and sees the cloak, now blood-stained by the lion, he assumes that Thisby has been killed by the lion and stabs himself to death. Thisby returns as he is dying and also kills herself.   15 **Oberon** /ˈəubərən/ 奥布朗   16 **Titania** /taiˈteiniə/ 提泰妮娅   17 **changeling** child taken by the fairies (usually exchanged for a fairy child)   18 **will** inclination (plays on the sense of 'sexual desire/penis')

Titania and Bottom,
1793—1794, Johann Heinrich Füssli

Puck reports to Oberon on Titania's new lover and that a group of "rude mechanicals" are rehearsing in the wood. After all the pranks, Oberon now relents and has Puck set things right again. Lysander and Hermia are reunited, and Demetrius, with the aid of the magic juice, rediscovers his love for Helena. Titania and Bottom are released from their enchantments, and she agrees to give Oberon the little boy about whom they had quarrelled. Unsure whether what occurred was fact or nightmare, the lovers come upon the Duke and his party hunting in the woods that morning. After hearing their stories, he proclaims that to his wedding will be added those of the four young lovers. Bottom awakens, is confused, but returns to Athens and, with his friends, prepares to give their play at the Duke's wedding.

The last scene begins with Theseus and Hippolyta marveling at the story of the lovers and conclude that "The lunatic, the lover and the poet/Are of imagination all compact." (5.1.7-8) After the triple wedding, the play, "Pyramus and Thisby," is presented as part of the entertainment. It is performed so earnestly and so badly that the assembled guests are weak from laughter. After the performance, the newlyweds adjourn to bed, and the fairies appear to confer a final blessing on the happy couples.

Beyond the Play: *Mendelssohn's "Wedding March"*

A Midsummer Night's Dream has inspired many literary, movie, musical as well as dramatic works. Among the German Romantic composer Felix Mendelssohn's best-known works, the overture and incidental music for *A Midsummer Night's Dream*, especially the Wedding March from the latter, remain popular at marriage ceremonies, and together with many other musical compositions, have contributed to the play's reputation for inspiring leading composers.

III SELECTED READINGS

Act I, scene 1

    HELENA How happy some o'er other some can be!
230   Through Athens I am thought as fair as she.
    But what of that? Demetrius thinks not so:
    He will not know what all but he doth know.
    And as he errs, doting on Hermia's eyes.
    So I, admiring of his qualities.
235   Things base and vile, folding no quantity,

1.1 229 **other some** some others 230 **Through** Throughout 232 **all** everyone else 235 **quantity** value/substance/proportion

        Love can transpose to form and dignity.
        Love looks not with the eyes, but with the mind,
        And therefore is winged Cupid painted blind.
        Nor hath Love's mind of any judgement taste,
240   Wings and no eyes figure unheedy haste.
        And therefore is Love said to be a child,
        Because in choice he is so oft beguiled.
        As waggish boys in game themselves forswear,
        So the boy Love is perjured every where.
245   For ere Demetrius look'd on Hermia's eyne,
        He hail'd down oaths that he was only mine.
        And when this hail some heat from Hermia felt,
        So he dissolved, and showers of oaths did melt.
        I will go tell him of fair Hermia's flight:
250   Then to the wood will he to-morrow night
        Pursue her; and for this intelligence
        If I have thanks, it is a dear expense.
        But herein mean I to enrich my pain,
        To have his sight thither and back again.

Act II, scene 1

Enter DEMETRIUS, HELENA, following him
DEMETRIUS I love thee not, therefore pursue me not.
        Where is Lysander and fair Hermia?
        The one I'll slay, the other slayeth me.
195   Thou told'st me they were stolen unto this wood;
        And here am I, and wood within this wood,
        Because I cannot meet my Hermia.
        Hence, get thee gone, and follow me no more.
    HELENA You draw me, you hard-hearted adamant;
200   But yet you draw not iron, for my heart
        Is true as steel: leave you your power to draw,
        And I shall have no power to follow you.
    DEMETRIUS Do I entice you? Do I speak you fair?
        Or, rather, do I not in plainest truth
205   Tell you, I do not, nor I cannot love you?
    HELENA And even for that do I love you the more.
        I am your spaniel; and, Demetrius,
        The more you beat me, I will fawn on you.
        Use me but as your spaniel, spurn me, strike me,
210   Neglect me, lose me; only give me leave,
        Unworthy as I am, to follow you.

---

236 **form** ordered, attractive appearance/substance   238 **blind** Cupid was often depicted as a blindfolded child   239 **of ... taste** the least bit of reason   240 **figure** symbolize   242 **beguiled** deceived, misguided   243 **waggish** playful, mischievous **game** jest/play **themselves forswear** break their word   245 **eyne** eyes   251 **intelligence** information   252 **dear expense** effort worth making 2.1 195 **were stolen** stole 196 **wood** angry/mad (puns on 'wooed') 199 **draw** attract (magnetically) **adamant** hard magnetic substance 201 **leave you** give up 203 **you fair** favourably, kindly to you 205 **nor I cannot** nor I can 209 **but** only 210 **leave** permission

What worser place can I beg in your love—
And yet a place of high respect with me—
Than to be used as you use your dog?
215 DEMETRIUS Tempt not too much the hatred of my spirit,
For I am sick when I do look on thee.
HELENA And I am sick when I look not on you.
DEMETRIUS You do impeach your modesty too much,
To leave the city and commit yourself
220 Into the hands of one that loves you not,
To trust the opportunity of night
And the ill counsel of a desert place
With the rich worth of your virginity.
HELENA Your virtue is my privilege: for that
225 It is not night when I do see your face,
Therefore I think I am not in the night.
Nor doth this wood lack worlds of company,
For you in my respect are all the world.
Then how can it be said I am alone,
230 When all the world is here to look on me?
DEMETRIUS I'll run from thee and hide me in the brakes,
And leave thee to the mercy of wild beasts.
HELENA The wildest hath not such a heart as you.
Run when you will, the story shall be changed:
235 Apollo flies, and Daphne holds the chase;
The dove pursues the griffin, the mild hind
Makes speed to catch the tiger. Bootless speed,
When cowardice pursues and valour flies.
DEMETRIUS I will not stay thy questions, let me go;
240 Or, if thou follow me, do not believe
But I shall do thee mischief in the wood.
HELENA Ay, in the temple, in the town, the field,
You do me mischief. Fie, Demetrius!
Your wrongs do set a scandal on my sex:
245 We cannot fight for love, as men may do;
We should be wooed and were not made to woo.
Exit DEMETRIUS
I'll follow thee and make a heaven of hell,
To die upon the hand I love so well. *Exit*

Act V, scene 1

Enter THESEUS, HIPPOLYTA, PHILOSTRATE, Lords and Attendants
HIPPOLYTA
'Tis strange my Theseus, that these lovers speak of.

---

218 **impeach** discredit 222 **desert** desolate, isolated 224 **privilege** safeguard **for that** because 231 **brakes** bushes 235 **Apollo ... chase** a reversal of the myth in which Daphne, being chased by Apollo, was spared violation by being turned into a laurel tree 236 **griffin** mythical beast, part lion part eagle **hind** female deer 237 **bootless** pointless 239 **stay** wait for 244 **set ... sex** make me behave in a way that disgraces womankind 248 **upon** by/at 5.1 1 **that** that which

> **THESEUS** More strange than true. I never may believe
> These antic fables, nor these fairy toys.
> Lovers and madmen have such seething brains,
> 5 Such shaping fantasies, that apprehend
> More than cool reason ever comprehends.
> The lunatic, the lover and the poet
> Are of imagination all compact.
> One sees more devils than vast hell can hold;
> 10 That is, the madman: the lover, all as frantic,
> Sees Helen's beauty in a brow of Egypt.
> The poet's eye, in fine frenzy rolling,
> Doth glance from heaven to earth, from earth to heaven,
> And as imagination bodies forth
> 15 The forms of things unknown, the poet's pen
> Turns them to shapes and gives to airy nothing
> A local habitation and a name.
> Such tricks hath strong imagination,
> That if it would but apprehend some joy,
> 20 It comprehends some bringer of that joy.
> Or in the night, imagining some fear,
> How easy is a bush supposed a bear!
> **HIPPOLYTA** But all the story of the night told over,
> And all their minds transfigured so together,
> 25 More witnesseth than fancy's images
> And grows to something of great constancy;
> But, howsoever, strange and admirable.

Questions for Comprehension and Reflection

Act I, scene 1
1. What is the property of love?
2. Why is Cupid normally painted blind?
3. What is the metaphor used to show Demetrius' fickleness?

Act II, scene 1
1. What does Helena say about her role in her relation to Demetrius?
2. What message does Helena want to convey with the changed story of Apollo and Daphne?
3. How does Helena comment on men and women where love is concerned?

Act V, scene 1
1. What does "see[ing] Helen's beauty in a brow of Egypt" show about a lover?
2. What can a poet do with things unknown?
3. How can you understand lines 19-20?

---

3 **antic** bizarre/grotesque, with pun on 'antique' **fairy toys** foolish stories about fairies 5 **shaping** creative **apprehend** grasp (intellectually) 8 **compact** composed 10 **frantic** mad, frenzied 11 **Helen's** Helen of Troy's **brow of Egypt** dark-skinned complexion (thought unattractive) 14 **bodies forth** gives shape to 19 **apprehend** conceive 20 **comprehends** incorporates 24 **transfigured** changed, affected 25 **More witnesseth** more certain testimony 26 **constancy** consistency, truth 27 **admirable** wondrous, extraordinary

IV. SHAKESPEAREAN RELEVANCE

A. Shakespeare in Everyday English
Please try to understand the following Shakespearean words and expressions in the contexts designated within parentheses and give their generally used meanings in the space provided.
1. fancy-free (2.1.167): _____
2. bootless speed (2.1.237): _____
3. more strange than true (5.1.2): _____

B. Shakespeare in Literature
Read the following literary excerpts, locate the Shakespearean allusions and explain their meanings according to the contexts where they appear.
1. She couldn't tell if he was smiling, or if his face always wore that puckish grin. (Doug Beason and Kevin J. Anderson, *Assemblers of Infinity*, 1993)
2. She lay curled up on the sofa in the back drawing-room in Harley Street, looking very lovely in her white muslin and blue ribbons. If Titania had ever been dressed in white muslin and blue ribbons, and had fallen asleep on a crimson damask sofa in a back drawing-room, Edith might have been taken for her. (Elizabeth Gaskell, *North and South*, 1854-1855)
3. Why Pia's brother had volunteered Jono was never clear; Jono had done so because he loved Charles and could not let him go alone. In the end they were parted early on, sent off to different regiments. Charles had fallen distressingly in love with Diana whom he met on his last leave before his departure for France in 1915. She had kissed him and given him a photograph which he carried until his death four weeks later. Jono, too, had kissed her, chastely, as Pyramus had kissed the Wall, which she still represented for him, dividing him from and uniting him with the golden Charles who had ridden off to war like one of Edith's troubadours, carrying Diana's favour in his breast. (Elizabeth Ironside, *Death in the Garden*, 1995)

C. Shakespeare in Music, Art and on Screen
1692: *The Fairy-Queen*, a semi-operatic by Henry Purcell.
1826, 1842: overture and incidental suite for the play by Felix Mendelssohn.
1960: *A Midsummer Night's Dream*, an operatic adaptation with music by Benjamin Britten.
1968: *A Midsummer Night's Dream*, a film version directed by Peter Hall with a cast of the Royal Shakespeare Company including such big names as Ian Richardson (King Oberon) and Judi Dench (Queen Titania).
1977: *A Midsummer Night's Dream*, a ballet by John Neumeier.
1982: *A Midsummer Night's Sex Comedy*, a film written and directed by Woody Allen.
1989: *Dead Poets Society*, a film directed by Peter Weir and starring Robin Williams, in which Neil Perry, a senior student of an elite prep school, tries and wins the role of Puck in a school play of *A Midsummer Night's Dream* despite his father's opposition.
2005: *ShakespeaRe-Told*, the BBC TV series which presented an adaptation of the play.

V SHAKESPEARE QUOTES

The course of true love never did run smooth. (1.1.136)
Love looks not with the eyes, but with the mind,
And therefore is winged Cupid painted blind. (1.1.237-238)
And yet, to say the truth, reason
and love keep little company together nowadays. (3.1.104-105)
Lord, what fools these mortals be! (3.2.115)
And sleep, that sometime shuts up sorrow's eye,
Steal me awhile from mine own company. (3.2.451-452)
The lunatic, the lover, and the poet, are of imagination all compact. (5.1.7-8)

2. The Merchant of Venice
威尼斯商人

I INTRODUCTION

《威尼斯商人》是一部令读者和观众颇费周章的戏。首先,该剧的作者是反犹太的吗? 众所周知,该剧是围绕犹太高利贷者夏洛克与基督教商人安东尼奥之间的冲突展开的。安东尼奥的朋友巴萨尼奥为向富家嗣女鲍西娅求婚,由安东尼奥做担保向夏洛克借了三千块钱。安东尼奥同意,若不能按期还款,夏洛克可取其身上一磅肉。期限至,安东尼奥未能还款,夏洛克遂要求对方履行承诺,最后,经过鲍西娅乔装打扮法庭上智斗夏洛克,使得他放弃了自己的权利,并被迫皈依基督教。根据剧情,该剧常被认为是歌颂基督教慈悲这一美德,同时也是对严苛的《旧约》"以牙还牙"律法的批判。这就是直至19世纪对《威尼斯商人》的标准阐释。今天,特别是在发生了德国纳粹屠杀犹太人(the Holocaust)之后,人们对该剧的看法发生了改变。比如,有人认为剧中的巴萨尼奥、葛莱西安诺和萨莱尼奥这样一些出没于威尼斯市场的犹太人时髦、幼稚、骄纵,而安东尼奥则以金钱将他们牢牢地缚在自己的周围。夏洛克也常被演绎成"过错无多而报应太重"("more sinned against than sinning")的犹太李尔王。所以,不同的时代、异样的视角产生出另类的解读,这也显示出莎翁作品主题所具有的永恒性和开放性。选段为著名的法庭审讯,其中鲍西娅那段有关慈悲的精彩陈述发挥了扭转乾坤的作用,而低头认罪服输的夏洛克的一句"我身子不大舒服"则显示高利贷者富有人性的一面,这或许也或多或少地改变了人们对他的看法。

II PLOT SUMMARY

The play begins with **Antonio**,[1] the merchant of Venice, musing that "In **sooth**[2] I know not why I am so sad." (1.1.1) To help his friend get over his moodiness, **Bassanio**,[3] a noble but bankrupt Venetian comes to borrow three thousand ducats to woo **Portia**[4] of **Belmont**,[5] "a lady richly left" and "fair and, fairer than word". The lady's wealth is such that "Renownèd suitors, and her sunny locks/Hang on her temples like a golden fleece". (1.1.171-172) Antonio is only too happy to assist his friend but his own money is invested in foreign ventures, the success or failure of which depends on the safe return of his ships. So he decides to borrow the money from **Shylock**,[6] a Jewish moneylender. Shylock has suffered at the hands of Antonio who habitually berates him and "lends out money **gratis**[7] brings down/The rate of **usance**[8] here with us in Venice". (1.3.31-32) When he cites the biblical story of how Jacob outwitted his uncle Laban to

---

[1] **Antonio** /ænˈtəuniəu/ 安东尼奥 [2] **sooth** truth [3] **Bassanio** /bəˈsɑːniəu/ 巴萨尼奥 [4] **Portia** /ˈpɔːʃjə/ 鲍西娅 [5] **Belmont** /belˈmɔnt/ 贝尔蒙特 [6] **Shylock** /ˈʃailək/ 夏洛克 [7] **gratis** for nothing (i.e. without changing interest) [8] **usance** lending money at interest

prove his point, Antonio quips, "**The devil can cite Scripture for his purpose.**"⁹ (1.3.89) Seeing a chance to get even with Antonio, Shylock finally agrees to lend him the money at no interest save "an equal pound/Of your fair flesh, to be cut off and taken/In what part of your body pleaseth me". (1.3.141-143)

In Belmont, a test unfolds that will find Portia the right husband. Portia's father decreed before his death that she will marry whichever suitor makes the correct choice when presented with three caskets, made respectively of gold, silver and lead. The Prince of Morocco, chooses the gold casket, attracted by the inscriptions: "Who chooseth me shall get as much as he deserves," only to find a skull with a written scroll warning: "All that glisters is not gold." (2.7.66) In Venice, **Jessica**,¹⁰ Shylock's daughter, plans to run away to become a Christian and marry **Lorenzo**.¹¹ Shylock soon finds his daughter missing and his ducats stolen, but he doesn't know what to lament first, his daughter or his money: "My daughter! /O my **ducats**!¹² O my daughter! /Fled with a Christian! O my Christian ducats! /Justice, the law, my ducats, and my daughter!" (2.8.15-17) Back in Belmont, Portia receives yet another suitor, the Prince of Aragon. Lured by the inscription: "Who chooseth me shall get as much as he deserves," the prince chooses the silver casket and finds the portrait of a blinking idiot accompanied by a scroll describing such choice as that of a fool.

The Merchant of Venice, a bas relief for Folger Shakespeare Library by John Gregory

In a Venetian street, **Salerio**¹³ and **Solanio**¹⁴ meet Shylock and ask him why he cares about his bond with Antonio. Aroused, Shylock unleashes a volley of angry protests and threat of revenge: "I am a Jew. Hath not a Jew eyes? Hath not a Jew hands, organs, **dimensions**,¹⁵ senses, **affections**,¹⁶ **passions**?¹⁷ Fed with the same food, hurt with the same weapons, subject to the same diseases, healed by the same means, warmed and cooled by the same winter and summer, as a Christian is? If you prick us, do we not bleed? If you tickle us, do we not laugh? If you poison us, do we not die? And if you wrong us, shall we not revenge?" (3.1.40-45) Again in Belmont, where the two princes fail, Bassanio succeeds by choosing the lead casket, with musical cues from Portia. His friend **Gratiano**¹⁸ marries Portia's lady-in-waiting **Nerissa**¹⁹ at the same time. Then news arrives that Antonio's ships "have all miscarried"; he is unable to pay his debt. Shylock's claim to his pound of flesh is heard in the law court before the duke. Unknown to their husbands, Portia disguises herself as Balthasara, a young lawyer sent by Doctor Bellario from Padua, Nerissa as a clerk. At the court, Portia loses no time in arguing for forgiveness: "The quality of mercy is not strained,/It droppeth as the gentle rain from heaven/Upon the place beneath…" (*See* the excerpt) When Shylock refuses, Portia then begins her ingenious defense that the Jew is entitled to his pound of flesh but not to spill any of Antonio's blood; she argues that the Jew should forfeit his life for having conspired against the life of a Venetian. Only until then does Shylock realize that

---

9 **The devil … purpose** 魔鬼也会引证《圣经》来替自己辩护。 10 **Jessica** /ˈdʒesikə/ 杰西卡 11 **Lorenzo** /lɔˈrenzəu/ 罗兰佐 12 **ducats** /ˈdʌkəts/ gold coins 13 **Salerio** /səˈleriəu/ 萨莱尼奥 14 **Solanio** /səˈlæniəu/ 萨拉里诺 15 **dimensions** parts of the body 16 **affections** inclinations/emotions/love 17 **passions** powerful emotions 18 **Gratiano** /grɑːʃiˈɑːnəu/ 葛莱西安诺 19 **Nerissa** /niˈrisə/ 尼莉莎

the tables have been turned on himself. The duke pardons Shylock on condition that he gives half his wealth to Antonio and half to the state. Antonio surrenders his claim on condition that Shylock converts to Christianity and leaves his property to his daughter Jessica, whom he has disinherited for running away with her Christian lover Lorenzo. Finally, Jessica and Lorenzo are found in a beautiful but ironic love-duet about ill-fated mythological lovers. Portia and Nerissa then assert their power over Bassanio and Gratiano by means by a trick involving rings that the men have promised never to part with. Antonio then thanks Portia for having given him life and living and announces that his ships are safely home.

Beyond the Play: *Anti-Semitism in Shakespeare's Time*

The earliest Jewish settlers came to England with the Normans in the 1060s. In 1189, the fledgling community fell victim to the first of London's anti-Semitic pogroms culmininating in their expulsion in 1290. Over the next 400 years, some Jews returned. When a Portugueses Jew, Dr. Roderigo Lopez, was executed in London in 1594 charged with trying to poison his patient, none other than Queen Elizabeth, a fresh wave of anti-Semitism swept through England.

Picture on the right: the yellow badge of shame associated with antisemitism.

III SELECTED READINGS

Act IV, scene 1

     DUKE You are welcome. Take your place...
        Are you acquainted with the difference
        That holds this present question in the court?
170 *PORTIA* I am informèd throughly of the cause.
        Which is the merchant here, and which the Jew?
     DUKE Antonio and old Shylock, both stand forth.
     PORTIA Is your name Shylock?
     SHYLOCK Shylock is my name.
175 *PORTIA* Of a strange nature is the suit you follow,
        Yet in such rule that the Venetian law
        Cannot impugn you as you do proceed
        You stand within his danger, do you not?
     ANTONIO Ay, so he says.
180 *PORTIA* Do you confess the bond?
     ANTONIO I do.
     PORTIA Then must the Jew be merciful.
     SHYLOCK On what compulsion must I? Tell me that.

---

170 **throughly** thoroughly   176 **rule** proper discipline   177 **impugn** call into question   178 **within his danger** in his power

	PORTIA The quality of mercy is not strained,
185	It droppeth as the gentle rain from heaven
	Upon the place beneath. It is twice blest:
	It blesseth him that gives, and him that takes,
	'Tis mightiest in the mightiest, it becomes
	The thronèd monarch better than his crown.
190	His sceptre shows the force of temporal power,
	The attribute to awe and majesty,
	Wherein doth sit the dread and fear of kings.
	But mercy is above this sceptred sway,
	It is enthroned in the hearts of kings,
195	It is an attribute to God himself;
	And earthly power doth then show likest God's,
	When mercy seasons justice. Therefore, Jew,
	Though justice be thy plea, consider this,
	That in the course of justice none of us
200	Should see salvation. We do pray for mercy,
	And that same prayer doth teach us all to render
	The deeds of mercy. I have spoke thus much,
	To mitigate the justice of thy plea,
	Which if thou follow, this strict court of Venice
205	Must needs give sentence 'gainst the merchant there.
	SHYLOCK My deeds upon my head! I crave the law,
	The penalty and forfeit of my bond.
	PORTIA Is he not able to discharge the money?
	BASSANIO Yes, here I tender it for him in the court,
210	Yea, twice the sum. If that will not suffice,
	I will be bound to pay it ten times o'er,
	On forfeit of my hands, my head, my heart.
	If this will not suffice, it must appear
	That malice bears down truth, and I beseech you,
215	Wrest once the law to your authority—
	To do a great right, do a little wrong,
	And curb this cruel devil of his will.
	PORTIA It must not be, there is no power in Venice
	Can alter a decree established:
220	'Twill be recorded for a precedent,
	And many an error by the same example
	Will rush into the state. It cannot be.
	SHYLOCK A Daniel come to judgement! Yea, a Daniel!
	O wise young judge, how I do honour thee!
225	PORTIA I pray you, let me look upon the bond.
	SHYLOCK Here 'tis, most reverend doctor, here it is.

184 **strained** constrained, forced; filtered, distilled   186 **is twice blest** bestows a double blessing   190 **shows** represents   196 **likest** most like   197 **seasons** modifies   199 **justice** i. e. God's justice (if He did not show mercy to humankind)   201 **render** perform in return   206 **My ... head**! possible echo of the crowd's acceptance of responsibility for Jesus' death (Matthew 27:25)   208 **discharge** pay   209 **tender** offer   213 **must appear** will be evident   214 **bears down truth** overwhelms integrity   220 **for** as   223 **Daniel** (in the Apocrypha) the young defender of Susannah against the elders who falsely accused her of adultery

PORTIA Shylock, there's thrice thy money offered thee.
SHYLOCK An oath, an oath, I have an oath in heaven.
Shall I lay perjury upon my soul?
230 No, not for Venice.
PORTIA Why, this bond is forfeit,
And lawfully by this the Jew may claim
A pound of flesh, to be by him cut off
Nearest the merchant's heart. Be merciful,
235 Take thrice thy money, bid me tear the bond.
SHYLOCK When it is paid according to the tenure.
It doth appear you are a worthy judge,
You know the law, your exposition
Hath been most sound: I charge you by the law,
240 Whereof you are a well-deserving pillar,
Proceed to judgement. By my soul I swear,
There is no power in the tongue of man
To alter me. I stay here on my bond.
ANTONIO Most heartily I do beseech the court
245 To give the judgement.
PORTIA Why then, thus it is.
You must prepare your bosom for his knife.
SHYLOCK O noble judge! O excellent young man!
PORTIA For the intent and purpose of the law
250 Hath full relation to the penalty,
Which here appeareth due upon the bond.
SHYLOCK 'Tis very true: O wise and upright judge!
How much more elder art thou than thy looks!
PORTIA Therefore, lay bare your bosom.
255 *SHYLOCK* Ay, his breast,
So says the bond, doth it not, noble judge?
'Nearest his heart,' those are the very words.
PORTIA It is so. Are there balance here, to weigh.
The flesh?
260 *SHYLOCK* I have them ready.
PORTIA Have by some surgeon, Shylock, on your charge,
To stop his wounds, lest he do bleed to death.
SHYLOCK Is it so nominated in the bond?
PORTIA It is not so expressed, but what of that?
265 'Twere good you do so much for charity
SHYLOCK I cannot find it, 'tis not in the bond.
PORTIA You merchant, have you any thing to say?
ANTONIO But little; I am armed and well prepared.
Give me your hand, Bassanio, fare you well!
270 Grieve not that I am fall'n to this for you,
For herein Fortune shows herself more kind
Than is her custom: it is still her use,

---

236 **tenure** terms of the bond   261 **on your charge** at your expense   272 **use** practice

	To let the wretched man outlive his wealth,
	To view with hollow eye and wrinkled brow
275	An age of poverty; from which ling'ring penance
	Of such misery doth she cut me off.
	Commend me to your honourable wife,
	Tell her the process of Antonio's end,
	Say how I loved you, speak me fair in death;
280	And when the tale is told, bid her be judge
	Whether Bassanio had not once a love.
	Repent but you that you shall lose your friend,
	And he repents not, that he pays your debt.
	For if the Jew do cut but deep enough,
285	I'll pay it instantly with all my heart.

<pre>
            BASSANIO Antonio, I am married to a wife
              Which is as dear to me as life itself,
              But life itself, my wife, and all the world,
              Are not with me esteemed above thy life.
290   I would lose all, ay, sacrifice them all
              Here to this devil, to deliver you.
            PORTIA Your wife would give you little thanks for that,
              If she were by, to hear you make the offer.
            GRATIANO   I have a wife, whom, I protest, I love—
295   I would she were in heaven, so she could
              Entreat some power to change this currish Jew.
            NERRISSA 'Tis well you offer it behind her back,
              The wish would make else an unquiet house.
            SHYLOCK These be the Christian husbands! I have a daughter.
300   Would any of the stock of Barrabas
              Had been her husband, rather than a Christian!
              We trifle time, I pray thee pursue sentence.
            PORTIA A pound of that same merchant's flesh, is thine,
              The court awards it, and the law doth give it.
305   SHYLOCK Most rightful judge!
            PORTIA And you must cut this flesh from off his breast,
              The law allows it, and the court awards it.
            SHYLOCK Most learned judge—a sentence come, prepare.
            PORTIA Tarry a little, there is something else.
310   This bond doth give thee here no jot of blood.
              The words expressly are 'a pound of flesh'.
              Take then thy bond, take thou thy pound of flesh,
              But, in the cutting it, if thou dost shed
              One drop of Christian blood, thy lands and goods
315   Are by the laws of Venice confiscate
              Unto the state of Venice.
            GRATIANO O upright judge! Mark, Jew. O learnèd judge!
</pre>

---

279 **me ... death** favourably of me when I am dead   300 **would** I wish   **Barrabas** (in the Bible) robber released instead of Christ when Pontius Pilate, Prefect of the Roman province of Judaea, bowed to the will of the mob; also, scoundrelly protagonist of Marlow's *Jew of Malta*.   302 **trifle** waste   **pursue** proceed with   315 **confiscate** confiscated

   SHYLOCK Is that the law?
   PORTIA Thyself shalt see the act,
320 For, as thou urgest justice, be assured
   Thou shalt have justice more than thou desirest.
   GRATIANO O learnèd judge! Mark, Jew: O learnèd judge!
   SHYLOCK I take this offer then—pay the bond thrice,
   And let the Christian go.
325 BASSANIO Here is the money.
   PORTIA Soft!
   The Jew shall have all justice. Soft, no haste.
   He shall have nothing but the penalty.
   GRATIANO O Jew! An upright judge, a learned judge!
330 PORTIA Therefore, prepare thee to cut off the flesh.
   Shed thou no blood, nor cut thou less nor more
   But just a pound of flesh. If thou tak'st more
   Or less than a just pound, be it but so much
   As makes it light or heavy in the substance,
335 Or the division of the twentieth part
   Of one poor scruple, nay, if the scale do turn
   But in the estimation of a hair,
   Thou diest and all thy goods are confiscate.
   GRATIANO A second Daniel, a Daniel, Jew!
340 Now, infidel, I have you on the hip.
   PORTIA Why doth the Jew pause? Take thy forfeiture.
   SHYLOCK Give me my principal, and let me go.
   BASSANIO I have it ready for thee, here it is.
   PROTIA He hath refused it in the open court.
345 He shall have merely justice and his bond.
   GRATIANO A Daniel, still say I, a second Daniel!
   I thank thee, Jew, for teaching me that word.
   SHYLOCK Shall I not have barely my principal?
   PORTIA Thou shalt have nothing but the forfeiture
350 To be so taken at thy peril, Jew.
   SHYLOCK Why then the devil give him good of it!
   I'll stay no longer question.
   PORTIA Tarry, Jew.
   The law hath yet another hold on you...
355 It is enacted in the laws of Venice,
   If it be proved against an alien,
   That by direct or indirect attempts
   He seek the life of any citizen,
   The party gainst the which he doth contrive
360 Shall seize one half his goods, the other half
   Comes to the privy coffer of the state,
   And the offender's life lies in the mercy

---

326 **Soft**! Wait a moment! 336 **scruple** tiny amount 337 **estimation ... hair** a hair's breadth or weight 340 **on the hip** at a disadvantage (wrestling term) 342 **principal** original capital sum, i.e. three thousand ducats 351 **good** good fortune 352 **stay** remain **question** to argue the case 361 **privy coffer** private treasury 362 **in** at

	Of the duke only, gainst all other voice.
	In which predicament, I say, thou stand'st,
365	For it appears by manifest proceeding,
	That indirectly and directly too
	Thou hast contrived against the very life
	Of the defendant; and thou hast incurred
	The danger formerly by me rehearsed.
370	Down, therefore, and beg mercy of the duke.
	GRATIANO Beg that thou mayst have leave to hang thyself,
	And yet thy wealth being forfeit to the state,
	Thou hast not left the value of a cord,
	Therefore thou must be hanged at the state's charge.
375	DUKE That thou shalt see the difference of our spirit,
	I pardon thee thy life before thou ask it.
	For half thy wealth, it is Antonio's,
	The other half comes to the general state,
	Which humbleness may drive unto a fine.
380	PORTIA Ay, for the state, not for Antonio.
	SHYLOCK Nay, take my life and all, pardon not that.
	You take my house, when you do take the prop
	That doth sustain my house; you take my life,
	When you do take the means whereby I live.
385	PORTIA What mercy can you render him, Antonio?
	GRATIANO A halter gratis. Nothing else, for God's sake.
	ANTONIO So please my lord the duke and all the court
	To quit the fine for one half of his goods,
	I am content, so he will let me have
390	The other half in use, to render it
	Upon his death unto the gentleman
	That lately stole his daughter.
	Two things provided more, that, for this favour,
	He presently become a Christian.
395	The other, that he do record a gift,
	Here in the court, of all he dies possessed,
	Unto his son Lorenzo and his daughter.
	DUKE He shall do this, or else I do recant
	The pardon that I late pronounced here.
400	PORTIA Art thou contented, Jew? What dost thou say?
	SHYLOCK I am content.
	PORTIA Clerk, draw a deed of gift.
	SHYLOCK I pray you give me leave to go from hence,
	I am not well, send the deed after me,
405	And I will sign it.

363 **gainst ... voice** despite any other appeals 369 **danger** damage or penalty **rehearsed** related 370 **Down** i. e. on your knees 374 **charge** cost 377 **For** as for 379 **humbleness** remorse (on Shylock's part) **drive** convert 380 **for ... Antonio** i. e. the state's portion of the goods may be reduced to a fine, but not Antonio's half 386 **halter** hangman's noose 387 **So** if it please 388 **quit** cancel, release (Shylock) from 389 **so** provided that 390 **use** (legal) trust 394 **presently** immediately 396 **possessed** possessed of 397 **son** i. e. son-in-law 399 **late** lately

DUKE Get thee gone, but do it.
GRATIANO In christening thou shalt have two godfathers.
　Had I been judge, thou shouldst have had ten more,
　To bring thee to the gallows, not the font.　　　　　　　　　　*Exit [Shylock]*

Questions for Comprehension and Reflection
Act IV, scene 1
1. What is meant by "The quality of mercy is not strained" (184)?
2. How does mercy compare with kingly power?
3. When can earthly power become that of God?
4. Can you see the fun in Bassanio's and Gratiano's avowals of friendship to Antonio and their wives' responses (286-298)
5. What is Portia's oratorical strategy?
6. What does "I am not well" (404) show about the character Shylock?

IV　SHAKESPEAREAN RELEVANCE

A. Shakespeare in Everyday English
Please try to understand the following Shakespearean words and expressions in the contexts designated within parentheses and give their generally used meanings in the space provided.
1. with bated breath (1.3.115): _____
2. sand-blind (2.2.48): _____
3. the short and the long (2.2.84): _____
3. in the twinkling (of an eye) (2.2.116): _____
4. a pound of flesh (4.1.311): _____

B. Shakespeare in Literature
Read the following literary excerpts, locate the Shakespearean allusions and explain their meanings according to the contexts where they appear.
1. "You want paying, that's what you want," she said quietly, "I know." She produced her purse from somewhere and opened it. "How much do you want, you little Shylock?" (L. P. Hartley, *The Go-Between*, 1953)
2. This court finds the defendant not guilty, and the cruiser shall wait a few days longer that he may have an opportunity to come and thank the divine Portia. (Edgar Rice Burroughs, *Tarzan of the Apes*, 1914)

C. Shakespeare in Music, Art and on Screen
1973: *The Merchant of Venice*, British video-taped television version directed by John Sichel with a cast including Laurence Olivier as Shylock.
1991: *Star Trek VI: The Undiscovered Country*, a science fiction film directed by Nicholas Meyer in which a general quotes the play, "Tickle us, do we not laugh? Prick us, do we not bleed? Wrong us, shall we not revenge?"
1993: *Schindler's List* directed by Steven Spielberg which depicts SS Lieutenant Amon Göth quoting Shylock's "Hath not a Jew eyes?" speech when deciding whether or not to rape his

---

408 **ten more** i.e. twelve, the number in a jury　　409 **fort** place of Christian baptism

Jewish maid.

2002: *The Pianist*, a historical drama film directed by Roman PolanskiIn in which Shylock's "Hath not a Jew eyes?" is quoted in a Jewish ghetto during the Nazi occupation of Poland in World War II.

2002: *The Maori Merchant of Venice*, directed by Don Selwyn in Maori with English subtitles.

2004: *The Merchant of Venice*, a film directed by Michael Radford and produced by Barry Navidi with Al Pacino as Shylock, Jeremy Irons as Antonio, Joseph Fiennes as Bassanio.

V SHAKESPEARE QUOTES

Superfluity comes sooner by white hairs, but competency lives longer. (1.2.5)
Such a hare is madness the youth, to skip o'er the meshes of good counsel the cripple. (1.2.13-14)
Holy men at their death have good inspirations. (1.2.19-20)
The devil can cite scripture for his purpose. (1.3.89)
It is a wise father that knows his own child. (2.2.49-50)
Our house is hell, and thou, a merry devil,
Didst rob it of some taste of tediousness. (2.3.2-3)
Fast bind, fast find. (2.5.51)
All that glisters is not gold. (2.7.66)
My daughter! O my ducats! O my daughter! (2.8.15)
Hanging and wiving goes by destiny. (2.9.83)
In converting Jews to Christians, you raise the price of pork. (3.5.24-25)
I never knew so young a body with so old a head. (4.1.161)
I am not well. (4.1.404)

3. As You Like It
皆大欢喜

I INTRODUCTION

　　该剧被认为是莎翁最优雅的一部戏,与《第十二夜》《仲夏夜之梦》并称为沙翁最伟大的三部喜剧。与频繁地进行对比强烈的场景转换的众多莎剧不同,《皆大欢喜》开始于宫廷篡权、兄弟阋墙以及姊妹情深的喧嚣尘世,但很快便移景至世外桃源般的亚登森林,这里有过着绿林好汉般快活生活的被放逐的公爵及其随从,有坠入爱河难以自拔而将爱人的名字罗瑟琳刻在树上并将情诗挂满树枝的奥兰多,更有篡位的弗莱德里克公爵路遇修道士而悔悟前非并与反目弟兄和好如初。作为爱情主线衬托的是忧郁的杰奎斯对理想的思想和行为刻薄而睿智的揶揄。他那著名的人生七阶段的精彩内心独白在英美已经家喻户晓,其首句 All the world's a stage 更是广为传诵,并荣登 1997 年落成的现代仿造环球剧场(Shakespeare's Globe)的门楣,以与该剧场 1599 年开张时所悬挂的拉丁文座右铭 *Totus Mundus agit histrionem* 相对应。戏剧尾声处,扮演罗瑟琳的男童[1] 以"好酒要用好招牌,好戏倘再加上一段好收场,岂不更好"(to good wine they do use good bushes, and good plays prove the better by the help of good epilogues)开始,继而恳请世间男女欢喜这出戏。戏中人物女扮男装,舞台上的伶人男扮女装,这或许令当时的观众产生如杰奎斯所总结的"全世界就是一个舞台,所有的男男女女不过是一些演员"的顿悟和感慨。的确是人生如戏、戏如人生。

II PLOT SUMMARY

　　Orlando,[2] the youngest son of the now deceased **Sir Roland de Bois**,[3] complains to Adam, the old family retainer, that his eldest brother, Oliver, has kept his inheritance from him and neglected training Orlando to be a proper gentleman. Oliver arrives on the scene, and a bitter quarrel takes place. Adam parts the fighting brothers, and Oliver coldly promises to give him part of his due. Learning that Orlando intends to challenge Duke Frederick's champion wrestler, a brute of a man called Charles, Oliver makes plans to have his brother killed in the ring. He convinces the slow-witted Charles that Orlando is plotting against him and that Orlando should be killed.

　　At the match the next day, Duke Frederick, his daughter **Celia**,[4] and his niece, **Rosalind**,[5] watch Charles and Orlando wrestle. Charles has seriously injured his first three opponents, but in

---

[1] 伊丽莎白一世时代舞台上的女角皆由男童扮演　[2] **Orlando** /ɔːˈlaɪndəʊ/ 奥兰多　[3] **Sir Roland de Bois** /rɔˈlɑŋdəˈbɔɪ/ 罗兰·德·鲍埃。**de Bois** French, meaning 'of the woods', though probably Anglicized to the pronunciation 'boys'.　[4] **Celia** /ˈsiːliə/ 西莉娅　[5] **Rosalind** /ˈrəʊsəlɪnd/ 罗瑟琳

The Wrestling Scene from "As You Like it",
1855, Daniel Maclise

the match with Orlando, the young man's great speed and agility defeat the duke's champion. At first, Frederick is very cordial to Orlando, but when he learns the youth's identity, he becomes furious and leaves. The reason for this is that Orlando's dead father, Sir Roland de Bois, had at one time been Frederick's bitter enemy. After Frederick stalks out, Rosalind makes it clear that she finds Orlando most attractive. Orlando returns her feelings, but he is tongue-tied: "What passion hangs these weights upon my tongue? I cannot speak to her, yet she urged **conference**."[6] (1. 2. 196-197)

At the ducal palace, Celia and her cousin Rosalind are found to be as close as sisters, "[W]heresoe'er we went, **like Juno's swans**,[7]/Still we went coupled and inseparable." (1. 3. 68-69) Rosalind is the daughter of the rightful duke, Duke Senior, whose throne has been usurped by his brother, Frederick. Frederick has banished Duke Senior, along with a band of his faithful followers, to the **Forest of Arden**[8] to "live like the old **Robin Hood**[9] of England" and "many young gentlemen flock to him every day, and **fleet**[10] the time **carelessly**[11] as they did in the **golden world**."[12] (1. 1. 78-80) Until now, it is only the strong bond between Rosalind and Celia that prevents Duke Frederick from sending Rosalind away to share her father's exile. But suddenly, Frederick storms into the palace, accuses Rosalind of plotting against him, and despite Celia's pleas for her cousin, he banishes Rosalind. After her father leaves, Celia decides to go into exile with her cousin, and the girls set out for the Forest of Arden. Fearing that "**Beauty provoketh thieves sooner than gold**,"[13] (1. 3. 105) Rosalind disguises herself as a young man "**Ganymede**"[14] and Celia as a young country lass, "**Aliena**."[15] Touchstone, Frederick's jester, accompanies them.

Meanwhile, Orlando returns home and is warned by the faithful Adam that Oliver is plotting to kill him. Together, they too decide to set out for the Forest of Arden, hoping that they will find safety there. When his daughter Celia is missed, Frederick sends his men out to find Orlando. When he is informed of Orlando's flight to the Forest of Arden, Frederick assumes that Orlando is responsible for Celia's disappearance, and in a rage he sends for Oliver and commands him to "seek him (Orlando) with candle" and "Bring him dead or living" or else forfeit his entire estate.

In the Forest of Arden, Duke Senior contents himself with his exile, noting that "Sweet are the **uses**[16] of adversity,/Which, like the **toad, ugly and venomous,/Wears yet a precious jewel in his head.**[17]/And this our life **exempt from public haunt**[18]/Finds **tongues**[19] in trees, books in the running brooks,/Sermons in stones and good in everything." (2. 1. 12-17) A lord attending Duke Senior recommends **Jaques**[20] who "can suck melancholy out of a song." (2. 5. 11) When the Duke observes that they are not all alone unhappy there, Jaques takes the cue and

---

6 **conference** conversation　7 **like Juno's swans** i. e. yoked together to pull the chariot of the Roman queen of the gods　8 **Forest of Arden** probably the one near Stratford-upon-Avon　9 **Robin Hood** 罗宾汉 a popular English outlaw who lived in a forest and robbed the rich to help the poor　10 **fleet** pass　11 **carelessly** in a carefree way　12 **golden world** in classical mythology (according Hesiod's *Theogony*), the earliest of ages, when life was idyllic　13 **Beauty … gold** 美貌比金银更容易引起盗心　14 **Ganymede** (/ˈgænimiː d/ 盖尼米德), named after a beautiful Trojan boy who was carried away by Zeus to serve as cupbearer to the Olympian gods　15 **Aliena** from the Latin for 'stranger'　16 **uses** benefits　17 **toad … head** supposedly, venomous toads had precious stones in their heads that were antidotes to poisons　18 **exempt … haunt** not visited by people　19 **tongues** speech　20 **Jaques** /ˈdʒeikwiz/ 杰奎斯

reflects satirically on the seven ages of man. Orlando and Adam join Rosalind's exiled father and his men, while Rosalind and Celia, still in disguise, purchase a little cottage and a small herd of sheep and settle down to a peaceful pastoral existence. One day, however, Rosalind finds that the trees in the forest are all covered with sheets of poetry, dedicated to her. The author of these poems, of course, is Orlando. So, still pretending to be the young man Ganymede, Rosalind meets Orlando, who is in the throes of lovesickness for having apparently lost Rosalind. Ganymede offers to cure Orlando of his lovesickness by pretending to be his lady-love, Rosalind—Orlando, she says, should woo Ganymede as though "he" were Rosalind. In turn, Ganymede will do "his best" to act as moody and capricious as a girl might just do and, eventually, Orlando will weary of all the coy teasing and forget all about love—and Rosalind. Orlando agrees to try out the plan.

Rosalind, meanwhile, continues to assume the guise of Ganymede and becomes accidentally involved in yet another complication: **Silvius**,[21] a young shepherd, falls in love with **Phoebe**,[22] a hard-hearted shepherdess, but Phoebe rejects Silvius's attentions and falls in love with the young, good-looking Ganymede. In the midst of all this confusion, Oliver arrives in the Forest of Arden. He tells Ganymede of a narrow escape he has just had with death. His brother, Orlando, he says, saved him from being poisoned by a deadly snake as he slept, and later, Orlando killed a lioness which was ready to pounce on Oliver. Oliver then tells Ganymede that he has been sent to this part of the forest to seek out a young man known as Ganymede and that Orlando cannot keep his appointment with him. And there is more news: while saving Oliver's life, Orlando was wounded, on whose arm "the lioness had torn some flesh away." Hearing this, Ganymede swoons. Later, Oliver and Celia meet and fall in love at first sight, and the jester, Touchstone, falls in love with a homely, simple-minded young woman named **Audrey**,[23] who tends a herd of goats. Touchstone chases off Audrey's suitor, a lout named William, and although he realizes that he will never instill in Audrey any understanding of, or love for, such things as poetry, he still feels that he must have her.

At this point, Rosalind, still disguised as Ganymede, promises to solve the problems of everyone by magic. Shedding her male attire in private, she suddenly appears as herself, and the play comes to a swift close as she and Orlando, Oliver and Celia, and Silvius and Phoebe are married, as emceed by Hymen, god of marriage. At this festive moment, Jaques de Bois, second brother of Orlando, arrives with the tidings that Duke Frederick came to the forest with a mighty army but "was converted both from his enterprise and from the world" after a meeting with an old religious man. Rosalind's father, the rightful duke, is joyous at finding his daughter again and is returned to his ducal status. Rosalind comes forward and addresses the audience in a short but charming epilogue. In particular, she talks to all the lovers in the audience and wishes them well.

Unraveling the Bard's Comedies: *the Green World Structure*

A Midsummer Night's Dream and *As You Like It* are both called "green world" plays. In them, the young heroes must venture into a wild and unconventional nearby forest, before emerging with their correct future mate and restoring society to balance. Could you, with the help of the following diagram, explain the themes and the Green World Structure of *As You Like It*?

---

21 **Silvius** /ˈsilvjəs/ 西尔维斯 22 **Phoebe** /ˈfiːbiː/ 菲苾 23 **Audrey** /ˈɔːdriː/ 奥德蕾

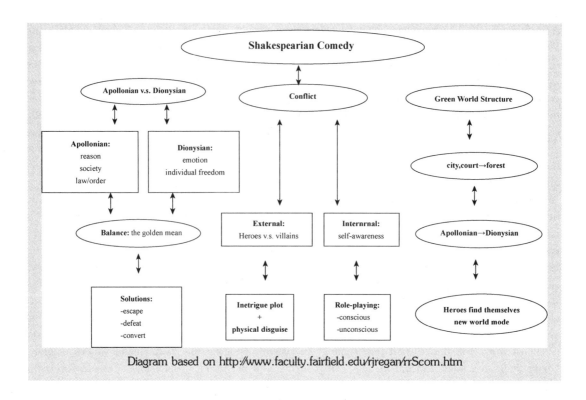

Diagram based on http://www.faculty.fairfield.edu/rjregan/rrScom.htm

III SELECTED READINGS

Act II, scene 7

The Seven Ages of Man, 1838, William Mulready

DUKE SENIOR
    Thou see'st we are not all alone unhappy:
    This wide and universal theatre

140 Presents more woeful pageants than the scene
     Wherein we play in.
     JAQUES All the world's a stage,
     And all the men and women merely players;
     They have their exits and their entrances,
145 And one man in his time plays many parts,
     His acts being seven ages. At first the infant,
     Mewling and puking in the nurse's arms.
     And then the whining school-boy, with his satchel
     And shining morning face, creeping like snail
150 Unwillingly to school. And then the lover,
     Sighing like furnace, with a woeful ballad
     Made to his mistress' eyebrow. Then a soldier,
     Full of strange oaths and bearded like the pard,
     Jealous in honour, sudden and quick in quarrel,
155 Seeking the bubble reputation
     Even in the cannon's mouth. And then the justice,
     In fair round belly with good capon lined,
     With eyes severe and beard of formal cut,
     Full of wise saws and modern instances.
160 And so he plays his part. The sixth age shifts
     Into the lean and slipper'd pantaloon,
     With spectacles on nose and pouch on side,
     His youthful hose, well saved, a world too wide
     For his shrunk shank; and his big manly voice,
165 Turning again toward childish treble, pipes
     And whistles in his sound. Last scene of all,
     That ends this strange eventful history,
     Is second childishness and mere oblivion,
     Sans teeth, sans eyes, sans taste, sans everything.

Act III, scene 2

     ROSALIND [*Aside to CELIA*] I will speak to him, like a saucy lackey
     and under that habit play the knave with him. — Do you hear, forester?
     ORLANDO Very well. What would you?
     ROSALIND I pray you, what is't o'clock?
230 ORLANDO You should ask me what time o' day: there's no clock in the forest.
     ROSALIND Then there is no true lover in the forest; else sighing every
     minute and groaning every hour would detect the lazy foot of Time as well
     as a clock.
     ORLANDO And why not the swift foot of Time? Had not that been as proper?
235 ROSALIND By no means, sir: time travels in divers paces with divers persons.

2.7 140 **pageants** scenes   143 **players** actors   146 **acts** actions/divisions of a play   147 **Mewling** whimpering, mewing **puking** vomiting   153 **strange** foreign   **bearded ... pard** with a bristling beard like a leopard's whiskers   154 **Jealous in** quick to defend his   156 **justice** judge   157 **capon lined** perhaps an allusion to the practice of bribing a judge with a capon   159 **saws** sayings   **modern instances** everyday examples   161 **pantaloon** ridiculous old man (from *Pantalone*, a stock figure in Italian comedy, who usually wore spectacles, pantaloons and slippers)   163 **hose** breeches   164 **shank** leg   167 **history** history play/ narrative   168 **mere** complete   169 **Sans** Without   3.2 226 **saucy lackey** insolent servant   227 **habit** guise   232 **detect** reveal 235 **divers** various

I'll tell you who Time ambles withal, who Time trots withal, who Time gallops withal and who he stands still withal.

ORLANDO I prithee, who doth he trot withal?

ROSALIND Marry, he trots hard with a young maid between the contract of her marriage and the day it is solemnized. If the interim be but a se'nnight, time's pace is so hard that it seems the length of seven year.

ORLANDO Who ambles Time withal?

ROSALIND With a priest that lacks Latin and a rich man that hath not the gout, for the one sleeps easily because he cannot study, and the other lives merrily because he feels no pain: the one lacking the burden of lean and wasteful learning, the other knowing no burden of heavy tedious penury. These Time ambles withal.

ORLANDO Who doth he gallop withal?

ROSALIND With a thief to the gallows, for though he go as softly as foot can fall, he thinks himself too soon there.

ORLANDO Who stays it still withal?

ROSALIND With lawyers in the vacation, for they sleep between term and term and then they perceive not how Time moves.

ORLANDO Where dwell you, pretty youth?

ROSALIND With this shepherdess, my sister; here in the skirts of the forest, like fringe upon a petticoat.

ORLANDO Are you native of this place?

ROSALIND As the cony that you see dwell where she is kindled.

ORLANDO Your accent is something finer than you could purchase in so removed a dwelling.

ROSALIND I have been told so of many: but indeed an old religious uncle of mine taught me to speak, who was in his youth an inland man, one that knew courtship too well, for there he fell in love. I have heard him read many lectures against it, and I thank God I am not a woman, to be touched with so many giddy offences as he hath generally taxed their whole sex withal.

ORLANDO Can you remember any of the principal evils that he laid to the charge of women?

ROSALIND There were none principal; they were all like one another as half-pence are, every one fault seeming monstrous till his fellow fault came to match it.

ORLANDO I prithee, recount some of them.

ROSALIND No, I will not cast away my physic but on those that are sick. There is a man haunts the forest, that abuses our young plants with carving 'Rosalind' on their barks; hangs odes upon hawthorns and elegies on brambles; all, forsooth, deifying the name of Rosalind. If I could meet that

---

236 **withal** with   238 **prithee** *interj.* shortened form of "pray thee"   239 **Marry** *interj.* Mary; by the Virgin (mild oath, used esp. to emphasize an assertion)   **hard** with difficulty   239-240 **contract ... marriage** formal betrothal   **solemnized** publicly completed   **se'nnight** week   243 **lacks Latin** does not understand Latin   245-246 **lean and wasteful learning** study that makes a man go thin and waste away   **tedious** troublesome/painful   249 **softly** slowly   252 **vacation** period during which the law courts are suspended   **term** period appointed for the sitting of courts of law   255 **skirts** outskirts   258 **cony** rabbit   **kindled** born   259 **purchase** acquire   260 **removed** remote   261 **religious** pious/monastic/scrupulous   262 **inland** of civilized society   263-264 **read many lectures** deliver many admonitions   264 **touched** tainted   265 **giddy offenses** capricious faults   **generally** without exception   **taxed** accused   266 **laid to the charge of** accused ... of   273 **physic** medicine   274 **haunts** who hangs around

fancy-monger I would give him some good counsel, for he seems to have the quotidian of love upon him.

ORLANDO   I am he that is so love-shaked. I pray you tell me your remedy.

280 ROSALIND   There is none of my uncle's marks upon you: he taught me how to know a man in love; in which cage of rushes I am sure you are not prisoner.

ORLANDO   What were his marks?

ROSALIND   A lean cheek, which you have not: a blue eye and sunken, which
285 you have not: an unquestionable spirit, which you have not, a beard neglected, which you have not—but I pardon you for that, for simply your having in beard is a younger brother's revenue. Then your hose should be ungartered, your bonnet unbanded, your sleeve unbuttoned, your shoe untied and every thing about you demonstrating a careless desolation: but
290 you are no such man: you are rather point-device in your accoutrements as loving yourself than seeming the lover of any other.

ORLANDO   Fair youth, I would I could make thee believe I love.

ROSALIND   Me believe it! You may as soon make her that you love believe it, which I warrant she is apter to do than to confess she does: that is one of
295 the points in the which women still give the lie to their consciences. But, in good sooth, are you he that hangs the verses on the trees, wherein Rosalind is so admired?

ORLANDO   I swear to thee, youth, by the white hand of Rosalind, I am that he, that unfortunate he.

300 ROSALIND   But are you so much in love as your rhymes speak?

ORLANDO   Neither rhyme nor reason can express how much.

ROSALIND   Love is merely a madness, and, I tell you, deserves as well a dark house and a whip as madmen do: and the reason why they are not so punished and cured is, that the lunacy is so ordinary that the whippers are
305 in love too. Yet I profess curing it by counsel.

ORLANDO   Did you ever cure any so?

ROSALIND   Yes, one, and in this manner. He was to imagine me his love, his Mistress, and I set him every day to woo me. At which time would I, being but a moonish youth, grieve, be effeminate, changeable, longing and liking,
310 proud, fantastical, apish, shallow, inconstant, full of tears, full of smiles, for every passion something and for no passion truly any thing, as boys and women are for the most part cattle of this colour: would now like him, now loathe him; then entertain him, then forswear him: now weep for him, then spit at him; that I drave my suitor from his mad humour of love to a living

315 humour of madness, which was, to forswear the full stream of the world, and to live in a nook merely monastic. And thus I cured him, and this way

---

277 **fancy-monger** dealer in love   278 **quotidian** daily recurring fever   279 **love-shaked** shaken by the fever of love   281 **cage of rushes** i. e. prison easy to escape from   283 **marks** signs, symptoms   284 **blue** i. e. with dark circles   285 **unquestionable** unwilling to be questioned   287 **your ... revenue** your beard is like a younger brother's income (i. e. small)   288 **ungartered** not tied up   **unbanded** without a coloured hat-band   290 **point-device** immaculate   **accoutrements** clothes   292 **would** wish   294 **apter** readier   295 **in the which** in which   **give ... consciences** lie about their real feelings   296 **sooth** truth   301 **reason** plain language   302-303 **dark ... do** imprisonment in the dark and whipping were "treatments" for the insane   309 **moorish** changeable   310 **fantastical** fanciful, impulsive   **apish** foolish   312 **cattle of this colour** beasts of this kind   313 **entertain** welcome, treat well   314 **drave** drove   **living** genuine   315 **forswear** deny, reject

will I take upon me to wash your liver as clean as a sound sheep's heart, that there shall not be one spot of love in't.
ORLANDO I would not be cured, youth.
320 ROSALIND I would cure you, if you would but call me Rosalind and come every day to my cote and woo me.
ORLANDO Now, by the faith of my love, I will. Tell me where it is.
ROSALIND Go with me to it and I'll show it you and by the way you shall tell me where in the forest you live. Will you go?
325 ORLANDO With all my heart, good youth.
ROSALIND Nay you must call me Rosalind. —Come, sister, will you go?
Exeunt

Questions for Understanding and Reflection
Act II, scene 7
1. What is the modern word for **players** (143)? And what are **exits and entrances**, **parts** and **acts** in the theatre? What are they in a person's life?
2. How is each person and age described by Shakespeare, flatteringly or cynically? Please elaborate.
3. Are the descriptions made so long ago still true today?

Act III, scene 2
1. How do people perceive time differently?
2. What are the symptoms of a man suffering from lovesickness?
3. How does Rosalind (Ganymede) offer to cure Orlando of his lovesickness?

IV SHAKESPEAREAN RELEVANCE

A. Shakespeare in Everyday English
Please try to understand the following Shakespearean words and expressions in the contexts designated within parentheses and give their generally used meanings in the space provided.
1. lay on with a trowel (1.2.74): _____
2. dead and buried (1.2.83): _____
3. lack-lustre (2.7.21): _____
4. thereby hangs a tale (2.7.28): _____
5. bag and baggage (3.2.128): _____
6. neither rhyme nor reason (3.2.294): _____
7. too much of a good thing (4.1.85): _____
8. meat and drink (5.1.7): _____
9. an ill-favoured thing sir, but mine own (5.4.49-50): _____

B. Shakespeare in Literature
Read the following literary excerpts, locate the Shakespearean allusions and explain their meanings according to the contexts where they appear.
1. "… what about that house, Mr. Chucks?" "Why, thereby hangs a tale," replied he, giving a

---
317 liver thought to be the seat of the passion **sound** healthy   321 **cote** cottage

sigh ... (F. Marryat, *Peter Simple*, 1834)
2. Young Cowperwood did not care very much for her relatives, and the Semples, bag and baggage, had been alienated by her second, and to them outrageous, marriage. (T. Dreiser, *The Financier*, 1912)
3. When she received it, who had long received no letters ... she ... sobbed, laughed, clasped her hands on her breast, and without rhyme or reason began singing ... (J. Galsworthy, *Caravan: The Assembled Tales of John Galsworthy*, 1925)

C. Shakespeare in Music, Art and on Screen
1936: *As You Like It*, a film directed by Paul Czinner and starring Laurence Olivier (Orlando).
1968: "Under The Greenwood Tree", a song from Act Ⅱ, scene 4 was set to music by British singer-songwriter Donovan and recorded for his fifth album *A Gift from a Flower to a Garden*.
1978: *As You Like It*, a BBC videotaped version, directed by Basil Coleman.
2006: *As You Like It*, a film set in 19th-century Japan, directed by Kenneth Branagh.
2014: *As You Like It*, a stage musical adapted by Scott Stroman and premiered for Shakespeare's 450th birthday.

SHAKESPEARE QUOTES

The dulness of the fool is the whetstone of the wits. (1.2.37-38)
O, how full of briars is this working-day world! (1.3.8-9)
Alas, what danger will it be to us,
Maids as we are, to travel forth so far!
Beauty provoketh thieves sooner than gold. (1.3.103-105)
Hath not old custom made this life more sweet
Than that of painted pomp? Are not these woods
More free from peril than the envious court? (2.1.2-4)
All the world's a stage,
And all the men and women merely players. (2.7.142-143)
If it be true that good wine needs no bush,
'tis true that a good play needs no epilogue. (5.4.174-175)

4. The Taming of the Shrew
驯悍记

I INTRODUCTION

《驯悍记》是莎士比亚最具争议的婚姻性别政治戏剧。帕多瓦富翁巴普提斯塔有两女，均已到了谈婚论嫁的年龄。大女儿凯瑟丽娜模样俊俏但性情暴躁，动辄高声叫骂甚至拳脚相向，成为恋爱、婚姻的"困难户"，而二女儿比恩卡温柔恬静、风度迷人，追求者众多。维洛那富绅彼特鲁乔为了获得丰厚的嫁妆，请求并得到了巴普提斯塔的允婚。大婚之日，彼特鲁乔姗姗来迟并衣着滑稽，随后将凯瑟丽娜携往其乡间住宅，从此开始了对悍妇的"调教"，使用的手段包括不给饭吃、不给觉睡、指鹿为马、颠倒黑白。"调教"似乎非常成功，因为在该剧的末尾处凯瑟丽娜已是对丈夫俯首听耳，并以谦卑的语气娓娓道出了妻子们应该恪守的为妇之道。对《驯悍记》的演绎多种多样，或闹剧、或两性争斗、或对夫权的抨击、或对女权的讥讽，但无论哪个导演和演员都无法回避凯瑟丽娜"臣服"告白，对此的处理可反映他们不同的价值取向。也不论是对莎翁时代妇女社会境况的客观反映还是对她们的戏虐描写，该剧所探讨的家庭中妇女的作用仍是娱乐界和现实生活中经久不衰的主题。

II PLOT SUMMARY

Christopher Sly, 1867, William Quiller Orchardson

Christopher Sly, a tinker, falls into a drunken stupor in an alehouse after an argument with the hostess. He is discovered in this state by a Lord and his train who stop at the alehouse after a hunt. The Lord, deciding to have a joke, orders Sly taken to the Lord's own chamber, dressed in fine clothes, and put to bed. When Sly awakens, the Lord and his party have little difficulty convincing him that he is really a nobleman who has been comatose for fifteen years. Refusing to believe his newly acquired status, Sly demands, "Am not I Christopher Sly, old Sly's son of **Burtonheath**,[1] by birth a pedlar, by education a **cardmaker**,[2] by **transmutation**[3] a **bear-herd**,[4] and now by

---

1 **Burtonheath** possibly Barton-on-th-heath, a village near Stratford-upon-Avon 2 **cardmaker** maker of cards, instruments for combing wool 3 **transmutation** change of condition 4 **bear-herd** keeper of a performing bear

present profession a **tinker**?"[5] (Induction 2: 14-16) A company of traveling players is employed to put on a play for the benefit of Sly. The play is *The Taming of the Shrew*.

Lucentio,[6] a young man from Pisa, arrives in **Padua**,[7] the "nursery of arts", with his servants, **Tranio**[8] and Biondello, to study philosophy "that treats of happiness". He sees and at once falls in love with **Bianca**.[9] She is the daughter of **Baptista**,[10] who has an elder daughter, **Katherina**.[11] Although Bianca has two suitors, Baptista refuses to allow her to marry until her older sister, a noisy shrew, has found a husband. **Hortensio**[12] and **Gremio**,[13] Bianca's suitors, agree between them to try to find a man for Katherina so that he "would thoroughly woo her, wed her and bed her and rid the house of her". (1.1.131-132) Lucentio, "t' achieve that maid/ **Whose sudden sight**[14] hath **thrilled**[15] my **wounded**[16] eye," (1.1.209-210) schemes to gain access to the confined Bianca by posing as a tutor, while his servant Tranio is to assume his identity and "keep house and port" as he normally does. At this point, Sly appears to be falling asleep and wishes the play were over. He is not heard from ever since.

The Shrew Katherina, 1898, Edward Robert Hughes

Petruchio[17], a gentleman of Verona, arrives from the country with his servant, **Grumio**,[18] intending to find himself a wife. He visits his old friend Hortensio, who jokingly suggests that he marry Katherina. Petruchio declares that "As wealth is burden of my wooing dance—/Be she as foul as was **Florentius' love**,[19]/As old as **Sibyl**[20] and as curst and shrewd/As Socrates' **Xanthippe**,[21] or a worse,/She **moves me not**,[22] or **not removes, at least,/Affection's edge in me**,[23] were she as rough/As are the swelling Adriatic seas./I come to wive it wealthily in Padua,/If wealthily, then happily in Padua." (1.2.62-70) Lucentio, in disguise, offers himself to Baptista as a suitor to Bianca, and Hortensio, in disguise, does otherwise. To avert Baptista's attention from Lucentio, Tranio becomes Lucentio as another suitor for Bianca's hand, assuming Lucentio's identity, at his master's instruction. Then Tranio invites all suitors to "do as **adversaries**[24] do in law/**Strike**[25] mightily, but eat and drink as friends." (1.2.268-269) Petruchio announces himself to Baptista as a suitor of Katherina and holds a stormy, private interview with the young lady, after which he sets a wedding date even though Katherina strongly objects. He then leaves for Venice to prepare for the wedding.

Baptista now informs Gremio and Tranio (posing as Lucentio) that whichever one of them offers the finest dowry may have Bianca in marriage. Tranio wins out, but Baptista says that he must have Lucentio's father's agreement to the dowry, since it is such a large one that he cannot believe Vincentio (Lucentio's father) would willingly part with it.

Petruchio arrives at his wedding very late, ridiculously attired, which as Baptista complains is

---

5 **tinker** pot-mender 6 **Lucentio** /luˈsentʃiəu/ 路森修 7 **Padua** (/ˈpædjuə/ 帕多瓦) a city in northern Italy 8 **Tranio** /ˈtrɑːniəu/ 特拉尼奥 9 **Bianca** /ˈbjɑːŋkə/ 比恩卡 10 **Baptista** /ˈbæptistə/ 巴普提斯塔 11 **Katherina** /ˌkæθəˈrinə/ 凯瑟丽娜 12 **Hortensio** /hɔˈtensiəu/ 霍坦西奥 13 **Gremio** /ˈgremiəu/ 葛莱米奥 14 **Whose sudden sight** the sudden sight whom 15 **thrilled** enslaved 16 **wounded** i.e. pierced by Cupid's arrow 17 **Petruchio** /pəˈtrɔtʃiəu/ 彼特鲁乔 18 **Grumio** /ˈgrumiəu/ 葛鲁米奥 19 **Florentius' love** in *Confessio Amantis* ("The Lover's Confession"), a narrative poem written by the English poet John Gower (c. 1330-1408), Florentius is a knight who agrees to marry an ugly hag if she helps him solve the riddle on which life depends 20 **Sibyl** (/ˈsɪbɪl/ 西比尔) ancient prophetess, who according to classical mythology was granted by Apollo as many years of life as she held grains of sand in her hand without any promise of accompanying youth 21 **Xanthippe** (/zænˈθipi/ 粘西比) wife of Socrates, notorious for her bad temper 22 **moves me not** do not affect me 23 **not ... me** cannot blunt the edge of my desire 24 **adversaries** opposing lawyers 25 **Strike** compete

"an eyesore to our solemn festival". (3.2.88) After marrying Katherina, he "kissed her lips with such a clamorous smack/That at the parting all the church did echo," (3.2.165-166) and forces her to return to the country with him immediately, leaving the wedding banquet to the guests. When they arrive home — cold, tired, and hungry - he refuses to let her eat or sleep. He finds fault with the meat and the making of the bed, pretending that they are not good enough for Katherina and she shall therefore have none. In a soliloquy, Petruchio boasts that he is taming his wife as he would tame a falcon.

Lucentio, in the guise of a tutor, declares himself to Bianca, who is at first cautious, but soon finds herself in love with him. Hortensio (as the tutor Licio) is horrified at Bianca's behavior toward Lucentio, and gives up his suit of her, declaring that he will marry a widow who has loved him for some time.

Tranio persuades a Pedant to assume the role of Lucentio's father, by telling him that as a citizen of Mantua he is in danger in Padua and must therefore pretend to be from Pisa. Petruchio continues his taming. He offers to purchase finery for Katherina for a trip to her father's house, but then finds fault with all that the haberdasher and tailor have to offer, concluding that she must wear what she has already, since their wares are beneath her.

While the Pedant plays Lucentio's father and affirms the dowry offered by Tranio, the real Lucentio secretly marries Bianca. Petruchio, Katherina, and Hortensio (who has been a guest with them) return to Padua. During the trip, Katherina is forced to call the sun the moon and an old man (Vincentio) a young virgin. Vincentio, discovering that Tranio is posing as his son, is convinced that Lucentio has been murdered. At the height of the confusion over mistaken identities, Lucentio returns with his bride and asks a blessing on his marriage from the two fathers.

In the final scene, the whole company enjoys a dinner together following Hortensio's marriage. Now thoroughly tamed, Katherina is summoned after dinner to explain to the other brides their duties toward their husbands. She is now more attuned to her husband's wishes than either Bianca or Hortensio's wife.

Beyond the Play: *Husband and Wife On and Off Screen*

Fascinated by the volatile dynamic between Petruchio and Katherina in the play, directors have often enjoyed casting real husbands and wives in the leading roles. In a 1967 riotous film version of the play, Franco Zeffirelli directed the tempestuous husband-and-wife-team Richard Burton and Elizabeth Taylor (left). Similarly, the earliest movie version of *The Taming of the Shrew*, from 1929, matched Mary Pickford with her spouse Douglas Fairbanks. (right)

III SELECTED READINGS

Act V, scene 1

Enter BAPTISTA, VINCENTIO, GREMIO, the Pedant, LUCENTIO and BIANCA, [PETRUCHIO, KATHARINA, HORTENSIO,] TRANIO, BIONDELLO, and Widow. The Serving-men with Tranio bringing in a banquet

LUCENTIO At last, though long, our jarring notes agree,
And time it is, when raging war is done,
To smile at scapes and perils overblown.
My fair Bianca, bid my father welcome,
5   While I with self-same kindness welcome thine.
Brother Petruchio, sister Katharina,
And thou, Hortensio, with thy loving widow,
Feast with the best, and welcome to my house.
My banquet is to close our stomachs up
10   After our great good cheer. Pray you sit down,
For now we sit to chat as well as eat.
PETRUCHIO Nothing but sit and sit, and eat and eat!
BAPTISTA Padua affords this kindness, son Petruchio.
PETRUCHIO Padua affords nothing but what is kind.
15 HORTENSIO For both our sakes, I would that word were true.
PETRUCHIO Now, for my life, Hortensio fears his widow.
Widow Then never trust me if I be afeard.
PETRUCHIO You are very sensible, and yet you miss my sense:
I mean, Hortensio is afeard of you.
20 Widow He that is giddy thinks the world turns round.
PETRUCHIO Roundly replied.
KATE Mistress, how mean you that?
Widow Thus I conceive by him.
PETRUCHIO Conceives by me! How likes Hortensio that?
25 HORTENSIO My widow says, thus she conceives her tale.
PETRUCHIO Very well mended. Kiss him for that, good widow.
KATE 'He that is giddy thinks the world turns round.'
I pray you tell me what you meant by that.
Widow Your husband, being troubled with a shrew,
30 Measures my husband's sorrow by his woe:
And now you know my meaning.
KATE A very mean meaning.
Widow Right, I mean you.
KATE And I am mean indeed, respecting you.
35 PETRUCHIO To her, Kate!

5.1 3 **scapes** escapes **overblown** now past 5 **kindness** kinship/good will 8 **with** on 9 **close** fill 10 **great good cheer** presumably the main wedding feat at Baptista's 16 **fears** is frightened of/frightens 17 **Then ... afeard** i.e. I can assure you I am not frightened 18 **sensible** perceptive 20 **He ... round** i.e. you attribute your own feelings to others—you, Petruchio, are afraid of your wife 21 **Roundly** boldly, soundly 23 **Thus ... him** that's how I understand him (Petruchio picks up on **roundly** and **conceive** to make a joke about pregnancy) 25 **conceives her tale** interprets her remark/is impregnated (tale puns on 'tail' – i.e. vagina) 26 **mended** retorted/rectified 32 **mean** average/poor 34 **mean ... you** moderate compared to you 35 **To her** attack her (a cry used to urge on animals in hunting or fighting)

HORTENSIO To her, widow!
PETRUCHIO A hundred marks, my Kate does put her down.
HORTENSIO That's my office.
PETRUCHIO Spoke like an officer; ha' to thee, lad!
Drinks to HORTENSIO
40 BAPTISTA How likes Gremio these quick-witted folks?
GREMIO Believe me, sir, they butt together well.
BIANCA Head, and butt! An hasty-witted body
   Would say your head and butt were head and horn.
VINCENTIO Ay, mistress bride, hath that awakened you?
45 BIANCA Ay, but not frighted me: therefore I'll sleep again.
PETRUCHIO Nay, that you shall not. Since you have begun,
   Have at you for a bitter jest or two!
BIANCA Am I your bird? I mean to shift my bush,
   And then pursue me as you draw your bow.
50   You are welcome all.
Exeunt BIANCA, [KATHARINA and Widow]
PETRUCHIO She hath prevented me. Here, Signior Tranio.
   This bird you aimed at, though you hit her not:
   Therefore a health to all that shot and missed.
TRANIO O, sir, Lucentio slipped me like his greyhound,
55   Which runs himself and catches for his master.
PETRUCHIO A good swift simile, but something currish.
TRANIO 'Tis well, sir, that you hunted for yourself:
   'Tis thought your deer does hold you at a bay.
BAPTISTA O, O, Petruchio! Tranio hits you now.
60 LUCENTIO I thank thee for that gird, good Tranio.
HORTENSIO Confess, confess, hath he not hit you here?
PETRUCHIO A has a little galled me, I confess.
   And as the jest did glance away from me,
   'Tis ten to one it maimed you two outright.
65 BAPTISTA Now, in good sadness, son Petruchio,
   I think thou hast the veriest shrew of all.
PETRUCHIO Well, I say no: and therefore for assurance
   Let's each one send unto his wife,
   And he whose wife is most obedient
70   To come at first when he doth send for her,
   Shall win the wager which we will propose.
HORTENSIO Content. What is the wager?
LUCENTIO Twenty crowns.
PETRUCHIO Twenty crowns!

---

37 **marks** coins, each worth two thirds of a pound **put her down** outdo her (Gremio plays on the sense of 'have sex with her')
38 **office** role/sexual duty 41 **butt** lock horns/thrust sexually 42 **butt** bottom **hasty-witted body** quick-witted person 43 **head and horn** a horned head (i.e. that of a cuckold; horn plays on the sense of 'penis/hunting horn') 47 **Have at you** be prepared for **bitter** shrewd, keen 48 **bird** prey **shift my bush** fly to another bush to hide in (plays on the idea of pubic hair) 49 **bow** refers to fowling – hunting sitting birds with bow and arrow (with phallic connotations) 51 **prevented** thwarted 52 **hit** shot with an arrow/penetrated sexually 53 **health** toast 54 **slipped** unleashed 56 **currish** ignoble/dog-like 58 **deer** puns on 'dear' **does ... bay** turns on you and holds you off with its horns/denies you sex 60 **gird** taunt 62 **galled** scratched, irritated 63 **glance away from** bounce off 65 **good sadness** all seriousness 66 **veriest** truest 67 **assurance** proof

75   I'll venture so much of my hawk or hound,
        But twenty times so much upon my wife.
      LUCENTIO   A hundred then.
      HORTENSIO   Content.
      PETRUCHIO   A match! 'tis done.
80   HORTENSIO   Who shall begin?
      LUCENTIO   That will I.
        Go, Biondello, bid your mistress come to me.
      BIONDELLO   I go.
      Exit
      BAPTISTA   Son, I'll be your half, Bianca comes.
85   LUCENTIO   I'll have no halves. I'll bear it all myself.
      Re-enter BIONDELLO
        How now! What news?
      BIONDELLO   Sir, my mistress sends you word
        That she is busy and she cannot come.
      PETRUCHIO   How? She is busy and she cannot come?
90   Is that an answer?
      GREMIO   Ay, and a kind one too:
        Pray God, sir, your wife send you not a worse.
      PETRUCHIO   I hope better.
      HORTENSIO   Sirrah Biondello, go and entreat my wife
95   To come to me forthwith.
      Exit BIONDELLO
      PETRUCHIO   O, ho, entreat her?
        Nay, then she must needs come.
      HORTENSIO   I am afraid, sir,
        Do what you can,
      Enter BIONDELLO
        yours will not be entreated.
100   Now, where's my wife?
      BIONDELLO   She says you have some goodly jest in hand.
        She will not come. She bids you come to her.
      PETRUCHIO   Worse and worse, she will not come! O vile,
        Intolerable, not to be endured!
105   Sirrah Grumio, go to your mistress.
        Say, I command her to come to me.
      Exit GRUMIO
      HORTENSIO   I know her answer.
      PETRUCHIO   What?
      HORTENSIO   She will not.
110   PETRUCHIO   The fouler fortune mine, and there an end.
      BAPTISTA   Now, by my holidame, here comes Katharina!
      Enter KATHARINA
      KATHARINA   What is your will, sir, that you send for me?
      PETRUCHIO   Where is your sister, and Hortensio's wife?

---

75 **of** on   84 **be your half** put up half your bet   89 **How**? What?   97 **needs** necessarily   110 **The ... mine** then I have the worst luck   111 **by my holidame** by Our Lady/by all that I hold holy

	KATHARINA They sit conferring by the parlor fire.
115	PETRUCHIO Go fetch them hither. If they deny to come,
	Swinge me them soundly forth unto their husbands.
	Away, I say, and bring them hither straight.

Exit KATE

LUCENTIO   Here is a wonder, if you talk of a wonder.
HORTENSIO   And so it is: I wonder what it bodes.
120   PETRUCHIO   Marry, peace it bodes, and love and quiet life,
And awful rule and right supremacy,
And, to be short, what not, that's sweet and happy.
BAPTISTA   Now, fair befall thee, good Petruchio!
The wager thou hast won; and I will add
125   Unto their losses twenty thousand crowns;
Another dowry to another daughter,
For she is changed, as she had never been.
PETRUCHIO   Nay, I will win my wager better yet
And show more sign of her obedience,
130   Her new-built virtue and obedience.
See where she comes and brings your froward wives
As prisoners to her womanly persuasion. —

Enter KATE, BIANCA and Widow

Katharina, that cap of yours becomes you not.
Off with that bauble, throw it underfoot.
135   Widow   Lord, let me never have a cause to sigh,
Till I be brought to such a silly pass!
BIANCA   Fie! What a foolish duty call you this?
LUCENTIO   I would your duty were as foolish too:
The wisdom of your duty, fair Bianca,
140   Hath cost me an hundred crowns since suppertime.
BIANCA   The more fool you, for laying on my duty.
PETRUCHIO   Katharine, I charge thee tell these headstrong women
What duty they do owe their lords and husbands.
Widow   Come, come, you're mocking. We will have no telling.
145   PETRUCHIO   Come on, I say, and first begin with her.
Widow   She shall not.
PETRUCHIO   I say she shall, and first begin with her.
KATHARINA   Fie, fie! Unknit that threatening unkind brow,
And dart not scornful glances from those eyes,
150   To wound thy lord, thy king, thy governor.
It blots thy beauty as frosts do bite the meads,
Confounds thy fame as whirlwinds shake fair buds,
And in no sense is meet or amiable.
A woman moved is like a fountain troubled,
155   Muddy, ill-seeming, thick, bereft of beauty,

---

114 **conferring** chatting   116 **Swinge** thrash   121 **awful** worthy of respect   **right** rightful   122 **what not** everything   123 **fair befall thee** good luck to you   127 **as ... been** as if the former Kate had never existed   136 **pass** state of affairs   137 **foolish** stupid (Lucentio shifts the sense to 'fond, doting')   141 **laying** betting   148 **Unknit** relax   **unkind** harsh/unnatural   151 **meads** meadows   152 **Confounds thy fame** destroys your reputation   153 **meet** appropriate   154 **moved** angered   155 **ill-seeming** ugly

        And while it is so, none so dry or thirsty
        Will deign to sip or touch one drop of it.
        Thy husband is thy lord, thy life, thy keeper,
        Thy head, thy sovereign: one that cares for thee,
160   And for thy maintenance commits his body
        To painful labour both by sea and land,
        To watch the night in storms, the day in cold,
        Whilst thou liest warm at home, secure and safe,
        And craves no other tribute at thy hands
165   But love, fair looks and true obedience;
        Too little payment for so great a debt. —
        Such duty as the subject owes the prince
        Even such a woman oweth to her husband.
        And when she is froward, peevish, sullen, sour,
170   And not obedient to his honest will,
        What is she but a foul contending rebel
        And graceless traitor to her loving lord?
        I am ashamed that women are so simple
        To offer war where they should kneel for peace,
175   Or seek for rule, supremacy and sway,
        When they are bound to serve, love and obey.
        Why are our bodies soft and weak and smooth,
        Unapt to toil and trouble in the world,
        But that our soft conditions and our hearts
180   Should well agree with our external parts? —
        Come, come, you froward and unable worms,
        My mind hath been as big as one of yours,
        My heart as great, my reason haply more,
        To bandy word for word and frown for frown;
185   But now I see our lances are but straws,
        Our strength as weak, our weakness past compare,
        That seeming to be most which we indeed least are.
        Then vail your stomachs, for it is no boot,
        And place your hands below your husband's foot:
190   In token of which duty, if he please,
        My hand is ready, may it do him ease.
        PETRUCHIO Why, there's a wench! Come on, and kiss me, Kate.
        LUCENTIO Well, go thy ways, old lad, for thou shalt ha't.
        VINCENTIO 'Tis a good hearing when children are toward.
195   LUCENTIO But a harsh hearing when women are froward.
        PETRUCHIO Come, Kate, we'll to bed.
        We three are married, but you two are sped.

---

161 **painful** grueling   162 **watch** be awake during   169 **peevish** stubborn, perverse   170 **honest** virtuous, upright   172 **graceless** sinful   173 **simple** foolish   175 **sway** authority, influence   176 **bound** i. e. by duty/in marriage   178 **Unapt** not designed   179 **soft** gentle, fragile   **conditions** constitutions/qualities   181 **unable** incapable   182 **big** strong/contentious/determined/proud   183 **haply** perhaps   184 **bandy** exchange   187 **That ... be** seeming to be that   188 **vail your stomachs** lower your pride/surrender your inclinations   **boot** use   191 **do him ease** give him pleasure/ease his burden   193 **go thy ways** well done   **ha't** have it (win the wager)   194 **'Tis ... toward** it is a good thing to hear when children are compliant   197 **three** three men   **you ... sped** you two (Lucentio and Hortensio) are done for

> *To* LUCENTIO
> 'Twas I won the wager, though you hit the white.
> And being a winner, God give you good night!
> *Exeunt* PETRUCHIO [*KATHARINA*]
200   HORTENSIO   Now, go thy ways; thou hast tamed a curst shrew.
        LUCENTIO   'Tis a wonder, by your leave, she will be tamed so.
        Exeunt

Questions for Comprehension and Reflection
Act V, scene 1
1. What does the widow mean by "He that is giddy thinks the world turns round" (20)?
2. How do Petruchio and Hortensio decide to find out whose wife is more obedient?
3. How do Bianca and Katherina each respond to their husbands' request to present themselves?
4. What does Katherina think of a woman who is given to hot temper?
5. Do you agree with Katherina's opinions concerning a wife's duties to her husband?

IV   SHAKESPEAREAN RELEVANCE

A. Shakespeare in Everyday English
Please try to understand the following Shakespearean words and expressions in the contexts designated within parentheses and give their generally used meanings in the space provided.
1. budge an inch (Induction 1:8-9): _____
2. wive and thrive (1.2.50): _____
3. break the ice (1.2.257): _____
4. an eye-sore (3.2.88): _____
4. kill with kindness (3.3.171): _____
5. Pitchers have ears. (4.2.52): _____
6. forever and a day (4.2.90): _____
7. more fool you (5.1.141): _____

B. Shakespeare in Literature
Read the following literary excerpts, locate the Shakespearean allusions and explain their meanings according to the contexts where they appear.

    In truth, Mrs Proudie was all but invincible; had she married Petruchio, it may be doubted whether that arch wife-tamer would have been able to keep her legs out of those garments which are presumed by men to be peculiarly unfitted for feminine use.
                                               (Anthony Trollope, *Barchester Towers*, 1875)

C. Shakespeare in Music, Art and on Screen
1756: *Catharine and Petruchio*, an adaptation of *The Taming of the Shrew* by British playwright and actor David Garrick.
1929: *The Taming of the Shrew*, the first sound version on film directed by Sam Taylor, starring Mary Pickford and Douglas Fairbanks.

---

198 **white** centre of the target (puns on Bianca's name, 'white' in Italian)   200 **shrew** pronounced 'shrow', the word provides the rhyme for this final couplet

1948: *Kiss Me, Kate*, a famous musical adaptation with music and lyrics by Cole Porter.
1957: *The Taming of the Shrew*, the best known Russian opera composed by Vissarion Shebalin.
1967: *The Taming of the Shrew*, the most widely seen film version, directed by Franco Zeffirelli and starring Elizabeth Taylor and Richard Burton.
1975: *The Shrew*, a play produced by Charles Marowitz and performed in the Sydney Opera House.

SHAKESPEARE QUOTES

Let the world slide. (Induction, 1:4)
I have Pisa left
And am to Padua come, as he that leaves
A shallow plash to plunge him in the deep
And with satiety to quench his thirst. (1.1.21-24)
No profit grows where is no pleasure ta'en:
In brief, sir, study what you most affect. (1.1.39-40)
There's small choice in rotten apples. (1.1.125)
Tis a world to see
How tame, when men and women are alone,
A meacock wretch can make the curstest shrew. (2.1.312-314)
I am no breeching scholar in the schools. (3.1.18)
Who woo'd in haste and means to wed at leisure. (3.2.11)
Our purses shall be proud, our garments poor,
For 'tis the mind that make the body rich,
And as the sun breaks through the darkest clouds,
So honor peereth in the meanest habit.
What, is the jay more precious than the lark,
Because his feathers are more beautiful?
Or is the adder better than the eel
Because his painted skin contents the eye? (4.1.164-171)

5. Twelfth Night, or "What You Will"
第十二夜（又名：各遂所愿）

I INTRODUCTION

　　同胞分离、身份错位（mistaken identity）、爱情心计、主仆阴谋，这些桥段都使得《第十二夜》更像是怪事迭出的悬疑剧。该剧的主要来源可能是 Brande Richede 的"Of Apolonius and Silla"，但莎翁的生花妙笔却令《第十二夜》超出了喜剧的界限。戏幕刚一开启，读者或观众便为死亡的阴影所笼罩：伯爵小姐奥丽维娅痛失亲哥，发誓为其服丧七年方可考虑婚姻大事；海难幸存者薇奥拉因担心同胞兄弟西巴斯辛已葬身海底而惴惴不安。于是，戏剧便围绕这双重损失发展下去，随后有了薇奥拉女扮男装自荐于伊利里亚公爵奥西诺做了侍童，并奉命代其主人向奥丽维娅求婚，结果自己却成了贵族小姐追求的对象。除了这些上层主人们之间的爱情纠葛之外，尚有下层仆人们之间的恶搞胡闹。这真是上层社会衣食无忧、悠闲谈情说爱，而下层则满腹忧患、热衷勾心斗角。或许英国影视剧导演及作家们所钟爱的反映等级森严的英国社会的"楼上、楼下"主题便是衍生于此。[1] 奥丽维娅的管家马伏里奥对女主人的一厢情愿以及所受到的仆人们的百般捉弄令人忍俊不禁，但他的最后一句"我一定要出这一口气，你们这批东西一个都不放过"（I'll be revenged on the whole pack of you）却使我们的笑声戛然而止。

II PLOT SUMMARY

　　The Duke **Orsino**,[2] the unmarried ruler of **Illyria**,[3] has been courting the Countess **Olivia**,[4] a local lady, like a moody adolescent who is infatuated by sentimental music: "If music be the food of love, play on/Give me excess of it, that **surfeiting**,[5]/The **appetite**[6] may sicken and so die./That strain again, it had a **dying fall**."[7] (1.1.1-4) Olivia has consistently rejected him, because of her resolve to mourn the recent death of her brother for seven years. Orsino loves her all the more for her sibling devotion. Meanwhile, **Sebastian**[8] and **Viola**,[9] a twin sister and brother, are separated when they were shipwrecked in a storm at sea, each fearing the other has been drowned. Viola, who is rescued by the ship's captain and obtains his promise to keep her identity and gender a secret, arrives in Illyria and decides to disguise herself as the boy "**Cesario**"[10] in order to seek service with Orsino. Having successfully ingratiated herself with the

---

[1] BBC 于 1971—1975 和 2010—2012 年间所推出的电视剧更是被旗帜鲜明地命名为 *Upstairs Downstairs*，其主题昭然若揭。
[2] **Orsino** /ɔːˈsinəu/ 奥西诺 [3] **Illyria** (/iˈliriə/ 伊利里亚) a country on the east of the Adriatic Sea, now Croatia [4] **Olivia** /ˈɔliviə/ 奥丽维娅 [5] **surfeiting** overindulging (in food or sex) [6] **appetite** hunger/sexual craving [7] **dying fall** dropping cadence (plays on the sense of 'orgasm and detumescence') [8] **Sebastian** /siˈbæstjən/ 西巴斯辛 [9] **Viola** /vaɪˈulə/ 薇奥拉

Duke, she is soon sent by him as a messenger—with a gift and declarations of love—to his beloved Countess.

In the meantime, we're introduced to several members of Olivia's household, the "downstairs" characters whose antics will advance the comic side of the plot, just as the problems of such "upstairs" characters as Orsino, Olivia and Viola will advance the romantic side. The leader of this group of characters is Sir Toby Belch, Olivia's fat, jolly, hard-drinking cousin, whose love for pranks and merry-making in general motivates much of the comic action. His companion, Sir Andrew **Aguecheek**,[11] is a wealthy, skinny, rather feeble-minded knight who has come to Illyria to woo Olivia. Sir Toby encourages this hopeless courtship because he wants Sir Andrew handy for the sake of his money. The three other important comic personages are Maria, Olivia's shrewd maid, who has designs on Sir Toby; **Malvolio**,[12] her unpleasant, Puritanical steward; and **Feste**,[13] the household jester, or "Fool."

Olivia, 1888, Edmund Blair Leighton

"Cesario" comes to court Olivia for the Duke, and she does her job with so much grace and wit that the unhappy lady falls passionately in love with the messenger, observing that "Thy tongue, thy face, thy limbs, actions and spirit,/Do give thee five-fold blazon." (1. 5. 226-227) She has her steward Malvolio follow the "boy" with favors and messages. But Viola has herself fallen in love with Orsino, so she's distressed for good reason when she discovers that her rival for his affection, Olivia, harbors a similar passion for her: "Fortune forbid my **outside**[14] have not charmed her!/She **made good view of**[15] me, indeed so much/That methought her eyes had lost her tongue,/For she did speak in **starts**[16] **distractedly**.[17]/She loves me, sure." (2. 2. 13-17) In the meantime, it turns out that Sebastian, Viola's twin brother, has also been rescued from drowning by Antonio, a kindly sea-captain, with whom he soon sets out to visit Illyria.

Viola and the Countess, 1859, Frederick Richard Pickersgill

While the romantic triangle of Olivia, Orsino, and Viola is thus stalemated, and before the arrival of Sebastian in town, the comic subplot begins to unfold with Sir Toby, Andrew, Feste, and Maria carousing late at night at Olivia's house, emboldened by Feste's vocal *carpe diem*: "What is love? 'Tis not **hereafter**,[18]/Present mirth hath present laughter./What's to come is **still**[19] unsure./In delay there lies no **plenty**.[20]/Then come kiss me, sweet **and twenty**,[21]/Youth's a **stuff**[22] will not endure." (2. 3. 34-39) While they are thus engaged, the priggish Malvolio bursts in and threatens to tell Olivia of their uncivil ways. Determined to revenge themselves and to show up his egotism and pretentiousness, the other comic characters plan to "gull him into a nayword and make him a common recreation" by sending him an anonymous "obscure epistles of love" that he'll think might be from Olivia herself. They leave

---

10 **Cesario** /siː'zariəu/ 西萨里奥 11 **Aguecheek** (/'eigjutʃiːk/, 艾古契克) suggesting the thin face of one suffering from a fever 12 **Malvolio** (/mæl'vɔuljəu/, 马伏里奥) probably from the Italian *Malvolio* ('I want Mall'), alluding to Sir William Knollys, who was infatuated with Mary Fitton, his protégé and the lady-in-waiting of Elizabeth I (支荩忠,1987:1) 13 **Feste** (/'fest/ 费斯特) from Latin or Italian, *festa* ('feast' or 'festival'), an appropriate name for a fool/clown 14 **outside** appearance 15 **made good view of** had a good look at 16 **starts** bursts 17 **distractedly** with agitation; madly 18 **hereafter** in the future 19 **still** always 20 **plenty** profit 21 **and twenty** an intensifier (the singer's lover is 'twenty times sweet') 22 **stuff** quality/material

the letter in the garden, where Malvolio discovers it when he's strolling already deep in fantasies of being the "Count," Olivia's husband. The unnamed letter-writer, supposedly Olivia, suggests to the egotistical steward that he can become "great" by wooing his lady, the Countess, in yellow-stockings and cross-garters, and by continually smiling at her while at the same time being "surly" with other members of the household. Naturally, the letter fires all his ambitions, and he determines to follow its instructions, deliberately designed by Maria to make a mockery of him.

Meanwhile, Olivia's own passion for Cesario has become so intense that she openly woos Orsino's "page," much to Viola's discomfort. Indeed, Viola has grown so desperately attached to Orsino that she herself is barely able to keep from confessing her love to him—and when Olivia makes her declaration, she emphatically swears that she can never give her heart to any woman—which is reasonable enough, since she's a woman herself. At this point, Sebastian and Antonio have arrived in Illyria, and because Antonio once opposed Orsino in a sea fight, arousing the permanent hostility of the Illyrians, the two decide to separate, Antonio to remain concealed at a nearby inn, and Sebastian to join him there after doing some sightseeing in the town.

Malvolio and the Countess, 1859, Daniel Maclise

By now Malvolio has followed the instructions of the false love-letter, and crazily costumed, he makes a fantastic approach to Olivia, as her wooer. The Countess, supposing him mad—which is just what the plotters intended—gives him into Sir Toby's care to be imprisoned as a lunatic. And with Malvolio "safely" out of the way, she herself once more resumes her own courtship of Viola. But her favors and attentions to the Duke's "man" have so enraged Sir Toby's friend, the foolish Andrew, that this basically cowardly knight actually challenges "Cesario" to a duel. Though both are anxious to avoid any real fighting, Sir Toby and Fabian, another of Olivia's servants, egg them on to the point where bloodshed is only avoided by the sudden appearance of Antonio, Sebastian's friend, who, thinking Viola is Sebastian, draws his sword in her defense and ends up battling Sir Toby himself. A group of police officers, however, also appear on the scene and quickly arrest Antonio. The beleaguered captain then asks "Sebastian" (Viola) for a purse he's lent the real Sebastian earlier, and when Viola doesn't know what he's talking about, he accuses her of ingratitude, calling her by her brother's name as the officers lead him away. Viola now realizes that her twin must be alive, and in Illyria, and she goes off in high excitement.

Soon Sebastian himself wanders in and he, in turn, is mistaken for "Cesario" (just as Viola was taken for him) by the clown, Feste, as well as by both Sir Andrew and Sir Toby, who (imagining that he's still as timid as the original "Cesario") attack him once more with their swords. This time, however, they don't find themselves opposed by a young girl with no knowledge of dueling, but by her brother, who spiritedly defends himself and is on the verge of soundly beating them both when Olivia arrives and, like the others, supposing Sebastian to be "Cesario," scolds her cousin for fighting with him and lovingly invites him into her house.

While Sebastian and Olivia are ripening their relationship in one part of the house, Feste, the clown, is persuaded by Maria and Toby to visit the imprisoned Malvolio disguised as "Sir Topas," the priest. Failing the madness test administered by Feste, Malvolio protested his unfair treatment: "Fool, there was never man so **notoriously**[23] abused." (4.2.65) After tormenting the unhappy steward for a bit, the jester then returns in his own person—again at the instigation of Toby (who

---

23 **notoriously** evidently/outrageously

has at last tired of the whole affair)—and provides Malvolio with pencil and paper so he can write to Olivia informing her of his plight. In the meantime, Olivia persuades Sebastian, who's fallen in love with her quickly enough, to marry her at once. She still thinks, of course, that he's "Cesario," and not trusting his sudden apparent change of heart, wants to make certain of him while she can. Sebastian is aware that there must be some mistake in all this, but he enjoys this hallucinating twist of events: "This is the air, that is the glorious sun,/This pearl she gave me, I do feel't and see't." (4.3.1-2).

At last Orsino, accompanied by Viola and his entire retinue, visits Olivia to renew his suit in person. There he encounters Sebastian and marvels at his physical resemblance to Viola: "One face, one voice, one **habit**,[24] and two persons,/A **natural perspective**,[25] that is and is not!" (5.1.200-201) Antonio is also puzzled: "An apple cleft in two is not more twin/Than these two creatures. Which is Sebastian?" (5.1.208-209) Then Olivia appears, and, to the Duke's surprise and anger, addresses "Cesario" as husband. Viola, of course, denies both Antonio's and Olivia's accusations, but the priest who married Olivia and the other "Cesario" (Sebastian) supports the Countess's claim. Orsino is ready to banish or condemn Viola, when Andrew and Toby also appear with a complaint; they accuse "Cesario" of having beaten them. Viola again denies all knowledge of the affair, but she seems to have become a general object of blame when Sebastian himself at last appears onstage, and all the complications are satisfactorily resolved.

It's clear, of course, that he, and not Viola, is responsible for Andrew's and Toby's injuries. The twins are reunited. Olivia discovers that, after having unluckily fallen in love with the sister, she's luckily married the brother. Antonio learns that Sebastian had kept faith with him after all. And finally Orsino, finding that his devoted "page" is really a woman, decides that he can easily return her devotion and lovingly proposes to the happy girl. In the midst of all this rejoicing, Olivia remembers Malvolio, and after Feste has given her the steward's letter, outlining his grievances, the miserable man himself is brought in to have the secret of his "madness"—Maria's letter—explained by Fabian. Fabian also reveals that Sir Toby has rewarded Maria for her cleverness by marrying her. At his meditative best, Feste thus comments on the caprices of fate: "'Some are born great, some achieve greatness, and some have greatness thrown upon them.' ... And thus the **whirligig**[26] of time brings in his revenges." (5.1.355-356, 358-359) The inconsolable Malvolio rushes off in a rage, vowing that "I'll be revenged on the whole pack of you." (5.1.360) Orsino pursues him and entreats peace, leaving Feste to sing a sad song about the different stages of an absurd life.

Beyond the Play: *Twelfth Night*

The title *Twelfth Night* refers to the twelfth night of Christmas, a festival celebrated in some branches of Christianity, marking the coming of the Epiphany (主显节) and concluding the Twelve Days of Christmas, the evening of the fifth of January. Celebrations briefly inverted standard hierarchies, overturned social orders and praised human folly.

(Picture on the right: Mervyn Clitheroe's Twelfth Night party, by "Phiz")

---

24 **habit** clothing 25 **natural perspective** optical illusion produced by nature 26 **whirligig** spinning top/merry-go-round

III SELECTED READINGS

Act II, scene 4

  ORSINO Let all the rest give place.
    Once more, Cesario,
80 Get thee to yond same sovereign cruelty:
    Tell her, my love, more noble than the world,
    Prizes not quantity of dirty lands.
    The parts that fortune hath bestow'd upon her
    Tell her, I hold as giddily as fortune.
85 But 'tis that miracle and queen of gems
    That nature pranks her in attracts my soul.
  VIOLA But if she cannot love you, sir?
  ORSINO I cannot be so answer'd.
  VIOLA Sooth, but you must.
90 Say that some lady, as perhaps there is,
    Hath for your love a great a pang of heart
    As you have for Olivia: you cannot love her.
    You tell her so; must she not then be answered?
  ORSINO There is no woman's sides
95 Can bide the beating of so strong a passion
    As love doth give my heart; no woman's heart
    So big, to hold so much. They lack retention.
    Alas, their love may be called appetite,
    No motion of the liver, but the palate,
100 That suffer surfeit, cloyment and revolt.
    But mine is all as hungry as the sea,
    And can digest as much. Make no compare
    Between that love a woman can bear me
    And that I owe Olivia.
105 VIOLA Ay, but I know—
  ORSINO What dost thou know?
  VIOLA Too well what love women to men may owe:
    In faith, they are as true of heart as we.
    My father had a daughter loved a man,
110 As it might be, perhaps, were I a woman,
    I should your lordship.
  ORSINO And what's her history?
  VIOLA A blank, my lord. She never told her love,
    But let concealment, like a worm i'th'bud,
115 Feed on her damask cheek: she pined in thought,

2.4 78 **give place** leave 82 **dirty** dishonourably acquired 83 **parts** wealth 84 **giddily** lightly **fortune** normally held to be capricious 85 **miracle ... gems** i.e. Olivia's beauty 86 **pranks** adorns 93 **be answered** satisfied 95 **bide** withstand 97 **retention** the power to retain 98 **appetite** desire/fancy 99 **motion** impulse/emotion **liver** thought to be the seat of strong passion **palate** organ of taste, i.e. easily satisfied 100 **suffer** undergo **surfeit** illness brought on by overindulgence in food or drink **cloyment** distaste or revulsion **revolt** revulsion (of appetite) 101 **mine** i.e. my love 102 **compare** comparison 104 **owe** have for 112 **history** story 115 **damask** pinkish white skin

And with a green and yellow melancholy
She sat like Patience on a monument,
Smiling at grief. Was not this love indeed?
We men may say more, swear more: but indeed
120 Our shows are more than will, for still we prove
Much in our vows, but little in our love.
ORSINO But died thy sister of her love, my boy?
VIOLA I am all the daughters of my father's house,
And all the brothers too, and yet I know not.
125 Sir, shall I to this lady?
ORSINO Ay, that's the theme.
To her in haste: give her this jewel: say
My love can give no place, bide no denay.

Act V, scene 1

Enter OLIVIA and Attendants
ORSINO Here comes the countess. Now heaven walks on earth.
85 But for thee, fellow—fellow, thy words are madness.
Three months this youth hath tended upon me.
But more of that anon. Take him aside.
OLIVIA What would my lord, but that he may not have,
Wherein Olivia may seem serviceable?
90 Cesario, you do not keep promise with me.
VIOLA Madam!
ORSINO Gracious Olivia—
OLIVIA What do you say, Cesario? Good my lord—
VIOLA My lord would speak, my duty hushes me.
95 OLIVIA If it be aught to the old tune, my lord,
It is as fat and fulsome to mine ear
As howling after music.
ORSINO Still so cruel?
OLIVIA Still so constant, lord.
100 ORSINO What, to perverseness? You uncivil lady,
To whose ingrate and unauspicious altars
My soul the faithfull'st offerings hath breathed out
That e'er devotion tender'd! What shall I do?
OLIVIA Even what it please my lord, that shall become him.
105 ORSINO Why should I not, had I the heart to do it,
Like to the Egyptian thief at point of death,
Kill what I love? —a savage jealousy
That sometimes savours nobly. But hear me this:

---

116 **green and yellow** sickly, pale and sallow   117 **Patience** statue personifying grief, often affixed to a tomb   **monument** carved figure on a memorial   120 **shows** outwards displays   **are more** have more substance   **will** our desires   **still** always   125 **to** to go to   128 **give no place** not give way   **denay** denial   5.1   85 **But for** as for   88 **but ... have** except that which I refuse him, i. e. love   93 **lord** if addressed to Viola, 'husband' (Viola uses the sense of 'master')   95 **aught** anything   96 **fat** gross   **fulsome** distasteful, nauseating   100 **uncivil** uncivilized   101 **ingrate** ungrateful   **unauspicious** ill-omened, unpromising   103 **tendered** offered (may play on 'tender', i. e. loving, gentle)   104 **Even what** whatever/exactly what   **become** suit   106 **Egyptian thief** character from a Greek romance who tried to kill a captive he loved when his own life was threatened   108 **savours nobly** has a taste of nobility

                Since you to non-regardance cast my faith,
110   And that I partly know the instrument
                That screws me from my true place in your favour,
                Live you the marble-breasted tyrant still.
                But this your minion, whom I know you love,
                And whom, by heaven I swear, I tender dearly,
115   Him will I tear out of that cruel eye,
                Where he sits crowned in his master's spite.
                Come, boy, with me. My thoughts are ripe in mischief:
                I'll sacrifice the lamb that I do love,
                To spite a raven's heart within a dove.
120   VIOLA   And I, most jocund, apt and willingly,
                To do you rest, a thousand deaths would die.
        OLIVIA Where goes Cesario?
        VIOLA   After him I love
                More than I love these eyes, more than my life,
125   More, by all mores, than e'er I shall love wife.
                If I do feign, you witnesses above
                Punish my life for tainting of my love!
        OLIVIA Ay me, detested! How am I beguiled!
        VIOLA   Who does beguile you? Who does do you wrong?
130   OLIVIA Hast thou forgot thyself? Is it so long?
                Call forth the holy father.
        ORSINO Come, away!
        OLIVIA Whither, my lord? Cesario, husband, stay.
        ORSINO Husband!
135   OLIVIA Ay, husband. Can he that deny?
        ORSINO Her husband, sirrah!
        VIOLA   No, my lord, not I.
        OLIVIA Alas, it is the baseness of thy fear
                That makes thee strangle thy propriety
140   Fear not, Cesario; take thy fortunes up.
                Be that thou know'st thou art, and then thou art
                As great as that thou fear'st.
        Enter Priest
                O, welcome, father!
                Father, I charge thee, by thy reverence
145   Here to unfold, though lately we intended
                To keep in darkness what occasion now
                Reveals before 'tis ripe, what thou dost know
                Hath newly pass'd between this youth and me.
        Priest A contract of eternal bond of love,

---

109 **non-regardance** disrespect/lack of attention   110 **that** since   111 **screws** forces   113 **minion** favourable/darling   114 **tender** care for/value   116 **in ... spite** to the vexation of his master   117 **ripe in mischief** ready to do harm   120 **jocund** cheerful   **apt** readily   121 **To ... rest** in order to give you ease   125 **mores** such comparisons   127 **tainting of** discrediting   128 **beguiled** deceived   136 **sirrah** sir (contemptuous; used to an inferior)   138 **baseness** cowardice/lowly nature   139 **strangle** stifle   **propriety** real identity   141 **that** that which   142 **that thou fear'st** him you fear, i. e. Orsino   145 **unfold** reveal

150　　　　Confirm'd by mutual joinder of your hands,
　　　　　　Attested by the holy close of lips,
　　　　　　Strengthen'd by interchangement of your rings,
　　　　　　And all the ceremony of this compact
　　　　　　Seal'd in my function, by my testimony.
155　　　　Since when, my watch hath told me, toward my grave
　　　　　　I have travell'd but two hours.
　　　　ORSINO　O thou dissembling cub! What wilt thou be
　　　　　　When time hath sow'd a grizzle on thy case?
　　　　　　Or will not else thy craft so quickly grow
160　　　　That thine own trip shall be thine overthrow?
　　　　　　Farewell, and take her; but direct thy feet
　　　　　　Where thou and I henceforth may never meet.
　　　　VIOLA　My lord, I do protest—
　　　　OLIVIA　O, do not swear!
165　　　　Hold little faith, though thou hast too much fear.

Questions for Comprehension and Reflection
Act II, scene 4
1. What attracts Orsino to Olivia?
2. How does Orsino compare his love and a woman's love?
3. What might Viola suggest to Orsino when she says "I am all the daughters of my father's house,/And all the brothers too"?

Act V, scene 1
1. What does Orsino intend to do with Viola? And why?
2. What is the priest's proof of Olivia's marriage to "Cesario"?
3. How long have they been married?

IV SHAKESPEAREAN RELEVANCE

A. Shakespeare in Everyday English
Please try to understand the following Shakespearean words and expressions in the contexts designated within parentheses and give their generally used meanings in the space provided.
1. a night owl (2.3.44): _____
2. cakes and ale (2.3.89): _____
3. horse of a different color (2.3.126): _____
4. in stitches (3.2.45): _____
5. midsummer madness (3.4.45): _____
6. out of the jaws of death (3.4.281): _____

B. Shakespeare in Literature
Read the following literary excerpts, locate the Shakespearean allusions and explain their meanings

---

150 **joinder** joining　151 **close** meeting　153 **compact** agreement　154 **Seal'd ... function** certified by my priestly authority　155 **watch** clock　158 **grizzle** sprinkling of grey hair　**case** (animal) skin　159 **craft** cunning　160 **trip** wrestling move to throw opponent　163 **protest** declare/swear　165 **Hold little faith** keep some part of your promise

according to the contexts where they appear.

1. Clive Barker, "*Sex, Death and Starshine*," a short story in a series of horror fiction published between 1984 and 1985, revolving around a doomed production of *Twelfth Night*.
2. Ken Ludwig, *Leading Ladies*, 2004, a play inspired by *Twelfth Night*.
3. Elizabeth Hand, *Illyria*, 2006, a novella featuring a high school production of *Twelfth Night* with many references to the play, especially Feste's song.
4. Cassandra Clare, *City of Glass*, 2009, a novel containing chapter names inspired by quotations of Antonio and Sebastian.
5. He smiled on me in quite a superior sort of way—such a smile as would have become the face of Malvolio. (Bram Stoker, *Dracula*, 1897)
6. At present I share Bafliol with one ... man ... who rather repels me at meals by his ... habit of shewing satisfaction with the food: Sir Toby Belch was not in it. (Aldous Huxley, *The Letters of Aldous Huxley*, 1915)
7. "This is midsummer madness," cried I; "and I for one will be no party to it." (R. Stevenson, *The Master of Ballantrae*, 1889)

C. Shakespeare in Music, Art and on Screen

1910: *Twelfth Night*, a silent, short adaptation released by Vitagraph Studios, starring Florence Turner, Julia Swayne Gordon and Marina Sais.
1980: *Twelfth Night*, a TV adaptation as part of the *BBC Television Shakespeare* series.
1996: *Twelfth Night*, a British film adaptation, directed by Trevor Nunn with an all-star cast.
1998: *Shakespeare in Love*, a British-American romantic comedy-drama film directed by John Madden with several references to *Twelfth Night* near the end of the movie.
2004: *Wicker Park*, a psychological drama/romantic mystery film directed by Paul McGuigan and loosely based on *Twelfth Night*.
2006: *She's the Man*, a film that modernises Shakespeare's story as a contemporary teenage comedy.

V SHAKESPEARE QUOTES

If music be the food of love, play on;
Give me excess of it. (1.1.1-2)
Better a witty fool than a foolish wit. (1.5.27)
O, stay and hear; your true love's coming (2.3.27)
I was adored once too. (2.3.136)
Some are born great, some achieve greatness, and some have greatness thrust upon 'em. (2.5.107-108)
There is no darkness but ignorance. (4.2.31)
I'll be revenged on the whole pack of you. (5.1.360)

6. The Tempest
暴 风 雨

I INTRODUCTION

几乎可以肯定的是,《暴风雨》是莎士比亚独立创作的最后一部戏剧,但常常又是他的全集版本中(包括第一对开本 the First Folio)排在首位的一出戏。对其个中原因专家学者议论纷纷、莫衷一是,而对于该剧的解读则已成为解读莎翁及其作品的试金石。该剧的所有情节均在一座岛上展开,引发了读者和观众有关世外桃源和政治乌托邦的种种想像。那不勒斯国王阿隆佐刚刚出席其女与突尼斯国王的大婚,正和继嗣腓迪南及其随从乘船返国。同行的还有12年前在那不勒斯国王的帮助下篡得其兄普洛斯彼罗米兰公爵爵位的安东尼奥。当年,被废黜的普洛斯彼罗和米兰达父女二人乘着腐朽的破船在海上随波逐流,最终登上一座小岛。后来,普洛斯彼罗运用多年苦修得来的法术解救了被女巫西考拉克斯幽禁在松树中的精灵爱丽儿,并将女巫丑陋的儿子凯列班变成了自己的奴仆。现在,当普洛斯彼罗得知阿隆佐的船队正经过小岛时,他决定实施复仇计划,一雪多年前的篡位之辱……该剧反映了莎士比亚时代对巫术的普遍信仰、对海外奇异新天地发现的兴奋以及对篡位夺权的不齿。在后帝国主义时代,它被认为是对殖民主义的抨击之作。而该剧末尾处普洛斯彼罗的辞别小岛告白则被认为是莎翁本人辞别伦敦戏剧舞台和创作生涯退隐家乡的宣言。选文的第一段是令人忍俊不禁的凯列班、斯丹法诺和特林鸠罗的"锵锵三人行",而第二个选段则是普洛斯彼罗那篇著名的告别演说。

II PLOT SUMMARY

A ship at sea is being tossed by a furious tempest and driven relentlessly against an island shore. The sailing master and the boatswain are on deck directing the seamen in the complicated handling of the sails, shouting through the storm. The royal passengers (**Alonso**,[1] King of Naples, his brother **Sebastian**,[2] and Prospero's brother **Antonio**[3] — the usurping Duke of Milan) and other members of the court group rush anxiously on deck and exhort the crew to do their best. The boatswain, utterly contemptuous of their rank: "What cares these roarers for the name of king?" (1.1.14) rudely orders them below deck. The royal party remains on deck for some time, but finally they go below to pray.

Meanwhile, **Prospero**,[4] exiled Duke of Milan, and his fifteen-year-old daughter, **Miranda**,[5] are stationed before the cave which has been their home for twelve years. It is Prospero who, by his magic art, has raised the storm and jeopardized the ship. Miranda has watched the mariners'

---

[1] **Alonso** /əˈlɒnzəʊ/ 阿隆佐 [2] **Sebastian** /sɪˈbæstjən/ 西巴斯辛 [3] **Antonio** /ænˈtəʊnɪəʊ/ 安东尼奥 [4] **Prospero** /ˈprɒspərəʊ/ 普洛斯彼罗 [5] **Miranda** /mɪˈrændə/ 米兰达

Miranda, 1888, Frederick Goodall

peril in anguish and begs her father to end the storm and save them. He assures her that no harm will come to any of these people. Then he proceeds to give her the history of their coming to the island. He tells her that he is the rightful Duke of Milan, who entrusted the general management of his dukedom to his brother, Antonio, "thus neglecting **worldly ends**,[6] all dedicated/To **closeness**[7] and the bettering my mind." (1.2.105-106) With the help of the King of Naples, Antonio staged an insurrection and seized power. Prospero was cast off alone with Miranda, who was then three years old. **Gonzalo**,[8] a nobleman of Naples appointed to carry out the plan, took pity on them and stocked their craft with food, water, cloth, and other necessities, including books from Prospero's library "with volumes that/I prize above my dukedom." (1.2.194-195) They were cast up on the shore of this island. Now, by the strangest accident, all of Prospero's enemies have been brought together within his power on one ship.

Prospero puts Miranda to sleep and gives audience to **Ariel**,[9] his servant, a spirit of airy quality, who performs his magic works. Ariel reports that he has done a very good job of raising a storm, frightening both passengers and crew, and then calming everything down without harm to anyone: the crew are below and the passengers are dispersed about the island and "The king's son have I landed by himself,/Whom I left cooling of the air with sighs/In an old angle of the isle,

and sitting,/His arms in this sad knot." (1.2.257-260) Prospero is pleased but takes occasion to remind Ariel of his past history and his obligations. Prospero points out that, were it not for him, Ariel would still be a prisoner in a "cloven pine" where he was left by **Sycorax**,[10] a witch who formerly ruled the island. Next **Caliban**[11] is introduced, a half-monster, son of Sycorax, and enslaved by Prospero's magic. Caliban was treated kindly and taught to speak by Prospero and his daughter, but fell from grace when he attempted to rape Miranda, for which the slave wished, "Wouldn't had been done! /Thou didst prevent me: **I had peopled else**[12]/This isle with Calibans." (1.2.408-410)

The Enchanted Island: Before the Cell of Prospero, 1797, Henry Fuseli

Ariel introduces some charming, light songs to bewitch **Ferdinand**,[13] Prince of Naples, whom he is leading by this method to the neighborhood of Prospero's cave so that he can meet Miranda. "At the first sight/They have changed eyes," (1.2.513-514) as has been Prospero's intention. However, to prevent this love affair from developing too rapidly, "lest too light winning/Make the prize light," (1.2.526-527) Prospero becomes rough and unfriendly to Ferdinand, disarms him by his magic, and puts him to work at the menial task of log piling. This serves only to increase Miranda's love and admiration for the prince.

We next find the rest of the shipwrecked passengers wandering around in dejection in another

---

6 **worldly ends** i.e. state or governmental duties   7 **closeness** solitude   8 **Gonzalo** /gɔnˈzɑːləu/ 贡柴罗   9 **Ariel** /ˈɛərɪəl/ 爱丽儿   10 **Sycorax** /ˈsikəræks/ 西考拉克斯   11 **Caliban** /ˈkælibæn/ 凯列班   12 **I had peopled else** otherwise I would have populated   13 **Ferdinand** /ˈfəːdinənd/ 腓迪南

part of the island, being kept strictly separate by Ariel from the others. They think that Ferdinand, Prince of Naples, is drowned, and, of course, Alonso, King of Naples, is grief-stricken to the point of indifference. Gonzalo attempts to comfort the king, while Sebastian and Antonio mock his attempts and blame the king for their troubles.

Ariel, invisible, arrives and puts all but Sebastian and Antonio to sleep. The latter convinces the former to agree to kill Sebastian's brother and old Gonzalo while they sleep, so that Sebastian can seize the throne of Naples as Antonio did the dukedom of Milan. They are about to put their evil design into effect when Ariel, still invisible, awakens Gonzalo who finds the two conspirators with their swords drawn ready to strike. They make the excuse of having heard the roaring of wild animals. The king accepts their excuse and the party moves off in search of Ferdinand.

The next episode shows Caliban, bringing in wood for Prospero and heartily cursing him, at the same time describing the pinches and cramps he is subjected to when disobedient. The king's jester, **Trinculo**,[13] also saved from the ship, encounters Caliban and is utterly at a loss to classify him. Nevertheless, he creeps under the monster's cloak to take shelter from a sudden downpour. **Stephano**,[14] the butler, having ridden ashore on a cask of wine, stumbles upon this ridiculous scene, quite drunk on the wine and carrying a supply in an improvised bark container. After some comic comment about the four-legged monster beneath the cloak, Stephano discovers Trinculo and Caliban, and offers them a drink. Caliban, new to the effects of alcohol, takes Stephano for a god and forthwith spurns any allegiance to Prospero.

The Temptest, Act V, Scene 1, c. 1795, Francis Wheatley

Miranda comes to speak with Ferdinand while he carries logs, a labour assigned him by Prospero which is made light by thoughts of Miranda: "There be some **sports**[15] are **painful**,[16] and **their labour/Delight in them sets off**:[17] some kinds of **baseness**/[18] Are nobly undergone, and most poor matters/Point to rich ends." (3.1.1-4) She offers herself in the sweetest and most innocent terms to Ferdinand as his wife; he accepts her in equally innocent terms and offers himself as her husband. Prospero, who surveys this scene, voices his approval of the "fair encounter/Of two most rare affections".

Then in another part of the island Ariel hovers about, bedeviling Trinculo and Stephano by mimicking Trinculo's voice while invisible. However, they make up after their quarrel, and Caliban suggests that they proceed to Prospero's cave, where Prospero will be asleep in the middle of the afternoon, and kill him. He suggests a number of brutal methods of doing this. Ariel goes off playing a tune, with Trinculo, Caliban, and Stephano in pursuit.

Meanwhile, the royal party has continued searching for Ferdinand. Antonio and Sebastian, unrepentant, are waiting for another opportunity to kill Alonso. Prospero, with his magic, sets a feast before them but, before they can touch it, causes the banquet to vanish. Ariel, in the guise of a harpy, accuses Alonso, Antonio, and Sebastian, recalling their past crimes to them. The king is conscience-stricken and desperate, while Sebastian and Antonio lash out at their accuser with swords.

---

13 **Trinculo** /ˈtrinkjuləu/ 特林鸠罗 14 **Stephano** /ˈstæfənəu/ 斯丹法诺 15 **sports** activities 16 **painful** arduous 17 **their ... off** the pleasure derived from the task is enhanced by the hard work/pleasure in undertaking the task removes the sense of effort 18 **baseness** contemptible work

The Tempest, Act Ⅴ, 1735, William Hogarth

  Satisfied that his enemies are in his power, Prospero turns his attention to Ferdinand and Miranda, relaxing restraints and handsomely sanctioning the union of the two lovers. He has Ariel arrange a masque in their honor. In the masque, Iris, messenger of the Greek gods, invites Ceres, goddess of the harvest and all earthly fertility, to meet Juno, queen of the gods, on a certain lawn to celebrate "a contract of true love." Ceres refuses to come if she must meet Venus. But when assured that Venus, goddess of sensual love, will not mar the celebration, she agrees to attend. Juno arrives and a marriage blessing is conferred on the young couple. The masque ends abruptly when Prospero remembers that Caliban, Trinculo, and Stephano, the dissolute trio, are on their way to murdering him. He waves the masque and spirits away, and accordingly they vanish.

  Ariel reports that he has bewitched the conspirators through all kinds of obstructions and left them floundering in a pond covered with filth not far away. Ordered by Prospero, Ariel hangs out some "glittering apparel" on a nearby line, and when the conspirators arrive, Stephano and Trinculo are so attracted to the clothing that they forget the object of their march, the murder of Prospero. Caliban is unimpressed and begs them to leave these things alone. Prospero and Ariel turn a pack of spirit dogs on the conspirators and they decamp in confusion and terror.

  Prospero has a long conversation with his "delicate Ariel" in which he tells him that he will take pity on his enemies. He has Ariel release the royal party from their magic imprisonment in a grove near the cave. When they arrive in a daze, Prospero indicts his enemies and expresses his gratitude to Gonzalo. He tells Antonio and Sebastian that he could expose them for their plot on the life of the king, but out of the pure spirit of reconciliation, he will "tell no tales." The implication is that they will have to behave in the future.

  Prospero leads Alonso to the cave to see his son playing chess with Miranda. They do not care for the chess game which they have abandoned, preferring loving conversation. Alonso is overcome and immediately gives his blessing on the marriage of the two. He is about to apologize to Miranda about his behavior twelve years before, when Prospero stops him and suggests, "Let us not burden our remembrances with/A heaviness that's gone." (5.1.225-226)

  Ariel magically fetches up the master and the boatswain of the ship, and they are properly astonished. Then Ariel produces the two drunken conspirators, Stephano and Trinculo, along with Caliban. The last is utterly disillusioned as to Stephano's being a god. The other two are left to the discipline of their master, the king. Caliban resolves to seek for grace. Prospero will put up the king and his followers for the night and will go into the details of his life during the last twelve years. With his staff broken and buried deep in the earth and his book drowned in the depth of the ocean, Prospero has renounced his magic and is ready to sail back to Milan to resume his dukedom.

Beyond the Play: *"Our Revels Now Are Ended"*

With so many lost years to retrieve in Shakespeare's career, biographers have resorted conveniently to the Bard's plays. The historical plays factored out, his career is often conjectured as beginning with the comedies, optimistic romances vibrant with the energy of youth. Next, the problem plays (plays that are neither comic nor purely tragic), hinting at an impending spiritual crisis. Finally, the tragedies, a period beginning with Hamlet's melancholy and gradually deepening into the harsh ugliness of Timon. But the period of inward calm that follows, reflected in the tranquil joyousness of the romances, belies this view. *The Tempest* is Shakespeare's requiem to the stage. As Prospero breaks his staff, flings his books into the sea, and leaves his enchanted island for Milan, so Shakespeare abandons his charmed stage and returns to cosy domesticity in Stratford-upon-avon.

III SELECTED READINGS

Act II, scene 2

    Enter CALIBAN with a burden of wood. A noise of thunder heard
    CALIBAN   All the infections that the sun sucks up
        From bogs, fens, flats, on Prosper fall and make him
        By inch-meal a disease! His spirits hear me
        And yet I needs must curse. But they'll nor pinch,
5   Fright me with urchin—shows, pitch me i' the mire,
        Nor lead me, like a firebrand, in the dark
        Out of my way, unless he bid 'em: but
        For every trifle are they set upon me,
        Sometime like apes that mow and chatter at me,

2.2 1 **infections** unhealthy vapors rising from the ground or other sources   3 **inch-meal** inch by inch   6 **firebrand** will-o'-the-wisp (磷火)   9 **mow** grimace, make faces

10   And after bite me, then like hedgehogs, which
Lie tumbling in my barefoot way and mount
Their pricks at my footfall: sometime am I
All wound with adders, who with cloven tongues
Do hiss me into madness.
      Enter TRINCULO
15   Lo, now, lo!
Here comes a spirit of his, and to torment me
For bringing wood in slowly. I'll fall flat:
Perchance he will not mind me.
     TRINCULO   Here's neither bush nor shrub, to bear off any weather at
20   all, and another storm brewing: I hear it sing i' the wind: yond same
black cloud, yond huge one, looks like a foul bombard that would
shed his liquor. If it should thunder as it did before, I know not
where to hide my head: yond same cloud cannot choose but fall by
pailfuls. What have we here? A man or a fish? Dead or alive? A fish:
25   he smells like a fish: a very ancient and fishlike smell: a kind of not-
of-the-newest Poor-John. A strange fish! Were I in England now — as
once I was — and had but this fish painted, not a holiday fool there
but would give a piece of silver: there would this monster make a
man: any strange beast there makes a man: when they will not give
30   a doit to relieve a lame beggar, they will lazy out ten to see a dead
Indian. Legged like a man and his fins like arms! Warm o' my troth!
I do now let loose my opinion, hold it no longer: this is no fish, but
an islander, that hath lately suffered by a thunderbolt. (*Thunder*)
Alas, the storm is come again! My best way is to creep under his
35   gaberdine; there is no other shelter hereabouts. Misery acquaints a
man with strange bed-fellows. I will here shroud till the dregs of the
storm be past.
      Enter STEPHANO, *singing with a bottle in his hand*
     STEPHANO   I shall no more to sea, to sea,
40   Here shall I die ashore—
This is a very scurvy tune to sing at a man's funeral: well, here's my comfort.
      Drinks
      Sings
The master, the swabber, the boatswain and I,
The gunner and his mate,
45   Loved Mall, Meg and Marian and Margery,
But none of us cared for Kate.
For she had a tongue with a tang,
Would cry to a sailor, 'Go hang!'
She loved not the savour of tar nor of pitch,

---

10 **after** afterward   13 **wound** wound round   **adders** venomous snakes   **cloven** split   18 **mind** notice   19 **bear off** ward off   21 **bombard** leather wine jug   26 **poor-John** dried and salted hake, a cheap fish eaten esp. by the poor   27 **fish painted** i.e. on a sign to attract passers-by   28-29 **make a man** make a man rich/be taken for a man   30 **doit** trifling sum (a small Dutch coin)   30-31 **dead Indian** American Indians were sometimes displayed to the paying public   **Legged** with legs   31 **o' my troth** by my faith   32 **let loose** take back   35 **gaberdine** long, loose coarse-textured cloak   36 **shroud** shelter   41 **scurvy** wretched, disagreeable   43 **swabber** sailor who washed the deck   47 **tang** sting   49 **savor** smell

50   Yet a tailor might scratch her where'er she did itch:
        Then to sea, boys, and let her go hang!
        This is a scurvy tune too: but here's my comfort.   *Drinks*
    CALIBAN Do not torment me: Oh!
    STEPHANO What's the matter? Have we devils here? Do you put
55   tricks upon's with savages and men of Ind, ha? I have not scaped
        drowning to be afeard now of your four legs; for it hath been said,
        'As proper a man as ever went on four legs cannot make him give
        ground'; and it shall be said so again while Stephano breathes at's
        nostrils.
60 CALIBAN The spirit torments me; Oh!
    STEPHANO This is some monster of the isle with four legs, who
        hath got, as I take it, an ague. Where the devil should he learn our
        language? I will give him some relief, if it be but for that. if I can
        recover him and keep him tame and get to Naples with him, he's a
65   present for any emperor that ever trod on neat's leather.
    CALIBAN Do not torment me, prithee; I'll bring my wood home
        faster.
    STEPHANO He's in his fit now and does not talk after the wisest. He
        shall taste of my bottle: if he have never drunk wine afore will go
70   near to remove his fit. If I can recover him and keep him tame, I will
        not take too much for him; he shall pay for him that hath him, and
        that soundly.
    CALIBAN Thou dost me yet but little hurt; thou wilt anon, I know it
        by thy trembling: now Prosper works upon thee.
75 STEPHANO Come on your ways; open your mouth; here is that which will give language
        to you, cat. Open your mouth: this will shake your shaking, I can tell you, and that
        soundly: you cannot tell who's your friend: open your chaps again.
    TRINCULO I should know that voice: it should be—but he is drowned;
80   and these are devils: O defend me!
    STEPHANO Four legs and two voices: a most delicate monster! His
        forward voice now is to speak well of his friend; his backward voice
        is to utter foul speeches and to detract. If all the wine in my bottle
        will recover him, I will help his ague. Come. Amen! I will pour some
85   in thy other mouth.
    TRINCULO Stephano!
    STEPHANO Doth thy other mouth call me? Mercy, mercy! This is
        a devil, and no monster: I will leave him; I have no long spoon.
    TRINCULO Stephano! If thou beest Stephano, touch me and speak to
90   me: for I am Trinculo—be not afeard—thy good friend Trinculo.
    STEPHANO If thou beest Trinculo, come forth: I'll pull thee by the

---

50 **tailor ... itch** she would let a tailor (proverbially lecherous) have sex with her (**itch** may suggest venereal disease)   55 **Ind** India   57-59 **proper** normal/fine   **give ground** yield   **at's nostrils** through his nostrils   62 **ague** sickness, shaking, fever   63 **relief** refreshment   64 **recover** revive   65 **neat's leather** cowhide   68 **after** in the manner of   70-71 **I ... him** i.e. no price can be too high for him   73 **anon** shortly   75 **Come on your ways** come on/come here   75-76 **language ... cat** 'ale will make a cat speak' (proverbial)   77 **shake** cast off   81 **delicate** extraordinary/ingeniously made/delightful   83 **detract** slander   88 **long spoon** 'he should have a long spoon that sups with the devil' (proverbial)

lesser legs: if any be Trinculo's legs, these are they. Thou art very Trinculo indeed! How camest thou to be the siege of this moon-calf? Can he vent Trinculos?

95 TRINCULO I took him to be killed with a thunder-stroke. But art thou not drowned, Stephano? I hope now thou art not drowned. Is the storm overblown? I hid me under the dead moon-calf's gaberdine for fear of the storm. And art thou living, Stephano? O Stephano, two Neapolitans 'scaped!

100 STEPHANO Prithee, do not turn me about; my stomach is not constant.

CALIBAN [Aside] These be fine things, an if they be not sprites. That's a brave god and bears celestial liquor. I will kneel to him.

STEPHANO How didst thou 'scape? How camest thou hither?
105 Swear by this bottle how thou camest hither. I escaped upon a butt of sack which the sailors heaved o'erboard, by this bottle; which I made of the bark of a tree with mine own hands since I was cast ashore.

CALIBAN I'll swear upon that bottle to be thy true subject; for the
110 liquor is not earthly.

STEPHANO Here; swear then how thou escapedst.

TRINCULO Swum ashore. man, like a duck: I can swim like a duck, I'll be sworn.

STEPHANO Here, kiss the book. Though thou canst swim like a
115 duck, thou art made like a goose.

TRINCULO O Stephano. hast any more of this?

STEPHANO The whole butt, man: my cellar is in a rock by the sea-side where my wine is hid. How now, moon-calf! How does thine ague?

120 CALIBAN Hast thou not dropp'd from heaven?

STEPHANO Out o' the moon, I do assure thee: I was the man i' th'moon when time was.

STEPHANO Come, kiss.

TRINCULO But that the poor monster's in drink: an abominable
125 monster!

CALIBAN I'll show thee the best springs; I'll pluck thee berries; I'll fish for thee and get thee wood enough. A plague upon the tyrant that I serve! I'll bear him no more sticks, but follow thee, thou wondrous man.

130 TRINCULO A most ridiculous monster, to make a wonder of a Poor drunkard!

CALIBAN I prithee, let me bring thee where crabs grow: and I with my long nails will dig thee pignuts: show thee a jay's nest and instruct thee how to snare the nimble marmoset: I'll bring thee to

---

92 **lesser legs** presumably Trinculo has shorter legs than Caliban   93 **siege** excrement (Stephano pulls Trinculo out from between Caliban's legs)   **moon-calf** monstrosity, misshapen creature, idiot (born under the moon's influence)   94 **vent** discharge/fart   97 **overblown** blown over   102 **an if** if   105-106 **butt of sack** barrel of Spanish white wine   114 **kiss the book** alludes to kissing the Bible to confirm an oath, and to the phrase 'kiss the cup' (i.e. have another drink)   115 **goose** simpleton; also suggests drunken giddiness   122 **when time was** once   132 **crabs** crab-apples   133 **pignuts** edible roots, earth chestnuts   134 **marmoset** small monkey

135   clustering filberts, and sometimes I'll get thee young scamels from the rock. Wilt thou go with me?
  STEPHANO   I prithee now, lead the way without any more talking.
    Trinculo, the king and all our company else being drowned, we will
    inherit here. – Here, bear my bottle. Fellow Trinculo, we'll fill him
140   by and by again.
  CALIBAN   [*Sings drunkenly*] Farewell master; farewell, farewell!
  TRINCULO   A howling monster: a drunken monster!
  CALIBAN   No more dams I'll make for fish,
    Nor fetch in firing at requiring,
145   Nor scrape trencher, nor wash dish,
    'Ban, 'Ban, Cacaliban
    Has a new master: get a new man.
    Freedom, high-day! High-day, freedom! Freedom, high-day, freedom!
  STEPHANO   O brave monster! Lead the way.
  Exeunt

Act V, scene 1

  EPILOGUE SPOKEN BY PROSPERO
    Now my charms are all o'erthrown,
    And what strength I have's mine own,
    Which is most faint: now, tis true,
    I must be here confined by you,
360   Or sent to Naples. Let me not,
    Since I have my dukedom got
    And pardoned the deceiver, dwell
    In this bare island by your spell,
    But release me from my bands
365   With the help of your good hands;
    Gentle breath of yours my sails
    Must fill, or else my project fails,
    Which was to please. Now I want
    Spirits to enforce, art to enchant,
370   And my ending is despair,
    Unless I be relieved by prayer,
    Which pierces so that it assaults
    Mercy itself and frees all faults.
    As you from crimes would pardoned be,
375   Let your indulgence set me free.

---

135 **filberts** hazelnuts   **scamels** of uncertain meaning, perhaps error for 'seamews' (seagulls) or 'shamois' (goat); a fish or shellfish has also been suggested   5.1 356 **charms ... o'erthrown** my magic is relinquished (**o'erthrown** plays on the sense of 'usurped')   359 **you** the audience   364 **bands** bonds   365 **hands** i.e. in applause   366 **Gentle breath** kind words/cries of approval   368 **want** lack   371 **prayer** approbation and forgiveness   372 **pierces ... assaults** penetrates so deeply that it moves   375 **indulgence** approval (playing on the Catholic sense of 'official release from sin')

Questions for Comprehension and Reflection
Act II, scene 2
1. How does Stephano describe Caliban?
2. What does Caliban think Stephano and Trinculo are?
3. What's your take on the character Caliban?

Act V, scene 1
1. Who is Prospero addressing?
2. What request is Prospero making?
3. What might "Let your indulgence set me free" (375) signify?

IV SHAKESPEAREAN RELEVANCE

A. Shakespeare in Everyday English
Please try to understand the following Shakespearean words and expressions in the contexts designated within parentheses and give their generally used meanings in the space provided.
1. a sea-change (1.2.464): _____
2. inch-meal (2.2.3): _____
3. strange bed-fellows (2.2.32): _____
4. melt into air, into thin air (4.1.163): _____
5. fair play (5.1.193): _____
6. brave new world (5.1.205): _____
7. in a pickle (5.1.316): _____

B. Shakespeare in Literature
Read the following literary excerpts, locate the Shakespearean allusions and explain their meanings according to the contexts where they appear.
1. Percy Bysshe Shelley, "With a Guitar, To Jane".
2. Robert Browning, "Caliban upon Setebos", 1864.
3. W. H. Auden, "The Sea and the Mirror: A Commentary on Shakespeare's *The Tempest*", 1942—1944.
4. He escorted them to their box with a sort of pompous humility, waving his fat jewelled hands, and talking at the top of his voice. Dorian Cray loathed him more than ever. He felt as if he had come to look for Miranda and had been met by Caliban. (Oscar Wilde, *The Picture of Dorian Gray*, 1891)
5. I was wrestling with my unconscious, an immense dark brother who seeped around me when I was awake, flowed over me when I slept ... a force with a baby's features, greedy orifices, a madman's cunning and an animal's endurance, a Caliban as quicksilver as Ariel. (Edmund White, *A Boy's Own Story*, 1982)
6. You were Prospero enough to make her what she has become. (Henry James, *Portrait of a Lady*, 1881)
7. She found herself standing, in the character of hostess, face to face with a man she had never seen before—moreover, looking at him with a Miranda-like curiosity and interest that she had never yet bestowed on a mortal. (Thomas Hardy, *A Pair of Blue Eyes*, 1873)

C. Shakespeare in Music, Art and on Screen

1667: *The Tempest, or The Enchanted Island*, an adaptation by John Dryden and Sir William Davenant.

1735: *A Scene from The Tempest*, painting by Willaim Hogarth.

1851: *Ferdinand Lured by Ariel*, a painting by John Everett Millais.

1873: *The Tempest*, an orchestral work composed by Pyotr Ilyich Tchaikovsky.

1925-1926: Incidental Music to Shakespeare's *The Tempest*, written by Jean Sibelius.

1956: *Forbidden Planet*, an MGM science fiction film directed by Fred M. Wilcox.

1991: *Prospero's Books*, a film adaptation written and directed by Peter Greenaway, starring John Gielgud (aged 87) as Prospero.

1992: "The Tempest", *Shakespeare: The Animated Tales*, abridged by Leon Garfield.

2010: *The Tempest*, a fantasy film directed by Julie Taymor, with Helen Mirren as Prospero.

V SHAKESPEARE QUOTES

The ivy which had hid my princely trunk
And sucked my verdure out on't. (1.2.101-102)
Your tale, sir, would cure deafness. (1.2.123)
My library was dukedom large enough. (1.2.126-127)
Good wombs have borne bad sons. (1.2.139)
There's nothing ill can dwell in such a temple:
If the ill-spirit have so fair a house,
Good things will strive to dwell with't. (1.2.533-535)
What's past is prologue. (2.1.255)
Misery acquaints men with strange bedfellows. (2.2.32)
Travellers ne'er did lie,
Though fools at home comdemn 'em. (3.3.30-31)
Our revels now are ended. (4.1.161)
We are such stuff as dreams are made on. (4.1.169-170)

Histories 历史剧

7. Henry IV, Part 1
亨利四世·上篇

I INTRODUCTION

《亨利四世》的剧名极易引起误解。实际上,亨利四世出镜/登台的次数极少,其作用是为亨利王子和福斯塔夫这两个更为有趣丰满的角色做支撑。该剧一开始,亨利四世如何保住王位、抵御曾经帮助他从理查二世手中篡得王位的潘西家族的叛乱似乎是该剧的主题。但随着情节的推进,亨利王子由寻欢作乐的公子哥变身为勇于担当的国君便成了中心。围绕这一中心的是以亨利四世为主宰的王宫庄重场景,以及以福斯塔夫为魁首的依斯特溪泊野猪头酒店(the Boar's Head Tavern in Eastcheap)中的喜剧情节,而游走于两者之间的亨利王子则是连接这一庄一谐设计的枢纽。该剧大体上基于史实,它始于霍美敦山英军对苏格兰的胜利(其中包括奥温·葛兰道厄所领导的威尔士叛乱),终于亨利王子在索鲁斯伯雷战役(the Battle of Shrewsbury)中对霍茨波其他潘西家族叛乱者的胜利。尽管如此,莎士比亚也根据需要运用了春秋笔法,比如令年龄相差二十好几的霍茨波和亨利王子年龄相仿并同场飙戏。这样处理的目的,一则是为了将性情迥异的二人进行对比,二则是为了铺陈剧中主角由浪荡公子到一代明君的嬗变。《亨利四世》常被称作"福斯塔夫剧"(Falstaffian play),因为该角色以其滑稽可笑和机巧睿智占了很大戏份。这个可爱的角色就连伊丽莎白一世也钟爱有加,以至于她曾不满福斯塔夫在《亨利四世下篇》中的过早离世而令莎士比亚在《温莎的风流娘儿们》中将其复活。该剧的语言丰富多彩,恰如其分地体现了人物的性格特点和社会地位。比如,左右逢源的亨利王子在酒肆操着市井俗语,而在宫中则谈吐高雅、韵律十足;霍茨波也是言语雅致,以与其刚烈而高尚的性格相称;福斯塔夫机智诙谐,为我们贡献了剧中最为精彩的台词。

II PLOT SUMMARY

When the play opens, King Henry's plan to lead a crusade to the Holy Land is delayed by "the tidings of this broil" from the battlefields. The Welsh rebel **Owen Glendower**[1] has defeated King Henry's army in the South and taken Lord Edmund **Mortimer**[2] prisoner while in the north the young Harry **Percy**[3] (or **Hotspur**),[4] who is supposedly loyal to King Henry, is refusing to send to the king the soldiers whom he has captured. The king contrasts the valiant Hotspur with his wastrel

---

1 **Owen Glendower** /ˈəuin, glenˈdauə/ 奥温·葛兰道厄　2 **Mortimer** /ˈmɔːtimə/ 摩提默　3 **Percy** /ˈpəːsi/ 潘西
4 **Hotspur** /ˈhɔtspəː/ 霍茨波

son, complaining that Lord Northumberland "Should be the father of so blest a son:/A son who is the **theme**[5] of honour's tongue;/Amongst a grove, the very **straightest plant**,/[6]Who is sweet Fortune's **minion**[7] and her pride,/Whilst I, by looking on the praise of him,/See **riot**[8] and dishonor stain the brow/Of my young Harry." (1.1.79-85) But he summons Hotspur back to the royal court so that he can explain his actions.

Falstaff with Big Wine Jar and Cup,
1896, Edward Grützner

Meanwhile, King Henry's son, Prince Harry, sits drinking in a bar with criminals and highwaymen. King Henry is very disappointed in his son; it is common knowledge that Harry, the heir to the throne, conducts himself in a manner unbefitting royalty. He spends most of his time in taverns on the seedy side of London, hanging around with vagrants and other shady characters. Harry's closest friend among the crew of rascals is **Falstaff**,[9] a surrogate father to Hal. Falstaff is a worldly and fat old man who steals and lies for a living. Falstaff is also an extraordinarily witty person who lives with great gusto. Harry claims that his spending time with these men is actually part of a scheme on his part to impress the public when he eventually changes his ways and adopts a more noble personality: "So, when this loose behavior I throw off/And pay the debt I never promisèd,/By so much better than my word I am,/By so much shall I **falsify men's hopes**,/[10] And like bright metal on a **sullen ground**,/[11] My reformation, glittering o'er my fault,/Shall show more goodly and attract more eyes/Than that which hath no foil to set it off." (1.2.145-152)

Falstaff's friend Poins arrives at the inn and announces that he has plotted the robbery of a group of wealthy travelers. Although Harry initially refuses to participate, Poins explains to him in private that he is actually playing a practical joke on Falstaff. Poins's plan is to hide before the robbery occurs, pretending to ditch Falstaff. After the robbery, Poins and Harry will rob Falstaff and then make fun of him when he tells the story of being robbed, which he will almost certainly fabricate. True to Poins's prediction, once at the **Boar's Head Tavern in Eastcheap**[12] after the robbery and the seizure of its spoils by the prince and Poins, Falstaff relishes a bogus version of the robbery until the Prince reveals his own involvement. Then Falstaff suggests they rehearse Hal's audience. Speaking as the prince, Falstaff complains about the prince's bad company except for "a good portly man" named Falstaff. Roles are switched, and Hal plays his father, accusing Falstaff as a "villainous abominable misleader of youth" and "old white-bearded Satan." (2.4.337-338) In the role of Prince Hal, Falstaff suggests the King banish everyone, but spare "sweet Jack Falstaff, kind Jack Falstaff, true Jack Falstaff, valiant Jack Falstaff," (2.4.347-348) for "banish plump Jack, and banish all the world." (2.4.350)

Hotspur arrives at King Henry's court and details the reasons why his family is frustrated with the king: the Percys were instrumental in helping Henry overthrow his predecessor, but Henry has failed to repay the favor. After King Henry leaves, Hotspur's family members explain to Hotspur their plan to build an alliance to overthrow the king. Harry and Poins, meanwhile, successfully carry out their plan to dupe Falstaff and have a great deal of fun at his expense.

---

5 **theme** subject, chief topic   6 **straightest plant** most upright tree   7 **minion** favourite   8 **riot** debauchery, corruption   9 **Falstaff** /ˈfɔːlstɑːf/ 福斯塔夫   10 **falsify men's hopes** prove expectations of me wrong   11 **sullen ground** dark background   12 **Boar's Head Tavern in Eastcheap** an inn located in Eastcheap, a western continuation of Great Tower Street towards Monument junction in central London, established before 1537, but destroyed in 1666 in the Great Fire of London, also the subject of essays by Oliver Goldsmith and Washington Irving. (http://www.buildinghistory.org/primary/inns/inns.shtml)

As they are all drinking back at the tavern, however, a messenger arrives for Harry. Harry's father has received news of the civil war that is brewing and has sent for his son; Harry is to return to the royal court the next day.

Falstaff at the Boar's Head Tavern,
before 1909, Edward Grützner

Although the Percys have gathered a formidable group of allies around them—leaders of large rebel armies from Scotland and Wales as well as powerful English nobles and clergymen who have grievances against King Henry—the alliance has begun to falter. Several key figures announce that they will not join in the effort to overthrow the king, and the danger that these defectors might alert King Henry to the rebellion necessitates going to war at once.

Heeding his father's request, Harry returns to the palace. King Henry expresses his deep sorrow and anger at his son's behavior and implies that Hotspur's valour might actually give him more right to the throne than Prince Harry's royal birth. Harry decides that it is time to reform, and he vows that he will abandon his wild ways and vanquish Hotspur in battle in order to reclaim his good name. Drafting his tavern friends to fight in King Henry's army, Harry accompanies his father to the battlefront.

The outcome of the civil war is decided in a great battle at **Shrewsbury**.[13] Harry boldly saves his father's life in battle and finally wins back his father's approval and affection. Harry also challenges and defeats Hotspur in a single combat. King Henry's forces win, and most of the leaders of the Percy family are put to death. Prince Henry kills Hotspur and laments the once ambitious Percy: "**Ill-weaved**[14] ambition, how much art thou shrunk? /When that this body did contain a spirit,/A kingdom for it was **too small a bound**,/[15] But now two paces of the vilest earth/Is room enough. This earth that bears thee dead/Bears not alive so **stout**[16] a gentleman." (5.3.89-94) Falstaff manages to survive the battle by avoiding any actual fighting.

Powerful rebel forces remain in Britain, however, so King Henry must send his sons and his forces to the far reaches of his kingdom to deal with them. When the play ends, the ultimate outcome of the war has not yet been determined; one battle has been won, but another remains to be fought.

---

13 **Shrewsbury** (/ˈʃruːzbəri/ 索鲁斯伯雷) a town in western England, situated on the River Severn near the border with Wales
14 **Ill-weaved** devious, tangled　15 **too small a bound** insufficient to contain it　16 **stout** strong, valiant

Beyond the Play: *Whose History Is It?*

The "Darnley Portrait" of Elizabeth I (ca. 1575)

Shakespeare's history plays refer to the two tetralogies, covering the reigns of English monarchs from Richard II to Richard III. The first tetralogy, *Henry VI, Part I*, *Henry VI, Part II*, *Henry VI, Part III* and *Richard III*, are recounted against the backdrop of the Wars of the Roses (1455—1487) fought between the House of Lancaster and that of York for the English crown. The second tetralogy, or the "Henriad", consists of *Richard II*, *Henry IV Part 1*, *Henry IV Part 2* and *Henry V*. set in the earlier era of the Hundred Years' War (1337—1453) between England and France. In the interim, Shakespeare also wrote *King John*, *Edward III*, *Henry VIII*. In these plays, Shakespeare has no interest in the accuracy of historical characters and events and takes immense liberties in recasting history for compelling drama on the stage. The Bard should be rightfully pardoned for historical errors, wildly altered chronologies and characterization and anachronisms. But he did take care not to rub the raw nerve of the Tudor dynasty: the then ruling sovereign was Queen Elizabeth I, the granddaughter of Henry Tudor, who had a dubious claim to the English throne after his victory over Richard at Bosworth. In an age of rigorous censorship, specifically of the so-called Tudor propaganda, a fool-hardy playwright who displeased the queen might have been penalized severely.

III SELECTED READINGS

Act I, scene 2

    PRINCE HENRY I know you all, and will awhile uphold
    The unyoked humour of your idleness.
    Yet herein will I imitate the sun,
135   Who doth permit the base contagious clouds
    To smother up his beauty from the world,
    That when he please again to be himself,
    Being wanted, he may be more wondered at,
    By breaking through the foul and ugly mists
140   Of vapours that did seem to strangle him.
    If all the year were playing holidays,
    To sport would be as tedious as to work;
    But when they seldom come, they wished for come,

1.2 132 **uphold** carry on with/support   133 **unyoked humour** unrestrained behavior, wild whim   134 **sun** common symbol of royalty   135 **contagious** noxious, infectious   **clouds** were thought to harbor disease   138 **wanted** missed, lacked   142 **sport** play, entertain oneself

And nothing pleaseth but rare accidents.
145 So, when this loose behavior I throw off
And pay the debt I never promisèd,
By how much better than my word I am,
By so much shall I falsify men's hopes,
And like bright metal on a sullen ground,
150 My reformation, glittering o'er my fault,
Shall show more goodly and attract more eyes
Than that which hath no foil to set it off.
I'll so offend, to make offence a skill.
Redeeming time when men think least I will.

Act II, Scene 4

PRINCE HENRY Do thou stand for my father, and examine me upon the particulars of my life.
FALSTAFF Shall I? Content. This chair shall be my state, this dagger my sceptre, and this cushion my crown.
280 PRINCE HENRY Thy state is taken for a joint-stool, thy golden sceptre for a leaden dagger, and thy precious rich crown for a pitiful bald crown!
FALSTAFF Well, an the fire of grace be not quite out of thee, now shalt thou be moved. Give me a cup of sack to make my eyes look red, that it may be thought I have wept, for I must speak in passion, and I will do it in King Cambyses' vein.
285 PRINCE HENRY Well, here is my leg.
FALSTAFF And here is my speech. Stand aside, nobility.
HOSTESS QUICKLY This is excellent sport, i' faith!
FALSTAFF Weep not, sweet queen, for trickling tears are vain.
HOSTESS QUICKLY O, the Father, how he holds his countenance!
290 FALSTAFF For God's sake, lords, convey my tristful queen;
For tears do stop the flood-gates of her eyes.
HOSTESS QUICKLY O, rare, he doth it as like one of these harlotry players as ever I see!
FALSTAFF Peace, good pint-pot, peace, good tickle-brain. — Harry, I do not only marvel where thou spendest thy time, but also how thou art accompanied,
295 for though the camomile, the more it is trodden on the faster it grows, yet youth, the more it is wasted the sooner it wears. That thou art my son, I have partly thy mother's word, partly my own opinion, but chiefly a villanous trick of thine eye and a foolish hanging of thy nether lip, that doth warrant me. If then thou be son to me, here lies the point: why, being son to me, art thou so
300 pointed at? Shall the blessed sun of heaven prove a micher and eat

---

144 **rare accidents** unusual events   152 **foil** contrast, background (technically, setting for a jewel)   153 **so offend** misbehave in such a way   **skill** art/cunning tactic   154 **Redeeming time** making up for lost time (**Redeeming** has religious connotations)   2.4 276 **stand for** stand in for, play the role of   **examine** question   277 **particulars** details   278 **Content** I'm content   280 **state** throne   **joint-stool** low stool made by a joiner   281 **crown** head   282 **an** and if   **fire of grace** effects of divine grace   283 **moved** affected emotionally   284 **King Cambyses' vein** ranting style; Cambyses was the tyrant in *Life of Cambyses, King of Persia* (Thomas Preston, 1569)   285 **leg** bow   288 **Weep ... vain** Falstaff addresses Mistress Quickly, who is presumably weeping from merriment (puns on 'quean', i.e. harlot, whore)   289 **O, the Father** i.e. in God's name, or Falstaff now playing the part of Hal's father   **holds his countenance** keeps a straight face, remains in character   290 **convey** take away/escort (to a seat)   **tristful** sorrowful   292 **rare** marvelous   **harlotry players** knavish actors   293 **pint-pot** Falstaff addresses Mistress Quickly with a nickname for one who sells beer   **tickle-brain** potent liquor   297 **trick** habit, feature   298 **foolish** affected/idiotic/lecherous   **warrant** assure

blackberries? A question not to be asked. Shall the sun of England prove a
thief and take purses? A question to be asked. There is a thing, Harry, which
thou hast often heard of and it is known to many in our land by the name of
pitch: this pitch, as ancient writers do report, doth defile; so doth the
305　company thou keepest. For, Harry, now I do not speak to thee in drink but in
tears: not in pleasure but in passion: not in words only, but in woes also.
And yet there is a virtuous man whom I have often noted in thy company,
but I know not his name.
PRINCE HENRY　What manner of man, an it like your majesty?
310　FALSTAFF　A goodly portly man, i' faith, and a corpulent: of a cheerful look, a
pleasing eye and a most noble carriage; and, as I think, his age some fifty, or,
by'r lady, inclining to three score; and now I remember me, his name is
Falstaff. If that man should be lewdly given, he deceives me; for, Harry, I see
virtue in his looks. If then the tree may be known by the fruit, as the fruit by
315　the tree, then, peremptorily I speak it, there is virtue in that Falstaff: him
keep with, the rest banish. And tell me now, thou naughty varlet, tell me,
where hast thou been this month?
PRINCE HENRY　Dost thou speak like a king? Do thou stand for me, and I'll play
my father.
320　FALSTAFF　Depose me? If thou dost it half so gravely, so majestically, both in
word and matter, hang me up by the heels for a rabbit-sucker or a poulter's
hare.
PRINCE HENRY　Well, here I am set.
FALSTAFF　And here I stand. Judge, my masters.
325　PRINCE HENRY　Now, Harry, whence come you?
FALSTAFF　My noble lord, from Eastcheap.
PRINCE HENRY　The complaints I hear of thee are grievous.
FALSTAFF　I'faith, my lord, they are false. — Nay, I'll tickle ye for a young prince.
PRINCE HENRY　Swearest thou, ungracious boy? Henceforth ne'er look on me.
330　Thou art violently carried away from grace: there is a devil haunts thee in
the likeness of an old fat man; a tun of man is thy companion. Why dost
thou converse with that trunk of humours, that bolting-hutch of
beastliness, that swollen parcel of dropsies, that huge bombard of sack, that
stuffed cloak-bag of guts, that roasted Manningtree ox with the pudding in
335　his belly, that reverend Vice, that grey Iniquity, that father ruffian, that
Vanity in years? Wherein is he good, but to taste sack and drink it? Wherein

300 **pointed at** gossiped about, mocked　**micher** truant/loiterer/petty thief　304 **pitch** black tar-like substance　**defile** stain, corrupt, alluding to Ecclesiastes (Apocrypha) 13:1: 'Whoso toucheth pitch shall be defiled.'　306 **passion** sincere emotion, distress　309 **an it like** if it please　310 **portly** dignified　**corpulent** solid, well-built/fat　311 **noblecarriage** dignified bearing　313 **lewdly given** wickedly, lasciviously inclined　315 **peremptorily** determinedly　316 **naughty** wicked　321 **rabbit-sucker** unweaned baby rabbit　**poulter's hare** hare hanging up in a poulter's shop (who sold fowl and game)　323 **set** seated (on the mock throne)　324 **Judge, my masters** the tavern audience must decide who is the more kingly　328 **tickle ye** amuse you in the role of　329 **ungracious** without grace, blasphemous　331 **tun** large barrel especially for wine or beer/ton weight　332 **converse** associate　**trunk** container/body　**humours** diseases/fluids that determine the disposition: blood, bile, choler, phlegm　**bolting-hutch** large bin used for sifting grain　333 **dropsies** diseases which made the body swell with an accumulation of fluid　**bombard** a leather wine jug　334 **cloak-bag** large bag for carrying clothes　**Manningtree** an Essex town with a well-known fair and cattle market　**pudding** stuffing/sausage　335 **reverend** worthy of respect　**Vice** comic character in medieval morality plays who tempted the youthful hero　**grey** grey-haired　**Iniquity** sinfulness/allegorical name for morality play character　**father** i.e. elderly　336 **Vanity** vain, proud, foolish, worthless character　**In years** i.e. advanced in years, aged　**Wherein ... good** what is he good for　**sack** white wine of Spain

neat and cleanly, but to carve a capon and eat it? Wherein cunning, but in craft? Wherein crafty, but in villany? Wherein villanous, but in all things? Wherein worthy, but in nothing?

340 FALSTAFF I would your grace would take me with you: whom means your grace?

PRINCE HENRY That villanous abominable misleader of youth, Falstaff, that old white-bearded Satan.

FALSTAFF My lord, the man I know.

345 PRINCE HENRY I know thou dost.

FALSTAFF But to say I know more harm in him than in myself, were to say more than I know. That he is old, the more the pity, his white hairs do witness it. But that he is, saving your reverence, a whoremaster, that I utterly deny. If sack and sugar be a fault, God help the wicked! If to be old and merry be a sin,

350 then many an old host that I know is damned: if to be fat be to be hated, then Pharaoh's lean kine are to be loved. No, my good lord, banish Peto, banish Bardolph, banish Poins, but for sweet Jack Falstaff, kind Jack Falstaff, true Jack Falstaff, valiant Jack Falstaff, and therefore more valiant, being, as he is, old Jack Falstaff, banish not him thy Harry's company, banish not him thy Harry's

355 company: banish plump Jack, and banish all the world.

PRINCE HENRY I do, I will.

Act V, Scene 1

PRINCE HENRY
Why, thou owest God a death. *Exit PRINCE HENRY*

FALSTAFF 'Tis not due yet. I would be loath to pay him before his day. What need I be so forward with him that calls not on me? Well, 'tis no matter, honour

130 pricks me on. But how if honour prick me off when I come on? How then? Can honour set to a leg? No. Or an arm? No. Or take away the grief of a wound? No. Honour hath no skill in surgery, then? No. What is honour? A word. What is in that word 'honour'? What is that honour? Air. A trim reckoning! Who hath it? He that died o' Wednesday. Doth he feel it? No. Doth he hear it? No. 'Tis

135 insensible, then. Yea, to the dead. But will it not live with the living? No. Why? Detraction will not suffer it. Therefore I'll none of it. Honour is a mere scutcheon: and so ends my catechism.

Questions for Understanding and Reflection
Act I, Scene 2
1. How would Prince Henry like to "imitate the sun"?
2. What are the benefits of the prince's behaving the way he does?
3. What does this monologue show about Prince Hal's personality?

---

337 **neat and cleanly** refined and skillful **cunning** knowledgeable, skillful 338 **craft** deceit **crafty** skillful 340 **take ... you** enable me to follow you, help me to understand 344 **the man I know** i.e. I recognize the man but not the description 348 **saving your reverence** begging your pardon/if you will excuse my language **whoremaster** user of whores, i.e. a wicked man 350 **host** innkeeper, pub landlord 351 **Pharaoh's lean kine** biblical reference to Pharoah's dream in which the seven lean kine (cattle) devour the seven fat kine, fortelling famine to come (Genesis 41:1-31) 5.1 130 **prick me off** marks me down (for a dead man) 131 **set to a leg** join together, set a broken leg **grief** pain 133 **trim** fine, neat 135 **insensible** cannot be felt by the senses 136 **Detraction** slander **scutcheon** heraldic shield, decorated with coats of arms and often used at funerals 137 **catechism** set series of questions and answers (used as a form of instruction by the Church)

Act II, Scene 4
1. What linguistic register does Falstaff employ when he plays King Henry?
2. Does Prince Hall have a positive opinion of Falstaff?
3. How does this play-within-a-play function?

Act V, Scene 1
What is Falstaff's sense of honour?

IV SHAKESPEAREAN RELEVANCE

A. Shakespeare in Everyday English
Please try to understand the following Shakespearean words and expressions in the contexts designated within parentheses and give their generally used meanings in the space provided.
1. sweet Fortune's minion (1.1.82): _____
2. give the devil its due (1.2.80): _____
3. madcap (1.2.95): _____
4. sink or swim (1.3.197): _____
5. send ... packing (2.4.221): _____
6. hue and cry (2.4.371): _____
7. ballad-monger (3.1.130): _____
8. out of compass (3.3.13): _____

B. Shakespeare in Literature
Read the following literary excerpts, locate the Shakespearean allusions and explain their meanings according to the contexts where they appear.
1. I must say anger becomes you; you would make a charming Hotspur. (Thomas Love Peacock, *Crotchet Castle*, 1831)
2. It was all so fine, so precise, and it was a wonder that this miracle was wrought by a whiskered Falstaff with a fat belly and a grubby singlet showing through the layers of wet, sour hessian. (Peter Carey, *Oscar and Luanda*, 1988)

C. Shakespeare in Music, Art and on Screen
1960: *An Age of Kings*, BBC TV mini-series, starring Tom Fleming as Henry IV, with Robert Hardy as Prince Hal, Frank Pettingell as Falstaff and Sean Connery as Hotspur.
1965: *Chimes at Midnight*, a film directed by and starring Orson Welles as Falstaff, John Gielgud as King Henry, Keith Baxter as Hal, Margaret Rutherford as Mistress Quickly and Norman Rodway as Hotspur.
1979: a BBC TV version, starring Jon Finch as Henry IV, David Gwillim as Prince Hal, Anthony Quayle as Falstaff and Tim Pigott-Smith as Hotspur.
1991: *My Own Private Idaho*, a film directed by Gus Van Sant, which is roughly based on *Part 1 of Henry IV*.
2012: *The Hollow Crown*, British TV film series, comprising the second tetralogy, *Henry IV, Part 1*, directed by Richard Eyre and starring Jeremy Irons as Henry IV, Tom Hiddleston as Prince Hal, Simon Russel Beale as Falstaff and Joe Armstrong as Hotspur.

V SHAKESPEARE QUOTES

Let us be Diana's foresters, gentlemen of the shade,
minions of the moon. (1.2.17-18)
What, in thy quips and thy quiddities? (1.2.31)
It would be argument for a week, laughter for a month,
and a good jest for ever. (2.2.67-68)
I am not in the roll of common men. (3.1.43)
I had rather be a kitten and cry mew?
Than one of these same metre ballad-mongers. (3.1.129-130)
The time of life is short!
To spend that shortness basely were too long. (5.2.83-84)
Two stars keep not their motion in one sphere;
Nor can one England brook a double reign,
Of Harry Percy and the Prince of Wales. (5.3.66-68)
The better part of valour is discretion. (5.3.117)

8. Henry IV, Part 2
亨利四世·下篇

I INTRODUCTION

作为《亨利四世上篇》的续篇,该剧叙述的是1403年索鲁斯伯雷战役和1413年亨利四世驾崩之间所发生的事情,国王日渐羸弱而王国则面临着内乱和外敌入侵的威胁。莎士比亚在剧中重点叙述了兰开斯特公爵(即约翰王子)如何巧用诈术剿灭了以约克大主教、理查·斯克鲁普和托阿斯·毛勃雷为首的叛军。之后,诺森伯兰伯爵起事,但很快被打败。威尔士的叛乱也被亨利王子镇压。与《亨利四世上篇》不同,亨利王子在此剧中大部分是缺席的,直至其父王弥留之际才出现与之和解。冗长的篇幅和苦涩的剧情以及缺少了上篇中展示霍茨波和亨利王子英雄气慨的场面,使得该剧不如上篇那么广受欢迎,而福斯塔夫的活力、胡闹和机巧则大大弥补了以上不足。他在野猪头酒店与大法官和快嘴妇人们的唇枪舌剑凸显了他的机智风趣,而屡次哄骗乡村法官夏禄的钱财则暴露了他的"英雄本色"。福斯塔夫最具风采的还是在他独处的时候,如他对夏禄的评价(3.2.217-235)以及关于葡萄酒作用的阐述(见 **Selected Readings**:Act Ⅳ, scene 1)。亨利四世的忧郁笼罩着全剧,其最著名的内心独白以"戴王冠的头是不能安于他的枕席的"结束(见 **Selected Readings**:Act Ⅲ, scene 1),揭示了为君者孤独、不安的内心。而该剧末尾处刚刚登基的亨利五世对昔日人生导师兼玩伴福斯塔夫的一句冷淡的"我不认识你,老头儿"(I know thee not, old man)一方面标志着哈尔从狂浪王子到冷峻国君转变的完成,同时也再次证明了人性的吊诡和世态的炎凉。

II PLOT SUMMARY

Now the Battle of **Shrewsbury**[1] is over, the Earl of **Northumberland**[2] receives false reports of the battle from Lord **Bardolph**,[3] but **Morton**,[4] whose "brow, like to a **title-leaf**,/[5]Foretells the nature of a tragic volume," (1.1.69-70) comes to report the rebel's defeat and his son's death. In a burst of grief, he wishes chaos upon the world. He is quickly reminded of his responsibilities to his people and of a way to get revenge. The Archbishop of York and the Lords **Mowbray**[6] and **Hastings**[7] are old friends of the dead King Richard. They have been enemies of Henry Ⅳ for many years. Now they see the diversion in the west as an opportunity to attack Henry in the east.

Back in London, Sir John Falstaff encounters the Lord Chief Justice who would like to question him about the Gadshill robbery (which took place in Act 5, *Henry Ⅳ Part Ⅰ*). Falstaff

---

1 **Shrewsbury** See footnote 13 in Henry Ⅳ Part Ⅰ 2 **Northumberland** /nɔːˈθʌmbələnd/ 诺森伯兰 3 **Bardolph** /ˈbɑːdɔlf/ 巴道夫 4 **Morton** /ˈmɔːtən/ 毛顿 5 **title-leaf** title page of a book describing the contents 6 **Mowbray** /ˈmaubrei/ 毛勃雷
7 **Hastings** /ˈheistiŋz/ 海司丁斯

answers that his commission to join Prince John against the Yorkist rebels has made him immune to arrest. Freed for the time being from the threat of imprisonment, Falstaff must still find a way of raising funds for the expedition.

In his palace at York, the Archbishop holds a council of war with Thomas Mowbray (son of the Duke of Norfolk, Henry's old enemy), Lord Hastings, and Lord Bardolph (Northumberland's emissary). Recalling Hotspur's defeat at Shrewsbury, Bardolph urges caution in engaging the King without adequate forces. The rebels decide that whether or not Northumberland joins them their numbers are sufficient to defeat the King.

On a London street, several officers attempt to arrest Falstaff for debt on a complaint lodged by Mistress Quickly, hostess of the Boar's Head Tavern. Mistress Quickly complains that "He hath eaten me out of house and home; he hath put all my substance into that fat belly of his," (2.1.51-52) and has broken a promise to marry her. The Lord Justice arrives and restores order. Falstaff manages to placate Mistress Quickly, who invites him to dinner and promises an additional loan.

On another street in London, Prince Hal and his friend Poins discuss the King's illness. The Prince is truly distressed by his father's poor health, but he knows that a show of grief now after his previous misconduct would cause the world to brand him a hypocrite. Rather than change appearances before he is ready, Prince Hal proposes that he and Poins disguise themselves as waiters and spy on Falstaff who is dining at the Boar's Head Tavern.

Back in Warkworth at Northumberland's castle, the Earl decides to join forces with the Archbishop. But his wife and Hotspur's widow, Kate, urge him to wait until the Yorkist party shows some signs of success. Northumberland agrees to retire to Scotland "[t]ill time and vantage crave my company." (2.3.70)

At the Boar's Head Tavern in Eastcheap of London, Falstaff, Doll Tearsheet, and Mistress Quickly are wining and dining. Pistol, a swaggering soldier under Falstaff's command, joins them, causes a commotion, and is driven out. The Prince and Poins listen as Falstaff gives Doll an unflattering description of the Prince. When the disguised waiters reveal their identities, Falstaff claims he has dispraised the young heir to spare him from unworthy followers. News of the King's waning strength sends the Prince flying to his side. Falstaff makes a false start to join Prince John at York and is last heard of sending for Doll to join him for the night.

In a chamber at Westminster Palace, the King is spending a restless night. Smitten by worries and unable to sleep, he admires the slumber of "happy low" including the sea-boy "upon the high and giddy mast," and concludes that "Uneasy lies the head that wears a crown." He then discusses the threat of the rebellion with **Warwick**[8] and **Surrey**[9] and recalls his own rebellion against King Richard, which he swears he had not intended. Nevertheless, he is conscience-stricken and promises that when the civil wars are over he will expiate his sins by leading an army to Jerusalem to restore the Holy Land to Christendom.

Falstaff has stopped at Gloucestershire to recruit men for his expedition. He accepts bribes from two recruits to release them from service and selects two less able-bodied men in their places. He tarries briefly with **Shallow**[10] and **Silence**,[11] two comical rural justices, whom Falstaff believes he can easily fleece once the war is over.

In Gaultree Forest, Yorkshire, the Archbishop learns of Northumberland's retreat and he also believes the king is weary of war for "His foes are so **enrooted**[12] with his friends/That, plucking to unfix an enemy,/He doth unfasten so and shake a friend,/So that his land, like an offensive wife/That hath **enraged him on**[13] to offer strokes,/As he is striking, holds his infant up/And **hangs resolved correction**[14] in the arm/That was upreared to **execution**."[15] (4.1.210-217) Thus, when

---

8 **Warwick** /ˈwɔrik/ 华列克 9 **Surrey** /ˈsʌri/ 萨立 10 **Shallow** 夏禄 11 **Silence** 赛伦斯 12 **enrooted** entangled 13 **enraged him on** provoked 14 **hangs resolved correction** forestalls the determined punishment 15 **execution** carry out the action

Westmoreland arrives with an offer of mercy from King Henry's third son, Prince John, Duke of Lancaster, he and Hastings are eager to negotiate a peace. Mowbray advises battle and only reluctantly agrees to parley with Prince John rather than fight. Still in Gaultree Forest, Prince John calls a meeting of the rebel leaders and promises to remedy their grievances if they will disband their armies and return allegiance to the King. As soon as they have done so, the Archbishop and his cohorts are seized and executed for treason.

In another part of Gaultree forest, Falstaff captures Sir John Coleville, a rebel knight. Prince John arrives, rebukes Falstaff for his delayed arrival, and gives him permission to return to London via Gloucestershire. Once alone, Falstaff dispraises Prince John, a cold-natured man, and contrasts him with Prince Hal whose natural coldness has been "manured, husbanded and tilled with excellent endeavor of drinking good and good store of fertile sherry, that he is become very hot and valiant." He observes that if he had a thousand sons, the first principle he would teach them should be to addict themselves to sack (an early version of sherry).

Henry Ⅳ is now seriously ill and feels death approaching. He intended to make a crusade to the Holy Land to expiate his sins in connection with the murder of Richard. In fact, it had been predicted that he would die in Jerusalem. He collapses in the Jerusalem Chamber, a room in Westminster, where he will die. Even on his deathbed, the King is worried about the future of England, especially since his heir apparent is so irresponsible. Prince Hal arrives later, mistakes the King for dead, and tries on the heavy crown of state, But the King awakens, delivers a lecture on royal conduct, and once again repents that "Heaven knows, my son,/By what **by-paths**[16] and indirect crooked ways/I **met**[17] this crown," (4.2.321-323) but reassures his son that "To thee it shall descend with better quiet,/Better opinion, better confirmation,/For all the **soil**[18] of the achievement goes/With me into the earth." (4.2.325-328) He also advises Prince Henry that "Be it thy course to busy **giddy**[19] minds/With foreign quarrels, that **action**,[20] **hence borne out**,/[21] May **waste**[22] the memory of the former days", (4.2.351-353) which foreshadows the Battle of Agincourt against the French in *Henry Ⅴ*. Once more Hal promises to reform. The King then asks to be taken to the Jerusalem chamber to die, thus fulfilling a prophecy that he should die but in Jerusalem, if not in the Holy Land but at least in name only.

The Banishment of Falstaff, 1846, Moritz Retzsch

When news of the King's death reaches Falstaff who has been carousing in Gloucestershire with Justice Shallow, he hurries to court, confident of special favors now that his friend Hal is King Henry Ⅴ. He is deeply disappointed, however, when Hal shows that he intends to keep his promise to his dying father. In a public scene, the new King dismisses Falstaff: "I know thee not, old man. ... That I have turned away my former self,/So will I those that kept me company." (5.5.41, 52-53) But he promises to pension his old friends, provided the latter show signs of reforming. He also promises to rely on the counsel of the older men who had supported and advised his father. Thus, Prince Hal is completely converted from a youthful reprobate to the perfect king, Henry Ⅴ.

---

16 **by-paths** obscure, indirect paths 17 **met** came by 18 **soil** grounds, foundation/stain, dishonor 19 **giddy** foolish, restless 20 **action** war 21 **hence borne out** undertaken abroad 22 **waste** dispel

Beyond the Play: *Falstaff—a "Misleader of Youth"?*

Buffoon, braggart, coward, parasite, and wit, Falstaff eclipses everyone else in *Henry IV*, the most earthly personality in Shakespeare's canon. As the only character to appear in four Shakepearean plays (others being *Henry V* and *The Merry Wives of Windsor*), he (and its derivative Falstaffian) has now become associated with someone who is "fat, jolly, and debauched." (The *New Oxford Dictionary of English*, 2005) He is more of a phenomenon than just a character in dramatic literature, an inspiration for music, paintings, operas, and even commercial products. Such an enchanting character has mesmerized some of the best actors (e.g. Orson Welles with his *Chimes at Midnight*) both on stage and screen. In spite of its popular interest, Shakespearean lovers are divided into two camps, the Falstaffians and the anti-Falstaffians. The former see Falstaff as the real central hero of *Henry IV*, praising his earthly vitality and philosophical depth. The latter disparage the character as a corrupter of youth, the seven deadly sins in human form and believe that Hal's rejection of him is both honorable and necessary. Debates of this kind undoubtedly will continue for the obvious reason that very few major Shakespearean characters are cardboard cut-out figures.

Poster for *Falstaff* (*Chimes at Midnight*), 1966

III   SELECTED READINGS

Act III, scene 1

    KING HENRY IV Go call the Earls of Surrey and of Warwick.
        But ere they come, bid them o'er-read these letters,
        And well consider of them. Make good speed.
        Exit Page
        How many thousand of my poorest subjects
5   Are at this hour asleep? O sleep, O gentle sleep,
        Nature's soft nurse, how have I frighted thee,
        That thou no more wilt weigh my eyelids down
        And steep my senses in forgetfulness?
        Why rather, sleep, liest thou in smoky cribs,
10   Upon uneasy pallets stretching thee
        And hushed with buzzing night-flies to thy slumber,
        Than in the perfumed chambers of the great,

3.1 9 **cribs** hovels   10 **pallets** straw mattresses

            Under the canopies of costly state,
            And lulled with sound of sweetest melody?
15   O thou dull god, why liest thou with the vile
            In loathsome beds, and leav'st the kingly couch
            A watch-case or a common 'larum-bell?
            Wilt thou upon the high and giddy mast
            Seal up the ship-boy's eyes, and rock his brains
20   In cradle of the rude imperious surge
            And in the visitation of the winds,
            Who take the ruffian billows by the top,
            Curling their monstrous heads and hanging them
            With deaf'ning clamour in the slipp'ry clouds,
25   That, with the hurly, death itself awakes?
            Canst thou, O partial sleep, give thy repose
            To the wet sea-boy in an hour so rude,
            And in the calmest and most stillest night,
            With all appliances and means to boot,
30   Deny it to a king? Then happy low, lie down!
            Uneasy lies the head that wears a crown.

Act IV, scene 1

         FALSTAFF   My lord, I beseech you give me leave to go through Gloucestershire,
425   and, when you come to court, stand my good, pray, in your good report.
         PRINCE JOHN   Fare you well, Falstaff. I, in my condition
            Shall better speak of you than you deserve. *Exeunt [all but Falstaff]*
         FALSTAFF   I would you had but the wit: 'twere better than your dukedom. Good
            faith, this same young sober-blooded boy doth not love me, nor a man cannot
430   make him laugh. But that's no marvel: he drinks no wine. There's never none
            of these demure boys come to any proof, for thin drink doth so over-cool their
            blood, and making many fish-meals, that they fall into a kind of male
            green-sickness, and then when they marry, they get wenches. They are
            generally fools and cowards; which some of us should be too, but for
435   inflammation. A good sherry sack hath a two-fold operation in it: it ascends me
            into the brain, dries me there all the foolish and dull and curdy vapours which
            environ it, makes it apprehensive, quick, forgetive, full of nimble fiery and
            delectable shapes, which, delivered o'er to the voice, the tongue, which is the
            birth, becomes excellent wit. The second property of your excellent sherry is
440   the warming of the blood, which, before cold and settled, left the liver white
            and pale, which is the badge of pusillanimity and cowardice. But the sherry

---

13 **state** splendor 15 **vile** mean, wretched, low-born 17 **watch-case** ticking watch in a case/sentry box **common 'larum-bell** public alarm bell, rung by a night watchman in an emergency 20 **rude imperious surge** rough, overwhelming swell of the sea 21 **visitation** violent, destructive force 22 **ruffian billows** rough waves 24 **slipp'ry** rapidly passing/unable to be grasped 25 **That** so that **hurly** tumult, uproar 26 **partial** unfair, biased/sympathetic 27 **rude** rough, dangerous 29 **to boot** besides 30 **happy low** fortunate humble men 4.1 426 **in my condition** according to my disposition/as military commander 432 **making many fish-meals** they eat such a lot of fish (as opposed to red meat) 433 **green-sickness** anaemia causing a greenish complexion; it often afflicted teenage girls **get wenches** father only daughters 435 **inflammation** roused emotions resulting from drink/swelling weight **sherry sack** sweet Spanish white wine **ascends me** ascends (**me** is used colloquially for emphasis) 436 **curdy** thick, curdled **vapours** noxious exhalations supposedly produced in the body and rising to the brain 437 **environ** surround 440 **liver** considered the seat of the passions 441 **pusillanimity** lack of courage, timidity

warms it and makes it course from the inwards to the parts extreme: it illumineth the face, which as a beacon gives warning to all the rest of this little kingdom, man, to arm. And then the vital commoners and inland petty spirits muster me all to their captain, the heart, who, great and puffed up with this retinue, doth any deed of courage, and this valour comes of sherry. So that skill in the weapon is nothing without sack, for that sets it a-work, and learning a mere hoard of gold kept by a devil, till sack commences it and sets it in act and use. Hereof comes it that Prince Harry is valiant, for the cold blood he did naturally inherit of his father, he hath, like lean, sterile and bare land, manured, husbanded and tilled with excellent endeavour of drinking good and good store of fertile sherry, that he is become very hot and valiant. If I had a thousand sons, the first principle I would teach them should be, to forswear thin potations and to addict themselves to sack.

Questions for Understanding and Reflection
Act III, scene 1
1. What is Henry IV suffering from?
2. Who can enjoy peaceful sleep?
3. How can you understand "Uneasy lies the head that wears a crown"?

Act IV, scene 1
1. What is the cause for Prince John's sober-bloodedness?
2. What are the properties of a good sherry sack?
3. What is the metaphor used to explain one of the properties?

IV SHAKESPEAREAN RELEVANCE

A. Shakespeare in Everyday English
Please try to understand the following Shakespearean words and expressions in the contexts designated within parentheses and give their generally used meanings in the space provided.
1. woe-begone (1.1.81): _____
2. smack of (1.2.70): _____
3. wake not a sleeping wolf (1.2.110): _____
4. eat ... out of house and home (2.1.52): _____
5. the hatch and brood of time (3.1.82): _____
6. chimes at midnight (3.2.157): _____
7. (as dead) as nail in door (5.3.98): _____

B. Shakespeare in Literature
Read the following literary excerpts, locate the Shakespearean allusions and explain their meanings according to the contexts where they appear.
The professor was a big, jovial man of Falstaffian appearance. (Marjorie Eccles, *A Species of Revenge*, 1996)

---

442 **parts extreme** extremities   444 **vital ... spirits** the 'vital spirits' were thought to be the essence of life   445 **muster me** assemble   447 **a-work** to work   448 **a** is a   **commences** initiates, unleashes   451 **husbanded** cultivated   454 **potations** liquors

C. Shakespeare in Music, Art and on Screen

1893: *Falstaff*, an opera by the Italian composer Giuseppe Verdi, libretto adapted by Arrigo Boito.
1913: *Falstaff*, a symphonic study by Edward Elgar.
1960: *An Age of Kings*, British TV miniseries.
1966: *Chimes at Midnight*, an English language Spanish-Swiss co-produced film, directed by and starring Orson Welles.
1979: *Henry IV, Part 2*, a BBC television film.
1990: *The War of the Roses*, a 7-play sequence, directly filmed from the stage of Shakespeare's history plays.
2012: *The Hollow Crown: Henry IV, Part 2*, a BBC2 production.

V SHAKESPEARE QUOTES

Rumour is a pipe
Blown by surmises, jealousies, conjectures
And of so easy and so plain a stop
That the blunt monster with uncounted heads,
The still-discordant wavering multitude,
Can play upon it. (Induction 15-20)
Some smack of age in you, some relish of the saltness of time. (1.2.70)
Let the end try the man. (2.2.30)
Uneasy lies the head that wears a crown. (3.1.31)
A soldier is better accommodated than with a wife. (3.2.47)
We have heard the chimes at midnight. (3.2.157)
I care not. A man can die but once: we owe God a death. (3.2.171)
Thy wish was father, Harry, to that thought. (4.2.230)
What wind blew you hither, Pistol?
Not the ill wind which blows none to good, sweet knight. (5.3.66)
I know thee not, old man. (5.5.41)

9. Henry V
亨利五世

I INTRODUCTION

《亨利五世》已成为英国爱国主义的代名词,是莎剧中唯一一部不以王位争夺为主题的历史剧。当年的公子哥王位既登,便将目光转向自己可能拥有其王位继承权的法国,而法国对其野心的回应则是网球礼物的羞辱。盛怒之下,亨利五世亲率英军讨伐法国并很快攻克了哈弗娄城。战事稍歇,莎翁又引我们入法国公主的闺房(boudoir)去领略该女士向侍女恶补英文时对陌生语言中的粗俗表达的震惊和好奇(注:莎剧原文该部分为法文)。经过战场内外的较量、博弈,英法两军最终在阿金库尔战役(the Battle of Agincourt)中一决雌雄。大战前夕,亨利为了鼓舞士气作了著名的"克里斯宾节演讲",成为后代众多将军备战的灵感来源,而英国战时首相丘吉尔要求劳伦斯·奥利弗拍摄该剧电影的良苦用心可见一斑。与以上英法交战的沉重主题相映衬的是野猪头酒店那帮粗人的插科打诨(gag)以及弗鲁爱林上尉对军人道德的坚持和浓重威尔士乡音这些轻松的情节。莎翁笔下的亨利五世是个矛盾的人物,他是个模范的君王但不是个完美的人。他当上国王之前与手下同乐,可谓平易近人,但等到成为亨利五世之际便无情地抛弃了他们。他虔诚而谦卑,但又是个冷酷的战争机器:违背不杀俘房的战争规则、下令将法国战俘割喉。总而言之,他勇武、阳刚、爱国,但同时又内心黑暗深不可测。而这些正是他的魅力所在。

II PLOT SUMMARY

King Henry V is planning on entering into a war with France over some disputed lands and titles. He has instructed the Archbishop to be sure that his claims are valid. When the play opens, the Archbishop explains to his Bishop how he plans to convince the king to enter into a war with France, thus protecting the church's property, which might otherwise be placed in the hands of the state rather than left in the church's control. They are also amazed at the young king's unexpected transformation, observing that "The strawberry grows underneath the nettle/And wholesome berries thrive and ripen best/Neighboured by fruit of baser quality./And so the prince **obscured**[1] his **contemplation**/[2]Under the veil of wildness, which, no doubt,/Grew like the summer grass, fastest by night,/Unseen, yet **crescive in his faculty**."[3] (1.1.62-68)

After the king is convinced of the validity of his claims, an ambassador from France arrives with a rejection of the claims; he also delivers an insulting barrel of tennis balls from the French **Dauphin**,[4] who still considers King Henry to be the silly and rowdy Prince Hal. This scornful jibe

---

1 **obscured** disguised, hid   2 **contemplation** meditation, thought   3 **crescive in his faculty** growing, in accordance with its natural function   4 **Dauphin** /ˈdɔːfæ/ the title given to the heir apparent to the throne of France between 1350 and 1824; it is the French word for "dolphin", the animal depicted on their coat of arms

at his "wilder days" spurs the king on to the immediate invasion of France, who warns that "many a thousand widows/Shall this his mock mock out of their dear husbands;/Mock mothers from their sons, mock castles down,/And some are yet **ungotten**[5] and unborn,/That shall have cause to curse the dauphin's scorn." (1.2.289-293)

Bardolph, 1853, Henry Stacy Marks

As they are on the verge of leaving for France, King Henry is tending to some business—releasing a prisoner for a minor offense—and then he turns to three of his trusted advisors and has them executed for conspiring with the French to assassinate him. The king's former companions from his days in the Eastcheap tavern hear of the death of Sir John Falstaff from Hostess Quickly, now the wife of **Pistol**.[6] Falstaff's friends reminisce fondly about the fat rascal before they set out to join King Henry's expeditionary army. Meanwhile, in the French court, no one seems to take Henry seriously. The entire court is contemptuous of the claims and abilities of the "vain, giddy, shallow, humorous youth" who leads England. They are so overconfident that they do not send help to the town of Harfleur. Before the gates of Harfleur, King Henry V threatens that if Harfleur does not surrender, "The blind and bloody soldier with foul hand/ Defile the **locks**[7] of your shrill-shrieking daughters,/Your fathers taken by the silver beards,/And their most reverend heads dashed to the walls,/Your naked infants **spitted**[8] upon **pikes**,/[9] Whiles the mad mothers with their howls confused/Do break the clouds …" (3.3.34-40) Seeing no hope of being relieved of the siege, the governor has to yield his town. After this bloodless victory, Henry gives strict instructions that all the citizens are to be treated with mercy and that his soldiers are not to loot, rob, or insult the native population. However, a companion from Hal's youth, Bardolph, an inveterate thief, steals a small communion plate, and, as a result, he is executed.

In spite of the English victory, the French still do not express concern, even though Princess Katharine is involved. That is, if Henry is victorious, she will become the Queen of England. As a result, she feels the necessity to learn the English language and is struggling to learn that language from Alice, her attendant. Act Ⅲ, scene 4, an amusingly feminine scene written in French, affords a glimpse of a young princess's boudoir. Meanwhile, the reports that the English are sick and tattered allow the French to prepare for the battle with complete confidence, especially since they outnumber the English 60,000 to 12,000 troops.

Katherine Learns English from her Gentlewoman Alice, 1888, Laura Alma-Tadema

Just before the crucial **Battle of Agincourt**,[10] Henry tours the camp in disguise and, sounding out the opinions of his men, is led to ruminate over the heavy responsibilities of kingship. When left alone, he wonders what, apart from ceremony,

---

5 **ungotten** not yet conceived 6 **Pistol** 毕斯托尔 7 **locks** hair/guarded chastity 8 **spitted** impaled 9 **pikes** weapons with long wooden handles and pointed metal heads 10 **Battle of Agincourt** (/ˈædʒɪnkɔːt/) 阿金库尔战役

distinguishes him from his soldiers. An emissary once again approaches King Henry with demands that he immediately surrender his person. His demands are rejected. Then in a patriotic speech, he encourages his men that "The fewer men, the greater share of honour" and reassures them that anyone who fights the next day on Saint Crispin's day will be remembered "from this day to the ending of the world." By miraculous means, the English are victorious, with 10,000 French casualties including 1,500 lords, barons, knights and squires, as against the English deaths of only 3 lords and 25 soldiers. The French are shamed into submission. At the end of the play, King Henry's demands are granted, and he is seen at his linguistic and romantic best in wooing and winning Princess Katharine as his future queen: "O fair Katherine, if you will love me soundly with your French heart, I will be glad to hear you confess it brokenly with your English tongue" (5.2.105-106); "I will tell thee in French, which I am sure will hang upon my tongue like a new-married wife about her husband's neck, hardly to be shook off"; (5.2.154-155) "You have witchcraft in your lips, Kate: there is more eloquence in a sugar touch of them than in the tongues of the French council; and they should sooner persuade Harry of England than a general petition of monarchs." (5.2.223-226)

Beyond the Play: *English Patriotism and the V Sign*

Winston Churchill and his Famous V Sign in 1943 (photo)

The historical and dramatic *Henry V* has long been an icon of English heroism and patriotism. Less than ten years before the play's premier in 1599, the English navy had destroyed the otherwise invincible Spanish Armada against great odds, as in the Battle of Agincourt. Throughout the Victorian era, the play served to eulogize imperial power. It was again performed as a patriotic anthem in WWI, while famous productions in the 1930s—Ralph Richardson played Henry in 1931 and Laurence Olivier in 1937—kept it constantly in the public eye. Understandably, the French fans of Shakespeare ignored the play that ridicules them so cruelly and didn't get the chance to see it performed on the French soil until 1999! Accidentally, the two-fingered sod-off sign (with the thumb and the index finger raised and parted, the remaining ones clenched, and the palm facing outwards) probably came from the Battle of Agincourt. The French, sure of their victory, had threatened to cut off the bow-fingers of all the English longbowmen. When it proved to the contrary, the archers held up their hands in insulting defiance. A variant of this gesture involving the index and middle fingers has been used to represent "victory", as used by Winston Churchill during WWII.

III SELECTED READINGS

Act IV, scene 1

105   KING HENRY V   By my troth, I will speak my conscience of the king: I think he would not wish himself any where but where he is.
    BATES   Then I would he were here alone; so should he be sure to be ransomed, and a many poor men's lives saved.
    KING HENRY V   I dare say you love him not so ill, to wish him here alone,
110   howsoever you speak this to feel other men's minds. Methinks I could not die any where so contented as in the king's company; his cause being just and his quarrel honourable.
    WILLIAMS   That's more than we know.
    BATES   Ay, or more than we should seek after; for we know enough, if we know
115   we are the king's subjects. If his cause be wrong, our obedience to the king wipes the crime of it out of us.
    WILLIAMS   But if the cause be not good, the king himself hath a heavy reckoning to make, when all those legs and arms and heads, chopped off in battle, shall join together at the latter day and cry all, 'We died at such a
120   place'— some swearing, some crying for a surgeon, some upon their wives left poor behind them, some upon the debts they owe, some upon their children rawly left. I am afeard there are few die well that die in a battle, for how can they charitably dispose of any thing, when blood is their argument? Now, if these men do not die well, it will be a black matter for the king that led them to
125   it—who to disobey were against all proportion of subjection.
    KING HENRY V   So, if a son that is by his father sent about merchandise do sinfully miscarry upon the sea, the imputation of his wickedness by your rule, should be imposed upon his father that sent him. Or if a servant, under his master's command transporting a sum of money, be assailed by robbers and
130   die in many irreconciled iniquities, you may call the business of the master the author of the servant's damnation. But this is not so: the king is not bound to answer the particular endings of his soldiers, the father of his son, nor the master of his servant; for they purpose not their death, when they purpose their services. Besides, there is no king, be his cause never so spotless, if it
135   come to the arbitrement of swords, can try it out with all unspotted soldiers: some peradventure have on them the guilt of premeditated and contrived murder; some, of beguiling virgins with the broken seals of perjury; some, making the wars their bulwark, that have before gored the gentle bosom of peace with pillage and robbery. Now, if these men have defeated the law and
140   outrun native punishment, though they can outstrip men, they have no wings to fly from

---

4.1 110 **feel** test   114 **seek after** try to find out   117 **reckoning** account of debts (both literal losses and spiritual debts)   118-119 **join together** remake whole bodies/unite in crying out   **latter day** Judgement Day   120 **upon** on account of   122 **rawly** too young/unprovided for   **afeard** afraid   123 **charitably** i.e. with Christian charity   **dispose of** make arrangements for/bestow (possessions in a will/souls to god)   **argument** theme   125 **proportion** natural order   **subjection** the condition of being a subject   126-127 **merchandise** trading, commerce   **sinfully miscarry** i.e. die in a state of sin   **imputation of** accusation of, responsibility for   130 **irreconciled** unreconciled to God, unabsolved   **iniquities** wicked acts, sins   **author** person responsible for, creator of   135 **arbitrement of swords** arbitration, determining of the matter through war   **try it out** i.e. put his cause to the test   **unspotted** pure, sin-free   136 **peradventure** perhaps   137 **beguiling** deceiving   **perjury** oath-breaking   138 **bulwark** (military) fortification/safeguard, means of escape (from punishment for crimes)   140 **native punishment** the punishment due to them at home

God. War is his beadle, war is vengeance, so that here men are punished for before-breach of the king's laws in now the king's quarrel: where they feared the death, they have borne life away; and where they would be safe, they perish: then if they die unprovided, no more is the king guilty of their

145 damnation than he was before guilty of those impieties for the which they are now visited. Every subject's duty is the king's; but every subject's soul is his own. Therefore should every soldier in the wars do as every sick man in his bed, wash every mote out of his conscience, and dying so, death is to him advantage; or not dying, the time was blessedly lost wherein such preparation

150 was gained: and in him that escapes, it were not sin to think that, making God so free an offer, He let him outlive that day to see His greatness and to teach others how they should prepare.

WILLIAMS 'Tis certain, every man that dies ill, the ill upon his own head, the king is not to answer it.

155 BATES But I do not desire he should answer for me; and yet I determine to fight lustily for him.

KING HENRY V I myself heard the king say he would not be ransomed.

WILLIAMS Ay, he said so, to make us fight cheerfully. But when our throats are cut, he may be ransomed, and we ne'er the wiser.

160 KING HENRY V If I live to see it, I will never trust his word after.

WILLIAMS You pay him then. That's a perilous shot out of an elder-gun, that a poor and private displeasure can do against a monarch. You may as well go about to turn the sun to ice with fanning in his face with a peacock's feather. You'll never trust his word after! Come, 'tis a foolish saying.

165 KING HENRY V Your reproof is something too round. I should be angry with you, if the time were convenient.

WILLIAMS Let it be a quarrel between us, if you live.

KING HENRY V I embrace it.

WILLIAMS How shall I know thee again?

170 KING HENRY V Give me any gage of thine, and I will wear it in my bonnet: then, if ever thou darest acknowledge it, I will make it my quarrel.

WILLIAMS Here's my glove. Give me another of thine.

KING HENRY V There.

WILLIAMS This will I also wear in my cap. If ever thou come to me and say,

175 after to-morrow, 'This is my glove,' by this hand, I will take thee a box on the ear.

KING HENRY V If ever I live to see it, I will challenge it.

WILLIAMS Thou dar'st as well be hanged.

KING HENRY V Well. I will do it, though I take thee in the king's company.

180 WILLIAMS Keep thy word. Fare thee well.

BATES Be friends, you English fools, be friends. We have French quarrels

---

141-143 **beadle** parish officer with the power to punish petty offenders **before-breach** previous breaking **now the king's quarrel** the war that is now being fought on behalf of the king **death** death penalty **borne life away** i. e. got away with their lives 145 **visited** punished 149 **blessedly** fortunately, in a holy manner **lost** spent 150-151 **making God so free an offer** in offering himself to God 152 **prepare** i. e. for death 153 **ill** i. e. unprepared, in sin 154 **to answer it** responsible for it 156 **lustily** heartily 160 **it** i. e. that outcome 161 **pay** punish **elder-gun** toy gun, pellet gun (made from an elder stick) 162 **a poor and private displeasure** the displeasure of a commoner 163 **go about** try 165 **round** blunt, plain-spoken 168 **embrace** heartily accept 170 **gage** pledge (usually signifying a commitment to duel; often a glove or gauntlet) 171 **darest** dare to 175 **take** give 179 **though** even if **take** find

enough, if you could tell how to reckon.
KING HENRY V Indeed, the French may lay twenty French crowns to one, they will beat us; for they bear them on their shoulders. But it is no English treason to cut French crowns, and tomorrow the king himself will be a clipper.

Exeunt soldiers

    Upon the king! Let us our lives, our souls,
    Our debts, our careful wives,
    Our children and our sins lay on the king!
    We must bear all. O hard condition,
    Twin-born with greatness, subject to the breath
    Of every fool, whose sense no more can feel
    But his own wringing. What infinite heart's-ease
    Must kings neglect, that private men enjoy?
    And what have kings, that privates have not too,
    Save ceremony, save general ceremony?
    And what art thou, thou idle ceremony?
    What kind of god art thou, that suffer'st more
    Of mortal griefs than do thy worshippers?
    What are thy rents? What are thy comings in?
    O ceremony, show me but thy worth!
    What is thy soul of adoration?
    Art thou aught else but place, degree and form,
    Creating awe and fear in other men?
    Wherein thou art less happy being fear'd
    Than they in fearing.
    What drink'st thou oft, instead of homage sweet,
    But poison'd flattery? O, be sick, great greatness,
    And bid thy ceremony give thee cure!
    Think'st thou the fiery fever will go out
    With titles blown from adulation?
    Will it give place to flexure and low bending?
    Canst thou, when thou command'st the beggar's knee,
    Command the health of it? No, thou proud dream,
    That play'st so subtly with a king's repose;
    I am a king that find thee, and I know
    'Tis not the balm, the sceptre and the ball,
    The sword, the mace, the crown imperial,
    The intertissued robe of gold and pearl,
    The farcèd title running 'fore the king,

---

182 **reckon** count   183 **crowns** coins/heads   185 **cut French crowns** cut French heads off/shave silver or gold from French coins   **clipper** clipper of coins/barber   187 **careful** full of cares or grief   188 **lay on** burden/assault   189 **condition** situation/social rank   190 **twin-born** born at the same birth   **breath** i.e. opinion   192 **wringing** aches and pains   **heart's-ease** inner peace, contentment   194 **privates** men who do not hold public office   195 **Save** except   **general** public   196 **idle** useless   198 **mortal** human   199 **comings in** income   201 **of adoration** made up of insubstantial admiration/of the things that provoke admiration   202 **aught** anything   **place, degree and form** i.e. social rank and eminence   210 **titles** puns on 'tittles', i.e. trifles   **blown** fanned, breathed (as if to cool fever)/corrupted, contaminated   211 **give place** retreat, give away   **flexure** kneeling   **bending** bowing   212 **command'st the beggar's knee** claim it as your right that the beggar kneels before you   214 **subtly** deceptively   **repose** rest   215 **find thee** find you out, discover your true nature   216 **balm** consecrated oil (used at a coronation)   **ball** monarch's orb   217 **mace** official scepter   218 **intertissued** interwoven   219 **farcèd** stuffed, pompous

220	The throne he sits on, nor the tide of pomp
	That beats upon the high shore of this world.
	No, not all these, thrice-gorgeous ceremony,
	Not all these, laid in bed majestical,
	Can sleep so soundly as the wretched slave,
225	Who with a body filled and vacant mind
	Gets him to rest, cramm'd with distressful bread;
	Never sees horrid night, the child of hell,
	But, like a lackey, from the rise to set,
	Sweats in the eye of Phoebus and all night
230	Sleeps in Elysium: next day after dawn,
	Doth rise and help Hyperion to his horse,
	And follows so the ever-running year,
	With profitable labour, to his grave.
	And, but for ceremony, such a wretch,
235	Winding up days with toil and nights with sleep,
	Had the forehand and vantage of a king.
	The slave, a member of the country's peace,
	Enjoys it; but in gross brain little wots
	What watch the king keeps to maintain the peace,
240	Whose hours the peasant best advantages.

Act IV, scene 3

	WESTMORELAND O that we now had here
	But one ten thousand of those men in England
	That do no work to-day!
20	KING HENRY V
	What's he that wishes so?
	My cousin Westmoreland? No, my fair cousin,
	If we are mark'd to die, we are enough
	To do our country loss; and if to live,
25	The fewer men, the greater share of honour.
	God's will! I pray thee, wish not one man more.
	By Jove, I am not covetous for gold,
	Nor care I who doth feed upon my cost,
	It yearns me not if men my garments wear;
30	Such outward things dwell not in my desires.
	But if it be a sin to covet honour,
	I am the most offending soul alive.
	No, faith, my coz, wish not a man from England.
	God's peace! I would not lose so great an honour

---

220 **pomp** ceremonious trappings, splendor   226 **distressful** earned by labour   228 **lackey** servant, specifically a footman who ran alongside his master's coach (here, Phoebus' chariot)   **the rise to set** sunrise to sunset   229 **Sweats in the eye of Phoebus** under the sun (Phoebus, the Roman sun god)   230 **Elysium** i. e. perfect contentment (the heaven of classical mythology)   231 **Hyperion** in classical mythology, father of the sun; sometimes the sun itself   233 **profitable** useful, valuable   236 **forehand and vantage of** advantage over   237 **member** sharer in   238 **gross** dull   **wots** knows   239 **watch** sleeplessness/guard   240 **advantages** benefits from   4.3 23-24 **we are enough/To do our country loss** there are enough of us for England to feel the loss   26 **wish** wish for   27 **Jove** supreme Roman god   28 **upon my cost** at my expense   29 **yearns** grieves   33 **coz** cousin

35 As one man more, methinks, would share from me
    For the best hope I have. O, do not wish one more.
    Rather proclaim it, Westmoreland, through my host,
    That he which hath no stomach to this fight,
    Let him depart, his passport shall be made
40 And crowns for convoy put into his purse:
    We would not die in that man's company
    That fears his fellowship to die with us. —
    This day is called the feast of Crispian:
    He that outlives this day, and comes safe home,
45 Will stand a tiptoe when the day is named,
    And rouse him at the name of Crispian.
    He that shall live this day, and see old age,
    Will yearly on the vigil feast his neighbours,
    And say 'Tomorrow is Saint Crispian.'
50 Then will he strip his sleeve and show his scars,
    And say 'These wounds I had on Crispin's day.'
    Old men forget; yet all shall be forgot,
    But he'll remember with advantages
    What feats he did that day. Then shall our names,
55 Familiar in his mouth as household words —
    Harry the king, Bedford and Exeter,
    Warwick and Talbot, Salisbury and Gloucester —
    Be in their flowing cups freshly rememberèd.
    This story shall the good man teach his son,
60 And Crispin Crispian shall ne'er go by,
    From this day to the ending of the world,
    But we in it shall be rememberèd;
    We few, we happy few, we band of brothers.
    For he today that sheds his blood with me
65 Shall be my brother, be he ne'er so vile,
    This day shall gentle his condition.
    And gentlemen in England now abed
    Shall think themselves accursed they were not here,
    And hold their manhoods cheap whiles any speaks
70 That fought with us upon Saint Crispin's day.

Questions for Understanding and Reflection
Act IV, scene 1
1. According to Williams, if the cause for a war is not just or honourable, who is responsible for all the casualties?
2. What does Henry V think of death in the battlefield?

---

35 **share** take away as his share   37 **proclaim it** declare, announce   38 **stomach to** appetite/courage for   39 **passport** document of authorization (to pass through France and board a ship)   40 **convoy** i. e. his journey   42 **his fellowship** duty as a companion   43 **feast of Crispian** Saint Crispin's day, 25 October   45 **stand a tiptoe** i. e. feel uplifted, proud, eager   48 **vigil** evening before a feast day   52 **all** all else   53 **advantages** additions   58 **Be in their flowing cups freshly remembered** i. e. a toast will be raised to them   60 **Crispin Crispian** Saint Crispin's day marks the martyring of two brothers, Crispin and Crispinus   63 **happy** fortunate   65 **vile** low-ranking   66 **gentle his condition** ennoble him   69 **manhoods** manliness   **any** anyone

3. How does Henry V compare the life of a slave with that of a king?

Act IV, scene 3
1. Why doesn't Henry IV want more men in the upcoming battle?
2. What is heartening to those who will survive the battle?
3. What does the king promise to those who will fight with him?

IV SHAKESPEAREAN RELEVANCE

A. Shakespeare in Everyday English
Please try to understand the following Shakespearean words and expressions in the contexts designated within parentheses and give their generally used meanings in the space provided.
1. wooden O (pro. 13):
2. cipher (pro. 17):
3. turning of the tide (2.3.9-10):
4. as cold as stone (2.3.16):
5. the Devil incarnate (2.3.23):
6. stiffen the sinews (3.1.7):
7. stand like greyhounds in the slips (3.1.31):
8. man of mould (3.2.20):
9. household words (4.3.54):

B. Shakespeare in Literature
Read the following literary excerpts, locate the Shakespearean allusions and explain their meanings according to the contexts where they appear.
1. ... I grew by degrees cold as a stone, and then my courage sank. (Charlotte Brontë, *Jane Eyre*, 1847)
2. If beauty is a matter of fashion, how is it that wrinkled skin, grey hair, hairy backs and Bardolph-like noses have never been 'in fashion'?
   (*Frontiers*: Penguin Popular Science, 1994)

C. Shakespeare in Music, Art and on Screen
1944: *Henry V*, a British Technicolor film adaptation, directed by and starring Laurence Olivier as Henry V and Asherson Renée as Katherine.
1989: *Henry V*, British drama film, directed by and starring Kenneth Branagh as Henry V.
2012: *The Hollow Crown: Henry V*, a BBC2 production.

V SHAKESPEARE QUOTES

> For once the eagle England being in prey,
> To her unguarded nest the weasel Scot
> Comes sneaking and so sucks her princely eggs,

Appreciating Shakespearean Plays

Playing the mouse in absence of the cat,
To, tame and havoc more than she can eat.(1.2.171-175)
Men are merriest when they are from home. (1.2.277)
Covering discretion with a coat of folly;
As gardeners do with ordure hide those roots
That shall first spring and be most delicate. (2.4.40-42)
Once more unto the breach, dear friends, once more,
Or close the wall up with our English dead! (3.1.1-2)
Would I were in an alehouse in London:
I would give all my fame for a pot of ale, and safety. (3.2.10-11)
Ill will never said well. (3.7.82)
That's a valiant flea that dare eat his
breakfast on the lip of a lion. (3.7.104-105)
There is some soul of goodness in things evil. (4.1.4)
I am afeard there are few die well that die in battle, for how can they charitably
dispose of anything, when blood is their argument? (4.1.121-123)
We few, we happy few, we band of brothers. (4.3.62)
The man that once did sell the lion's skin
While the beast lived, was killed with hunting him. (4.3.96-97)
The empty vessel makes the greatest sound. (4.4.56)

10. Richard III
理查三世

I INTRODUCTION

Richard III (1452—1485)

大幕开启,一个长相丑陋、弯腰驼背之人孤独地跛行而来,接着便开始了他那段著名的内心独白:"现在我们严冬般的宿怨已给这颗约克的红日照耀成为融融的夏景;那笼罩着我们王室的片片愁云全都埋进了海洋深处。……"旷日持久的红白玫瑰战争终告结束,约克家族的爱德华四世无可争议地登上王位。国王的弟弟葛罗斯特公爵理查自知仪容乏善可陈,遂决定以韬略和阴谋弥补。他计划篡夺长兄的王位,但需清除一个个障碍,其中包括国王、克莱伦斯公爵、国王的继嗣,他还需休掉原配并娶亨利六世太子的遗孀以确立他王位诉求的合法性。在第一幕第二场,莎士比亚便为我们生动地呈现了理查向安夫人求婚的场面。正在哭灵的安夫人面对导致自己丈夫、父亲、公公死亡元凶的求爱厌恶至极,她不停地对他诅咒、吐唾沫,但最终还是架不住他的甜言蜜语而就范。芳心既得,理查自鸣得意:"哪有一个女子是这样求到手的? 哪有一个女子是这样求到手的?"在第四幕第三场,莎士比亚又借提瑞尔之口讲述了行将就死的两位王子是如何的手足情深、可爱单纯。接下来的一场则是几个同是理查受害者的怨妇在争先诉说所遭受的丧夫丧子之痛。在最后的波士委战役(the Battle of Bosworth)中,理查落了个坐骑战死、四面楚歌的境地,但高声喊出的"一匹马! 一匹马! 我的王位换一匹马!"却表现出阴谋野心家绝望但倔强的一面。

II PLOT SUMMARY

After years of civil unrest between the royal Houses of York and Lancaster (recounted in *2 Henry VI* and *3 Henry VI*), the Yorkist Edward IV becomes king. His brother, Richard Duke of Gloucester determines to seize the throne for himself: "Now is the winter of our discontent/Made glorious summer by this son of York. ... since I cannot prove a lover,/To entertain these fair well-spoken days,/I am determinèd to prove a villain/And hate the idle pleasures of these days." He first manages to turn Edward against the Duke of Clarence, who is imprisoned in the Tower on the charge of treason. Next, he wins the hand of Lady Anne, even as she follows the hearse bearing the body of the murdered Henry VI, and gloats: "Was ever woman in this humour wooed? /Was

Richard, Duke of Gloucester, and the Lady Anne, 1896, Edwin Austin Abbey

ever woman in this humour won?" (1.2.237-238) As part of his plan, Richard succeeds in convincing Hastings and Buckingham that the queen and her faction are to blame for Clarence's imprisonment. Hired murderers carry out his instructions to put Clarence to death.

Richard joins the other members of the hostile factions in solemnly vowing in the presence of the dying Edward to hold the peace. The remorseful king learns that Clarence has been put to death before he himself dies. When the young Prince Edward is sent for from Ludlow to be crowned, Richard moves quickly to meet this turn of events. **Buckingham**,[1] now Richard's "second self," promises to separate the prince from the queen's kindred. Lord Rivers, Lord Grey, and Sir Thomas **Vaughan**[2] are imprisoned by Richard and are executed. The frightened queen seeks sanctuary for her son.

With a great display of courtesy and devotion, Richard has Prince Edward and his brother lodged in the Tower. Finding that Hastings remains loyal to the prince, the villain-hero denounces him as a traitor and orders his execution. Soon thereafter Rivers, Grey, and Vaughan meet similar fates. Next, Richard convinces the Lord Mayor of London that he has acted only for the security of the realm. He has Buckingham slander the dead Edward, implying that the late king's children are illegitimate and that Edward himself was basely born. When citizens of London, headed by the lord mayor, offer him the crown, Richard accepts it with pretended reluctance. Arrangements are made for his coronation.

The Princes in the Tower, 1878, John Everett Millais

The despairing queen-mother fails in an attempt to visit her sons in the Tower just before Richard is crowned. To secure his position, the new king suggests to Buckingham that the young princes be put to death. But the duke falters at the thought of such a monstrous deed. **Dorset**,[3] it is learned, has fled to **Britanny**[4] to join Henry, Earl of Richmond. This turn of events does not deter King Richard. He has rumors spread that his wife is mortally ill; he arranges a lowly match for Margaret, Clarence's daughter; he imprisons Clarence's son; he engages Sir James **Tyrrel**[5] to undertake the murder of the little princes, "... the gentle babes ... girdling one another/Within their alabaster innocent arms./Their lips were four red roses on a stalk,/And in their summer beauty kisses each other." (4.3.9-13) Buckingham, now treated disdainfully and denied the promised earldom of Hereford, resolves to join Richmond. Richard is gladdened that "my wife (Anne) hath bid the world good night" as Tyrrel kills the two young princess. In the palace, each of Richard's female victims—Queen Margaret, widow of Henry VI, Queen Elizabeth, King Edward IV's widow, Duchess of York, mother of Gloucester, Clarence and Edward IV—vies with one another in denouncing what Richard, "that bottled spider, that foul bunch-backed toad" and "hell's black intelligencer," has done to her and her family: "I had an Edward, till a Richard killed him:/I had a husband, till a Richard killed him:/Thou hadst an Edward, till a Richard killed him:/Thou hadst a Richard, till a Richard killed him." Richmond lands at Milford at the head of a mighty army. Joined by many nobles, he marches inland to claim the throne.

---

1 **Buckingham** /ˈbʌkiŋəm/ 勃金汉 2 **Vaughan** /vɔːn/ 伏根 3 **Dorset** /ˈdɔːsit/ 道塞特 4 **Britanny** /ˈbritəni/ 布列塔尼 a region in the north-west of France 5 **Tyrrel** /ˈtirəl/ 提瑞尔

Buckingham is captured and slain.

David Garrick as Richard III, 1745, William Hogarth

The two armies meet at **Bosworth Field**,[6] and the two leaders are encamped on either side. That night the ghosts of Richard's victims appear in the sleep of both Richard and Richmond. They indict Richard and prophesy that he will "despair and die". In contrast, Richmond has "fair-boding dreams" and is assured that "God and good angels" stand ready to assist him and that he will "live and flourish". Both Richard and Richmond address their troops before the battle begins. Richard fights courageously but is overcome and slain in personal combat with Richmond after he loses his horse and concedes "A horse! A horse! My kingdom for a horse!" Richmond accepts the crown and proposes to marry Elizabeth of York, thus ending the Wars of the Roses between the two great factions and ushering in the Tudor dynasty.

Beyond the Play: *the Real Richard III?*

Laurence Olivier (1907—1989) as Richard III

Anthony Sher as Richard III

"That bottled spider", "a hellhound", "this poisonous bunch-backed toad", "hell's black intelligencer" ... Shakespeare, through the mouth of Richard's victims, heaps the severest curses imaginable upon the evilly crafty personality. The English are arguably known for getting their history from Shakespeare as they do their theology from John Milton (e.g. his ever-evolving perception of Satan). In fact, Shakespeare's influence on perceptions of the historical English kings has reached a point where Richard III is thought to be a deformed and blood-thirsty usurper. He was a lady killer too, evidenced by his successful wooing of Lady Anne and the now famous William-the-Conqueror-was-before-Richard-the-Third anecdote, which involves the Bard, Richard Burbage, the star of Shakespeare's theatre company, and a female fan of Burbage. These images, further strengthened by the superbly riveting performances of such Richards as Edmund Kean, Laurence Olivier and Antony Sher, have been somewhat rectified through the unremitting efforts of members of The Richard III Society and the 2013 unearthing of Richard III's skeleton made by an archeological team of the University of Leicester, England.

---

6 **Bosworth** (/ˈbɔswəːθ/) **Field** 博斯沃思原野 site of the Battle of Bosworth near Ambion Hill, south of the town of Market Bosworth in Leicestershire, England

III SELECTED READINGS

Act I, scene 1

    RICHARD Now is the winter of our discontent
          Made glorious summer by this son of York:
          And all the clouds that loured upon our house
          In the deep bosom of the ocean buried.
5   Now are our brows bound with victorious wreaths,
          Our bruisèd arms hung up for monuments,
          Our stern alarums changed to merry meetings,
          Our dreadful marches to delightful measures.
          Grim-visaged war hath smoothed his wrinkled front,
10   And now, instead of mounting bardèd steeds
          To fright the souls of fearful adversaries,
          He capers nimbly in a lady's chamber
          To the lascivious pleasing of a lute.
          But I, that am not shaped for sportive tricks,
15   Nor made to court an amorous looking-glass:
          I, that am rudely stamped, and want love's majesty
          To strut before a wanton ambling nymph:
          I, that am curtailed of this fair proportion,
          Cheated of feature by dissembling nature,
20   Deformed, unfinished, sent before my time
          Into this breathing world, scarce half made up,
          And that so lamely and unfashionable
          That dogs bark at me as I halt by them —
          Why, I, in this weak piping time of peace,
25   Have no delight to pass away the time,
          Unless to spy my shadow in the sun
          And descant on mine own deformity.
          And therefore, since I cannot prove a lover,
          To entertain these fair well-spoken days,
30   I am determinèd to prove a villain
          And hate the idle pleasures of these days.
          Plots have I laid, inductions dangerous,
          By drunken prophecies, libels and dreams,
          To set my brother Clarence and the king

1.1 2 **son of York** refers to Edward IV, whose father was Richard Duke of York, the emblem of which was the "sun"   6 **arms** armour, weapons   **for** as   7 **alarums** calls to arms/sudden attacks   8 **dreadful** fearsome, inspiring dread   **measures** stately dances   9 **Grim-visaged war** war with a grim expression   **front** forehead   10 **bardèd** armoured   11 **fearful** frightened/frightening   12 **capers** dances   with   13 **pleasing** attraction, delight   14 **sportive** pleasurable/amorous/sex   **tricks** behaviour, skills/sexual acts   15 **court ... looking-glass** i.e. gaze lovingly at myself in a mirror, flirt with my own reflection   16 **rudely stamped** crudely formed, roughly printed with an image   **want** lack   17 **wanton** flirtatious, lascivious   **ambling** sauntering, walking with a sexy rolling gait   18 **curtailed** deprived, cut short (literally refers to the docking of a dog's tail)   19 **feature** a pleasing shape   **dissembling** cheating, deceitful   20 **sent ... time** i..e. born prematurely   21 **made up** fully formed   22 **unfashionable** odd-looking, inelegant/poorly shaped   23 **halt** limp   24 **piping** characterized by pastoral pipes, rather than warlike instruments/shrill, weak, contemptible   27 **descant** improvise variations on (musical term), i.e. ponder, comment   29 **entertain** pass enjoyably   **well-spoken** courteous, harmonious   30 **determinèd** resolved/destined   32 **inductions** initial steps, preparations

35   In deadly hate the one against the other.
     And if King Edward be as true and just
     As I am subtle, false and treacherous,
     This day should Clarence closely be mewed up,
     About a prophecy, which says that 'G'
40   Of Edward's heirs the murderer shall be.
     Dive, thoughts, down to my soul.

Act IV, scene 4

   QUEEN MARGARET   So, now prosperity begins to mellow
     And drop into the rotten mouth of death.
     Here in these confines slyly have I lurked,
     To watch the waning of mine enemies.
5   A dire induction am I witness to,
     And will to France, hoping the consequence
     Will prove as bitter, black, and tragical.
     Withdraw thee, wretched Margaret. Who comes here?
   Enter QUEEN ELIZABETH and the DUCHESS OF YORK
   QUEEN ELIZABETH   Ah, my young princes! Ah, my tender babes!
10   My unblowed flowers, new-appearing sweets!
     If yet your gentle souls fly in the air
     And be not fixed in doom perpetual,
     Hover about me with your airy wings
     And hear your mother's lamentation!
15 QUEEN MARGARET   Hover about her: say, that right for right
     Hath dimmed your infant morn to agèd night.
   DUCHESS OF YORK   So many miseries have crazed my voice,
     That my woe-wearied tongue is still and mute.
     Edward Plantagenet, why art thou dead?
20 QUEEN MARGARET   Plantagenet doth quit Plantagenet:
     Edward for Edward pays a dying debt.
   QUEEN ELIZABETH   Wilt thou, O God, fly from such gentle lambs,
     And throw them in the entrails of the wolf?
     When didst thou sleep when such a deed was done?
25 QUEEN MARGARET   When holy Harry died, and my sweet son.
   DUCHESS OF YORK   Blind sight, dead life, poor mortal living ghost,
     Woe's scene, world's shame, grave's due by life usurped,
     Brief abstract and record of tedious days,
     Rest thy unrest on England's lawful earth,
     Sitting down
30   Unlawfully made drunk with innocents' blood!

---

37 **subtle** cunning, sly false dishonest, disloyal   38 **mewed up** imprisoned, cooped up (like a caged bird of prey)   39 **About** as a result of 'G' Clarence's first name is George; Richard, however, is the Duke of Gloucester   4.4 1 **mellow** ripen   3 **confines** regions, territories (of England)   5 **induction** introduction, opening scene   6 **consequence** unfolding events and their conclusion   10 **unblowed** young and unopened, not yet in bloom   **sweets** flowers/dear ones   12 **in doom perpetual** eternally in the place appointed for you   15 **right for right** even-handed justice   17 **crazed** cracked   19 **Edward Plantagenet** could refer to Edward IV or his son   20 **quit** requite, repay   21 **Edward for Edward** probably refers to Elizabeth's son and Margaret's (with Henry VI)   23 **entrails** insides, intestines   25 **Harry** Henry VI (Margaret's husband)   27 **grave's ... usurped** i.e. one who should have died but remains living   28 **abstract** summary/epitome   29 **lawful** own proper, that is rightfully England's

> QUEEN ELIZABETH O, that thou wouldst as well afford a grave
> As thou canst yield a melancholy seat!
> Then would I hide my bones, not rest them here.
> O, who hath any cause to mourn but I?
> *Sitting down by her*
35 QUEEN MARGARET If ancient sorrow be most reverend,
> Give mine the benefit of seniory,
> And let my woes frown on the upper hand.
> If sorrow can admit society,
> *Sitting down with them*
> I had an Edward, till a Richard killed him;
40 I had a husband, till a Richard killed him:
> Thou hadst an Edward, till a Richard killed him;
> Thou hadst a Richard, till a Richard killed him;
> DUCHESS OF YORK I had a Richard too, and thou didst kill him;
> I had a Rutland too, thou holp'st to kill him.
45 QUEEN MARGARET Thou hadst a Clarence too, and Richard killed him.
> From forth the kennel of thy womb hath crept
> A hell-hound that doth hunt us all to death:
> That dog, that had his teeth before his eyes,
> To worry lambs and lap their gentle blood,
50 That foul defacer of God's handiwork,
> That reigns in gallèd eyes of weeping souls,
> That excellent grand tyrant of the earth,
> Thy womb let loose, to chase us to our graves.
> O upright, just, and true-disposing God,
55 How do I thank thee, that this carnal cur
> Preys on the issue of his mother's body,
> And makes her pew-fellow with others' moan!
> DUCHESS OF YORK O Harry's wife, triumph not in my woes!
> God witness with me, I have wept for thine.
60 QUEEN MARGARET Bear with me; I am hungry for revenge,
> And now I cloy me with beholding it.
> Thy Edward he is dead, that stabbed my Edward,
> Thy other Edward dead, to quit my Edward:
> Young York he is but boot, because both they
65 Match not the high perfection of my loss.

---

31 **thou** i. e. the earth **afford** offer   36 **seniory** seniority   37 **on ... hand** from the superior position   38 **admit society** permit company   39 **Edward** Margaret's son with Henry VI (murdered by Richard, Edward IV and Clarence; see *3 Henry VI*, Act 5 scene 5)   40 **husband** Henry VI (murdered by Richard; see *3 Henry VI*, Act 5 scene 6)   41 **Edward** Elizabeth's eldest son with Edward IV   42 **Richard** Elizabeth's second son, the young Duke of York   43 **Richard** the Duke of York, the Duchess' husband (killed by Margaret and Clifford; see *3 Henry VI*, Act 1 scene 4)   44 **Rutland** the Duchess' youngest son (murdered by Clifford; see *3 Henry VI*, Act 1 scene 3)   **holp'st** helped   48 **teeth ... eyes** i. e. could bite before he could see properly; Richard was born with teeth   49 **worry** seize by the throat   50 **defacer ... handiwork** i. e. murderer (perhaps also alludes to Richard's own deformed physique)   51 **gallèd** irritated, swollen (from weeping)   52 **excellent** supreme   54 **upright** righteous, just   **true-disposing** arranging all justly   55 **carnal cur** flesh-eating dog   56 **issue** offspring, children   57 **pew-fellow** fellow mourner   **moan** lamentations, grief   58 **triumph** glory, exult   61 **cloy me** gorge myself   62 **Thy Edward** Edward IV   **my Edward** Margaret's son with Henry VI   63 **other Edward** Elizabeth's eldest son with Edward IV   64 **Young York** Elizabeth's second son, the young Duke of York   **but boot** merely added to make up the total   **both they** Edward IV and his eldest son   65 **perfection ... loss** completeness, extent of the loss I experience/excellence of the people I have lost

	Thy Clarence he is dead that killed my Edward;
	And the beholders of this frantic play,
	Th' adulterate Hastings, Rivers, Vaughan, Grey,
	Untimely smothered in their dusky graves.
70	Richard yet lives, hell's black intelligencer,
	Only reserved their factor, to buy souls
	And send them thither: but at hand, at hand,
	Ensues his piteous and unpitied end:
	Earth gapes, hell burns, fiends roar, saints pray.
75	To have him suddenly conveyed away.
	Cancel his bond of life, dear God, I prey,
	That I may live to say, 'The dog is dead!'
	QUEEN ELIZABETH O, thou didst prophesy the time would come
	That I should wish for thee to help me curse
80	That bottled spider, that foul bunch-backed toad!
	QUEEN MARGARET I called thee then vain flourish of my fortune:
	I called thee then poor shadow, painted queen,
	The presentation of but what I was,
	The flattering index of a direful pageant,
85	One heaved a-high, to be hurled down below,
	A mother only mocked with two sweet babes,
	A dream of what thou wast, a garish flag,
	To be the aim of every dangerous shot;
	A sign of dignity, a breath, a bubble;
90	A queen in jest, only to fill the scene.
	Where is thy husband now? Where be thy brothers?
	Where are thy children? Wherein dost thou joy?
	Who sues, and kneels and says, 'God save the queen'?
	Where be the bending peers that flattered thee?
95	Where be the thronging troops that followed thee?
	Decline all this, and see what now thou art:
	For happy wife, a most distressed widow:
	For joyful mother, one that wails the name:
	For one being sued to, one that humbly sues:
100	For queen, a very caitiff crowned with care:
	For one that scorned at me, now scorned of me:
	For one being feared of all, now fearing one:
	For one commanding all, obeyed of none.

---

67 **frantic** mad, frenzied   68 **Th' adulterate** the adulterous (Hastings; refers to his affair with Jane Shore)   70 **intelligencer** spy, secret agent   71 **Only reserved** solely kept alive (to be)/exclusively selected (as)   **factor** agent, representative   80 **bottled** swollen (with venom), rounded, bottle-shaped   **bunch-backed** hunchbacked   81 **vain flourish** meaningless, frivolous adornment   82 **shadow** illusory, fragile image/actor   **parted** artificial/made-up with cosmetics   83 **presentation** imitation   84 **flattering index** deceptively attractive prologue   **pageant** play   86 **mocked** taunted/imitated, play-acted   87 **dream** mere image   **flag** army's identifying banner, highly visible in battle/type of flower belonging to the iris family   89 **sign** mere symbol/military banner   **dignity** monarchy   90 **in jest** for entertainment/pretend   **fill the** fulfill the requirements of/make up numbers in   93 **sues** pays court, entreats   94 **bending** bowing/yielding   95 **troops** retinues   96 **Decline** go through in order (grammatical term)   97 **For** instead of   98 **name** i.e. of mother   100 **caitiff** wretch   **care** troubles, grief   101 **of** by

	Thus hath the course of justice whirled about,
105	And left thee but a very prey to time,

        Thus hath the course of justice whirled about,
105   And left thee but a very prey to time,
        Having no more but thought of what thou wast,
        To torture thee the more, being what thou art.
        Thou didst usurp my place, and dost thou not
        Usurp the just proportion of my sorrow?
110   Now thy proud neck bears half my burthened yoke,
        From which even here I slip my wearied head,
        And leave the burthen of it all on thee.
        Farewell, York's wife, and queen of sad mischance:
        These English woes will make me smile in France.
115   QUEEN ELIZABETH   O thou well skillrd in curses, stay awhile,
        And teach me how to curse mine enemies!
        QUEEN MARGARET   Forbear to sleep the night, and fast the day:
        Compare dead happiness with living woe:
        Think that thy babes were fairer than they were,
120   And he that slew them fouler than he is.
        Bett'ring thy loss makes the bad causer worse:
        Revolving this will teach thee how to curse.
        QUEEN ELIZABETH   My words are dull. O, quicken them with thine!
        QUEEN MARGARET   Thy woes will make them sharp, and pierce like mine.
        Exit
125   DUCHESS OF YORK   Why should calamity be full of words?
        QUEEN ELIZABETH   Windy attorneys to their client's woes,
        Airy succeeders of intestine joys,
        Poor breathing orators of miseries!
        Let them have scope: though what they do impart
130   Help nothing else, yet do they ease the heart.
        DUCHESS OF YORK   If so, then be not tongue-tied: go with me.
        And in the breath of bitter words let's smother
        My damnèd son, which thy two sweet sons smothered.
        The trumpet sounds: be copious in exclaims.

Questions for Understanding and Reflection

Act I, scene 1
1. Now that war, death, and winter are over, what are people busy doing?
2. What hinders Richard from enjoying "this weak piping time of peace"?
3. What does he pledge himself to?

Act IV, scene 4
1. How does Queen Margaret differ from the two women in her state of mind?
2. What is the verbal abuse that Richard III gets from the three women?

---

104 **course ... about** an image that recalls the popular conception of fortune as a wheel that raised humans up and cast them down as it came full circle   105 **very** absolute   106 **thought** i. e. memory   113 **mischance** misfortune   117 **Forbear** refrain, refus 121 **Bett'ring** amplifying   **bad causer** person responsible for the evil   122 **Revolving** considering, reflecting on   123 **dull** lifeless, sluggish/blunt   **quicken** enliven/sharpen   126 **Windy ... woes** (words are) empty, wind-blown representatives of the grief of the speakers   127 **intestine** internal (both in the sense of 'experienced within' and in the sense of 'digestive', the latter making words into farts)   129 **scope** range, room   134 **exclaims** outcries, exclamations

3. Can you see the humour in the way each woman tries to outspeak the others in their denunciations?

IV SHAKESPEAREAN RELEVANCE

A. Shakespeare in Everyday English
Please try to understand the following Shakespearean words and expressions in the contexts designated within parentheses and give their generally used meanings in the space provided.
1. Now is the winter of our discontent. (1.1.1): _____
2. the piping time of peace (1.1.24): _____
3. snow in harvest (1.4.221): _____
4. short shrift (3.4.94): _____
5. not in the vein (4.2.104): _____
6. the bowels of (5.2.3): _____
7. a tower of strength (5.3.13): _____

B. Shakespeare in Literature
Read the following literary excerpts, locate the Shakespearean allusions and explain their meanings according to the contexts where they appear.
1. They are like to meet short shrift and a tight cord. (W. Scott, *Quentin Durward*, 1823)
2. ... an affectionate husband who is a tower of strength to her. (B. Shaw, *The Devil's Disciple*, 1897)
3. No doubt, if a King Richard III were worsted on a modern battlefield, his instinctive cry would be, "My Kingdom for a telephone." (Herbert Newton Casson, *The History of the Telephone*, 2009)

C. Shakespeare in Music, Art and on Screen
1955: *Richard III*, a film adaptation, directed, produced by and starring Laurence Olivier as Richard.
1995: *Richard III*, a film version starring Ian McKellen, set in a fictional 1930s fascist England.
1996: *Richard III*, *Looking for Richard*, a documentary film directed by Al Pacino.
2008: *Richard III*, a film directed by Scott M. Anderson, a modern-day retelling set in contemporary Hollywood.

V SHAKESPEARE QUOTES

Now is the winter of our discontent
Made glorious summer by this son of York. (1.1.1-2)
Was ever woman in this humour wooed?
Was ever woman in this humour won? (1.2.237-238)
The world is grown so bad
That wrens make prey where eagles dare not perch. (1.3.69-70)
Talkers are no good doers. (1.3.352)
Small herbs have grace, great weeds do grow apace. (2.4.13)

> *So wise so young do never live long. (3.1.79)*
> *Eighty odd years of sorrow have I seen,*
> *And each hour's joy wrecked with a week of teen. (4.1.97-98)*
> *I know a discontented gentleman,*
> *Whose humble means match not his haughty spirit:*
> *Gold were as good as twenty orators,*
> *And will, no doubt, tempt him to anything. (4.2.38-41)*
> *Thou didst usurp my place, and dost thou not*
> *Usurp the just proportion of my sorrow? (4.4.108-109)*
> *A horse! A horse! My kingdom for a horse! (5.3.361)*

Tragedies 悲剧

11. The Tragedy of Romeo and Juliet
罗密欧与朱丽叶

I INTRODUCTION

"故事发生在维洛那名城,有两家门第相当的巨族,累世的宿怨激起了新争,鲜血把市民的白手污渎……"——莎士比亚第一部伟大悲剧刚一开始便向我们预示了一场爱情令人唏嘘不已的结局,从而成就了跨越时空的戏剧绝响。该剧情节的主要来源是 Arthur Broke(卒于 1562 年)的叙事长诗 *The Tragicall Historye of Romeus and Juliet*,其灵感则来自意大利作家 Matteo Bandello(1485-1561)相关故事的法文翻译。Arthur Broke 的版本早已失传,独有莎翁的戏剧流传至今,并对文学、音乐、舞蹈、戏剧等领域产生了巨大的影响,而剧中蒙太古和凯普莱特两个家族的交恶、罗密欧和朱丽叶的双双殉情,都使得这两个主人公成为世人想像中的不幸恋人(star-crossed lovers)的代表,类似于中国的牛郎织女、梁山伯和祝英台。除了炙热的情感、曲折的情节之外,《罗密欧与朱丽叶》还以其优美的诗歌语言使人陶醉其中,如被广为引用(包括语言学界)的"姓名本来是没有意义的;我们叫做玫瑰的这一种花,要是换个名字,它的香味还是同样的芬芳。"(What's in a name? That which we call a rose/By any other word would smell as sweet.),以及貌似自相矛盾的"啊,吵吵闹闹的相爱,亲亲热热的怨恨!啊,无中生有的一切!啊,沉重的轻浮,严肃的狂妄,整齐的混乱,铅铸的羽毛,光明的烟雾,寒冷的火焰,憔悴的健康,永远觉醒的睡眠,否定的存在!"(O brawling love, O loving hate,/O anything of nothing first create! /O heavy lightness, serious vanity,/Misshapen chaos, of well-seeming form,/Feather of lead, bright smoke, cold fire, sick health,/Still-waking sleep that is not what it is!)所选的两个片段,一段是著名的阳台幽会,另一段是晨曦话别。

II PLOT SUMMARY

A feud has been raging for many years between the houses of **Capulet**[1] and **Montague**[2] in **Verona**,[3] Italy. The Prince, incensed at the latest disturbance, orders the disputing parties to depart "on pain of death". **Romeo**,[4] the only son of the Montagues, absent from the riot, hears about the commotion from his friend **Benvolio**.[5] Benvolio finds Romeo brooding over his unrequited love for Rosaline and pointing out the contradictory nature of love: "Why, then, O

---

1 **Capulet** /ˈkpjulet/ 凯普莱特　2 **Montague** /ˈmɔntəgjuː/ 蒙太古　3 **Verona** /vəˈrəunə/ 维洛那　4 **Romeo** /ˈrəumiu/ 罗密欧　5 **Benvolio** /benˈvəulju/ 班伏里奥　6 **create** created

brawling love, O loving hate,/O anything of nothing first **create**!⁶/O heavy lightness, serious vanity,/Misshapen chaos of well-seeming forms,/Feather of lead, bright smoke, cold fire, sick health./Still-waking sleep that is not what it is!" (1.1.163-168) He suggests they go, as uninvited masked guests, to a party given by Capulet so that Romeo can compare Rosaline with other beauties. At the party, Romeo notices and is struck by **Juliet**'s⁷ beauty: "O, she doth teach the torches to burn bright!/It seems she hangs upon the cheek of night/As a rich jewel in an **Ethiope's**⁸ ear:/**Beauty**⁹ too rich for **use**,¹⁰ for **earth**¹¹ too **dear**!"¹² (1.4.161-164) At the first opportunity he approaches her and gives her worshipful kisses: " My lips, two blushing pilgrims, read stand/To smooth that rough touch with a tender kiss." (1.4.215-216) They fall in love immediately and only after parting do they realize that they belong to rival families.

Romeo and Juliet, 1884, Frank Dicksee

Romeo, reluctant to leave the grounds of the Capulet household, eludes his friends and hides in an orchard where he overhears Juliet, at a window, professing her love for him: "O Romeo, Romeo, **wherefore**¹³ art thou Romeo? / ... / What's in a name? That which we call a rose/By any other word would smell as sweet ...". (2.1.80-91) The two exchange vows and decide to marry the next day. The Friar, though skeptical about young men's love: "Young men's love then lies/Not truly in their hearts, but in their eyes", (2.2.68-69) agrees to perform such a hasty ceremony, hoping that the union will bring peace to the feuding families.

Tybalt,¹⁴ a relative of Capulet who recognized Romeo at the party, meets Romeo and insults him. Romeo mitigates Tybalt's anger with a soft reply. However, **Mercutio**,¹⁵ Romeo's friend, is provoked and challenges Tybalt to a duel. Mercutio receives a death wound from Tybalt under Romeo's arm. Romeo then engages Tybalt, kills him, and flees. Romeo takes refuge in Friar Laurence's cell, where he later learns that he has been banished from Verona. Desperate at being separated from Juliet, Romeo attempts to take his own life, but he is calmed by the Friar, who advises him to say farewell to Juliet and remain in Mantua until it is safe to return to Verona.

In the hope that marriage will make Juliet forget her sorrow over the death of her cousin Tybalt, Capulet consents to Paris's request for Juliet's hand. The marriage is to take place in three days. Having spent his wedding night with Juliet, Romeo prepares to leave at dawn. Juliet at first won't let him go, arguing that "[i]t is not yet near day./It was the nightingale, and not the lark,/That pieced the fearful hollow of thine ear". (3.5.1-3) But realizing the danger of any delay, she urges him to leave: "It is, it is; **hie**¹⁶ hence, begone, away!/It is the lark that sings so out of tune,/**Straining**¹⁷ harsh

Romeo and Juliet with Friar Laurence, 1792—96, William Bunbury

---

7 **Juliet** /ˈdʒuːljət/ 朱丽叶   8 **Ethiope's** Ethiopian's   9 **Beauty** possibly puns on 'booty'   10 **use** plays on the sense of 'financial interest'   11 **earth** life on earth/death and burial   12 **dear** beloved/costly   13 **wherefore** why   14 **Tybalt** /ˈtibəlt/ 提伯尔特   15 **Mercutio** /məˈkjuːʃjəu/ 茂丘西奥   16 **hie** hurry   17 **Straining** singing (plays on the sense of 'forcing, making an unnatural effort')

discords and unpleasing sharps." (3.5.26-28) After the departure of Romeo, Juliet attempts to persuade her parents to absolve her of her marriage to Paris, but her father threatens to disown her if she will not obey him.

Juliet goes to the Friar for advice; he gives her a potion that will produce the effect of death until Romeo can be summoned. Juliet returns home and pretends submission to her parents' wishes. Delighted, Capulet decides to have the wedding the next day. Once alone, Juliet imagines the grim possibility of reviving before Romeo comes into the Capulet tomb next to "the bones of all [her] buried ancestors" and "bloody Tybalt, yet but green in earth." Finally, she drinks the vial and falls onto the bed. The following morning, the Nurse finds Juliet apparently dead. The intended wedding celebration becomes a funeral.

A Monument Belonging to the Capulets, 1789, James Northcote

Balthasar, Romeo's servant, brings his master word in **Mantua**[18] that Juliet has been buried in the family tomb. Since the Friar's messenger failed to reach Mantua, Romeo has not been informed that Juliet is only apparently dead. Saddened by the supposed death of Juliet, Romeo buys poison and returns to Verona. At the tomb, Romeo is discovered by Paris who, thinking Romeo has some evil intent, challenges him. Romeo kills Paris. He then kisses Juliet, drinks the poison, and dies. The Friar arrives at the tomb just as Juliet awakens. He tries to hurry her away from the tomb, but after seeing Romeo's body she refuses to leave. The Friar is frightened away by the voices of the watch, and Juliet stabs herself. The members of the rival families and the Prince are summoned to the tomb and hear the Friar's story. In the presence of their children's bodies, Capulet and Montague agree to end their feud, thus fulfilling what is foretold in the prologue: "A pair of star-crossed lovers take their life,/ Whose misadventured piteous overthrows;/Doth with their death bury their parents' strife."

Beyond the Play: "[S]he is not Fourteen."

In spite of its popularity, *Romeo and Juliet* has always been a daunting play to produce, especially when it comes to the casting of the adolescent Romeo and Juliet. The early 20th-century British leading Shakespearean actress Ellen Terry once remarked that as soon as a woman is old enough to understand Juliet, she's too old to play her. It is quite true that directors always find it a mission impossible to strike a balance between age and experience when casting Romeo and Juliet. At age 19 in 1924, John Gielgud was found to be too old for Romeo. Norma Shearer was 35 when she played the 13-year-old virgin in the 1936 movie version, with Leslie Howard (aged 40) as her middle-aged Romeo. For his 1968 film, Franco Zeffirelli cast a 17-year-old Romeo and a 15-year-old Juliet, whose youth was applauded but whose teenage delivery of the Shakespearean English left much to be desired. (Left: *Romeo and Juliet*, 1936. Right: *Romeo and Juliet*, 1968.)

---

18 **Mantua** /ˈmæntjuə/ 曼图亚

III SELECTED READINGS

Act II, scene 1

[*Enter JULIET above*]

But, soft, what light through yonder window breaks?
It is the east, and Juliet is the sun.
Arise, fair sun, and kill the envious moon,
50 Who is already sick and pale with grief,
That thou her maid art far more fair than she:
Be not her maid, since she is envious:
Her vestal livery is but sick and green
And none but fools do wear it; cast it off.
55 It is my lady, O, it is my love!
O, that she knew she were!
She speaks yet she says nothing: what of that?
Her eye discourses: I will answer it.
I am too bold, 'tis not to me she speaks:
60 Two of the fairest stars in all the heaven,
Having some business, do entreat her eyes
To twinkle in their spheres till they return.
What if her eyes were there, they in her head?
The brightness of her cheek would shame those stars,
65 As daylight doth a lamp; her eyes in heaven
Would through the airy region stream so bright
That birds would sing and think it were not night.
See, how she leans her cheek upon her hand!
O, that I were a glove upon that hand,
70 That I might touch that cheek!
JULIET Ay me!
ROMEO She speaks:
O, speak again, bright angel, for thou art
As glorious to this night, being o'er my head
75 As is a wingèd messenger of heaven
Unto the white-upturnèd wondering eyes
Of mortals that fall back to gaze on him
When he bestrides the lazy-pacing clouds,
And sails upon the bosom of the air.
80 JULIET O Romeo, Romeo, wherefore art thou Romeo?
Deny thy father and refuse thy name,
Or, if thou wilt not, be but sworn my love,
And I'll no longer be a Capulet.
ROMEO Shall I hear more, or shall I speak at this?
85 JULIET 'Tis but thy name that is my enemy;
Thou art thyself, though not a Montague.
What's Montague? It is nor hand, nor foot,

2.1 51 **maid** votary (Diana, Roman goddess of the moon and chastity)   53 **vestal livery** virginal clothing   58 **discourses** relates or recounts   62 **spheres** orbits   74 **glorious** magnificent/shining   80 **wherefore** why

                    Nor arm, nor face, nor any other part
                    Belonging to a man. O, be some other name.
90   What's in a name? That which we call a rose
                    By any other name would smell as sweet,
                    So Romeo would, were he not Romeo called,
                    Retain that dear perfection which he owes
                    Without that title. Romeo, doff thy name,
95   And for that name, which is no part of thee,
                    Take all myself.
            ROMEO
                    I take thee at thy word:
                    Call me but love, and I'll be new baptized,
                    Henceforth I never will be Romeo.
100   JULIET What man art thou that thus bescreened in night
                    So stumblest on my counsel?
            ROMEO By a name
                    I know not how to tell thee who I am:
                    My name, dear saint, is hateful to myself,
105   Because it is an enemy to thee.
                    Had I it written, I would tear the word.
            JULIET My ears have not yet drunk a hundred words
                    Of that tongue's utterance, yet I know the sound:
                    Art thou not Romeo and a Montague?
110   ROMEO   Neither, fair saint, if either thee dislike.
            JULIET How cam'st thou hither, tell me, and wherefore?
                    The orchard walls are high and hard to climb,
                    And the place death, considering who thou art,
                    If any of my kinsmen find thee here.
115   ROMEO   With love's light wings did I o'er-perch these walls,
                    For stony limits cannot hold love out,
                    And what love can do that dares love attempt:
                    Therefore thy kinsmen are no let to me.
            JULIET If they do see thee, they will murder thee.
120   ROMEO   Alack, there lies more peril in thine eye
                    Than twenty of their swords: look thou but sweet,
                    And I am proof against their enmity.
            JULIET I would not for the world they saw thee here.
            ROMEO   I have night's cloak to hide me from their sight;
125   And but thou love me, let them find me here:
                    My life were better ended by their hate,
                    Than death proroguèd, wanting of thy love.
            JULIET By whose direction found'st thou out this place?
            ROMEO   By love, who first did prompt me to inquire:
130   He lent me counsel and I lent him eyes.
                    I am no pilot, yet, wert thou as far

---

93 **owes** owns 94 **doff** cast off 100 **bescreened** hidden; obscured 115 **o'er-perch** fly over 120 **Alack** *interj.* an exclamation of despair 122 **proof** impenetrable 125 **but** unless 127 **proroguèd** postponed **wanting of** lacking 130 **counsel** advice, guidance 131 **pilot** navigator **wert** old form of **were**

98 APPRECIATING SHAKESPEAREAN PLAYS

As that vast shore wash'd with the farthest sea,
I would adventure for such merchandise.
JULIET Thou know'st the mask of night is on my face,
135 Else would a maiden blush bepaint my cheek
For that which thou hast heard me speak tonight
Fain would I dwell on form, fain, fain deny
What I have spoke: but farewell compliment!
Dost thou love me? I know thou wilt say 'Ay',
140 And I will take thy word. Yet if thou swear'st,
Thou mayst prove false: at lovers' perjuries
Then say Jove laughs. O gentle Romeo,
If thou dost love, pronounce it faithfully:
Or if thou think'st I am too quickly won,
145 I'll frown and be perverse and say thee nay,
So thou wilt woo, but else, not for the world.
In truth, fair Montague, I am too fond,
And therefore thou mayst think my behavior light:
But trust me, gentleman, I'll prove more true
150 Than those that have more coying to be strange.
I should have been more strange, I must confess,
But that thou overheard'st, ere I was ware,
My true love's passion: therefore pardon me,
And not impute this yielding to light love,
155 Which the dark night hath so discoverèd.
ROMEO Lady, by yonder blessèd moon I swear
That tips with silver all these fruit-tree tops—
JULIET O, swear not by the moon, the inconstant moon,
That monthly changes in her circlèd orb,
160 Lest that thy love prove likewise variable.
ROMEO What shall I swear by?
JULIET Do not swear at all:
Or, if thou wilt, swear by thy gracious self,
Which is the god of my idolatry,
165 And I'll believe thee.
ROMEO If my heart's dear love—
JULIET Well, do not swear. Although I joy in thee,
I have no joy of this contract tonight:
It is too rash, too unadvised, too sudden,
170 Too like the lightning, which doth cease to be
Ere one can say 'It lightens'. Sweet, good night!
This bud of love, by summer's ripening breath,
May prove a beauteous flower when next we meet.
Good night, good night, as sweet repose and rest
175 Come to thy heart as that within my breast!

---

133 **adventure** risk   137 **Fain** willingly   **form** formality   138 **compliment** etiquette   142 **Jove** Jupiter, Roman king of the gods   146 **So** so long as   148 **light** frivolous; unchaste   150 **coying** affected reluctance   **strange** aloof, reserved   152 **ere** before   **ware** aware (of you)   155 **discoverèd** revealed   159 **circlèd orb** celestial sphere   163 **gracious** full of divine grace   168 **contract** mutual declarations of love

ROMEO O, wilt thou leave me so unsatisfied?
JULIET What satisfaction canst thou have tonight?
ROMEO Th' exchange of thy love's faithful vow for mine.
JULIET I gave thee mine before thou didst request it:
180   And yet I would it were to give again.
ROMEO Wouldst thou withdraw it? For what purpose, love?
JULIET But to be frank, and give it thee again.
And yet I wish but for the thing I have.
My bounty is as boundless as the sea,
185   My love as deep; the more I give to thee,
The more I have, for both are infinite.
I hear some noise within. Dear love, adieu! —
[*Nurse*] *calls within*
Anon, good nurse! — Sweet Montague, be true.
Stay but a little, I will come again.   [*Exit, above*]

Act III, scene 5

Enter Romeo and Juliet above aloft
JULIET Wilt thou be gone? it is not yet near day.
It was the nightingale, and not the lark,
That pierced the fearful hollow of thine ear;
Nightly she sings on yon pom'granate tree.
5   Believe me, love, it was the nightingale.
ROMEO It was the lark, the herald of the morn,
No nightingale: look, love, what envious streaks
Do lace the severing clouds in yonder east:
Night's candles are burnt out, and jocund day
10   Stands tiptoe on the misty mountain tops.
I must be gone and live, or stay and die.
JULIET Yon light is not daylight, I know it, I:
It is some meteor that the sun exhales,
To be to thee this night a torch-bearer,
15   And light thee on thy way to Mantua.
Therefore stay yet: thou need'st not to be gone.
ROMEO Let me be ta'en, let me be put to death,
I am content, so thou wilt have it so.
I'll say yon grey is not the morning's eye,
20   'Tis but the pale reflex of Cynthia's brow,
Nor that is not the lark, whose notes do beat
The vaulty heaven so high above our heads.
I have more care to stay than will to go:
Come, death, and welcome! Juliet wills it so.
25   How is't, my soul? Let's talk, it is not day.
JULIET It is, it is: hie hence, be gone, away!

3.5 7 **envious** malicious; jealous   8 **severing** separating   9 **jocund** merry, sprightly   13 **meteor ... exhales** ill-omened meteors were believed to be formed of vapours drawn up from the earth by the sun   17 **ta'en** arrested   18 **so** provided   20 **reflex** reflection **Cynthia** another name for the goddess of the moon   22 **vaulty** vaulted, arched   23 **care** concern; inclination   26 **hie** hurry

                It is the lark that sings so out of tune,
                Straining harsh discords and unpleasing sharps.
                Some say the lark makes sweet division;
30   This doth not so, for she divideth us:
                Some say the lark and loathèd toad change eyes,
                O, now I would they had changed voices too!
                Since arm from arm that voice doth us affray,
                Hunting thee hence with hunt's-up to the day.
35   O, now be gone; more light and light it grows.
        ROMEO   More light and light; more dark and dark our woes!

Questions for Comprehension and Reflection
Act II, scene 1
1. Why is Juliet described as "her maid" (51)?
2. What is meant by "the more I give to thee,/The more I have, for both are infinite." (185-186)?
3. What does this poetically romantic exchange show about Juliet's personality?

Act III, scene 5
1. Why does Juliet insist that "it is not yet near day" (1)?
2. What does day mean to Romeo?
3. Is Romeo optimistic or pessimistic about his life with Juliet?

IV SHAKESPEAREAN RELEVANCE

A. Shakespeare in Everyday English
Please try to understand the following Shakespearean words and expressions in the contexts designated within parentheses and give their generally used meanings in the space provided.
1. star-crossed (pro. 6): _____
2. on pain of (1.1.71): _____
3. a man of wax (1.3.56-57): _____
4. a rose by any other name would smell as sweet (2.1.90-91): _____
5. a wild-goose chase (2.3.54): _____
6. a fool's paradise (2.3.124): _____
7. a plague on both your houses (3.1.78): _____
8. Fortune's fool (3.1.123): _____

B. Shakespeare in Literature
Read the following literary excerpts, locate the Shakespearean allusions and explain their meanings according to the contexts where they appear.
1. I told them I liked it when things were vast and made of iron. And I described a courtyard I went into where there was an iron girder strung between two houses. It seemed to be holding the two buildings apart, as if one was the Capulet house and the other was the house of the Montagues. (Rose Tremain, *The Way I Found Her*, 1998)

---

28 **Straining** singing   33 **arm from arm** from one another's arms

2. Fleur's in love, I understand, with Phil Merrick—a Romeo-and-Juliet affair disapproved of by his grandfather; though his grandfather already has an Olympic bronze in disapproval. (Staynes and Storey, *Dead Serious*, 1995)
3. His personal feeling that loving Phoebe Wilson was a thing beyond the scope of the most determined Romeo he concealed. It could, apparently be done. (P. G. Wodehouse, *Cocktail Time*, 1958)
4. It's that middle stretch of the night, when the curtains leak no light, the only streetnoise is the grizzle of a returning Romeo, and the birds haven't begun their routine yet cheering business. (Julian Barnes, *A History of the World in $10^1/_2$ Chapters*, 1989)

C. Shakespeare in Music, Art and on Screen

1867: *Roméo et Juliette*, an opera composed by Gounod, libretto by Jules Barbier and Michel Carré.
1839: *Roméo et Juliette*, a "symphonie dramatique" by berlioz.
1869: *Romeo and Juliet* Fantasy-Overture, a symphonic poem by Tchaikovsky.
1936: *Romeo and Juliet*, a film version directed by George Cukor, starring Leslie Howard as Romeo and Norma Shearer as Juliet.
1957: *West Side Story*, a musical adaptation with music by Leonard Bernstein and lyrics by Stephen Sondheim.
1968: *Romeo and Juliet*, a highly-acclaimed film adaptation directed by Franco Zeffirelli, starring Olivia Hussey as Juliet and Leonard Whiting as Romeo.
1996: *Romeo + Juliet*, a modernized version directed by Baz Luhrmann, starring Leonardo DiCaprio and Claire Danes in the leading roles.

V SHAKESPEARE QUOTES

For you and I are past our dancing days. (1.4.146)
O, she doth teach the torches to burn bright. (1.4.161)
But soft! What light through yonder window breaks?
It is the East and Juliet is the sun! (2.1.47-48)
See how she leans her cheek upon her hand!
O, that I were a glove upon that hand,
That I might touch that cheek! (2.1.68-70)
O Romeo, Romeo! wherefore art thou Romeo? (2.1.80)
What's in a name? That which we call a rose
By any other name would smell as sweet. (2.1.90-91)
Good Night, Good night! Parting is such sweet sorrow,
That I shall say good night till it be morrow. (2.1.239-240)
Wisely and slow: they stumble that run fast. (2.2.97)
Not stepping o'er the bounds of modesty. (4.2.25)
Tempt not a desperate man. (5.3.59)

12. The Tragedy of Julius Caesar
裘力斯·凯撒

I INTRODUCTION

伊丽莎白一世的国务大臣 Francis Walsingham(1532—1590)曾向女王谏言:"读史之要义在观往昔为政者处事决断之道,以事今日今朝者也。"(... in the reading of histories as you have principally to mark how matters have passed in government in those days, so have you apply them to these our times and states and see how they may be made serviceable to our age.)罗马位居世界中心位置一千多年,即便在其衰落之后仍以其文治武功、政治体制、道德规范继续引领风骚数百年。莎士比亚的英国则是偏安于世界西北一隅的小国,由于亨利八世早与罗马教廷脱离关系,国内处于分裂的边缘。但是,在伊丽莎白一世统治期间,英国的贵族、知识分子及普通的老百姓均爱国热情高涨,希望自己的弹丸岛国最终能够励精图治而成为雄踞世界的第二个罗马帝国。同时,由于都铎王朝篡位的不光彩的历史,年事渐高的独身女王伊丽莎白一世也更加迫切地感受到来自各方的威胁和册立继嗣人的必要。在此背景下,莎士比亚根据罗马作家普鲁塔克(Plutarch)的《希腊罗马名人传》(*Lives of the Noble Grecians and Romans*)创作除了这部借古喻今的"正剧",并赋予了剧中人物矛盾的特性:凯撒似神仙附体但又难免一死、安东尼忠诚不二但又蝇营狗苟、勃鲁托斯品格高贵但又极端自负。个人的矛盾和悲剧也放大为整个罗马的历史讽刺:遏制独裁的谋杀分裂了罗马并导致了内战的爆发,而这场内乱最终是以屋大维(Octavius)登基称皇从而开启帝国时代而结束的。莎翁借助历史所探讨的问题意义深远(比如:权利集中的度在哪里? 民主体制非常强大可以制约潜在的独裁者吗? 街头暴民是可能改变历史的唯一力量? 从政者能够做到大公无私而值得信赖吗?)。所以,当英国在18、19世纪成为称霸四海的大英帝国时,《裘力斯·凯撒》便成为贵族、政客、公务员教育和品格塑造的活教材,而马克·安东尼的那篇扭转乾坤的演讲(见选读)也成为学童诵读和修辞研究的范本。

II PLOT SUMMARY

The action begins in February, 44 B.C., **Julius Caesar**[1] has just reentered Rome in triumph after a victory in Spain over the sons of his old enemy, **Pompey**[2] the Great. A spontaneous celebration is interrupted and broken up by Flavius and Marullus, two political enemies of Caesar. It soon becomes apparent from their words that there are powerful and secret forces working against Caesar.

Caesar appears, attended by a train of friends and supporters, and is warned by a Soothsayer to "Beware the **Ides of March**,"[3] but he ignores the warning and leaves for the games and races

---

1 **Julius Caesar** /ˈdʒuːljəs, ˈsiːzə/ 裘力斯·凯撒 2 **Pompey** /ˈpɔmpi/ 庞培 3 **Ides** (/aidz/) **of March** 15 March

marking the celebration of the **Feast of Lupercal**.[4] Seeing Brutus and Cassius whispering, he observes that the latter "has a lean and hungry look", "thinks too much", and is dangerous. He prefers men "that are fat,/**Sleek-headed**[5] men, and such as sleep a-nights." (1.2.198-199)

After Caesar's departure, only two men remain behind—**Marcus Brutus**,[6] a close personal friend of Caesar, and **Cassius**,[7] a longtime political foe of Caesar. Both men are of aristocratic origin and see the end of their ancient privilege in Caesar's political reforms and conquests. Envious of Caesar's power and prestige, Cassius cleverly probes to discover where Brutus's deepest sympathies lie. As a man of highest personal integrity, Brutus opposes Caesar on principle, despite his friendship for him. Cassius cautiously inquires about Brutus's feelings if a conspiracy were to unseat Caesar; he finds Brutus not altogether against the notion. The two men part, promising to meet again for further discussions.

The Ides of March, 1883, Edward John Poynter

In the next scene, it is revealed that the conspiracy which Cassius spoke of in veiled terms is already a reality. He has gathered together a group of disgruntled and discredited aristocrats who are only too willing to assassinate Caesar. Partly to gain the support of the respectable element of Roman society, Cassius persuades Brutus to head the conspiracy, and Brutus apparently agrees to do so.

Shortly afterward, plans are made at a secret meeting in Brutus's orchard. The date is set: it will be on the day of the "Ides of March". Caesar is to be murdered in the Senate chambers by the concealed daggers and swords of the assembled conspirators. But when Cassius suggests that Mark Antony be murdered together with Caesar, Brutus disagrees, "Our course will seem too bloody, Caius Cassius,/To cut the head off and then hack the limbs—/Like wrath in death and envy afterwards—/For Antony is but a limb of Caesar./Let's be sacrificers, but not butchers." (2.1.169-173)

After the meeting, Brutus's wife, Portia, seeing her husband "steal out of his **wholesome**[8] bed/To dare the vile contagion of the night", (2.1.275-276) fears for his safety and questions him. Touched by her love and devotion, Brutus promises to reveal his secret to her later.

The next scene takes place in Caesar's house. The time is the very early morning; the date, the fateful Ides of March. The preceding night has been a strange one—wild, stormy, and full of strange and unexplainable sights and happenings throughout the city of Rome. Caesar's wife, **Calpurnia**,[9] terrified by horrible nightmares, persuades Caesar not to go to the Capitol, convinced that her dreams are portents of disaster. Caesar finally decides to go when Decius tells him that his wife's dream of his statue, "Which, like a fountain with an hundred spouts,/Did run pure blood,/and many lusty Romans/Came smiling and did bathe their hands in it" (2.2.81-83) is actually an allegory for Caesar's upcoming revival of Rome, and that his failure to present himself at the Senate would make him an object of mockery: "Break up the senate till another time/When Caesar's wife shall meet with better dream." (2.2.102-103)

By prearrangement, Brutus and the other conspirators arrive to accompany Caesar, hoping to fend off any possible warnings, until they have him totally in their power at the Senate. Unaware

---

4 **Feast of Lupercal** (/ˈljuːpəkæl/) 卢柏克节 a Roman festival held on 15 February in honour of Lupercus, the god of shepherds; festivities centred around the Lupercal, a cave in which a wolf was believed to have suckled Rome's founders, Romulus and Remus   5 **Sleek-headed** well-groomed, smooth-haired   6 **Marcus Brutus** /ˈmɑːkəs ˈbruːtəs/ 马可·勃鲁托斯   7 **Cassius** /ˈkæsiəs/ 凯歇斯   8 **wholesome** healthful   9 **Calpurnia** /kælˈpəːnjə/ 凯尔普妮娅

Death of Julius Caesar, Vincenzo Camuccini (1773—1844)

that he is surrounded by assassins, Caesar goes with them. Despite the conspirators' best efforts, a warning is pressed into Caesar's hand on the very steps of the Capitol, but he refuses to read it. Wasting no further time, the conspirators move into action. Purposely asking Caesar for a favor—they know he will refuse, they move closer, as if begging a favor, and then, reaching for their hidden weapons, they kill him before the shocked eyes of the Senators and spectators.

Hearing of Caesar's murder. Mark Antony, Caesar's closest friend begs permission to speak at Caesar's funeral. Brutus grants this permission over the objections of Cassius and goes to deliver his own speech first, explaining that he has risen against Caesar "not that I loved Caesar less, but that I loved Rome more," and vowing that "as I slew my best lover for the good of Rome, I have the same dagger for myself, when it shall please my country to need my death." (3.2.36-38) He is confident that his words will convince the populace of the necessity for Caesar's death. After Brutus leaves, Antony begins to speak. The crowd has been swayed by Brutu's words, and it is an angry crowd that Antony addresses. Using every oratorical device available to him, however, Antony turns the audience into a howling mob, screaming for the blood of Caesar's murderers. Alarmed by the furor caused by Antony's speech, the conspirators and their supporters are forced to flee from Rome, and finally from Italy.

At this point, Antony, together with Caesar's young grand-nephew and adopted son, **Octavius**[10] and a wealthy banker, **Lepidus**,[11] gathers an army to pursue and destroy Caesar's killers. Months pass, during which the conspirators and their armies are pursued relentlessly into the far reaches of Asia Minor. When finally they decide to stop at the town of Sardis, Cassius and Brutus quarrel bitterly over finances. Their differences are resolved, however, and plans are made to meet the forces of Antony, Octavius, and Lepidus in one final battle. Against his own better judgment, Cassius allows Brutus to over-rule him. Instead of holding to their well-prepared defensive positions, Brutus orders an attack on Antony's camp on the plains of Philippi.

Just before the battle, Brutus is visited by the ghost of Caesar. "I shall see thee at Philippi," the spirit warns him. But Brutus's courage is unshaken and he goes on. The battle rages hotly. At first, the conspirators seem to have won the day, but in the confusion, Cassius becomes mistakenly convinced that all is lost, and he kills himself. Leaderless, his forces are quickly defeated, and Brutus finds himself fighting a hopeless battle. Unable to face the prospect of humiliation and shame as a captive chained to the wheels of Antony's chariot and dragged through the streets of Rome, he too takes his own life.

Brutus and the Ghost of Caesar, 1802, Richard Westall

As the play ends, Antony delivers a eulogy over Brutus's body, calling him "the noblest

---

10 **Octavius** (/ɔkˈteiviəs/ 屋大维) great-nephew of Julius Caesar   11 **Lepidus** (/ˈlepədəs/ 莱必多斯) appointed, together with Octavius and Antony, the Second Triumvirate (/traɪˈʌmvɪrət/ 三人执政) after the death of Julius Caesar

Roman of them all." Caesar's murder has been avenged, order has been restored, and, most importantly, Rome has been preserved.

Beyond the Play: *Tidbits about Julius Caesar*

- For its manageable length and lack of sexy puns and allusions, Julius Caesar remains embedded in British and American school curriculum, whose austere and static plots and language only serve to turn kids away from Shakespeare altogether.
- Julius Caesar has been used to indict totalitarian regimes, with Caesar variously appearing as De Gaulle, Mussolini, and Hitler figures, and the changes of its setting.
- On April 14, 1865, American President Lincoln was assassinated by John Wilkes Booth, a member of one of the most famous acting families of the day. His father, Junius Brutus Booth, was named after Brutus, the assassin who killed Julius Caesar. Four months before the assassination, the three Booth brothers had taken part in a charity performance of *Julius Caesar*. In a final dramatic gesture after he shot and killed the President, John Wilkes, an ardent secessionist, leaped from the presidential box onto the stage, screaming "Sic Semper Tyrannis" ("Thus Be It Ever to Tyrants," the motto of the state of Virginia).

III SELECTED READINGS

Act III, scene 2

    Enter BRUTUS and goes into the pulpit, and CASSIUS with the Plebeians
    PLEBEIANS We will be satisfied: let us be satisfied.
    BRUTUS Then follow me, and give me audience, friends.
        Cassius, go you into the other street
        And part the numbers:
5   Those that will hear me speak, let 'em stay here;
        Those that will follow Cassius, go with him
        And public reasons shall be renderèd
        Of Caesar's death.
    First Plebeian I will hear Brutus speak.
10   *Second Plebeian* I will hear Cassius, and compare their reasons
        When severally we hear them rendered.
    Exit CASSIUS, with some of the Plebeians.
    Third Plebeian The noble Brutus is ascended: silence!
    BRUTUS Be patient till the last.
15   Romans, countrymen, and lovers! hear me for my cause, and be silent, that you may

---

3.2 2 **give me audience** listen to me   4 **part the numbers** divide the crowd   7 **public** given in pubic   11 **severally** separately   14 **last** end (of my speech)

hear. Believe me for mine honour and have respect to mine honour, that you may believe. Censure me in your wisdom and awake your senses, that you may the better judge. If there be any in this assembly, any dear friend of Caesar's, to him I say, that Brutus' love to Caesar was no less than

20   his. If then that friend demand why Brutus rose against Caesar, this is my answer: not that I loved Caesar less, but that I loved Rome more. Had you rather Caesar were living and die all slaves, than that Caesar were dead, to live all free men? As Caesar loved me, I weep for him; as he was fortunate, I rejoice at it; as he was valiant, I honour him: but, as he was ambitious, I slew

25   him. There is tears for his love: joy for his fortune: honour for his valour: and death for his ambition. Who is here so base that would be a bondman? If any, speak, for him have I offended. Who is here so rude that would not be a Roman? If any, speak, for him have I offended. Who is here so vile that will not love his country? If any, speak, for him have I offended. I pause for a

30   reply.

All   None, Brutus, none.

BRUTUS   Then none have I offended. I have done no more to Caesar than you shall do to Brutus. The question of his death is enrolled in the Capitol: his glory not extenuated, wherein he was worthy, nor his offences enforced, for

35   which he suffered death.

Enter MARK ANTONY with CAESAR's body

Here comes his body, mourned by Mark Antony, who, though he had no hand in his death, shall receive the benefit of his dying, a place in the commonwealth, as which of you shall not? With this I depart, that, as I slew my best lover for the good of Rome, I have the same dagger for myself, when

40   it shall please my country to need my death.

All   Live, Brutus, live, live!

First Plebeian   Bring him with triumph home unto his house.

Second Plebeian   Give him a statue with his ancestors.

Third Plebeian   Let him be Caesar.

45 *Fourth Plebeian*   Caesar's better parts
Shall be crowned in Brutus.

First Plebeian   We'll bring him to his house with shouts and clamours.

BRUTUS   My countrymen —

Second Plebeian   Peace, silence! Brutus speaks.

50 *First Plebeian*   Peace, ho!

BRUTUS   Good countrymen, let me depart alone,
And, for my sake, stay here with Antony:
Do grace to Caesar's corpse, and grace his speech
Tending to Caesar's glories, which Mark Antony —

55   By our permission — is allowed to make.
I do entreat you, not a man depart
Save I alone, till Antony have spoke. *Exit*

---

15 **lovers** friends   **cause** grounds for action   16 **for** because of   17 **Censure** judge   **senses** minds, wits   27 **rude** uncivilized   28 **vile** lowly   33 **question of** considerations behind   **enrolled** officially recorded   33 **extenuated** lessened, minimized   **enforced** exaggerated   37 **place ... commonwealth** i. e. his rights as a free man in the Roman republic   42 **triumph** pomp, ceremony   45 **parts** qualities   46 **crowned** literally crowned/rewarded/surpassed   53 **Do grace to** honour, respect   **grace** listen courteously to   54 **Tending** relating

First Plebeian　Stay, ho! and let us hear Mark Antony.
Third Plebeian　Let him go up into the public chair.
60　　We'll hear him. — Noble Antony, go up.
ANTONY　For Brutus' sake, I am beholding to you.　*Goes into the pulpit*
Fourth Plebeian　What does he say of Brutus?
Third Plebeian　He says, for Brutus' sake,
　　He finds himself beholding to us all.
65　*Fourth Plebeian*　'Twere best he speak no harm of Brutus here.
First Plebeian　This Caesar was a tyrant.
Third Plebeian　Nay, that's certain:
　　We are blest that Rome is rid of him.
Second Plebeian　Peace! Let us hear what Antony can say.
70　ANTONY　You gentle Romans,
Plebeians　Peace, ho! Let us hear him.
ANTONY　Friends, Romans, countrymen, lend me your ears:
　　I come to bury Caesar, not to praise him.
　　The evil that men do lives after them;
75　　The good is oft interrèd with their bones.
　　So let it be with Caesar. The noble Brutus
　　Hath told you Caesar was ambitious:
　　If it were so, it was a grievous fault,
　　And grievously hath Caesar answered it.
80　　Here, under leave of Brutus and the rest—
　　For Brutus is an honourable man;
　　So are they all, all honourable men —
　　Come I to speak in Caesar's funeral.
　　He was my friend, faithful and just to me;
85　　But Brutus says he was ambitious,
　　And Brutus is an honourable man.
　　He hath brought many captives home to Rome,
　　Whose ransoms did the general coffers fill:
　　Did this in Caesar seem ambitious?
90　　When that the poor have cried, Caesar hath wept:
　　Ambition should be made of sterner stuff.
　　Yet Brutus says he was ambitious,
　　And Brutus is an honourable man.
　　You all did see that on the Lupercal,
95　　I thrice presented him a kingly crown,
　　Which he did thrice refuse. Was this ambition?
　　Yet Brutus says he was ambitious,
　　And sure he is an honourable man.
　　I speak not to disprove what Brutus spoke,
100　　But here I am to speak what I do know.

---

59 **public chair** pulpit, platform for public orations　61 **beholding** obliged, indebted　75 **interrèd** buried　79 **answered** paid for　80 **leave** permission　88 **general coffers** public treasury

You all did love him once, not without cause:
What cause withholds you then, to mourn for him?
O judgment! thou art fled to brutish beasts
And men have lost their reason. — Bear with me:
105 My heart is in the coffin there with Caesar,
And I must pause till it come back to me.
First Plebeian   Methinks there is much reason in his sayings.
Second Plebeian   If thou consider rightly of the matter,
Caesar has had great wrong.
110 *Third Plebeian*   Has he, masters?
I fear there will a worse come in his place.
Fourth Plebeian   Marked ye his words? He would not take the crown:
Therefore 'tis certain he was not ambitious.
First Plebeian   If it be found so, some will dear abide it.
115 *Second Plebeian*   Poor soul, his eyes are red as fire with weeping.
Third Plebeian   There's not a nobler man in Rome than Antony.
Fourth Plebeian   Now mark him, he begins again to speak.
ANTONY   But yesterday the word of Caesar might
Have stood against the world: now lies he there,
120 And none so poor to do him reverence.
O masters, if I were disposed to stir
Your hearts and minds to mutiny and rage,
I should do Brutus wrong, and Cassius wrong,
Who—you all know—are honourable men.
125 I will not do them wrong: I rather choose
To wrong the dead, to wrong myself and you,
Than I will wrong such honourable men.
But here's a parchment, with the seal of Caesar.
I found it in his closet, 'tis his will.
130 Let but the commons hear this testament—
Which, pardon me, I do not mean to read—
And they would go and kiss dead Caesar's wounds
And dip their napkins in his sacred blood,
Yea, beg a hair of him for memory,
135 And, dying, mention it within their wills,
Bequeathing it as a rich legacy
Unto their issue.
Fourth Plebeian   We'll hear the will. Read it, Mark Antony.
All   The will, the will! We will hear Caesar's will.
140 ANTONY   Have patience, gentle friends, I must not read it.
It is not meet you know how Caesar loved you.
You are not wood, you are not stones, but men:
And, being men, bearing the will of Caesar,

---

110 **masters** sirs   111 **worse** i. e. worse tyrant   114 **dear abide it** suffer grievously for it   118 **But** only   119 **stood against** resisted, fought against   120 **poor** humble   129 **closet** cabinet   133 **dip ... blood** i. e. as if Caesar were a martyr   **napkins** handkerchiefs   137 **issue** children   141 **meet** fit

It will inflame you, it will make you mad;
145 'Tis good you know not that you are his heirs,
For, if you should, O, what would come of it!
Fourth Plebeian Read the will. We'll hear it, Antony;
You shall read us the will, Caesar's will.
ANTONY Will you be patient? Will you stay awhile?
150 I have o'ershot myself to tell you of it.
I fear I wrong the honourable men
Whose daggers have stabbed Caesar: I do fear it.
Fourth Plebeian They were traitors: honourable men?
All The will, the testament!
155 *Second Plebeian* They were villains, murderers. The will, read the will.
ANTONY You will compel me, then, to read the will:
Then make a ring about the corpse of Caesar,
And let me show you him that made the will.
Shall I descend? And will you give me leave?
160 *All* Come down.
Second Plebeian Descend.
Third Plebeian You shall have leave.
ANTONY comes down
Fourth Plebeian A ring. Stand round.
165 *First Plebeian* Stand from the hearse, stand from the body.
Second Plebeian Room for Antony, most noble Antony.
ANTONY Nay, press not so upon me. Stand far off.
Several Plebeians Stand back: room, bear back.
ANTONY If you have tears, prepare to shed them now.
170 You all do know this mantle. I remember
The first time ever Caesar put it on.
'Twas on a summer's evening in his tent,
That day he overcame the Nervii.
Look, in this place ran Cassius' dagger through:
175 See what a rent the envious Casca made:
Through this the well-belovèd Brutus stabbed,
And as he plucked his cursèd steel away,
Mark how the blood of Caesar followed it,
As rushing out of doors, to be resolved
180 If Brutus so unkindly knocked, or no,
For Brutus, as you know, was Caesar's angel. —
Judge, O you gods, how dearly Caesar loved him. —
This was the most unkindest cut of all.
For when the noble Caesar saw him stab,
185 Ingratitude, more strong than traitors' arms,
Quite vanquished him: then burst his mighty heart,

---

150 **o'ershot myself** gone further than I intended   165 **from** back from   **hearse** coffin or stand on which the body rests   173 **Nervii** Belgian tribe of warriors defeated by Caesar   175 **rent** tear, slash   179 **As** as if it were   180 **unkindly** cruelly/unnaturally   181 **angel** favourite, dearest friend/protective spirit

	And in his mantle muffling up his face,

And in his mantle muffling up his face,
Even at the base of Pompey's statue —
Which all the while ran blood — great Caesar fell.
190 O, what a fall was there, my countrymen!
Then I, and you, and all of us fell down,
Whilst bloody treason flourished over us.
O, now you weep, and, I perceive, you feel
The dint of pity: these are gracious drops.
195 Kind souls, what, weep you when you but behold
Our Caesar's vesture wounded? Look you here,
Here is himself, marred, as you see, with traitors.
First Plebeian O piteous spectacle!
Second Plebeian O noble Caesar!
200 *Third Plebeian* O woeful day!
Fourth Plebeian O traitors, villains!
First Plebeian O most bloody sight!
Second Plebeian We will be revenged.
All Revenge! About! Seek! Burn! Fire! Kill! Slay!
205 Let not a traitor live!
ANTONY Stay, countrymen.
First Plebeian Peace there, hear the noble Antony.
Second Plebeian We'll hear him, we'll follow him, we'll die with him.
ANTONY Good friends, sweet friends, let me not stir you up
210 To such a sudden flood of mutiny.
They that have done this deed are honourable.
What private griefs they have, alas, I know not,
That made them do it: they are wise and honourable
And will no doubt with reasons answer you.
215 I come not, friends, to steal away your hearts:
I am no orator, as Brutus is;
But, as you know me all a plain blunt man
That love my friend, and that they know full well
That gave me public leave to speak of him,
220 For I have neither wit, nor words, nor worth,
Action, nor utterance, nor the power of speech,
To stir men's blood: I only speak right on:
I tell you that which you yourselves do know.
Show you sweet Caesar's wounds, poor poor dumb mouths,
225 And bid them speak for me. But were I Brutus,
And Brutus Antony, there were an Antony
Would ruffle up your spirits, and put a tongue
In every wound of Caesar that should move

---

192 **flourished** triumphed/prospered/brandished (its sword)   194 **dint** impression, mark   **gracious** virtuous/blessed   196 **vesture** clothing   197 **marred** spoiled, stained   **with** by   212 **private griefs** personal grievances   216 **orator** eloquent speaker, master of rhetoric   217 **plain blunt** plain-speaking and forthright   220 **wit** intelligence   221 **Action** gestures (used by a skilled orator to reinforce his words)   222 **right on** directly, truthfully   225 **Brutus** i.e. a skilled orator   227 **ruffle up** incite, enrage

|||The stones of Rome to rise and mutiny.
230 *All* We'll mutiny.
First Plebeian We'll burn the house of Brutus.
Third Plebeian Away, then, come, seek the conspirators.
ANTONY Yet hear me, countrymen; yet hear me speak.
All Peace, ho! Hear Antony. Most noble Antony.
235 ANTONY Why, friends, you go to do you know not what:
Wherein hath Caesar thus deserved your loves?
Alas, you know not: I must tell you then:
You have forgot the will I told you of.
All Most true. The will! Let's stay and hear the will.
240 ANTONY Here is the will, and under Caesar's seal.
To every Roman Plebeian he gives,
To every several man, seventy-five drachmas.
Second Plebeian Most noble Caesar! We'll revenge his death.
Third Plebeian O royal Caesar!
245 ANTONY Hear me with patience.
All Peace, ho!
ANTONY Moreover, he hath left you all his walks,
His private arbours and new-planted orchards,
On this side Tiber. He hath left them you
250 And to your heirs for ever: common pleasures
To walk abroad, and recreate yourselves.
Here was a Caesar: when comes such another?
First Plebeian Never, never. Come, away, away:
We'll burn his body in the holy place,
255 And with the brands fire the traitors' houses.
Take up the body.
Second Plebeian Go fetch fire.
Third Plebeian Pluck down benches.
Fourth Plebeian Pluck down forms, windows, anything.
Exeunt Plebeians with the body
260 ANTONY Now let it work. Mischief, thou art afoot:
Take thou what course thou wilt. —
Enter a Servant How now, fellow?
Servant Sir, Octavius is already come to Rome.
ANTONY Where is he?
265 *Servant* He and Lepidus are at Caesar's house.
ANTONY And thither will I straight to visit him:
He comes upon a wish. Fortune is merry,
And in this mood will give us anything.
Servant I heard him say, Brutus and Cassius

---

236 **Wherein** for what   242 **several** individual   **seventy-five** would be a generous sum   **drachmas** silver coins   248 **orchards** gardens   250 **common pleasures** public parks, pleasure gardens   251 **recreate** enjoy   255 **brands** burning logs   **fire** set fire to   259 **forms** benches   **windows** shutters   260 **Mischief** evil, harm   266 **straight** (go) straight away   267 **upon a wish** just as I would have wished   **merry** in good spirits, inclined towards us

270   Are rid like madmen through the gates of Rome.
    ANTONY Belike they had some notice of the people
        How I had moved them. Bring me to Octavius. *Exeunt*

Questions for Comprehension and Reflection
Act I, scene 1
1. What is Brutus' accusation against Caesar?
2. What image of himself does Brutus intend to create in the mind of his audience?
3. How can you account for the way Antony begins his speech?
4. What are the rhetorical devices employed by Antony to sway the audience?
5. How does the audience respond to Antony's speech?

IV SHAKESPEAREAN RELEVANCE

A. Shakespeare in Everyday English
Please try to understand the following Shakespearean words and expressions in the contexts designated within parentheses and give their generally used meanings in the space provided.
1. tongue-tied (1.1.59):
2. gamesome (1.2.32):
3. a lean and hungry look (1.2.200):
4. It was Greek to me. (1.2.274):
5. a dish fit for the gods (2.1.180):
6. stand on ceremonies (2.2.13):
7. dogs of war (3.1.292):
8. be made of sterner stuff (3.2.89):

B. Shakespeare in Literature
Read the following literary excerpts, locate the Shakespearean allusions and explain their meanings according to the contexts where they appear.
1. I rose to my feet with some of the emotions of a man who has just taken the Cornish Express in the small of the back. She was standing looking at me with her hands on her hips, grinding her teeth quietly, and I gazed back with reproach and amazement, like Julius Caesar at Brutus. (P. G. Wodehouse, *Laughing Gas*, 1936)
2. I heard the woman yell, "Gaston! Get out here!" and then a man appeared and engulfed them both with bearlike arms. I had a sinking feeling as I watched them, like Brutus might've felt just before he stabbed Caesar. (John Dunning, *The Bookman's Wake*, 1995)

C. Shakespeare in Music, Art and on Screen
1937: *Julius Caesar*, a modern dress drama directed (together with John Houseman) by and starring Orson Welles as Brutus.
1953: *Julius Caesar*, a film adaptation, directed by Joseph L. Mankiewicz, starring Marlon Brando as Mark Antony, James Mason as Brutus, and John Gielgud as Cassius.
1973: *Heil Caesar*, a television adaption of the BBC with a modern setting in an unnamed country,

---
270 **Are rid** have ridden 271 **Belike** probably **notice of** news about

2012: *Julius Caesar*, an all-black production of the Royal Shakespeare Company directed by Gregory Doran; an all-female production directed by Phyllida Lloyd, starring Harriet Walter as Brutus and Frances Barber as Caesar.

V SHAKESPEARE QUOTES

Beaware the Ides of March. (1.2.21)
'Tis a common proof,
Lowliness is young ambition's ladder
Whereto the climber upward turns his face.
But when he once attains the upmost round,
He then unto the ladder turns his back,
Looks in the clouds, scorning the base degrees
By which he did ascend. (2.1.21-27)
Let's kill him boldly, but not wrathfully:
Let's carve him as a dish fit for the gods,
Not hew him as a carcass fit for hounds. (2.1.179-181)
When beggars die there are no comets seen:
The heavens themselves blaze forth the death of princes. (2.2.31-32)
Cowards die many times before their deaths,
The valiant never taste of death but once. (2.2.33-34)
Mischief, thou art afoot:
Take thou what course thou wilt. (3.2.257-258)
This was the noblest Roman of them all (5.5.73)

13. The Tragedy of Macbeth
麦 克 白

I INTRODUCTION

  暗影、淫雨、狂风、暮光、午夜这些日后黑色电影(*film noir*)的元素构成了《麦克白》的基调。苏格兰将军麦克白凯旋归来路遇三女巫,她们分别预言他将渐次升至葛莱密斯爵士、考特爵士及最后的苏格兰国王。前两个预言的很快实现再加上麦克白夫人的催促,麦克白终将在他城堡做客的邓肯国王杀死。弑君像是打开了一只潘多拉盒子,打破了天地间原先的秩序:黑夜不羁(unruly)、风暴骤起、大地颤动、御马狂嘶。王位既得,麦克白开始了巩固其地位的谋杀,但也陷入了深深的烦恼、自责之中,于是便又有了第二次占卜于三女巫,从由她们所引出的三个幽灵口中得到了"留心麦克德夫"([B]eware Macduff)、"没有一个妇人所生下的人可以伤害麦克白"([N]one of woman born/Shall harm Macbeth)和"麦克白永远不会被人打败,除非有一天勃南德树林会冲着他向邓西嫩高山移动"(Macbeth shall never vanquished be until/Great Birnam Wood to high Dunsinane Hill)的警示和预言。最终,麦克白众叛亲离,而他的夫人则由于饱受精神折磨而患上了梦游之症,后以自杀结束了自己的生命。全剧以麦克白败在麦克德夫手下殒命战场而告终。《麦克白》是一出关于梦想如何变成噩梦、白天似乎是小鸟安乐之窝的城堡如何在夜幕降临之后变成了地狱以及整个世界如何乾坤颠倒,特别是贤德、忠勇之士如何蜕变成十恶不赦的邪恶之人的悲剧。在第一个选段中,麦克白夫人担心丈夫"充满了太多的人情的乳臭"(too full o' th' milk of human kindness)而不能成就大事,所以决定"解除我的女性的柔弱"(unsex me)而采取必要的手段。第二选段描写了麦克白夫人梦游以及不停地擦手以除去血迹的习惯。最后的选段包含有麦克白在得知夫人已死之后所阐发的人生感悟:"人生不过是一个行走的影子……一个愚人所讲的故事,充满着喧哗和躁动,却找不到一点意义。"(Life's but a walking shadow … a tale/Told by an idiot, full of sound and fury,/ Signifying nothing.)

II PLOT SUMMARY

  In Scotland, **Macbeth**[1] and **Banquo**,[2] generals of the king's army, have been victorious in battle against the traitors Macdonwald and the **Thane**[3] of Cawdor. King Duncan hears of their courage before their return home from the battlefield and in gratitude bestows the title of Cawdor on the absent Macbeth. While they are returning from battle, Macbeth and Banquo encounter three

---

1 **Macbeth** /mək'beθ, mæk'beθ/ 麦克白 2 **Banquo** /'bæŋkwəu/ 班柯 3 **Thane** /θeɪn/ a man who held land from a Scottish king and ranked with an earl's son

witches on a desolate heath who greet Macbeth as Thane of Glamis, Thane of Cawdor, and "King hereafter." They prophesy that Banquo will beget kings though he will not himself be one. Macbeth, who is already Thane of Glamis, is startled when two messengers from the king greet him as the new Thane of Cawdor, thus fulfilling the witches' prophecy in part. When Macbeth learns that Duncan's son **Malcolm**[4] has been appointed Prince of Cumberland, automatic successor to the throne, he momentarily entertains the idea of killing the king and the prince consort: "Stars, hide your fires;/Let not light see my black and deep desires./The eye **wink at the hand**;[5] yet let that be/[6] Which the eye fears when it is done to see." (1.4.55-58) Lady Macbeth falls in with Macbeth's plot with greater energy than Macbeth himself but is worried that her husband is "too full of the **milk of human kindness**[7]/To catch the nearest way." (1.5.12-13) She is determined that "I may pour my spirits in thine ear/And **chastise**[8] with the valour of my tongue/All that **impedes**[9] thee from the **golden round**"[10] (1.5.21-23) and declares that "Come, you spirits/That **tend on**[11] **mortal**[12] thoughts, unsex me here/And fill me from the crown to the toe top-full/Of direst cruelty." (1.5.38-41) When Duncan and his retinue pay a visit to Macbeth's castle, Lady Macbeth vows ominously that the king "must be provided for."

Macbeth, 1768, Johann Zoffany

Banquo resists any thoughts that might hasten the witches' prophecy that his children will be kings. Elsewhere in the castle, however, Lady Macbeth is steeling her husband to kill the king, saying that "I have **given suck**,[13] and know/How tender 'tis to love the babe that milks me:/I would, while it was smiling in my face,/Have plucked my nipple from his boneless gums,/And dashed the brains out, had I so sworn as you/Have done to this." (1.7.58-63) He drugs the grooms in the king's bedchamber and stabs the sleeping Duncan, killing him. In the morning, when the murder is discovered, Macbeth, in pretended fury and grief, kills the grooms, who have denied committing the murder. The king's sons, Malcolm and Donalbain, seeing a similar fate for themselves, flee Scotland. Macbeth proceeds to Scone, where he is crowned as Duncan's successor to the throne.

Banquo half-suspects Macbeth of Duncan's murder but accepts an invitation to be the chief guest at the new king's feast. He tells Macbeth that he and his son Fleance will be riding that afternoon, and Macbeth employs two murderers to kill both father and son, thus negating the second part of the witches' prophecies. The murderers waylay the pair, killing Banquo, but Fleance escapes. That night at the feast Macbeth speaks glowingly of Banquo, whom he has killed. The ghost of Banquo enters and occupies the place of Macbeth, who is the only one who can see the ghostly apparition. Macbeth speaks to the ghost in horror, and the queen dismisses the guests before they become more suspicious. They discover that Duncan's son Malcolm has been joined by the powerful Lord **Macduff**[14] in opposition to Macbeth and are busy enlisting the help of Northumberland, Old Siward, in their cause. The three witches meet on the heath with their

---

4 **Malcolm** /ˈmælkəm/ 马尔康   5 **wink at the hand** shut itself to the deeds carried out by the hand   6 **be** come to pass   7 **milk of human kindness** compassion/natural humanity   8 **chastise** rebuke   9 **impedes** hinders   10 **golden round** crown   11 **tend on** attend   12 **mortal** deadly/human   13 **given suck** i.e. breast-fed a baby   14 **Macduff** /mækˈdʌf/ 麦克德夫

mistress **Hecate**[15] to bring about Macbeth's fall.

The Three Witches, after 1783, Henry Fuseli

Macbeth resolves to find the witches and demand further assurances. He encounters them on their dismal heath, where they answer him with a procession of apparitions: an armed head which warns him against Macduff; a child covered in blood which says that "none of woman born shall harm Macbeth"; a child holding a tree, who says Macbeth will be safe until "Birnam Wood" comes to Dunsinane; and eight kings followed by Banquo's ghost, which points to them with a smile as his descendants. While he is leaving, Macbeth encounters the nobleman Lennox, who denies having seen "the weird sisters" and tells him that Macduff has fled to England. Vengefully, Macbeth vows to kill Macduff's wife and children. At Macduff's castle, Lady Macduff questions her husband's wisdom "To leave his wife, to leave his babes,/His mansion and his **titles**[16] in a place/From whence himself does fly?" (4.2.8-10) A messenger arrives to warn her, but it is too late and Lady Macduff and her children are killed by Macbeth's assassins. Malcolm is at the king's palace in England, where he tests Macduff's loyalty in the cause against Macbeth. Satisfied, he welcomes him as an ally. When Ross enters with the terrible news of the massacre of Macduff's wife and children, Macduff refuses to believe what has been imparted. Then Malcolm urges him to "Be this the **whetstone**[17] of your sword. Let grief/Convert to anger: blunt not the heart, enrage it." (4.3.262-263) Macduff swears to exact revenge on Macbeth, the "fiend of Scotland."

At Dunsinane, Lady Macbeth has begun walking in her sleep. She enters in this state while her doctor and a waiting lady watch in horror. As she walks, unconscious of the others, she gives vent to her guilt and anguish over the crimes she and her husband have committed. She imagines her hands covered in blood, whose smell "All the perfumes of Arabia will not sweeten...," (5.1.37-38) echoing Macbeth's doubt: "Will all great Neptune's ocean wash this blood/Clean from my hand?" (2.2.71-72) as he stumbled out of the murder scene. Macbeth is deeply agitated over her disorder but is frenziedly preparing for the attack by the English invaders under Malcolm and the Earl of Northumberland, who have joined with rebellious Scottish forces. Malcolm has his soldiers cut boughs from Birnam Wood to carry as camouflage in the assault. Thus the prophecy "Till Birnam forest come to Dunsinane" begins to be fulfilled. Macbeth simultaneously learns that Lady Macbeth has died, possibly by suicide. In despair, he goes forth to battle and kills Young Siward, son of the Earl of Northumberland. Macbeth then encounters Macduff, who destroys his last confidence by admitting that he was "from his mother's womb untimely ripp'd"—born by Caesarian section, therefore not entirely born of woman. With this part of the prophecy no longer the protection it seemed, Macbeth dies at Macduff's hands. Macduff brings the head of Macbeth to Malcolm and hails the son of the murdered Duncan as the new King of Scotland.

---

15 **Hecate** (/ˈhekəti/ 赫卡特) a goddess of dark places, often associated with ghosts and sorcery   16 **titles** all to which he is entitled (lands, his thaneship)   17 **whetstone** stone on which swords are sharpened

Beyond the Play: *the Curse of "the Scottish Play"*

Because of the sinister atmosphere that shrouds Macbeth and a series of murders that happen therein, the bad luck that is associated with the play has given rise to what is known as "The Curse of the Scottish Play." For example, in 1849, years of tense rivalry between the American actor Edwin Forrest and the British actor John Macready finally reached a head when 31 people were killed in a riot in front of Astor Opera House in Manhattan, New York where the British actor was appearing in *Macbeth*. In one memorable week at the Old Vic of London in 1934, the play went through four different Macbeths: one came down with laryngitis, one caught a chill, one was fired, and only the fourth one survived to finish the run. Critics are not immune from the bad luck associated with the play, either. After the first night's performance of "Voodoo Macbeth" in New York, Percy Hammond, the drama critic of *the New York Herald Tribune*, wrote a review criticizing scathingly the production. Several days after his harassment he suffered from the group of African drummers in the play, Percy Hammond reportedly died of pneumonia. The theatrical superstition is such that any direct reference to or even quotation from the play is considered a taboo. For hundreds of years, the play has been delicately referred to as "The Scottish Play" or "The Bard's Play" and the lead character as "The Scottish King" or "Scottish Lord".

Astor Place Opera-House riots

III SELECTED READINGS

Act I, scene 5

    Enter LADY MACBETH, reading a letter
    LADY MACBETH   'They met me in the day of success: and I have learned
      by the perfect'st report, they have more in them than mortal
      knowledge. When I burned in desire to question them further, they
      made themselves air, into which they vanished. Whiles I stood rapt in
5   the wonder of it, came missives from the king, who all-hailed me
      'Thane of Cawdor', by which title, before, these weird sisters saluted
      me, and referred me to the coming on of time, with "Hail, king that
      shalt be!" This have I thought good to deliver thee, my dearest partner
      of greatness, that thou mightst not lose the dues of rejoicing, by being
10   ignorant of what greatness is promised thee. Lay it to thy heart, and

---

1.5 2 **perfect'st report** most accurate testimony   4 **whiles** while   5 **missives** messengers   8 **deliver thee** report to you   9 **dues** rightful claims   10 **Lay ... heart** reflect seriously on it/keep it secret

farewell.'
Glamis thou art, and Cawdor; and shalt be
What thou art promised: yet do I fear thy nature:
It is too full o' th' milk of human kindness
15 To catch the nearest way. Thou wouldst be great,
Art not without ambition, but without
The illness should attend it. What thou wouldst highly,
That wouldst thou holily: wouldst not play false,
And yet wouldst wrongly win. Thou'dst have, great Glamis,
20 That which cries 'Thus thou must do' if thou have it,
And that which rather thou dost fear to do
Than wishest should be undone. Hie thee hither,
That I may pour my spirits in thine ear
And chastise with the valour of my tongue
25 All that impedes thee from the golden round,
Which fate and metaphysical aid doth seem
To have thee crowned withal. —

Enter a Messenger   What is your tidings?
Messenger   The king comes here tonight.
30 LADY MACBETH   Thou'rt mad to say it.
Is not thy master with him? Who, were't so,
Would have informed for preparation.
Messenger   So please you, it is true: our thane is coming:
One of my fellows had the speed of him,
35 Who, almost dead for breath, had scarcely more
Than would make up his message.
LADY MACBETH   Give him tending;
He brings great news.
Exit Messenger   The raven himself is hoarse
40 That croaks the fatal entrance of Duncan
Under my battlements. Come, you spirits
That tend on mortal thoughts, unsex me here,
And fill me from the crown to the toe top-full
Of direst cruelty! Make thick my blood,
45 Stop up the access and passage to remorse,
That no compunctious visitings of nature
Shake my fell purpose, nor keep peace between
Th' effect and it! Come to my woman's breasts,
And take my milk for gall, you murdering ministers,
50 Wherever in your sightless substances
You wait on nature's mischief! Come, thick night,

---

15 **catch** seize   **nearest** most obvious, most direct   **wouldst** want to   17 **illness ... it** wickedness that must go with it   **highly** greatly/ambitiously   18 **holily** virtuously   **play false** be deceptive, treacherous   19 **Thou'dst have** Thou wouldst have   21-22 **And ... undone** i. e. you fear carrying out the deed (murder) rather than its consequences (the crown)   **Hie** hurry   24 **chastise** purify; drive away   25 **impedes** hinders   **golden round** royal crown   26 **metaphysical** supernatural   27 **withal** with   32 **informed for preparation** sent news so that preparations might be made   34 **had the speed of** overtook   37 **tending** attention, care   39 **raven** considered a bird of ill omen   42 **tend on** attend   **unsex** rid of sexual attributes; here, divest of womanly frailties   45 **remorse** pity   46 **compunctious** remorseful, filled with conscience   47 **fell** fierce, cruel   48 **Th' effect and it** the outcome and my intention   49 **take** exchange   **gall** bile, bitterness   **ministers** agents/attendants   50 **sightless** invisible

	And pall thee in the dunnest smoke of hell,
	That my keen knife see not the wound it makes,
	Nor heaven peep through the blanket of the dark,
55	To cry 'Hold, hold!'

Enter MACBETH   Great Glamis, worthy Cawdor!
　　Greater than both, by the all-hail hereafter!
　　Thy letters have transported me beyond
　　This ignorant present, and I feel now
60　　The future in the instant.
　　MACBETH   My dearest love,
　　Duncan comes here tonight.
　　LADY MACBETH   And when goes hence?
　　MACBETH Tomorrow, as he purposes.
65　　LADY MACBETH   O, never
　　Shall sun that morrow see!
　　Your face, my thane, is as a book where men
　　May read strange matters. To beguile the time,
　　Look like the time; bear welcome in your eye,
70　　Your hand, your tongue: look like the innocent flower,
　　But be the serpent under't. He that's coming
　　Must be provided for: and you shall put
　　This night's great business into my dispatch,
　　Which shall to all our nights and days to come
75　　Give solely sovereign sway and masterdom.
　　MACBETH We will speak further.
　　LADY MACBETH   Only look up clear;
　　To alter favour ever is to fear:
　　Leave all the rest to me.
　　Exeunt

Act V, scene 1

Enter a Doctor of Physic and a Waiting-Gentlewoman
　　DOCTOR   I have two nights watched with you, but can perceive no truth
　　　in your report. When was it she last walked?
　　GENTLEMAN   Since his majesty went into the field, I have seen her rise
　　　from her bed, throw her nightgown upon her, unlock her closet, take
5　　　forth paper, fold it, write upon't, read it, afterwards seal it, and again
　　　return to bed; yet all this while in a most fast sleep.
　　DOCTOR   A great perturbation in nature, to receive at once the benefit of
　　　sleep, and do the effects of watching. In this slumbery agitation,

---

51 **wait on** wait upon/lie in wait for   **nature's mischief** human evil   52 **pall** envelop, wrap (as if with a pall, or cloth used to cover a coffin)   **dunnest** darkest/murkiest   57 **all-hail hereafter** the future prophesied by the witches/the salutation of "king" that followed Glamis and Cawdor   59 **ignorant** unknowing   60 **instant** present moment   64 **purposes** intends   68 **strange** mysterious/unnatural/unfamiliar   **beguile** deceive   69 **Look ... time** look ordinary, appear to be like everyone else   72 **provided for** prepared for, taken care of (relates to hospitality and to murder)   73 **dispatch** management   75 **solely** entirely, exclusively   **sway** rule   77 **look up clear** appear to be untroubled and innocent   78 **alter favour** change your accustomed facial expression   5.1 *Physic* medicine   1 **watched** remained awake   2 **walked** sleepwalked   3 **field** battlefield (i. e. prepared for war)   4 **closet** cabinet   7 **perturbation** disturbance   8 **effects of watching** appearance and actions of waking   **agitation** disturbed state of mind/nervous activity

besides her walking and other actual performances, what—at any time,
10 have you heard her say?
GENTLEMAN   That, sir, which I will not report after her.
DOCTOR   You may to me: and 'tis most meet you should.
GENTLEMAN   Neither to you nor any one, having no witness to confirm
my speech.
Enter LADY MACBETH, with a taper
15 Lo you, here she comes. This is her very guise, and, upon my life, fast
asleep. Observe her: stand close.
DOCTOR   How came she by that light?
GENTLEMAN   Why, it stood by her. She has light by her continually: 'tis
her command.
20 DOCTOR   You see, her eyes are open.
GENTLEMAN   Ay, but their sense is shut.
DOCTOR   What is it she does now? Look, how she rubs her hands.
GENTLEMAN   It is an accustomed action with her, to seem thus washing
her hands: I have known her continue in this a quarter of an hour.
25 LADY MACBETH   Yet here's a spot.
DOCTOR   Hark, she speaks. I will set down what comes from her, to
satisfy my remembrance the more strongly.
LADY MACBETH   Out, damned spot! Out, I say! —One: two: why, then, 'tis
time to do't. —Hell is murky! —Fie, my lord, fie, a soldier, and afeard?
30 What need we fear who knows it, when none can call our power to
account? —Yet who would have thought the old man to have had so
much blood in him?
DOCTOR   Do you mark that?
LADY MACBETH   The Thane of Fife had a wife: where is she now?
35 —What, will these hands ne'er be clean? —No more o' that, my
lord, no more o' that: you mar all with this starting.
DOCTOR   Go to, go to: you have known what you should not.
GENTLEMAN   She has spoke what she should not, I am sure of that:
heaven knows what she has known.
40 LADY MACBETH   Here's the smell of the blood still. All the perfumes of
Arabia will not sweeten this little hand. O. O. O!
DOCTOR   What a sigh is there! The heart is sorely charged.
GENTLEMAN   I would not have such a heart in my bosom for the dignity
of the whole body.
45 DOCTOR   Well, well, well.
GENTLEMAN   Pray God it be, sir.
DOCTOR   This disease is beyond my practice. Yet I have known those
which have walked in their sleep who have died holily in their beds.
LADY MACBETH   Wash your hands, put on your nightgown, look not so
50 pale. I tell you yet again, Banquo's buried; he cannot come out on's

---

12 **meet** suitable **taper** candle   26 **set down** write down   27 **satisfy** meets the needs of, confirm   28 **One:two** Lady Macbeth imagines she hears the striking of a clock or perhaps the bell she was to strike as a signal to Macbeth   30-31 **none ... account** no one can hold us responsible as we are now so powerful   34 **Thane of Fife** Macduff   36 **starting** nervousness/fits, outbursts   37 **Go to** expression of reproof similar to "come come"   42 **sorely charged** grievously burdened   43 **dignity** worth, high status   46 **be** i. e. is that how it is   47 **practice** medical skill

grave.
DOCTOR Even so?
LADY MACBETH To bed, to bed. There's knocking at the gate. Come, come, come, come, give me your hand. What's done cannot be undone. To bed, to bed, to bed!
Exit
DOCTOR Will she go now to bed?
GENTLEMAN Directly.
DOCTOR Foul whisperings are abroad. Unnatural deeds
    Do breed unnatural troubles: infected minds
    To their deaf pillows will discharge their secrets.
    More needs she the divine than the physician.
    God, God forgive us all! Look after her;
    Remove from her the means of all annoyance,
    And still keep eyes upon her. So, good night.
    My mind she has mated, and amazed my sight.
    I think, but dare not speak.
GENTLEMAN Good night, good doctor.
Exeunt

Act V, scene 5

Enter MACBETH, SEYTON, and Soldiers, with drum and colours
MACBETH Hang out our banners on the outward walls;
    The cry is still 'They come.' Our castle's strength
    Will laugh a siege to scorn: here let them lie
    Till famine and the ague eat them up.
    Were they not forced with those that should be ours,
    We might have met them dareful, beard to beard,
    And beat them backward home.
A cry of women within
    What is that noise?
SEYTON It is the cry of women, my good lord.
Exit
MACBETH I have almost forgot the taste of fears:
    The time has been, my senses would have cooled
    To hear a night-shriek; and my fell of hair
    Would at a dismal treatise rouse and stir
    As life were in't: I have supped full with horrors;
    Direness, familiar to my slaughterous thoughts
    Cannot once start me.
Re-enter SEYTON
    Wherefore was that cry?
SEYTON The queen, my lord, is dead.
MACBETH She should have died hereafter:
    There would have been a time for such a word.

---

61 **divine** priest 63 **annoyance** injury 64 **still** continually 65 **mated** bewildered 5.5 4 **ague** fever 5 **forced** reinforced 6 **dareful** defiantly/boldly 12 **fell of hair** entire head of hair 13 **treatise** tale 14 **As** as if **supped full** had my fill of horror/dined in the company of horrors (i.e. Banquo's ghost) 15 **Direness** dreadfulness, horror 16 **start me** make me start 19 **She ... hereafter** she should have died at a future time/she would have died at some point anyway 20 **such a word** i.e. news of her death

>   Tomorrow, and tomorrow, and tomorrow,
>   Creeps in this petty pace from day to day
>   To the last syllable of recorded time;
>   And all our yesterdays have lighted fools
> 25   The way to dusty death. Out, out, brief candle.
>   Life's but a walking shadow, a poor player
>   That struts and frets his hour upon the stage
>   And then is heard no more. It is a tale
>   Told by an idiot, full of sound and fury,
> 30   Signifying nothing.
>   *Enter a Messenger*
>   Thou com'st to use thy tongue; thy story quickly.
>   MESSENGER   Gracious my lord,
>   I should report that which I say I saw,
>   But know not how to do't.
> 35   MACBETH   Well, say, sir.
>   MESSENGER   As I did stand my watch upon the hill,
>   I looked toward Birnam, and anon, methought
>   The wood began to move.
>   MACBETH   Liar and slave!
> 40   MESSENGER Let me endure your wrath, if't be not so.
>   Within this three mile may you see it coming;
>   I say, a moving grove.
>   MACBETH   If thou speak'st false,
>   Upon the next tree shalt thou hang alive
> 45   Till famine cling thee; if thy speech be sooth,
>   I care not if thou dost for me as much. —
>   I pull in resolution, and begin
>   To doubt the equivocation of the fiend
>   That lies like truth. 'Fear not, till Birnam wood
> 50   Do come to Dunsinane', and now a wood
>   Comes toward Dunsinane. Arm, arm, and out!
>   If this which he avouches does appear,
>   There is nor flying hence nor tarrying here.
>   I 'gin to be aweary of the sun,
> 55   And wish th' estate o' the world were now undone.
>   Ring the alarum-bell! Blow, wind, come, wrack,
>   At least we'll die with harness on our back. *Exeunt*

Questions for Understanding and Reflection
Act I, scene 5
1. Which nature of Macbeth's might prevent him becoming the king of Scotland according to Lady

---

22 **petty** slow/insignificant   23 **syllable** most minute portion/basic element of a word   **recorded** written/narrated/remembered
25 **dusty** i.e. characterized by the dust to which all mortals return   26 **shadow** insubstantial thing/illusion/ghost/actor   **poor** wretched/unskilled   31 **thy story quickly** relate your news at once   36 **did ... watch** was on guard   45 **cling** shrink up   **sooth** truth   46 **dost ... much** do the same for me   47 **pull in resolution** (am forced to) rein in my firmness of purpose   48 **fiend** i.e. the Third Apparition   52 **avouches** affirms   53 **nor ... here** no point either fleeting from here or remaining   54 **'gin** begin   55 **th' estate** the kingdom/condition/settled order   56 **wrack** ruin, destruction   57 **harness** armour

Macbeth?
2. What does Lady Macbeth mean by "unsex me" (42)?
3. What does Lady Macbeth advise her husband to do when Duncan comes?

Act V, scene 1
1. How can you explain Lady Macbeth's habit of rubbing her hands?
2. What might Lady Macbeth mean by "All the perfumes of Arabia will not sweeten this little hand"?
3. Whose help does the doctor think Lady Macbeth needs to have her disease cured?

Act V, scene 5
1. What is human life compared to?
2. Is Macbeth positive or negative about human life?
3. What does Macbeth decide to do in spite of the prophecy of the Third Apparition?

IV SHAKESPEAREAN RELEVANCE

A. Shakespeare in Everyday English
Please try to understand the following Shakespearean words and expressions in the contexts designated within parentheses and give their generally used meanings in the space provided.
1. come what come may (1.3.159): _____
2. the milk of human kindness (1.5.12): _____
3. the be-all and the end-all (1.7.5): _____
4. screw your courage to the sticking-place (1.7.66): _____
5. a sorry sight (2.2.25): _____
6. the primrose way (2.3.14): _____
7. What's done is done (3.2.14): _____
8. eye of newt and toe of frog, wool of bat and tongue of dog (4.1.14-15): _____
9. till the crack of doom (4.1.126): _____
10. at one fell swoop (4.3.252): _____
11. full of sound and fury (5.5.27): _____
12. a charmed life (5.7.49): _____

B. Shakespeare in Literature
Read the following literary excerpts, locate the Shakespearean allusions and explain their meanings according to the contexts where they appear.
1. Hovering like Banquo's ghost around the conference will be the former Chancellor Kenneth Clarke. (*The Observer*, 1997)
2. 'In a way her son was a much nastier character. Sophie was Lady Macbeth writ large. She pulled the trigger on Jean-Louis and Caterina Tozharska herself.' He smiled wryly. 'But even Lady Macbeth couldn't bring herself to kill!' (Max Marquis, *Written in Blood*, 1995)
3. Whatever else the years give me cause to forgive him for I shall never forgive him for wrecking my party and making a fool of Claude. Why am I clutching this orange, she wondered. She stared down at her hand, like lady Macbeth. What, in our house? When she returned to her guests—the perfumed blood under her nails—the performance was over. (Hilary Mantel, *A Place of Greater Safety*, 1992)

4. He wasn't listening. His eyes had swivelled away from me, drawn back to the house. I looked, too, and saw that his wife had emerged. She'd upped the melodrama, wringing her hands Lady Macbeth style. (Gillian Slovo, *Close Call*, 1995)
5. When the curtain call came, some of the girls who had been serving as ushers rushed to the footlights like Birnam Wood moving to Dunsinane, loaded with bouquets. (Robertson Davies, *The Manticore*, 1972)

C. Shakespeare in Music, Art and on Screen

1847: *Macbeth*, an opera in four acts by Giuseppe Verdi, with an Italian libretto by Francesco Maria Piave and additions by Andrea Maffei.
1886—1888: *Macbeth*, a symphonic poem written by Richard Strauss.
1948: *Macbeth*, an American film adaptation by Orson Welles.
1955: *Joe MacBeth*, a modern retelling of *Macbeth*, directed by Ken Hughes, starring Paul Douglas, Ruth Roman, and Bonar Colleano.
1957: *Throne of Blood* (蜘蛛巢城), a Japanese film adaptation directed by Akira Kurosawa with the play reset to feudal Japan.
1971: *Macbeth*, a British-American film adaptation, directed by Roman Polanski, starring Jon Finch as Macbeth and Francesca Annis as Lady Macbeth.
2001: *Scotland, PA*, a film directed, starring James LeCros, Maura Tierney and Christopher Walken.
2006: *Macbeth*, an Australian film adaptation, directed by Geoffrey Wright.
2000: *Thane to the Throne*, a studio album based on *Macbeth*, released by American power metal band Jag Panzer.

  SHAKESPEARE QUOTES

Fair is foul, and foul is fair:
Hover through fog and filthy air.(1.1.12-13)
Unsex me here.(1.5.39)
Knock, knock! Who's there? (2.3.3)
It provokes the desire,
but it takes away the performance.(2.3.22)
Double, double, toil and trouble:
Fire burn, and cauldron bubble.(4.1.10-11)
Tomorrow, and tomorrow, and tomorrow,
Creeps in this petty pace from day to day,
To the last syllable of recorded time:
And all our yesterdays have lighted fools
The way to dusty death. Out, out, brief candle.
Life's but a walking shadow, a poor player
That struts and frets his hour upon the stage
And then is heard no more. It is a tale
Told by an idiot, full of sound and fury,
Signifying nothing.(5.5.19-28)

14. The Tragedy of Hamlet, Prince of Denmark
哈姆雷特

I INTRODUCTION

《哈姆雷特》被认为是莎士比亚的第一部杰作,也可能是英语世界最具影响力的伟大悲剧。丹麦国王老哈姆雷特驾崩,其遗孀乔特鲁德匆忙下嫁国王的兄弟克劳狄斯,使得王位由其继承。父王的蹊跷离世和母亲的不忠和乱伦使哈姆雷特王子陷入了深深的忧郁之中。当父王的鬼魂向他倾诉叔父便是杀父的凶手时,哈姆雷特发誓要为父王报仇。接下来便是王子的装疯卖傻、生死思量、演戏试奸、大臣误伤、爱人溺亡以及最终的报仇雪恨和自我凋亡。该剧自创作演出至今广受剖析和争论,对于《哈姆雷特》的处理成为导演、演员和学者们职业生涯的标志(rite of passage)。它的魅力不仅在于其作为复仇剧的强大震撼力,还在于它对于人性的洞察力。正如英国"湖畔派诗人"塞缪尔·泰勒·柯尔律治(Samuel Taylor Coleridge)在其1811—1812年间所发表的演讲中所指出的那样:"莎士比亚(创作的)初衷是要我们记住这样一条真理:人类存在的主要目的是为了行动。"的确,在多数人看来,莎士比亚借丹麦王子哈姆雷特之口表达了人类所面对的种种困惑。剧中的大量词语业已在当今英语中广为使用,而使用者却可能浑然不知,遍布全剧的内心独白(如哈姆雷特的"To be or not to be")和演讲更是人们喜爱引用的段落。《哈姆雷特》影响之深远、巨大,就连"哈姆雷特"这个名字本身成了一个代名词,有关该剧的研究——Hamletology——也成为莎翁研究中的显学。

II PLOT SUMMARY

The play begins with the mysterious appearance of a ghost in small hours witnessed by two sentinels and **Horatio**,[1] Hamlet's close friend. Old Hamlet, King of Denmark, is dead and has been succeeded by his brother **Claudius**,[2] who married **Gertrude**,[3] the widowed queen. These events are suitably described by the new king as "mirth in funeral" and "dirge in marriage". Revolted by his mother and uncle's "most wicked speed, to post with such dexterity to incestuous sheets", Hamlet contemplates suicide but sets aside this thought when Horatio tells him about the Ghost and is now eager to see the Ghost himself. After attending the coronation of Claudius, **Laertes**[4] is about to return to France. He bids his sister **Ophelia**[5] farewell, warning her against taking Hamlet's courtship seriously. Ophelia agrees to heed her brother's advice but retorts that

---

1 **Horatio** /hɔˈreiʃiəu/ 霍拉旭 2 **Claudius** /ˈklɔːdiəs/ 克劳狄斯 3 **Gertrude** /ˈgəːtruːd/ 乔特鲁德 4 **Laertes** /leiˈəːtiːz/ 雷欧提斯 5 **Ophelia** /əuˈfiːliə/ 奥菲立娅

"Show me the steep and thorny way to heaven,/Whilst, like a **puffed**[6] and reckless **libertine**/[7]Himself the primrose path of dalliance treads,/And **recks**[8] not his own **rede**."[9] (1. 3. 50-53) **Polonius**[10] offers some fatherly advice to his departing son. Having met his father's ghost, Hamlet now finds his instincts confirmed: "O, my prophetic soul!" and pledges to revenge his father's murder by Claudius. Though Hamlet accepts the ghost's words while with him, seeds of doubt about the ghost's authenticity have been sown from the very beginning of the play and continue to torment Hamlet for much of its remainder. For it may be that the figure of the ghost is actually a diabolic impersonation of the spirit of Hamlet's father coming to tempt him to his damnation. To investigate Claudius' guilt, Hamlet feigns madness, though the sight of his father's spirit has caused his already unstable spirit to totter on the brink of actual insanity. This combination of real and assumed mental instability results in so worrying Claudius that he begins to spy on Hamlet to try to understand whether Hamlet represents a danger to him. He first sets **Rosencrantz**[11] and **Guildensfern**[12] to spy on Hamlet and then spies upon a prearranged meeting between Hamlet and his estranged sweetheart, Ophelia.

The Play Scene in "Hamlet", Daniel Maclise (1806—1870)

A company of actors arrive, providing Hamlet a means to test Claudius' guilt and the authenticity of the ghost: he will stage a performance of a play called *the Murder of Gonzago*, which, with some adaptation, will reenact Claudius' crime and observe his reaction to it: "the play's the thing/Wherein I'll catch the conscience of the king." (2. 2. 536-537) Within the hearing of the king and his councilor Polonius, Hamlet in his famed soliloquy questions whether he should go on with his revenge and life itself: "To be, or not to be, that is the question." (3. 1. 62) Hamlet then meets Ophelia and rejects her violently by urging her to "Get thee to a nunnery" to avoid breeding sinners. Hamlet's plan with the play is successful since the guilty Claudius breaks down during the performance. But it also alerts Claudius to Hamlet's knowledge of his crime and consequent danger to him, so he decides to exile Hamlet to England to be rid of him. Polonius begs Claudius to permit one final spying attempt upon Hamlet before his departure; his mother is to call Hamlet to her room, where Polonius will be hidden behind the arras to overhear the conference, and prevail upon him to confide in her.

Doubt cleared of his mind, Hamlet has an immediate opportunity for revenge when he accidentally comes upon the guilt-ridden Claudius alone in prayer. Again he rationalizes himself into delay, this time on the grounds that his revenge would not be horrible enough as Claudius's penitence might save his soul from hell. He goes to his mother's room, but in such an unnaturally

---

6 **puffed** swollen with pride and vanity   7 **libertine** (/ˈlibətiːn/) one who is sexually immoral and is unconcerned about the consequences of their behaviour   8 **recks** heeds   9 **rede** advice   10 **Polonius** /pəˈləuniəs/ 波洛涅斯   11 **Rosencrantz** /ˈrəusənkrænts/ 罗森格兰兹   12 **Guildensfern** /ˈgildənsfəːn/ 吉尔登斯吞

excited state that he scares his mother and the hidden Polonius into crying for help. His enraged murderous impulse, restrained from releasing itself upon Claudius or upon his mother, madly lashes out at the hidden figure: "A rat? Dead, for a ducat, dead!" (3.4.27) and results in the death of Polonius. This unpremeditated act seals Hamlet's own doom.

The first consequence of this rash act is to cause Claudius to alter his order for Hamlet's exile so that he will be executed in England. While on board the ship to England, however, Hamlet again acts rashly; he discovers the letter ordering his death and changes it so that the bearers, Rosencrantz and Guildenstern, will be put to death in his place. Escaping from the ship during an attack upon it by pirates, he returns to Denmark with a clear conscience both about his coming revenge against Claudius and his own order for the executions of Rosencrantz and Guildenstern. But he makes no plans for his revenge since he has come to place his full confidence upon Providence.

Ophelia, 1851—1852, John Everett Millais

This is not true, however, of Claudius or of Laertes, the son of Polonius, who has also returned to Denmark to revenge his own father's death. Forewarned of Hamlet's return, they lay plans for his death through a fencing match in which Laertes will use an illegally sharp and poisoned sword backed up by a poisoned drink. Laertes' grievance against Hamlet is increased by the madness and death of his sister, Ophelia, who, maddened by grief, drowned herself while trying to hang her coronet weeds on the drooping boughs by a "weeping brook." In a churchyard, Hamlet returns with Horatio to marvel at a gravedigger throwing up bones. He imagines the bones to be those of a politician, a courtier, a lawyer and a great buyer of land and comments on the fertility of all their worldly achievements and possessions. When shown the skull of **Yorick**,[13] the king's jester, Hamlet becomes even more philosophically nostalgic: "… a fellow of infinite jest, of most excellent **fancy**.[14] … Where be your gibes now, your gambols, your songs, your flashes of merriment that were wont to set the table on a roar?" (5.1.141-142, 144-145) Ophelia's hearse soon arrives and an inconsolable Laertes leaps into his sister's grave, causing a tussle with Hamlet who claims to be a greater mourner.

The day of ultimate showdown comes, but the plans of Claudius and Laertes backfire with the unexpected deaths of Gertrude who drinks from a poisoned cup intended for Hamlet, of Laertes who is struck by Hamlet with his own poisoned sword. Hamlet, wounded by the poisoned sword, kills the king: "The point envenomed too! /Then, venom, to thy work." (5.2.266-267) When Horatio declares "I am more an antique Roman than a Dane," suggestive of suicide to follow his close friend,[15] Hamlet requests, "If thou didst ever hold me in thy heart,/Absent thee from **felicity** awhile,/And in this harsh world draw thy breath in pain,/To tell my story." (5.2.294-297) Hamlet dies with a wish that **Fortinbras**,[16] Prince of Norway, who is returning triumphantly from Poland would be the new king of Denmark.

Laurence Olivier's *Hamlet*, 1948

Celebrated for his nobility of spirit, he is finally given a hero's funeral by the sovereign in question.

---

13 **Yorick** /ˈjɔrɪk/ 郁利克   14 **fancy** imagination   15 **felicity** happiness, bliss   16 **Fortinbras** /ˈfɔːtinbrɑːs/ 福丁布拉斯

Beyond the Play: *Hamlet, the Most Quoted Play*

As one of the most quoted works in the English language, *Hamlet* has contributed many words and expressions to contemporary English, from the famous "To be, or not to be" to a few less known, but still in currency today. Here are some examples (for more, see Shakespeare in Everyday English next): *the primrose path* (1.3.52), *more honoured in the breach than the observance* (1.4.18), *something is rotten in the state of Denmark* (1.4.72), *the time is out of joint* (1.5.205). In particular, the line "To be, or not to be" is so widely quoted that liberties have been taken with the original to serve different purposes, including advertising personality custom T-shirts (see the above picture), campaigning for abstinence (e.g. "TWO BEER OR NOT TWO BEER").

Interestingly, Prince Charles of Wales light-heartedly translated the Prince of Denmark's famous monologue into a flat, slangy modern British English in sharp contrast to the grand Shakespearean original: *Well, frankly, the problem as I see it/At this moment in time is whether I/Should just lie down under all this hassle/And let them walk all over me, / Or, whether I should just say, "OK, / I get the message," and do myself in/I mean, let's face it, I'm in a no win / Situation, and quite honestly, / I'm so stuffed up to here with the whole/Stupid mess that, I can tell you, I've just/God a good mind to take the quick way out. / That's the bottom line. The only problem is: / What happens if I find out that when I've bumped/Myself off, there's some kind of a, you know, / All that mystical stuff about when you die, / You might find you're still—know what I mean?*

Prince Charles, 1981, Mark Boxer

III SELECTED READINGS

Act I, scene 3

> POLONIUS
>   Yet here, Laertes! Aboard, aboard, for shame!
>   The wind sits in the shoulder of your sail,
> 60 And you are stayed for there. My blessing with you!
>   And these few precepts in thy memory
>   See thou character. Give thy thoughts no tongue,
>   Nor any unproportioned thought his act.
>   Be thou familiar, but by no means vulgar.

1.3 60 **stayed** waited   62 **See thou character** make sure that you inscribe   63 **unproportioned** immoderate/unruly   64 **familiar** friendly, sociable

65	The friends thou hast, and their adoption tried,
	Grapple them to thy soul with hoops of steel,
	But do not dull thy palm with entertainment
	Of each new-hatched, unfledged comrade: beware
	Of entrance to a quarrel, but being in,
70	Bear't that th' opposed may beware of thee.
	Give every man thy ear, but few thy voice:
	Take each man's censure, but reserve thy judgment:
	Costly thy habit as thy purse can buy,
	But not expressed in fancy; rich, not gaudy:
75	For the apparel oft proclaims the man,
	And they in France of the best rank and station
	Are of a most select and generous chief in that.
	Neither a borrower nor a lender be,
	For loan oft loses both itself and friend,
80	And borrowing dulls the edge of husbandry.
	This above all: to thine ownself be true,
	And it must follow, as the night the day,
	Thou canst not then be false to any man.
	Farewell: my blessing season this in thee!

Act III, scene 1

	HAMLET To be, or not to be, that is the question:
	Whether 'tis nobler in the mind to suffer
	The slings and arrows of outrageous fortune,
65	Or to take arms against a sea of troubles,
	And by opposing end them? To die, to sleep—
	No more—and by a sleep to say we end
	The heartache and the thousand natural shocks
	That flesh is heir to: 'tis a consummation
70	Devoutly to be wished. To die, to sleep:
	To sleep, perchance to dream: ay, there's the rub,
	For in that sleep of death what dreams may come
	When we have shuffled off this mortal coil,
	Must give us pause: there's the respect
75	That makes calamity of so long life,
	For who would bear the whips and scorns of time,
	The oppressor's wrong, the proud man's contumely,
	The pangs of despised love, the law's delay,
	The insolence of office and the spurns

65 **adoption tried** worthiness to be adopted as friends having been tested   66 **Grapple** fasten firmly   67 **dull thy palm** i. e. by shaking hands too often   68 **unfledged** still unfeatured (i. e. new, untried)   70 **Bear't that th' opposed** manage it so that your opponent   72 **censure** judgement/opinion   73 **habit** clothing   74 **fancy** elaborate, fanciful style   77 **Are ... that** are of a most distinguished and noble pre-eminence in their choice garments   80 **husbandry** economy   83 **false** dishonest, disloyal   84 **season** ripen   3.1 64 **slings** catapults, ballista, cannons or the missiles hurled by them   **outrageous** excessively wicked/violent, cruel   68 **shocks** violent blows/clashes with the enemy   69 **consummation** ending   71 **perchance** possibly; perhaps   **rub** obstacle   73 **shuffled off** cast off   **mortal coil** bustle or turmoil of this mortal life   74 **respect** consideration   75 **makes calamity of so long life** makes living so long a calamity   76 **scorns** insults, mockeries   77 **contumely** insolence, contempt, insulting language or behavior   78 **despised** undervalued/dishonoured   79 **office** office-holders   **spurns** kicks

80	That patient merit of the unworthy takes,
	When he himself might his quietus make
	With a bare bodkin? Who would fardels bear,
	To grunt and sweat under a weary life,
	But that the dread of something after death,
85	The undiscovered country from whose bourn
	No traveller returns, puzzles the will
	And makes us rather bear those ills we have
	Than fly to others that we know not of?
	Thus conscience does make cowards of us all:
90	And thus the native hue of resolution
	Is sicklied o'er with the pale cast of thought,
	And enterprises of great pith and moment
	With this regard their currents turn away,
	And lose the name of action. Soft you now,
95	The fair Ophelia. —Nymph, in thy orisons
	Be all my sins remembered.

OPHELIA   Good my lord,
How does your honour for this many a day?
HAMLET   I humbly thank you: well, well, well.
100   OPHELIA   My lord, I have remembrances of yours,
That I have longèd long to re-deliver:
I pray you, now receive them.
HAMLET   No, not: I never gave you aught.
OPHELIA   My honoured lord, you know right well you did,
105   And with them words of so sweet breath composed
As made the things more rich: their perfume lost,
Take these again, for to the noble mind
Rich gifts wax poor when givers prove unkind.
There, my lord.
110   HAMLET   Ha, ha! Are you honest?
OPHELIA   My lord?
HAMLET   Are you fair?
OPHELIA   What means your lordship?
HAMLET   That if you be honest and fair, your honesty should admit no discourse
115   to your beauty.
OPHELIA   Could beauty, my lord, have better commerce than with honesty?
HAMLET   Ay, truly, for the power of beauty will sooner transform honesty from
   what it is to a bawd than the force of honesty can translate beauty into his
   likeness: this was sometime a paradox, but now the time gives it proof. I did
120   love you once.
OPHELIA   Indeed, my lord, you made me believe so.

---

80 **of the unworthy takes** receives from those who are unworthy   81 **quietus** discharge of debts (i.e. death)   82 **bare bodkin** mere/unsheathed dagger   **fardels** burdens   85 **bourn** boundary   86 **puzzles** bewilders, confounds   89 **conscience** consciousness/introspection/awareness of right and wrong   90 **native hue** natural colour   91 **cast** tinge, shade   92 **pith and moment** substance and importance   94 **Soft you** wait a moment   95 **orisons** prayers   100 **remembrances** keepsake, love tokens   110 **honest** chaste   112 **fair** beautiful   114-115 **your ... beauty** your chastity should permit no approach to your beauty   116 **commerce** interaction   118 **bawd** pander or procurer   119 **sometime** once   **paradox** seemingly absurd statement/observation that contradicts commonly held beliefs

HAMLET You should not have believed me; for virtue cannot so inoculate our old stock but we shall relish of it: I loved you not.

OPHELIA I was the more deceived.

125 *HAMLET* Get thee to a nunnery. Why wouldst thou be a breeder of sinners? I am myself indifferent honest, but yet I could accuse me of such things that it were better my mother had not borne me: I am very proud, revengeful, ambitious, with more offences at my beck than I have thoughts to put them in, imagination to give them shape, or time to act them in. What should such
130 fellows as I do crawling between earth and heaven? We are arrant knaves all: believe none of us. Go thy ways to a nunnery. Where's your father?

OPHELIA At home, my lord.

HAMLET Let the doors be shut upon him, that he may play the fool no where but in 's own house. Farewell.

135 *OPHELIA* O, help him, you sweet heavens!

HAMLET If thou dost marry, I'll give thee this plague for thy dowry: be thou as chaste as ice, as pure as snow, thou shalt not escape calumny. Get thee to a nunnery: go, farewell. Or, if thou wilt needs marry, marry a fool; for wise men know well enough what monsters you make of them. To a nunnery, go, and
140 quickly too. Farewell.

OPHELIA O heavenly powers, restore him!

HAMLET I have heard of your paintings too, well enough. God has given you one face, and you make yourselves another: you jig, you amble, and you lisp, and nickname God's creatures, and make your wantonness your ignorance. Go
145 to, I'll no more on't: it hath made me mad. I say, we will have no more marriages: those that are married already, all but one, shall live: the rest shall keep as they are. To a nunnery, go.

Exit

OPHELIA O, what a noble mind is here o'erthrown!
The courtier's, soldier's, scholar's, eye, tongue, sword;
150 Th' expectancy and rose of the fair state,
The glass of fashion and the mould of form,
Th' observed of all observers, quite, quite down!
And I, of ladies most deject and wretched,
That sucked the honey of his music vows,
155 Now see that noble and most sovereign reason
Like sweet bells jangled, out of tune and harsh,
That unmatched form and feature of blown youth
Blasted with ecstasy. O, woe is me,
T' have seen what I have seen, see what I see!

122-123 **virtue ... it** virtue cannot be so successfully grafted onto an old sinful tree without some flavor of sin being retained   125 **nunnery** convent/brothel   126 **indifferent honest** moderately virtuous   128 **beck** command   130 **arrant knaves** out-and-out rogues/villains   137 **calumny** slander   139 **monsters** horned beasts, cuckolds (men with unfaithful wives were traditionally supposed to grow horns)   142 **paintings** use of cosmetics   143 **amble** walk with an easy motion   **lisp** speak in an affected manner   144 **make your wantonness your ignorance** use innocence as an excuse for behavior that is willful/affected/promiscuous   145 **on't** of it   150 **expectancy** hope   151 **glass of fashion** mirror on whose image men model themselves   **mould of form** pattern of excellent behaviour   157 **blown** blooming   158 **Blasted with ecstasy** destroyed by madness

Act V, scene 1

50   HAMLET   Has this fellow no feeling of his business, that he sings at
        grave-making?
    HORATIO   Custom hath made it in him a property of easiness.
    HAMLET   'Tis e'en so: the hand of little employment hath the daintier sense.
    First Clown [*Sings*]
55   But age, with his stealing steps
      Hath claw'd me in his clutch,
      And hath shipped me intil the land,
      As if I had never been such.
    Throws up a skull
    HAMLET   That skull had a tongue in it, and could sing once: how the knave jowls it
60   to th' ground, as if it were Cain's jaw-bone, that did the first murder. It might
      be the pate of a politician, which this ass o'er-offices, one that would
      circumvent God, might it not?
    HORATIO   It might, my lord.
    HAMLET   Or of a courtier; which could say 'Good morrow, sweet lord! How dost
65   thou, good lord?' This might be my lord Such-a-one, that praised my lord
      Such-a-one's horse, when he meant to beg it, might it not?
    HORATIO   Ay, my lord.
    HAMLET   Why, e'en so, and now my Lady Worm's, chapless, and knocked about
      the mazzard with a sexton's spade: here's fine revolution, an we had the trick
70   to see 't. Did these bones cost no more the breeding, but to play at loggats with
      'em? Mine ache to think on 't.
    First Clown [*Sings*]
      A pickaxe, and a spade, a spade,
      For and a shrouding sheet:
      O, a pit of clay for to be made
75   For such a guest is meet.
    Throws up another skull
    HAMLET   There's another: why may not that be the skull of a lawyer? Where be
      his quiddities now, his quillets, his cases, his tenures, and his tricks? Why does
      he suffer this rude knave now to knock him about the sconce with a dirty
      shovel, and will not tell him of his action of battery? Hum. This fellow might be
80   in 's time a great buyer of land, with his statutes, his recognizances, his fines,
      his double vouchers, his recoveries: is this the fine of his fines, and the
      recovery of his recoveries, to have his fine pate full of fine dirt? Will his

---

5.1 52 **property of easiness** easy for him   53 **hath the daintier sense** is more sensitive   57 **shipped ... land** dispatched me into the earth (i.e. my grave/dust)   58 **been such** been a young man in love   59 **jowls** hurls (a pun on 'jowl', i.e. jawbone)   60 **Cain** the first murderer in the Bible (Genesis 4) who killed his elder brother Abel   61 **politician** crafty schemer   **o'er-offices** lords it over   62 **circumvent** cheat, outwit   68 **chapless** jawless   69 **mazzard** head   **revolution** change/turn of the wheel of fortune   **trick** knack   70-71 **Did ... 'em?** Did these people cost so little to bring up that we may play games with their bones?   **loggats** a game where pieces of wood shaped like bowling pins were thrown at a stake fixed in the ground   73 **For and** and furthermore   **shrouding sheet** sheet in which the corpse was wrapped   77 **quiddities ... quillets** subtleties, verbal and distinctions, quibbling arguments   **tenures** (documents or cases relating to) conditions on which property is held   78 **rude** ignorant/rough   **sconce** head   79 **action of battery** litigation concerning physical assault   80-81 **statutes** legal documents that secured a debt on land and property (similar to a mortgage)   **recognizances** legal documents that formally acknowledged a debt   **fines ... recoveries** legal process concerned with securing the outright ownership of land   **double vouchers** refers to the practice of having two people vouch for a claimant's ownership of the land   **fine of his fines** end of his fines

85 vouchers vouch him no more of his purchases, and double ones too, than the length and breadth of a pair of indentures? The very conveyances of his lands will hardly lie in this box; and must the inheritor himself have no more, ha?
HORATIO Not a jot more, my lord.

...

HAMLET Whose was it?
First Clown A whoreson mad fellow's it was: whose do you think it was?
135 HAMLET Nay, I know not.
First Clown A pestilence on him for a mad rogue! A poured a flagon of Rhenish on my head once. This same skull, sir, was Yorick's skull, the king's jester.
HAMLET This?
First Clown E'en that.
140 HAMLET Let me see. (*Takes the skull*) Alas, poor Yorick! I knew him, Horatio: a fellow of infinite jest, of most excellent fancy. He hath borne me on his back a thousand times—and now, how abhorred in my imagination it is! My gorge rises at it. Here hung those lips that I have kissed I know not how oft. —Where be your gibes now? Your gambols? Your songs? Your flashes of merriment, that
145 were wont to set the table on a roar? No one now, to mock your own jeering? Quite chap-fallen? Now get you to my lady's chamber, and tell her, let her paint an inch thick, to this favour she must come; make her laugh at that. —Prithee, Horatio, tell me one thing.
HORATIO What's that, my lord?
150 HAMLET Dost thou think Alexander looked o' this fashion i' the earth?
HORATIO E'en so.
HAMLET And smelt so? Pah! (*Puts down the skull*)
HORATIO E'en so, my lord.
HAMLET To what base uses we may return, Horatio! Why may not imagination
155 trace the noble dust of Alexander, till he find it stopping a bung-hole?
HORATIO 'Twere to consider too curiously, to consider so.
HAMLET No, faith, not a jot; but to follow him thither with modesty enough, and likelihood to lead it: as thus: Alexander died, Alexander was buried, Alexander returneth into dust; the dust is earth; of earth we make loam; and why of that
160 loam, whereto he was converted, might they not stop a beer-barrel?
Imperious Caesar, dead and turn'd to clay,
Might stop a hole to keep the wind away.
O, that that earth, which kept the world in awe,
Should patch a wall to expel the winter's flaw!
165 But soft, but soft, aside: here comes the king.

...

83-84 **vouch** guarantee **the ... indentures** land (i. e. his grave) only as long and wide as a legal document **conveyances** deeds relating to the transfer of land and property 85 **box** deed-box/coffin 134 **whoreson** wretched (an abusive intensifier) 136 **A** he **Rhenish** German wine from the area around the River Rhine 141 **fancy** imagination 142–143 **abhorred** filled with horror **My gorge rises** i.e. I feel like vomiting **gorge** stomach contents 145-146 **No ... jeering?** there's no one left to laugh at the way you mocked and made fun of people **chap-fallen** lacking the lower jaw 155 **bung-hole** hole in a barrel stopped with a bung 156 **too curiously** too closely/overly ingeniously 157 **modesty** moderation 159 **loam** mortar made of clay, sand and straw 164 **flaw** squall, violent gust of wind

Questions for Understanding and Reflection

Act I, scene 3
1. What does Polonius think of making friends?
2. Does Polonius warn his son against buying costly clothing?
3. Why should one not lend or borrow money?

Act III, scene 1
1. Does Hamlet think that human beings are an admirable lot?
2. What prevents Hamlet from killing himself to shake off those "headache", "shocks" and injustices?
3. What is the dilemma facing Hamlet?

Act V, scene 1
1. What did a politician, a courtier and a lawyer like to do while they were alive?
2. How were Hamlet and Yorick related to each other?
3. Why is Alexander the Great mentioned?

IV SHAKESPEAREAN RELEVANCE

A. Shakespeare in Everyday English
Please try to understand the following Shakespearean words and expressions in the contexts designated within parentheses and give their generally used meanings in the space provided.
1. not a mouse stirring (1.1.11): _____
2. in mind's eye (1.2.186): _____
3. primrose path (1.3.52): _____
4. caviar to the general (2.2.383-384): _____
5. the slings and arrows of outrageous fortune (3.1.64): _____
6. There's the rub. (3.1.71): _____
7. mortal coil (3.1.73): _____
8. woe is me (3.1.158) _____
9. out-Herod Herod (3.2.9): _____
10. smell to heaven (3.3.39): _____
11. hoist with his own petard (3.4.208): _____
12. hugger-mugger (4.4.79): _____

B. Shakespeare in Literature
Read the following literary excerpts, locate the Shakespearean allusions and explain their meanings according to the contexts where they appear.
1. How do you know that Hetty isn't floating at the present moment in some star-lit pond, with lovely water-lilies round her, like Ophelia? (Oscar Wilde, *The Picture of Dorian Gray*, 1891)
2. I said I wanted to be best man, I said I wanted a church wedding. I went on about it. I started shouting. I came the Hamlets a bit. I was drunk at the time, if you must know. (Julian Barnes, *Talking It Over*, 1991)
3. To what extent was he, Closter Ridley, justified in imposing his taste upon the newspaper's subscribers? Still, was it not for doing so that he drew his excellent salary and his annual bonus, reckoned upon the profits? What about the barber's chair; might there not be a few

buttocks for Shillito? But he could go on in this Hamlet-like strain all day. (Robertson Davies, *Leaven of Malice*, 1954)

C. Shakespeare in Music, Art and on Screen
1948: *Hamelt*, a British film adaptation, directed by and starring Sir Laurence Olivier.
1990: *Hamelt*, a film adaptation, directed by Franco Zeffirelli, casting Mel Gibson.
1990: *Rosencrantz & Guilderstern Are Dead*, comedy-drama film written and directed by Tom Stoppard, which depicts two minor characters from Shakespeare's *Hamlet*.
1996: *Hamelt*, a film containing every word of the Bard's play, directed by and starring Kenneth Branagh.

V SHAKESPEARE QUOTES

A little more than kin and less than kind. (1.2.64)
Frailty, thy name is woman. (1.2.146)
Something is rotten in the state of Denmark. (1.4.72)
O, my prophetic soul! (1.5.46)
The time is out of joint. (1.5.205)
What a piece of work is a man! (2.2.284)
To be, or not to be, that is the question. (3.1.62)
Purpose is but the slave to memory,
Of violent birth, but poor validity. (3.2.159-160)
Never alone did the king sigh, but with a general groan. (3.3.23-24)
Diseases desperate grown
By desperate appliance are relieved. (4.2.9-10)
What is a man
If his chief good and market of his time
Be but to sleep and feed? A beast, no more. (4.4.106-108)
There's a special providence in the fall of a sparrow. If it be now, 'tis not to come: if it be not to come, it will be now: if it be not now, yet it will come: the readiness is all. (5.2.150-152)

15. The Tragedy of King Lear
李 尔 王

I INTRODUCTION

《李尔王》创作于詹姆斯一世登基之初,并在其白厅的宫中演出过。该剧对人的尊严做了深刻的探讨,揭示了一位年迈的国王在失去王权、回归基本生存状态时脆弱但又高贵的人性。两条密切关联、彼此交叉的情节贯穿全剧,一条叙述的是不列颠李尔王与三个女儿的关系,揭示了大女儿高纳里尔和二女儿里根的奸佞不孝以及小女儿考狄利娅的善良忠诚;另一条类似的情节是关于葛罗斯特伯爵和他的两个儿子爱德伽和爱德蒙的关系。李尔王根据三个女儿对他爱的不同表白决定王国的分配,高纳里尔和里根由于"娓娓动人的口才"(glib and oily art)和逢迎谄媚的本事赢得了最大的份额,而爱心比口才更富有(my love's more ponderous than my tongue)的考狄利娅却因为不善表白而未得到任何份额并被李尔王断绝了父女关系。同样作为父亲的葛罗斯特伯爵也相信其庶子爱德蒙的谗言而将无辜的爱德伽放逐。王国既分、忠良被逐,井然有序的世界遂变得混沌不堪,连自然界也出现暴风、日食等乱象。失去了王权钳制的邪恶如脱缰的野马恣意横行,内心邪恶的里根更是变本加厉。她与丈夫康华尔狼狈为奸,在众目睽睽之下将葛罗斯特伯爵的双眼挖出:"出来,可恶的浆块!现在你还会发光吗?"作为该剧的高潮,"荒原暴风"一景已与李尔王紧密联系在一起,它反映出主人公内心从悲愤、痴癫到醒悟的蜕变过程。在经历了种种磨难和变故之后,李尔王终于和真心爱他的考狄利娅团聚,但却是在监牢之中。当考狄利娅被处死之后,李尔王怀抱着女儿,并在"为什么一条狗、一匹马、一只耗子,都有它们的生命,你却没有一丝呼吸?"的扣问中死去。同其他的莎剧一样,《李尔王》的主题是模棱两可、难以确定的:它似乎在宣扬虚无主义(nihilism),但同时又肯定生命的价值;它提出抽象、无法回答的问题,但又直面现实且永恒的命题,如:父母年迈、手足之争、父子/女关系、无家可归以及对他人苦难的态度等。

II PLOT SUMMARY

Lear,[1] aged ruler of Britain, wishing to shake off the responsibilities of kingship, plans to divide his realm among his three daughters. In order to determine what share each should get, he proposes to make his gifts dependent upon each daughter's testimony of love. **Goneril**[2] and **Regan**,[3] wives of the Duke of Albany and of the Duke of Cornwall, vie with each other in fulsome protestations of their love. Goneril says she loves him "more than word can **wield**[4] the matter,/Dearer than eyesight, space, and liberty,/Beyond what can be valued rich or rare,/No less than life, with **grace**,[5] health, beauty, honour." (1.1.46-49) Regan professes that her only joy in life is to love her father. Much pleased, Lear gave them each a third of his kingdom. He then

---

1 **Lear** /liə/ 李尔   2 **Goneril** /ˈgɔnəril/ 高纳里尔   3 **Regan** /ˈriːgən/ 里根   4 **wield** express   5 **grace** virtue

Cordelia's Portion, 1843—1844, Ford Madox

turns to **Cordelia**,⁶ the youngest, expecting from her an even more eloquent declaration. But Cordelia's restrained expression that she will divide her love and duty between her husband and father enrages him. She is cast off completely and her share of the kingdom is divided between her elder sisters. The King declares that he will make his home with Goneril and Regan in turn. The Duke of Burgundy, one of the wooers of Cordelia, promptly loses interest in her; but the King of France, aware of her spiritual beauty and honest worth, declares that "She is herself a dowry" and gladly takes her as his wife. The Earl of Kent, faithful and outspoken, vainly tries to make Lear recognize the folly of his action, but earns for himself only the sentence of banishment. Left to themselves, Goneril and Regan agree to join forces against any new demonstrations of their father's willfulness which may affect them adversely.

Elsewhere in the kingdom, the Earl of **Gloucester**⁷ also misjudges a dutiful child and endows an undeserving one with power. The Earl is easily deceived by Edmund, his bastard son, who by means of a forged letter convinces him that Edgar, the legitimate son, plans to murder his father. On Edmund's advice, the unsuspecting Edgar flees.

Kent, who had not gone into exile, returns in disguise, determined to protect Lear, who accepts him as a servant. Although he had relinquished his kingdom, Lear expects prompt obedience and recognition of his status as king and father. The behavior of Oswald, Goneril's timeserving and well-instructed steward, and more especially the bitterly ironic commentaries of Lear's Fool, make it clear that he is to receive neither. Goneril shows no respect for Lear either as a father or as a king. She complains that his "hundred knights and squires,/Men so disordered, so debauched and **bold**,/⁸That this our court, infected with their manners,/Shows like a riotous inn: **epicurism**⁹ and lust/Makes it more like a tavern or a brothel/Than a **graced**¹⁰ palace," (1.4.185-190) and insists that they be reduced in number. Cursing that Goneril would be sterile or have a thankless child of spleen, the old King calls for his horse and leaves at once for Regan's place, Kent having been sent ahead to inform the second sister of his impending arrival.

The hypocritical Edmund succeeds in completing his father's conviction that Edgar is a "strong and fastened villain" just before Cornwall and Regan arrive at Gloucester's castle. The Duke praises Edmund for "virtue and obedience" and states that he has need for such a trustworthy person. Kent arrives and, motivated by his loyalty to Lear, excoriates Oswald as a "brazen-faced varlet" and upstart. Learning of this, Regan and Cornwall order that Kent be placed in the **stocks**.¹¹ When Lear appears, accompanied by the Fool, he is appalled to find that his emissary should be so treated. In a stormy exchange with her father, Regan states that she will not offer Lear hospitality until he apologizes to her sister. When Goneril arrives, the old king soon learns that the two jointly oppose him and that he is to be stripped of all the appurtenances of authority. He sets out in the raging storm and tempest, accompanied by Kent and the Fool.

Within the kingdom there are rumors of dissension between Albany and Cornwall and of possible invasion from France. As the terrifying storm still rages, Lear hurls his defiance at the elements and then, with Kent and the Fool, seeks haven in a hovel which is occupied by Edgar,

---

6 **Cordelia** /kɔːˈdiːljə/ 考狄利娅   7 **Gloucester** /ˈglɔstə/ 葛罗斯特   8 **bold** presumptuous, audacious   9 **epicurism** gluttony/pleasure-seeking   10 **graced** honourable   11 **stocks** a device of punishment consisting of a framework with holes for securing the ankles and, sometimes, the wrists, used to expose an offender to public ridicule

King Lear and the Fool in the Storm, 1851, William Dyce

who has disguised himself as mad Tom o' Bedlam. Lear questions Edgar and concludes that he represents "the thing itself"—man, stripped of all appearances and thus akin to the animal. Gloucester, who had braved the anger of Goneril and Regan, finds Lear and persuades him to take refuge in a farmhouse near the castle. But Gloucester had informed Edmund of his intentions to find and help the King, and the wicked son had promptly informed Cornwall of the Earl's intentions. Furthermore, he had produced another letter implicating his father in a plot with France in opposition to Cornwall. The Duke vows that he will have vengeance and promises that Edmund's "loyalty" will be rewarded.

Lear's mind now becomes unbalanced. In his madness he appoints the Fool and Poor Tom as judges and proceeds to arraign Coneril and Regan as criminals. At last Kent persuades the oppressed King to rest himself. "I'll go to bed at noon," says the Fool, who makes his last appearance in the play. Gloucester, who had left to get what supplies he could lay his hands on, returns to report that the evil daughters are plotting to kill their father. Lear must be taken at once to Dover, where, Gloucester believes, friends will protect him.

At Gloucester's castle, the wicked three—Goneril, Regan, and Cornwall—vindictively turn on Gloucester when they hear that an army of France has landed. At Cornwall's command, Edmund leaves the castle so that they may deal with his father, their host. Oswald is sent to bring in the Earl. Gloucester is denounced as a vicious traitor, and his eyes are plucked out in full view of the audience: "Out, vile jelly! /Where is thy lustre now?". (3.7.88-89) Finally, he is thrust out of the castle gates and left to "smell his way to Dover."

Still disguised as Poor Tom, Edgar finds his blinded father led by an old tenant and listens to his moving confession of mistaken judgment and his prayer that he might live to "see" Edgar again by means of touch. The loyal son, preferring not yet to identify himself, becomes his father's guide and humors him in his determination to reach the cliffs of Dover, where he plans to commit suicide. At Dover, Edgar employs a ruse by means of which Gloucester is made to believe that he has fallen from the cliff but miraculously survives. In scenes that balance this episode, Cordelia discovers her abused father fantastically dressed

Lear and Cordelia, 1874, Marcus Stone

with wild flowers and weeds. So tender is her care of him that he awakes, believing that he too has been saved by some miracle. Seeing Gloucester, Lear forgives the earl for his sin of adultery, observing that "The wren **goes to't**[12] and the small gilded fly/Does **lecher**[13] in my sight. Let copulation thrive,/For Gloucester's batard son was kinder to his father/Than were my daughters **got**[14] 'tween the lawful sheets." (4.5.120-123) Meanwhile, Albany, aware of what has been

---

12 **goes to't** does it, has sex   13 **lecher** fornicate

happening, denounces Goneril for her heartless cruelty. Both Goneril and Regan now compete lustfully for Edmund, who, after the news that Cornwall has died (killed by one of Gloucester's servants), becomes commander-in-chief of the English forces.

King Lear Weeping over the Dead Body of Cordelia, 1786—1788, James Barry

Because of his duty to defend Britain against a foreign power, Albany joins forces with Edmund. France is defeated in the ensuing battle. Lear and Cordelia are made prisoners by Edmund. Resigning to his lot, the king invites his daughter to "sing like birds i'th'cage ... and tell old tales, and laugh/At **gilded butterflies**,[15] and hear **poor rogues**/[16] Talk of court news ..." (5.3.10, 13-15) Determined to prevent Albany from helping them, Edmund gives secret orders for their execution. Goneril poisons Regan and then stabs herself when her adulterous conduct is revealed. While all this has been transpiring, Edgar reveals himself to his father, who, having been told by Kent of all that has happened to Lear, dies of a broken heart. Albany arrests Edmund for capital treason on Edgar's charge. In formal combat the noble son of Gloucester maintains his charge against his half brother and wounds him mortally. Lear's happiness in his reunion with Cordelia is short-lived. The repentant Edmund acts too late to countermand his order for their execution. The old king fights to save his daughter, but Cordelia is hanged. Lear is unable to bear Cordelia's death: "And my poor fool is hanged! No, no, no life?/Why should a dog, a horse, a rat have life,/And thou no breath at all? Thou'lt come no more,/Never, never, never, never, never!" (5.3.322-325) While trying to revive his daughter, the old king himself dies. Determined to follow his master King Lear (that is, to die with him), Kent declines Albany's invitation to jointly rule Britain, leaving the duke and Edgar to restore order in the kingdom.

Beyond the Play: *No-Holds Bard*[17]

When he forgives Gloucester for his adultery, King Lear sees human life as one gigantic orgy: "The wren goes to't, and the small fly / Does lecher in my sight." Bestial imagery like this suggests that beneath civilized behavior lurks an animal driven by crude appetites. The unusual use of common expressions like "go to't" is quite common in Shakespeare's plays. In fact, the Bard could be disgustingly bawdy and stunningly vulgar at once in order to cater to the Elizabethan audience who had a penchant for such sensitive discussions as human anatomy (as in *The Comedy of Errors*, 3.2.104-124 and words with sexual connotations like *cod*, *count*, *bottom*, *nothing*, *thing*), sexual behaviour (e.g. *die*, *hell*, *pricks* and *bowls*, *will*). In Shakespeare's language, the most neutral words are often capable of more than one meaning. Once you know the Elizabethan meaning of one or two words, a whole passage suddenly takes on a startling brand-new significance. Therefore,

---

14 **got** begot, conceived 15 **gilded butterflies** actual butterflies/lavishly dressed courtiers 16 **poor rogues** wretched fellows 17 **No-Holds Bard** a wordplay on the expression **no-holds-barred**, meaning 'free of any restrictions, censorship.'

slang hunting in Shakespeare is a worthwhile endeavour, and the underlying crudity or vulgarity doesn't necessarily detract from the beauty of the lines—it only adds another dimension. Admittedly, the knowledge of Elizabethan sexual slangs might raise the brows of those who ride the moral high horse (the sanitized version published by Harriet and Thomas Bowdler was such a response from that esteemed altitude, from whom *bowdlerize* derives), but earthiness is what makes Shakespeare a humanist playwright. A sufficiently annotated version of Complete Works of William Shakespeare will be of great help in this aspect.

Advertisement for 1819 edition of *The Family Shakespeare*

III   SELECTED READINGS

Act III, scene 2

Storm still. Enter KING LEAR and FOOL

KING LEAR   Blow, winds, and crack your cheeks! Rage, blow,
   You cataracts and hurricanoes, spout
   Till you have drenched our steeples, drown the cocks!
   You sulphurous and thought-executing fires,
5   Vaunt-couriers to oak-cleaving thunderbolts,
   Singe my white head! And thou, all-shaking thunder,
   Strike flat the thick rotundity o' th' world!
   Crack nature's moulds, an germens spill at once
   That make ingrateful man!
10 **FOOL**   O nuncle, court holy-water in a dry house is better than this rain-water
   out o' door. Good nuncle, in, and ask thy daughters' blessing: here's a night
   pities neither wise man nor fools.
KING LEAR   Rumble thy bellyful! Spit, fire! Spout, rain!
   Nor rain, wind, thunder, fire, are my daughters.
15   I tax not you, you elements, with unkindness;
   I never gave you kingdom, called you children;
   You owe me no subscription. Then let fall
   Your horrible pleasure: here I stand, your slave,
   A poor, infirm, weak, and despised old man:
20   But yet I call you servile ministers,
   That have with two pernicious daughters join
   Your high engendered battles gainst a head
   So old and white as this. O, ho, 'tis foul!

3.2 2 **cataracts** floods   **hurricanoes** waterspouts   3 **cocks** weathercocks   4 **thought-executing** i. e. lightning (as swift as thought/thought-destroying)   5 **Vaunt-couriers** forerunners   8 **nature's moulds** the moulds in which nature makes living creatures   **germens** seeds   10 **nuncle** variation of **uncle**   **court holy-water** courtly flattery   15 tax ... with accuse ... of   17 **subscription** allegiance   20 **ministers** agents   21 **pernicious** destructive/wicked   22 **high engendered** battalions created in the heavens   **gainst** short form of against   23 **foul** wicked/bad

	FOOL	He that has a house to put's head in has a good head-piece:
25		The cod-piece that will house
		Before the head has any,
		The head and he shall louse,
		So beggars marry many.
		The man that makes his toe
30		What he his heart should make
		Shall of a corn cry woe,
		And turn his sleep to wake.
		For there was never yet fair woman but she made mouths in a glass.
	KING LEAR	No, I will be the pattern of all patience;
35		I will say nothing.

Enter KENT

KENT Who's there?

FOOL Marry, here's grace and a codpiece: that's a wise man and a fool.

KENT Alas, sir, are you here? Things that love night
 Love not such nights as these: the wrathful skies
40 Gallow the very wanderers of the dark,
 And make them keep their caves. Since I was man,
 Such sheets of fire, such bursts of horrid thunder,
 Such groans of roaring wind and rain, I never
 Remember to have heard: man's nature cannot carry
45 Th' affliction nor the fear.

KING LEAR Let the great gods,
 That keep this dreadful pudder o'er our heads,
 Find out their enemies now. Tremble, thou wretch,
 That hast within thee undivulgèd crimes
50 Unwhipped of justice: hide thee, thou bloody hand,
 Thou perjured, and thou simular man of virtue
 That art incestuous: caitiff, to pieces shake,
 That under covert and convenient seeming
 Hast practised on man's life: close pent-up guilts,
55 Rive your concealing continents, and cry
 These dreadful summoners grace. I am a man
 More sinned against than sinning.

KENT Alack, bare-headed?
 Gracious my lord, hard by here is a hovel:

---

24 **put's** put his **headpiece** helmet/brain 25 **codpiece** penis (literally, appendage worn on the front of a man's breeches to cover and emphasise the genitals) **house** find a house for itself, i.e. have sex 27 **louse** get lice (in pubic and head hair) 28 **So ... many** in this way beggars end up with a string of mistresses (or a quantity of lice) 29-30 **makes ... make** values most what he should value least/considers his penis (sex) more important than his heart (love/moral integrity) 31 **corn** may suggest a syphilitic sore 33 **made ... glass** posed before a mirror 37 **grace ... codpiece** royalty and a fool (who sometimes wore exaggerated codpieces and was proverbially well-endowed) 40 **Gallow** gally, i.e. frighten **wanderers ... dark** nocturnal animals 47 **pudder** turmoil 50 **Unwhipped of** unpunished by 51 **perjured** perjurer **simular** faker, pretender 52 **caitiff** villain, wretch 53 **seeming** false appearance 54 **practised on** plotted against 55-56 **Rive** split open **continents** containers **cry ... grace** beg for mercy from these terrifying **summoners** (officers who summoned the accused to court) 57 **More sinned against than sinning** Less guilty than those who have injured one

60	Some friendship will it lend you gainst the tempest.
	Repose you there while I to this hard house—
	More harder than the stones whereof 'tis raised,
	Which even but now, demanding after you,
	Denied me to come in—return, and force
65	Their scanted courtesy.

KING LEAR My wits begin to turn.
Come on, my boy; how dost, my boy? Art cold?
I am cold myself—Where is this straw, my fellow?
The art of our necessities is strange,
70 That can make vile things precious. Come, your hovel. —
Poor fool and knave, I have one part in my heart
That's sorry yet for thee.

FOOL [*Singing*]
He that has and a little tiny wit—
With hey, ho, the wind and the rain,—
75 Must make content with his fortunes fit,
For the rain it raineth every day.

KING LEAR True, my good boy. Come, bring us to this hovel.

Exeunt KING LEAR *and* KENT

FOOL This is a brave night to cool a courtesan.
I'll speak a prophecy ere I go:
80 When priests are more in word than matter;
When brewers mar their malt with water;
When nobles are their tailors' tutors;
No heretics burned, but wenches' suitors;
When every case in law is right;
85 No squire in debt, nor no poor knight;
When slanders do not live in tongues;
Nor cutpurses come not to throngs;
When usurers tell their gold i' th' field;
And bawds and whores do churches build,
90 Then shall the realm of Albion
Come to great confusion:
Then comes the time, who lives to see't,
That going shall be used with feet.
This prophecy Merlin shall make, for I live before his time.

Exit

---

61 **hard house** pitiless household 63 **demanding after** asking for 65 **scanted** withheld 69 **The ... strange** necessity has a strange power 73 **and a** a very 75 **Must ... fit** must be satisfied with a fortune as tiny as his wit 78 **brave** fine **cool** i. e. cool the lust of **courtesan** courtier's mistress, high-class prostitute 80 **in ... matter** more concerned with words than substance (i. e. do not practise what they preach) 81 **mar** spoil 82 **are ... tutors** i. e. teach their tutors about fashion 83 **heretics** religious dissenters 87 **cutpurses** thieves who cut the strings of moneybags at their victims' waists **throngs** crowds 88 **tell ... i' th' field** count their money openly 89 **bawds** pimps 90 **Albion** ancient name for Britain 91 **confusion** destruction, overthrow 92 **who** whoever 93 **going ... feet** people will walk on their feet 94 **Merlin** King Arthur's great magician who, according to Holinshed's *Chronicles*, lived later than Lear

Questions for Understanding and Reflection

Act III, scene 2

1. What is King Lear's purpose of such a minute description of the storm?
2. In what ways are the elements "servile minister" (20)?
3. What is the rhyme pattern of the Fool's speech (25-32)
4. What is meant by "I am a man/More sinned against than sinning"?
5. How does the Fool predict the future of Britain?

IV SHAKESPEAREAN RELEVANCE

A. Shakespeare in Everyday English

Please try to understand the following Shakespearean words and expressions in the contexts designated within parentheses and give their generally used meanings in the space provided.

1. the last, not least. (1.1.75): _____
2. brazen-faced (2.2.21): _____
3. Every inch a king (4.5.115): _____
4. pell-mell (4.5.124): _____
5. forget and forgive (4.6.88): _____
6. come full circle (5.3.187): _____

B. Shakespeare in Literature

Read the following literary excerpts, locate the Shakespearean allusions and explain their meanings according to the contexts where they appear.

1. It was, Ralph thought in a remote and detached way, better to labour for a sane king than mad Lear. (Thomas Keneally, *The Playmaker*, 1987)
2. We are all scared of it, be honest. Madness. Don't tell me, as you flick through these pages in that rather airy way of yours, that you have never considered the dark, almost subliminal fear that you might awake one morning as barking as Lear, for I know better. (*The Guardian*, 1997)
3. Mrs. Whittaker was Cordelia-like to her father during his declining years. She came to see him several times a month, bringing him jelly or potted hyacinths. Sometimes she sent her car and chauffeur for him, so that he might take an easy drive through the town, and Mrs. Bain might be afforded a chance to drop her cooking and accompany him. (Dorothy Parker, *The Wonderful Old Gentleman*, 1944)

C. Shakespeare in Music, Art and on Screen

1971: *King Lear*, a British film adaptation, directed by Peter Brook and starring Paul Scofield.
1983: *King Lear*, a video production, directed by Michael Elliott with Laurence Olivier as Lear.
1985: *Ran* (乱), a Japanese-French epic film, directed and co-written by Akira Kurosawa.
1997: *A Thousand Acres*, an American film drama, directed by Jocelyn Moorhouse, and starring Michelle Pfeiffer, Jessica Lange, Jennifer Jason Leigh and Jason Robards.

2002: *King of Texas*, an American television film, directed by Uli Edel.

SHAKESPEARE QUOTES

Nothing will come of nothing: speak again. (1.1.82)
Fairest Cordelia, that art most rich being poor,
Most choice, forsaken, and most loved, despised. (1.1.258-259)
Why brand they us
With base? With baseness? Bastardy? Base, base?
Who in the lusty stealth of nature take
More composition and fierce quality
Than doth within a dull, stale, tired bed,
Go to th' creating a whole tribe of fops
Got 'tween asleep and wake? (1.2.9-15)
How sharper than a serpent's tooth it is
To have a thankless child! (1.4.236-237)
Keep thy foot out of brothels, thy hand out of plackets,
thy pen from lenders' books, and defy the foul fiend. (3.4.81-82)
As flies to wanton boys, are we to th' gods:
They kill us for their sport. (4.1.41-42)

16. The Tragedy of Othello, the Moor of Venice
奥 赛 罗

I INTRODUCTION

效力于威尼斯城邦的摩尔族将军奥赛罗英勇无比、屡建奇功,博得了元老勃拉班修之女苔丝狄蒙娜的芳心并与之秘密成婚。奥赛罗对凯西奥的提拔激起了其旗官、"忠实可靠"的伊阿古的嫉妒和仇恨,于是便上演了莎士比亚笔下最大的恶棍搬弄是非、费尽心机陷害苔丝狄蒙娜和凯西奥莫须有的奸情,最终导致男女主人公双双殒命的悲剧。《奥赛罗》迎合了伊丽莎白一世时代揶揄戴绿帽者(cuckold)的品味,但原本粗俗、低级的主题却经由莎翁之手被赋予了震撼、感人的力量。贯穿全剧的是表象与实质的矛盾和冲突:奥赛罗皮肤黝黑却内心高贵,伊阿古外表忠实却又包藏祸心(连他自己都承认:"世人知道的我,并不是实在的我"),苔丝狄蒙娜贤淑贞洁却遭毁誉。语言方面,《奥赛罗》一剧多精巧的演讲、惊心动魄的交锋以及种类繁多的修辞(如苔丝狄蒙娜对奥赛罗动人的爱情倾诉,奥赛罗骇人的醋意的迸发,伊阿古披露其邪恶心机的令人窒息的内心独白等)。《奥赛罗》的结构就像是一曲将反差很大的旋律融为一体的复调音乐,其中奥赛罗的语言多为诗歌体,音律纯净悦耳、词藻华丽工整,而以伊阿古为代表的普通百姓则使用的是口语体,时有秽言但又透着机敏。两者相得益彰,使得该剧不至流于粗俗(squalid)和做作(histrionic)。

II PLOT SUMMARY

The story takes place in the great and powerful city-state of Venice. It is late at night. **Roderigo**,[1] a young gentleman and former suitor of Senator **Brabantio**'s[2] daughter, **Desdemona**,[3] is angry with **Iago**,[4] a soldier in the Venetian army. Iago knew about Desdemona's elopement with the leader of the Venetian forces, a Moor named **Othello**,[5] yet, Roderigo complains that Iago did not tell him. Roderigo reminds Iago that he has said that he hates the Moor, but if this is so, why did he not report Othello's conquest of Desdemona to Roderigo immediately? Iago is defensively adamant: he hates Othello, and he is burning with jealousy that he, Iago, has been passed over for a promotion. For years Iago has been Othello's faithful ensign and he expected to be promoted to the rank of lieutenant; instead, the post went to a young man from Florence, **Michael Cassio**,[6] whom Iago holds in great contempt because "Mere **prattle**[7] without practice/Is all his soldiership." (1.1.26-27) Iago, on the other hand, is a veteran of many hard-fought campaigns.

---

1 **Roderigo** /ˌrɔdəˈrigəu/ 罗德利哥　2 **Brabantio** /brəˈbæntiəu/ 勃拉班修　3 **Desdemona** /ˌdezdiˈməunə/ 苔丝狄蒙娜　4 **Iago** /iˈɑːgəu/ 伊阿古　5 **Othello** /əuˈθeləu/ 奥赛罗　6 **Cassio** /ˈkæsiəu/ 卡西奥　7 **prattle** idle talk

Desdemonna, ca. 1888, Frederic Leighton

Iago tells Roderigo to awaken Desdemona's father and inform him that his daughter has run off with the Moor.

The two stand before Brabantio's house and call to him. When the senator appears at a window, Iago takes pleasure in telling him the news: "an old black **ram**/[8] is **tupping**[9] your white **ewe**."[10] (1.1.92-93) But before the old man comes running down to see exactly what the trouble is, Iago leaves quickly, telling Roderigo that as the Moor's trusted ensign it is not right that he should be involved. He must still pretend love and loyalty to Othello, who is about to embark for Cyprus with the army to fight the Turks.

A distraught Brabantio, with his servants, appears downstairs and demands to know where he may find Othello and his daughter. Roderigo agrees to take him to Othello.

In the next scene, we find Othello with Iago and several attendants on another street. Now Iago is telling Othello about Brabantio's reaction to his daughter's marriage. Iago warns Othello that her father will do whatever he can to take his daughter from the Moor. Cassio then enters to tell Othello that the Duke of Venice has sent for him to come immediately, for there is alarming news from Cyprus. A moment later, the enraged Brabantio burst upon the scene, along with several armed followers. But Othello will not allow his men to draw their swords against his new father-in-law. Instead, they all agree to appear before the Duke. Brabantio is sure that the Duke will take his side against Othello.

However, the war news is critically urgent, and the Duke, who admires Othello, needs him to lead the Venetian forces. He listens to Othello's story of his newfound love: "She loved me for the dangers I had passed,/And I loved her that she did pity them" (1.3.181-182), and then, when Dosdemona appears to note a "divided duty": "To you I am bound for life and **education**[11] ... But here's my husband,/And so much duty as my mother showed/To you, **preferring**[12] you before her father,/So much I **challenge**[13] that I may profess/Due to the Moor my lord." (1.3. 197, 201-205), the Duke attempts to reconcile Brabantio, Desdemona, and Othello—but to no avail. Brabantio will have no more to do with Desdemona and will not even allow her to remain in his house while Othello is off to war. Desdemona, at this point, speaks up and insists on following her new husband to Cyprus. Othello decides to leave his bride in the care of her maid, **Emilia**,[14] and Emilia's husband, Iago, Othello's most trusted friend; the Moor and his new bride then go off to spend their last few hours alone together. Iago tells Roderigo not to give up hope of Desdemona; he may still win her, for she will undoubtedly soon tire of the Moor. When Roderigo, somewhat encouraged, leaves, Iago reveals his deep hatred and jealousy of Othello and he mulls over a possible way to destroy him. He decides, at last, to use Cassio the man he deeply resents, as the instrument of his revenge.

The scene of the drama now changes to the island of Cyprus. There has been great storm at sea which has wrecked the Turkish fleet and held up Othello's arrival. Cassio's ship arrives first, and a short while later Desdemona lands, along with Emilia and Iago. Desdemona is concerned for Othello, and to take her mind off her worries, Cassio engages her in lighthearted conversation. Iago, seeing how well they get on together, visualizes the crystallization of his plan. When the victorious Othello arrives at last and goes off happily with his bride, Iago tells Roderigo that he is

---

8 **ram** a proverbially lustful beast   9 **tupping** mounting sexually   10 **ewe** /juː/ an adult female sheep   11 **education** upbringing
12 **preferring** promoting/esteeming   13 **challenge** claim, assert as a right   14 **Emilia** /əˈmiliə/ 爱米利娅

convinced that it is really Cassio whom Desdemona loves. Skillfully, Iago induces Roderigo to pick a quarrel with Cassio that same evening.

Shortly afterward, a herald appears and announces that the night will be given over to feasting and celebration in honor of Othello's victory and, belatedly, a celebration for the newly married couple.

Later that night, Cassio is left in charge of the night watch while Othello and Desdemona retire to their chambers. Iago plies Cassio with wine and teases him until his mood becomes irritable. Then Roderigo appears, and as planned, begins to fight with Cassio. Montano, governor of the island, tries to stop the fight and is wounded by the drunken Cassio.

Othello appears, and when he is told what happened, he removes Cassio from his position as lieutenant. Cassio, now somewhat sobered and deeply sorry for all the trouble, is about to plead with Othello, but Iago quickly persuades him that his chances will be better if he asks Desdemona to intercede for him with her husband. Iago then helps Cassio arrange to meet Desdemona privately, and Desdemona naively promises Cassio that she will do everything she can to restore him to Othello's good graces: "I'll **watch him tame**[15] and talk him out of patience;/His bed shall seem a school, his **board a shrift**."[16] (3.3.25-26)

Desdemona's Death Song,
Dante Gabriel Rossetti (1828—1882)

As Cassio is leaving, Iago and Othello appear. Seeing Othello's puzzle at Cassio's speedy departure, Iago quickly points out that Cassio seemed to be trying to avoid the Moor. Desdemona immediately and enthusiastically begins to beg Othello to pardon Cassio, "A man that languishes in your displeasure," (3.3.47) and will not stop her pleading until Othello agrees. The moment Desdemona and Emilia leave, however, Iago begins to plant seeds of doubt and suspicion in Othello's mind. Over and over again, all the while pretending to speak plainly and honestly, Iago subtly suggests that Desdemona and Cassio are having a love affair. When Iago is gone, Othello laments that "the plague to great ones,/**Prerogatived**[17] are they less than the base:/'Tis destiny unshunnable, like death:/Even then this **forkèd plague**[18] is fated to us/When we **do quicken**."[19] (3.3.303-307) Desdemona returns and finds her formerly gentle and loving husband in an overwrought emotional condition. She tries to soothe him by stroking his head with her handkerchief, but he irritably pushes it aside; it falls to the ground, and he leaves.

A while later, Emilia finds the handkerchief and gives it to Iago. It is a very special handkerchief, embroidered with a strawberry pattern, and was Othello's first present to Desdemona. Then Othello returns, demanding of Iago some proof of his wife's infidelity. The quick-witted Iago, thinking of the handkerchief in his pocket, says that he overheard Cassio talk in his sleep about Desdemona, and that, furthermore, he noticed Cassio wiping his face with a strawberry-embroidered handkerchief. Othello is now convinced that Desdemona has been unfaithful to him. He angrily vows revenge against both Cassio and Desdemona. Impulsively, he also promotes "honest" Iago to be his new lieutenant.

Now Othello cannot wait to ask Desdemona where the handkerchief is, and when she cannot

---

15 **watch him tame** tame him by preventing him from sleeping (a method for training hawks)   16 **board a shrift** table (shall seem) a confessional   17 **Prerogatived** privileged, advantaged   18 **forkèd plague** horned (cuckolds were traditionally supposed to grow horns)   19 **do quicken** are conceived

produce it, he flies into a rage of jealousy. Meanwhile, Iago has left the handkerchief where Cassio cannot fail to find it. He then arranges for Othello to actually see the handkerchief in Cassio's possession. Othello and Iago agree that Othello should kill Desdemona; Iago will dispose of Cassio. At this moment, Lodovico arrives from Venice with orders for Othello to return at once, leaving Cassio as Governor of Cyprus. Events move swiftly to a climax as Othello accuses Desdemona of infidelity and refuses to believe her protestations of innocence. He orders her to go to bed. Once alone, Desdemona tells Emilia about her mother's maid, Barbary, who was in love with a man who proved mad and deserted her. She died singing a song called "Willow". Desdemona then asks Emilia if she would commit adultery. Emilia thinks that she would, arguing that "for all the whole world, why, who would not make her husband a cuckold to make him a monarch? I should venture purgatory for 't." (4.3.79-81)

Iago, meanwhile, persuades the gullible Roderigo to kill Cassio. Later that night, Iago and Roderigo attack Cassio on a dark street. However, things do not work out as Iago planned, for it is Cassio who wounds Roderigo. Iago rushes out and stabs Cassio in the leg. Othello, hearing Cassio's cries for help, believes that half of the revenge plan is completed, and he hastens to fulfill his own act of revenge. But neither Cassio nor Roderigo is dead, and Iago, fearful that Roderigo will talk, quickly and secretly kills him. Emilia then enters and is sent off to tell Othello what has happened.

Othello with Desdemona in Bed Asleep, 1859, Christian Köhler

In the bedroom, Othello observes Desdemona in her bed and contemplates murdering her: "It is the cause, it is the cause:/ ... I'll not shed her blood,/Nor scar that whiter skin of hers than snow,/And smooth as monumental alabaster:/Yet she must die...". (5.2.1,3-6) Deaf to Desdemona's pleas and prayers, he has smothered her in her bed. Emilia tries to get into the room, but not until he is sure that his wife is dead will Othello unlock the doors and let Emilia enter. Desdemona revives briefly, tries to take the blame from Othello, and then dies. Othello then tells Emilia what he has done. Stricken with horror, Emilia tells him that Iago's accusations were all lies, and runs for help. The others enter, and Othello says he has killed Desdemona simply because "She was false as water" and "Cassio did top her." Emilia then tells him that it was she who took the fateful handkerchief and gave it to her husband. Iago stabs and kills his wife and he himself is wounded by the Moor, who then, remorseful and heartbroken, stabs himself. He dies, falling across Desdemona's body.

Beyond the Play: *Should Othello Be Black?*

Since its debut in front of King James at Whitehall Palace in 1604, *Othello* has raised more "politically correct" issues than any other Shakespearean play, the major one being whether the protagonist should be cast in a black actor. As the subtitle of the play suggests, Othello was a moor, a term applied to a person of either African or Middle

Paul Robeson with Uta Hagen in the Theatre Guild production of *Othello* (1943—1944)

Eastern origin, not necessarily black. This being the case, a black Othello remained unacceptable for centuries to white readers and audiences, simply because it would have been impossible for a girl to fall in love with a black. To play Othello then, such famous Shakespearean actors as Richard Burbage, David Garrick, Edmund Kean usually performed in blackface. Since the 19th century onwards, through the efforts of Ira Aldridge, Paul Robeson, Charles Dutton, etc., it has been politically correct to cast Othello with a black actor.

III SELECTED READINGS

Act IV, scene 3

Enter OTHELLO, LODOVICO, DESDEMONA, EMILIA and Attendants
LODOVICO   I do beseech you, sir, trouble yourself no further.
OTHELLO   O, pardon me: 'twill do me good to walk.
LODOVICO   Madam, good night. I humbly thank your ladyship.
DESDEMONA   Your honour is most welcome.
5   OTHELLO   Will you walk, sir? — O, Desdemona!
DESDEMONA   My lord?
OTHELLO   Get you to bed on th' instant; I will be returned forthwith: dismiss
    your attendant there: look 't be done.
DESDEMONA   I will, my lord.
Exeunt OTHELLO, LODOVICO, and Attendants
10   EMILIA   How goes it now? He looks gentler than he did.
DESDEMONA   He says he will return incontinent,
    He hath commanded me to go to bed,
    And bade me to dismiss you.
EMILIA   Dismiss me!
15   DESDEMONA   It was his bidding: therefore, good Emilia
    Give me my nightly wearing, and adieu.
    We must not now displease him.
EMILIA   I would you had never seen him!
DESDEMONA   So would not I my love doth so approve him,
20   That even his stubbornness, his checks, his frowns—
    Prithee, unpin me—have grace and favour.
EMILIA   I have laid those sheets you bade me on the bed.
DESDEMONA   All's one. Good father, how foolish are our minds! —
    If I do die before thee, prithee, shroud me

4.3 11 **incontinent** immediately, plays on the sense of 'loosely, unchastely'   16 **nightly wearing** nightclothes   19 **approve** commend   20 **stubbornness** inflexibility, obstinacy/ruthlessness, ferocity   21 **unpin me** i.e. loosen or detach parts of my clothing   23 **All's one** it makes no difference/all right   **Good father** i.e. God in heaven   24 **shroud** wrap (ready for burial)

25   In one of those same sheets.
          EMILIA   Come, come, you talk.
          DESDEMONA   My mother had a maid called Barbara:
            She was in love, and he she loved proved mad
            And did forsake her. She had a song of 'willow',
30   An old thing 'twas, but it expressed her fortune,
            And she died singing it: that song tonight
            Will not go from my mind: I have much to do
            But to go hang my head all at one side
            And sing it like poor Barbara. Prithee dispatch.
35   *EMILIA*   Shall I go fetch your nightgown?
          DESDEMONA   No, unpin me here.
            This Lodovico is a proper man.
          EMILIA   A very handsome man.
          DESDEMONA   He speaks well.
40   *EMILIA*   I know a lady in Venice would have walked barefoot to Palestine for a touch of his nether lip.
          DESDEMONA   [*Singing*] The poor soul sat sighing by a sycamore tree,
                    Sing all a green willow:
            Her hand on her bosom, her head on her knee,
45   Sing willow, willow, willow.
            The fresh streams ran by her, and murmured her moans,
            Sing willow, willow, willow:
            Her salt tears fell from her, and softened the stones,
            Sing willow—
50   Lay by these—
Singing
                    Willow, willow, willow;
            Prithee, hie thee: he'll come anon—

Singing
                    Sing all a green willow must be my garland.
                    Let nobody blame him, his scorn I approve—
55   Nay, that's not next. —Hark, who is 't that knocks?
          EMILIA   It's the wind.
          DESDEMONA   [*Singing*] I called my love false love; but what said he then?
                    Sing willow, willow, willow:
                    If I court more women, you'll couch with more men! —
60   So, get thee gone; good night. Mine eyes do itch:
            Doth that bode weeping?
          EMILIA   'Tis neither here nor there.
          DESDEMONA   I have heard it said so. O, these men, these men!

---

26 **talk** talk nonsense, talk on idly   28 **mad** insane/wild/faithless   29 **willow** a symbol of loss or unrequited love   32 **I ... to it** is all I can do not to   37 **proper** handsome/accomplished   41 **nether** lower   42 **sycamore** (/ˈsɪkəmɔː/) a type of fig-tree; puns on "sick amour"   50 **Lay by these** put these (her clothing or accessories) aside   52 **hie thee** hurry yourself   59 **couch** lie, sleep   61 **bode** foretell

	Dost thou in conscience think—tell me, Emilia,—
65	That there be women do abuse their husbands
	In such gross kind?

EMILIA There be some such, no question.
DESDEMONA Wouldst thou do such a deed for all the world?
EMILIA Why, would not you?
70 DESDEMONA No, by this heavenly light!
EMILIA Nor I neither by this heavenly light:
I might do 't as well i' th' dark.
DESDEMONA Wouldst thou do such a deed for all the world?
EMILIA The world's a huge thing: it is a great price
75 For a small vice.
DESDEMONA In troth, I think thou wouldst not.
EMILIA In troth, I think I should; and undo't when I had done. Marry, I would not do such a thing for a joint-ring, nor for measures of lawn, nor for gowns, petticoats, nor caps, nor any petty exhibition: but for the whole world, why,
80 who would not make her husband a cuckold to make him a monarch? I should venture purgatory for 't.
DESDEMONA Beshrew me, if I would do such a wrong
For the whole world.
EMILIA Why the wrong is but a wrong i' th' world, and having the world for
85 your labour, 'tis a wrong in your own world, and you might quickly make it right.
DESDEMONA I do not think there is any such woman.
EMILIA Yes, a dozen, and as many to th' vantage as
Would store the world they played for.
90 But I do think it is their husbands' faults
If wives do fall. Say that they slack their duties
And pour our treasures into foreign laps,
Or else break out in peevish jealousies,
Throwing restraint upon us, or say they strike us,
95 Or scant our former having in despite:
Why, we have galls, and though we have some grace,
Yet have we some revenge. Let husbands know
Their wives have sense like them: they see and smell
And have their palates both for sweet and sour,
100 As husbands have. What is it that they do
When they change us for others? Is it sport?
I think it is. And doth affection breed it?

---

65 **abuse** deceive, wrong 66 **gross kind** a great way/a coarse manner 74 **price** prize 78 **joint-ring** ring consisting of two joined halves **lawn** fine linen 79 **exhibition** gift 81 **venture** risk (going to) 82 **Beshrew me** used as a mild oath with the general sense of "May evil befall me" 88 **th' vantage** in addition, besides 89 **store** populate **played** gambled/had sex 91 **fall** succumb sexually **duties** marital and sexual duties 92 **our treasures into foreign laps** the semen that is due to us into other women's bodies 93 **peevish** senseless/perverse/willful 95 **scant** reduce/withhold **our former having** what we had before/our former financial means **despite** spite, malice 96 **have galls** are capable of feeling bitterness and resentment **grace** charm/virtue/mercy 97 **revenge** desire for revenge 101 **change** exchange **sport** entertainment/sex 102 **affection** desire, lust

	I think it doth. Is't frailty that thus errs?
	It is so too. and have not we affections?
105	Desires for sport? And frailty, as men have?
	Then let them use us well: else let them know,
	The ills we do, their ills instruct us so.

DESDEMONA Good night, good night: heaven me such uses send
    Not to pick bad from bad, but by bad mend!
Exeunt

Act V, scene 2

Enter OTHELLO and DESDEMONA in her bed
    OTHELLO It is the cause, it is the cause, my soul:
    Let me not name it to you, you chaste stars:
    It is the cause. Yet I'll not shed her blood,
    Nor scar that whiter skin of hers than snow,
5   And smooth as monumental alabaster:
    Yet she must die, else she'll betray more men.
    Put out the light, and then put out the light.
    If I quench thee, thou flaming minister,
    I can again thy former light restore,
10   Should I repent me: but once put out thy light,
    Thou cunning'st pattern of excelling nature,
    I know not where is that Promethean heat
    That can thy light relume. When I have plucked the rose,
    I cannot give it vital growth again:
15   It must needs wither. I'll smell it on the tree.
Kissing her
    O balmy breath, that dost almost persuade
    Justice to break her sword! One more, one more.
    Be thus when thou art dead, and I will kill thee
    And love thee after. One more, and this the last.
20   So sweet was ne'er so fatal. I must weep,
    But they are cruel tears: this sorrow's heavenly,
    It strikes where it doth love. She wakes.
DESDEMONA Who's there? Othello?
OTHELLO Ay. Desdemona.
25 *DESDEMONA* Will you come to bed, my lord?
OTHELLO Have you prayed tonight, Desdemona?
DESDEMONA Ay, my lord.
OTHELLO If you bethink yourself of any crime

---

106 **use** treat/employ sexually   108 **uses** habits (of thought)   109 **Not ... mend** not to learn bad habits from the bad behaviour of others, but to learn from such example to improve myself   5.2 1 **cause** offense/reason for action   8 **flaming minister** i. e. the torch or candle   **minister** servant   11 **cunning'st pattern** most skillfully made model   12 **Promethean** Prometheus was a Titan in Greek mythology who created mankind and stole fire from heaven for their use   13 **relume** relight   14 **vital** living   17 **Justice** traditionally depicted as a blindfolded woman carrying scales and a sword   20 **fatal** destructive/doomed   22 **strikes** delivers a blow/withers   27 **Ay** yes

            Unreconciled as yet to heaven and grace,
30   Solicit for it straight.
     DESDEMONA   Alas, my lord, what do you mean by that?
     OTHELLO   Well, do it, and be brief: I will walk by.
        I would not kill thy unprepared spirit,
        No, heaven forfend! I would not kill thy soul.
35   DESDEMONA   Talk you of killing?
     OTHELLO   Ay, I do.
     DESDEMONA   Then heaven have mercy on me!
     OTHELLO   Amen, with all my heart!
     DESDEMONA   If you say so, I hope you will not kill me.
40   OTHELLO   Hum!
     DESDEMONA   And yet I fear you; for you are fatal then
        When your eyes roll so: why I should fear I know not,
        Since guiltiness I know not, but yet I feel I fear.
     OTHELLO   Think on thy sins.
45   DESDEMONA   They are loves I bear to you.
     OTHELLO   Ay, and for that thou diest.
     DESDEMONA   That death's unnatural that kills for loving.
        Alas, why gnaw you so your nether lip?
        Some bloody passion shakes your very frame:
50   These are portents; but yet I hope, I hope,
        They do not point on me.
     OTHELLO   Peace, and be still!
     DESDEMONA   I will so. What's the matter?
     OTHELLO   That handkerchief which I so loved and gave thee
55   Thou gav'st to Cassio.
     DESDEMONA   No, by my life and soul!
        Send for the man, and ask him.
     OTHELLO   Sweet soul, take heed, take heed of perjury:
        Thou art on thy deathbed.
60   DESDEMONA   Ay, but not yet to die.
     OTHELLO   Presently:
        Therefore confess thee freely of thy sin,
        For to deny each article with oath
        Cannot remove nor choke the strong conception
65   That I do groan withal. Thou art to die.
     DESDEMONA   Then Lord have mercy on me!
     OTHELLO   I say, amen.
     DESDEMONA   And have you mercy too! I never did
        Offend you in my life, never loved Cassio
70   But with such general warranty of heaven
        As I might love: I never gave him token.

---

30 **Solicit** beg forgiveness   34 **forfend** forbid   61 **Presently** imminently   63 **article** item forming part of an accusation   64 **conception** belief/plan   65 **do groan withal** suffer with/am in labour with (play on the sense of pregnancy)   69 **Offend** sin against, commit a crime against   70 **warranty** authorization

OTHELLO By heaven, I saw my handkerchief in's hand.
O perjured woman, thou dost stone my heart,
And makest me call what I intend to do
75 A murder, which I thought a sacrifice:
I saw the handkerchief.
DESDEMONA He found it then:
I never gave it him. Send for him hither,
Let him confess a truth.
80 OTHELLO He hath confessed.
DESDEMONA What, my lord?
OTHELLO That he hath used thee.
DESDEMONA How? Unlawfully?
OTHELLO Ay.
85 DESDEMONA He will not say so.
OTHELLO No, his mouth is stopped:
Honest Iago hath ta'en order for 't.
DESDEMONA O, my fear interprets! What, is he dead?
OTHELLO Had all his hairs been lives, my great revenge
90 Had stomach for them all.
DESDEMONA Alas, he is betrayed and I undone!
OTHELLO Out, strumpet! Weep'st thou for him to my face?
DESDEMONA O, banish me, my lord, but kill me not!
OTHELLO Down, strumpet!
95 DESDEMONA Kill me to-morrow, let me live tonight!
OTHELLO Nay, if you strive—
DESDEMONA But half an hour!
OTHELLO Being done, there is no pause.
DESDEMONA But while I say one prayer!
100 OTHELLO It is too late.
He stifles her
EMILIA [*Within*] My lord, my lord! What, ho! my lord, my lord!
OTHELLO What noise is this? Not dead? Not yet quite dead?
I that am cruel am yet merciful:
I would not have thee linger in thy pain: so, so.
105 EMILIA [*Within*] What, ho! My lord, my lord!
OTHELLO Who's there?
EMILIA [*Within*] O, good my lord, I would speak a word with you!
OTHELLO Yes. — 'tis Emilia. — By and by. — She's dead.
'Tis like she comes to speak of Cassio's death. —
110 The noise was high. Ha, no more moving?
Still as the grave. Shall she come in? Were't good? —

---

73 **perjured** forsworn **stone** harden, turn to stone 82 **used** had sex with (Desdemona responds to a more general sense of "employed") 87 **ta'en order** made arrangements 90 **stomach** appetite 92 **strumpet** prostitute with emphasis on her fickleness 96 **strive** struggle 98 **Being done** i.e. as I am resolved to do the deed/while it is being done **is no pause** must be no hesitation 108 **By and by** in a moment 109 **like** likely 110 **noise** i.e. following the attack on Cassio **high** loud

                I think she stirs again. No. What's best to do?
                If she come in, she'll sure speak to my wife:
                My wife, my wife! What wife? I have no wife.
115   O insupportable! O heavy hour!
                Methinks it should be now a huge eclipse
                Of sun and moon, and that the affrighted globe
                Should yawn at alteration.
                EMILIA [*Within*] I do beseech you
120   That I may speak with you, O, good my lord!
                OTHELLO   I had forgot thee. —O, come in, Emilia. —
                Soft, by and by: let me the curtains draw. — *Unlocks the door*
                Where art thou? What's the matter with thee now?
                Enter EMILIA
                EMILIA   O, my good lord, yonder's foul murders done!
125   OTHELLO   What? Now?
                EMILIA   But now, my lord.
                OTHELLO   It is the very error of the moon:
                She comes more nearer earth than she was wont,
                And makes men mad.
130   EMILIA   Cassio, my lord, hath killed a young Venetian
                Called Roderigo.
                OTHELLO   Roderigo killed! And Cassio killed!
                EMILIA   No, Cassio is not killed.
                OTHELLO   Not Cassio killed! Then murder's out of tune,
135   And sweet revenge grows harsh.
                DESDEMONA   O, falsely, falsely murdered!
                EMILIA   Alas! What cry is that?
                OTHELLO   That? What?
                EMILIA   Out, and alas! That was my lady's voice.
140   Help! help, ho, help! O lady, speak again!
                Sweet Desdemona! O sweet mistress, speak!
                DESDEMONA   A guiltless death I die.
                EMILIA   O, who hath done this deed?
                DESDEMONA   Nobody; I myself. Farewell!
145   Commend me to my kind lord. O, farewell!
                Dies

Questions for Comprehension and Reflection
Act IV, scene 3
1. How does the willow song foretell what is to come?
2. What is Emilia's attitude towards women's "abusing" their husbands?
3. How much does Desdemona agree with Emilia's attitude?

---

118 **yawn at alteration** gape open at this great change in nature   122 **Soft** wait a moment   127 **error** roaming, wandering off course/mistake   128 **wont** accustomed   135 **harsh** jarring, discordant   136 **falsely** wrongfully, unjustly   139 **Out, and alas**! i.e. alas (**out** is an intensifier)

Act V, scene 2
1. What is the "cause"?
2. Is Othello fully resolved to kill Desdemona?
3. Why does Desdemona inspire our pity?

IV SHAKESPEAREAN RELEVANCE

A. Shakespeare in Everyday English
Please try to understand the following Shakespearean words and expressions in the contexts designated within parentheses and give their generally used meanings in the space provided.
1. wear one's heart (up) on one's sleeve (1.1.66): _____
2. out-tongue (1.2.21): _____
3. posthaste (1.2.41): _____
4. between the sheets (1.3.376): _____
5. green-eyed monster (3.3.188): _____
6. pomp and circumstance (3.3.392): _____

B. Shakespeare in Literature
Read the following literary excerpts, locate the Shakespearean allusions and explain their meanings according to the contexts where they appear.
1. Politicians who peddle their sincerity between whiles become transparent liars. Men who trade on integrity turn Iagos. (Peter Preston, *The Guardian*, 1995)
2. "Who was Iago?" Jack grinned. "You didn't come here to ask me that! You're quite right, but I'd still like to know." "He's a character from Othello. A Machiavelli who manipulated people's emotions in order to destroy them!" (Minette Walters, *The Scold's Bridle*, 1994)
3. As we got out of the car I warned Vico not to talk in the Stairwell. "We don't want the dogs to hear me and wake Mr. Contreras!" "He is a malevolent neighbor? You need me perhaps to guard you?" "He's the best-natured neighbor in the world. Unfortunately, he sees his role in my life as Cerberus, with a whiff of Othello thrown in!" (Sara Paretsky, *V. I. for Short*, 1995)
4. But it is when jealousy turns into pathological jealousy, or the Othello syndrome as it is now called, that problems begin to surface and treatment becomes necessary. (*The Independent*, 1998)

C. Shakespeare in Music, Art and on Screen
1833: *Othello*, the first time Othello was played a black actress on the London stage by Ira Aldridge.
1887: *Otello*, a four-act opera, composed by Giuseppe Verdi to an Italian libretto by Arrigo Boito.
1952: *Othello*, a film adaptation directed by and starring Orson Welles as Othello.
1965: *Othello*, a film adaptation directed by Stuart Burge, starring Laurence Olivier.
1986: *Othello*, a film version of Verdi's opera, directed by Franco Zeffirelli, starring Placido Domingo as Othello.
1995: *Othello*, a film adaptation, directed by Oliver Parker and starring Laurence Fishburne as Othello, Irene Jacob as Desdemona, and Kenneth Branagh as Iago, the first ever cinematic

reproduction of the play that casts a coloured actor to play the role of Othello.

V SHAKESPEARE QUOTES

But that I love the gentle Desdemona,
I would not my unhousèd free condition
Put into circumscritption and confine
For the sea's worth. (1.2.27-30)
When remedies are past, the griefs are ended
By seeing the worst, which late on hopes depended.
To mourn a mischief that is past and gone
Is the next way to draw new mischief on.
What cannot be preserved when fortune takes,
Patience her injury a mock'ry makes.
The robbed that smiles steals something from the thief:
He robs himself that spends a bootless grief. (1.3.218-225)
Our bodies are our gardens, to the which our wills are gardeners. (1.3.333-334)
Put money in thy purse. (1.3.346)
He hath achieved a maid
That paragons description and wild fame,
One that excels the quirks of blazoning pens,
And in th' essential vesture of creation
Does tire the engineer. (2.1.67-71)
Reputation is an idle and most false imposition: often got without merit and
lost without deserving. (2.3.252-253)
He that is robbed, not wanting what is stol'n,
Let him not know't and he's not robbed at all. (3.3.380-381)

17. The Tragedy of Antony and Cleopatra
安东尼与克莉奥佩特拉

I INTRODUCTION

　　《安东尼与克莉奥佩特拉》是莎士比亚最华丽的悲剧。该剧时间跨度十多年,涉及整个地中海世界,在其恢宏的历史经纬间具化了爱神维纳斯与战神马尔斯的神话邂逅及冲突。它围绕着一系列彼此对立体建构、铺陈:男性与女性、欲望与责任、床笫与战场、迟暮与青春,特别是埃及与罗马。"嘿,咱们主帅这样迷恋,真太不成话啦。"——戏剧的开始便是罗马士兵对其统帅安东尼拜倒在埃及女王裙下的微词。在罗马人看来,拥有显赫名声且权倾朝野的三巨头之一竟耽溺如此,一定是老朽昏聩所致。而在埃及人的价值观中,欲望力量巨大,足可超越狭隘的部族政治。安东尼挣扎在这两个迥异的世界之间,他一会儿吻着克莉奥佩特拉,信誓旦旦:"生命的光荣存在于一双心心相印的情侣的及时互爱和热烈拥抱之中",但很快又是义断情绝:"我必须挣断这副坚强的埃及镣铐,否则我将在沉迷中丧失自我了。"克莉奥佩特拉则是个演技高超的尤物,可以瞬间性情更变,使陪侍之人对其真正意图莫衷一是。但她又是莎士比亚悲剧中唯一一个在智慧方面可比肩《皆大欢喜》中的罗瑟琳和《威尼斯商人》中的鲍西娅的人物。一般认为,罗马将军与埃及艳后的感情纠葛是政治上的各取所需:安东尼为的是可以资助其东方征战的埃及财富,而克莉奥佩特拉则需要借助安东尼的罗马军团来重振自己的托勒密王朝。不管动机如何,这对情人在安东尼与屋大维的阿克兴海战和随后的陆战败北之后相继自杀。悲剧业已酿成,但各种原因仍扑朔迷离:安东尼的自杀是因为对克莉奥佩特拉的爱还是自己的屈辱? 克莉奥佩特拉的自我献祭是出于对安东尼的爱还是自身的傲骨? 如果自信能够在情场上俘获屋大维,她还会想到自杀吗? 对于莎士比亚作品中人物的理解都不是那么黑白分明的,这也是正是莎剧的魅力所在。

II PLOT SUMMARY

　　Mark Antony, Lepidus and Octavius Caesar are the triumvirs, the three-men team, who have divided the Roman world after their victory at Philippi over Cassius and Brutus, the assassins of Julius Caesar. Antony, who is the eastern commander, has become so devoted to **Cleopatra**,[1] the Queen of Egypt, that he is neglecting his duties and his wife in Rome. That's why his follower Philo laments, "this dotage of our general's/O'erflows the measure" (1.1.1-2) and "The triple pillar of the world transformed/Into a strumpet's fool." (1.1.12-13) When he realises from the rebellion of his wife, **Fulvia**,[2] and his brother against Caesar, how much danger and resentment

---

[1] **Cleopatra** /ˌklɪəˈpætrə/ 克莉奥佩特拉　[2] **Fulvia** /ˈfulviə/ 富尔维娅

Antony and Cleopatra, 1883, Sir Laurence Alma-Tadema

his prolonged stay in **Alexandria**³ has caused, he decides that he must leave Cleopatra: "These strong Egyptian fetters I must break,/Or lose myself in dotage." (1.2.110-111) Then he is informed that his wife Fulvia is dead but is comforted by **Enobarbus**⁴ that "This grief is crowned with consolation: your old/smock brings forth a new petticoat." (1.2.155-156) Learning of Fulvia's death, Cleopatra retorts, "Now I see, I see,/In Fulvia's death, how mine received shall be." (1.3.75-76) But she gives him her best wishes, "Upon your sword/Sit laurel victory, and smooth success/be strewed before your feet." (1.3.118-120)

In Rome, Caesar complains to Lepidus that Antony in Alexandria "fishes, drinks and wastes/The lamps of night in revel" (1.4.4-5) and has become "A man who is th' abstract of all faults/That all men follow." (1.4.9-10) But when informed that Pompey's navy and pirates are roaming the seas, he wishes the once-brave Antony back in Rome. After a cheerless meeting with Caesar and Lepidus, Antony agrees, in an effort to keep the alliance together, to marry Octavia, Caesar's sister. Sextus, the younger son of Pompey the Great, emboldened by Antony's absence in Egypt, has become so popular and powerful at sea that the reunited triumvirs arrange to meet him at Misenum, north of Rome.

Back in Egypt the news brought to the impatient Cleopatra of Antony's remarriage enrages her, and she demands to hear the fullest description of Octavia's attractions. From the frightened messenger's words, she is comforted to think her rival is "dull of tongue and dwarfish" (3.3.23) and "shows a body rather than a life,/A statue than a **breather**."⁵ (3.3.28-29)

In Caesar's house, the soothsayer warns Antony that his guardian angel, though noble, always feels overcome in the presence of Caesar, and so tells him to leave Rome. Antony admits that he must return to Egypt because, although he has made the marriage for his peace, his pleasure lies back in the East with Cleopatra.

After the banquet given on board Pompey's ship to celebrate their treaty, while Lepidus is carried off drunk, Caesar coolly retires early, leaving Antony and Pompey, now reconciled, to finish their drinking ashore.

However, not long after Antony has gone eastwards to Athens with Octavia, news comes that Caesar has broken the treaty and has first used Lepidus to help him to defeat Pompey, then treacherously imprisoned him. So Antony understands that the world is now divided between him and Caesar, who is becoming so powerful that Octavia goes to Rome to make peace between them, while he speeds back to Cleopatra. To convince the queen of his good faith he bestows upon her and her children the eastern kingdoms of the Roman Empire, in an elaborate public ceremony.

For Caesar, this, with the unannounced arrival in Rome of Octavia, is the final outrage. He informs his "most wronged sister" that her husband Antony has "given his empire /Up to a whore." Although he agrees to give Antony half his new acquisitions, he demands the same in return, knowing that this will never be granted, and that war must inevitably follow.

At **Actium**⁶ in northern Greece, with war imminent, Enobarbus, Anton's chief lieutenant, urges Cleopatra not to join Antony in the wars, arguing that her presence will be a distractor: "If we should serve with horse and mares together,/The horse were merely lost. The mares would

---

3 **Alexandria** /ˌælɪgˈzɑːndriə/ 亚历山大里亚 4 **Enobarbus** /ˌɪnəˈbɑːbəs/ 埃诺巴布斯 5 **breather** living creature
6 **Actium** /ˈæktɪəm/ 阿克兴

bear/A soldier and his horse." (3. 7. 9-11) In the ensuing sea battle, Caesar is victorious, because Antony, against all the warnings of Enobarbus and his generals, agrees with Cleopatra to fight at sea, and then, when she flees during the battle, follows her to Egypt. This is the beginning of the end for the lovers. Antony is disgusted with himself and with the queen, and is so unable to bear the thought of defeat by the young, despised Caesar that he contemplates suicide. Yet her apologies for her "fearful sails" (3. 11. 58) and his restraint bring about reconciliation, and to Caesar, arriving in Egypt with his army, he sends for peace terms.

The Battle of Actium, 1672, Lorenzo A. Castro

Caesar, however, replies that he will listen only to the queen, if she will send Antony away or kill him. This stings Antony into challenging him to fight alone, "sword against sword." Disregarding this challenge, Caesar sends Thidias with instructions to win Cleopatra from Antony, because he wants her for his triumph in Rome.

Antony, feeling authority melting from him, suspects Cleopatra of flirting, and perhaps betraying him, so has Thidias flogged, while fiercely attacking the queen for her behaviour.

Accepting her passionate excuses, he again relents and decides that he will fight Caesar, who has now reached the gates of Alexandria. Enobarbus, who has made up his mind to desert, is distressed, as is the queen, when Antony in thanking his servants for their devotion asks for their best service at the feast they are preparing, as though it would be his last. And, indeed, the soldiers on night watch at the palace, hearing a strange music, take it as a bad omen that the god Hercules whom Antony loved is now abandoning him.

The next day Cleopatra lovingly helps Eros to arm Antony, who hears, just before the battle, that Enobarbus has gone over to Caesar, sends all his treasure after him. Antony wins the first round and returns overjoyed for what, now, will really be his last night's celebration with Cleopatra. In Caesar's camp, Enobarbus, ashamed of his treachery, dies with Antony's name on his lips.

The following morning, on seeing the queen's navy surrendering to the enemy, Antony turns upon her furiously by calling her "**triple-turned whore**."[7] (4. 12. 15) For fear of her dear life, Cleopatra takes refuge with her ladies in her unfinished tomb, and sends him a message that she has killed herself. On being told this, Antony, who is already in a suicidal mood, immediately commands Eros to kill him. Eros stabs himself instead, and Antony falls on his own sword. But, humiliated by finding that he is only wounded, and that no one else will finish him off, he asks Diomedes to take him, uncomplaining, to the still living Cleopatra.

The dying hero is hoisted in through the window, and after a final cup of wine and kisses, he welcomes death, in the queen's arms. Desolate, she resolves to follow him:

The Death of Cleopatra, 1892, Reginald Arthur

---

7 **triple-turned whore** alluding to Cleopatra's three affairs with Julius Caesar, Gneius Pompey and Antony

"Shall I abide/In this dull world, which in thy absence is/No better than a **sty**?".[8] (4. 15. 69-71) Caesar, on news of Antony's death, speaks highly of him but sends Proculeius to encourage Cleopatra not to kill herself.

This he does, having by trickery entered the "monument" and captured the queen. Caesar then visits her but she, mistrustful, outwits him and goes ahead with her preparations to join Antony. Dressed once more in all her regalia, she takes the snake from a basket of figs, brought to her, as planned, by a countryman, and dies of poison. Caesar accepts his defeat by the lovers, and orders that Cleopatra shall be buried with Antony, with all the solemnity of a state funeral.

Beyond the Play: *Shakespeare—a Plagiarist*!

Arkins, B., *What Shakespeare Stole from Rome*, 2012

The American-British Nobel laureate in literature, T.S. Eliot once said, "Bad poets borrow, good poets steal." In this sense, Shakespeare was the prince of thieves. Taking advantage of world literature, from epics of the Greeks and the Romans to contemporary prose romances, he liberally helped himself to whatever he liked and made use of it in fashioning his plots. Sir Thomas North's 1579 English translation of Plutarch's *Lives of the Noble Grecians and Romans* was the main source for Shakespeare's Roman plays: *Julius Caesar*, *Coriolanus* and *Antony and Cleopatra*. In *Antony and Cleopatra*, Shakespeare stays close to Plutarch, but takes liberties with events and historical events. As with other plays, he paraphrased parts of Thomas North's translation *and* occasionally quoted from them verbatim, but with the golden touch of a literary genius. Just compare the following North's translation and Shakespeare's version (see II. Selected Readings: Act II, scene 2): *[She would] take her barge in the river Cydnus, the poop where of was of gold, the sails of purple, and the oars of silver, which kept stroke in rowing after the sound of the music of flutes, hautboys, citherns, viols, and such other instruments s they played upon the barge. And now for the person of her selfe: she was laid under a pavilion of cloth of gold of tissue, appareled and attired like the goddess of Venus, commonly drawn in picture; and hard by her, on either hand of her, pretty fair boys appareled as painters do set forth god Cupide, with little fans in their hands, with the which they fanned wind upon her. Her ladies and gentlemen also, the fairest of them were appareled like the nymphs.*

III SELECTED READINGS

Act I, scene 3
    Enter CLEOPATRA, CHARMIAN, IRAS, and ALEXAS
    CLEOPATRA   Where is he?

---

8 **sty** pigsty/place inhabited by whores and lustful people

CHARMIAN I did not see him since.
CLEOPATRA See where he is, who's with him, what he does.
   I did not send you: if you find him sad,
5 Say I am dancing; if in mirth, report
   That I am sudden sick. Quick, and return.
Exit ALEXAS
CHARMIAN Madam, methinks, if you did love him dearly,
   You do not hold the method to enforce
   The like from him.
10 CLEOPATRA What should I do I do not?
CHARMIAN In each thing give him way: cross him nothing.
CLEOPATRA Thou teachest like a fool, the way to lose him.
CHARMIAN Tempt him not so too far. I wish, forbear:
   In time we hate that which we often fear.
15 But here comes Antony.
Enter ANTONY
CLEOPATRA I am sick and sullen.
ANTONY I am sorry to give breathing to my purpose—
CLEOPATRA Help me away, dear Charmian! I shall fall.
   It cannot be thus long: the sides of nature
20 Will not sustain it.
ANTONY Now, my dearest queen—
CLEOPATRA Pray you stand further from me.
ANTONY What's the matter?
CLEOPATRA I know by that same eye there's some good news.
25 What, says the married woman you may go?
   Would she had never given you leave to come.
   Let her not say 'tis I that keep you here.
   I have no power upon you: hers you are.
ANTONY The gods best know—
30 CLEOPATRA O, never was there queen
   So mightily betrayed! Yet at the first
   I saw the treasons planted.
ANTONY Cleopatra—
CLEOPATRA Why should I think you can be mine and true—
35 Though you in swearing shake the thronèd gods,
   Who have been false to Fulvia? Riotous madness,
   To be entangled with those mouth-made vows
   Which break themselves in swearing!
ANTONY Most sweet queen—
40 CLEOPATRA Nay, pray you, seek no colour for your going,

1.3 2 **did not see him since** have not seen him recently 4 **I ... you** do not say I sent you **sad** serious/sorrowful 8 **hold** follow, adopt 9 **like** same 11 **give him away** let him have his own way **cross** thwart, obstruct 13 **Tempt** provoke/test **forbear** (you would) desist 16 **sullen** serious/melancholy 17 **give breathing to** utter, announce 19-20 **thus long** so long (before I die) **the ... it** my constitution won't survive the strain **sides** frame, body 22 **stand ... me** i.e. give me air 24 **eye** look in your eye 25 **the married woman** i.e. Fulvia 31 **at the first** from the beginning 35 **thronèd** enthroned (on Mount Olympus) 36 **false** unfaithful **Riotous madness** unrestrained, wanton folly (on my part) 37 **mouth-made** i.e. insincere, not from the heart 38 **break themselves in swearing** are broken as soon as they are spoken 40 **colour** pretext, pretence

	But bid farewell, and go: when you sued staying,
	Then was the time for words: no going then.
	Eternity was in our lips and eyes,
	Bliss in our brows' bent: none our parts so poor
45	But was a race of heaven. They are so still,
	Or thou, the greatest soldier of the world,
	Art turned the greatest liar.
	ANTONY How now, lady!
	CLEOPATRA I would I had thy inches: thou shouldst know
50	There were a heart in Egypt.
	ANTONY Hear me, queen:
	The strong necessity of time commands
	Our services awhile, but my full heart
	Remains in use with you. Our Italy
55	Shines o'er with civil swords; Sextus Pompeius
	Makes his approaches to the port of Rome.
	Equality of two domestic powers
	Breed scrupulous faction: the hated, grown to strength,
	Are newly grown to love: the condemned Pompey,
60	Rich in his father's honour, creeps apace
	Into the hearts of such as have not thrived
	Upon the present state, whose numbers threaten,
	And quietness, grown sick of rest, would purge
	By any desperate change. My more particular,
65	And that which most with you should safe my going,
	Is Fulvia's death.
	CLEOPATRA Though age from folly could not give me freedom,
	It does from childishness. Can Fulvia die?
	ANTONY She's dead, my queen.
70	Look here, and at thy sovereign leisure read
	The garboils she awaked: at the last, best,
	See when and where she died.
	CLEOPATRA O most false love!
	Where be the sacred vials thou shouldst fill
75	With sorrowful water? Now I see, I see,
	In Fulvia's death how mine received shall be.
	ANTONY Quarrel no more, but be prepared to know

---

41 **sued staying** begged to stay   43 **our** my (Cleopatra uses the royal plural as she reminds Antony of his former praises of her)   44 **brows' bent** arched eyebrows   **none our parts** not one of my feature (was)   45 **a race of heaven** a child of heaven/inherently divine   48 **How now** exclamation of reproach   49 **inches** height/manly strength (with phallic connotations)   50 **heart** courage, resolution   **Egypt** Cleopatra/the country   54 **in use** as (financial) security/in trust (legal term)/for your use (with connotations of sexual employment)   55 **civil swords** swords drawn in civil war   56 **port** city gate/harbour   57-59 **Equality ... faction** having an equal division of power in the state (between Octavius Caesar and Lepidus) produces factional squabbles over small details   **hated ... love** those who were hated, having grown strong, are now loved   59 **the condemned Pompey** Sextus Pompeius by the Senate for being a threat to peace   60 **apace** rapidly   62 **Upon ... state** under the present government   63 **purge** cleanse, purify itself through purgation (bloodletting)   64 **particular** personal concern   65 **safe** make safe   71 **garboils** brawls, disturbances   **best** best of all (or possibly, referring to Fulvia, 'when showed herself to be at her best')   74 **sacred vials** lachrymatory bottles; small vessels placed in Roman graves and thought to have contained mourners' tears   75 **water** tears   76 **how mine received shall be** how my death will be received by you   77 **know** learn

	The purposes I bear, which are, or cease,
	As you shall give th' advice. By the fire
80	That quickens Nilus' slime, I go from hence
	Thy soldier, servant, making peace or war
	As thou affects.
	CLEOPATRA Cut my lace, Charmian, come!
	But let it be: I am quickly ill, and well,
85	So Antony loves.
	ANTONY My precious queen, forbear,
	And give true evidence to his love, which stands
	An honourable trial.
	CLEOPATRA So Fulvia told me.
90	I prithee turn aside and weep for her,
	Then bid adieu to me, and say the tears
	Belong to Egypt. Good now, play one scene
	Of excellent dissembling, and let it look
	Life perfect honour.
95	ANTONY You'll heat my blood no more!
	CLEOPATRA You can do better yet, but this is meetly.
	MARK ANTONY Now, by my sword—
	CLEOPATRA And target. Still he mends,
	But this is not the best. Look, prithee, Charmian,
100	How this Herculean Roman does become
	The carriage of his chafe.
	ANTONY I'll leave you, lady.
	CLEOPATRA Courteous lord, one word:
	Sir, you and I must part, but that's not it:
105	Sir, you and I have loved, but there's not it:
	That you know well. Something it is I would:
	O, my oblivion is a very Antony,
	And I am all forgotten.
	MARK ANTONY But that your royalty
110	Holds idleness your subject, I should take you
	For idleness itself.
	CLEOPATRA 'Tis sweating labour
	To bear such idleness so near the heart
	As Cleopatra this. But, sir, forgive me,
115	Since my becomings kill me, when they do not

78 **The ... bear** my intentions   **are, or cease** stand or fall   79-80 **th' advice** the judgement   **fire ... slime** sun that brings fertility to the mudbanks of Egypt's River Nile   82 **thou affects** you desire   83 **lace** the ties of her bodice as she struggles for breath   84 **let it be** leave it alone   85 **So Antony loves** Antony loves in just such a changeable manner/depending on whether or not Antony loves me   86 **forbear** be patient/control yourself   87 **give true evidence** bear witness   **stands** will sustain
92 **Belong to Egypt** are shed for the Queen of Egypt   93 **dissembling** play-acting   95 **heat my blood** make me angry/passionate
96 **meetly** fairly good   98 **target** small shield; Cleopatra completes Antony's phrase and makes it into a blustering theatrical oath
mends improve (in his act)   100 **Herculean** heroic, prodigiously strong; Antony's family claimed descent from the Greek hero Hercules   101 **become ... chafe** carry off his anger convincingly   107 **oblivion** forgetfulness/loss, abandonment   108 **all forgiven** forgetful/completely forgotten   109 **But** were it not   110 **holds ... subject** considers frivolity beneath you/means that you are in control of frivolity   111 **idleness** foolishness/frivolity/triviality/worthlessness   112 **sweating labour** the language of childbirth, continued with **bear**   115 **becomings** attractive qualities

    Eye well to you. Your honour calls you hence:
    Therefore be deaf to my unpitied folly,
    And all the gods go with you! Upon your sword
    Sit laurel victory, and smooth success
120 Be strewed before your feet.
  ANTONY Let us go. Come:
    Our separation so abides and flies
    That thou, residing here, goest yet with me,
    And I, hence fleeting, here remain with thee.
125 Away!
  Exeunt

Act II, scene 2

  ENOBARBUS I will tell you.
    The barge she sat in, like a burnished throne,
    Burned on the water: the poop was beaten gold,
225 Purple the sails, and so perfumèd that
    The winds were lovesick with them: the oars were silver,
    Which to the tune of flutes kept stroke, and made
    The water which they beat to follow faster,
    As amorous of their strokes. For her own person,
230 It beggared all description: she did lie
    In her pavilion, cloth-of-gold of tissue,
    O'er-picturing that Venus where we see
    The fancy outwork nature: on each side her
    Stood pretty dimpled boys, like smiling Cupids,
235 With divers-coloured fans, whose wind did seem
    To glow the delicate cheeks which they did cool,
    And what they undid did.
  AGRIPPA O, rare for Antony!
  ENOBARBUS Her gentlewomen, like the Nereides,
240 So many mermaids, tended her i' th' eyes,
    And made their bends adornings. At the helm
    A seeming mermaid steers: the silken tackle
    Swell with the touches of those flower-soft hands
    That yarely frame the office. From the barge
245 A strange invisible perfume hits the sense
    Of the adjacent wharfs. The city cast

---

116 **Eye** look, seem 119-120 **laurel ... feet** on his return to Rome, a victorious general wore a laurel wreath, and had flowers and rushes strewn in his path 2.2 223 **barge** a long ornamental flat-bottomed boat used for pleasure or ceremony **burnished** shining, as if made of metal 224 **Burned** gleamed as though it were in flames **poop** highest deck at the stern or back of a ship 229 **strokes** beats of the oars/caresses/blows (eroticized violence) 231 **cloth-of-gold of tissue** rich cloth, woven with gold thread 232-233 **O'erpicturing ... nature** more beautiful than a painted image of Venus in which (the artist's) imagination has surpassed nature **her** of her 234 **like** resembling/in the guise of **Cupid** Roman god of love, son of Venus and Mercury; always depicted as a child 235 **divers-coloured** multicoloured 236 **glow** make glow (with amorous excitement) 238 **rare** splendid, magnificent 239 **gentlemen ... Nereides** female attendants resembling (or 'in the guise of') beautiful sea nymphs 240 **tended her i' th' eyes** attended to her every glance 241 **made ... adornings** made the scene more beautiful with their graceful bows 242 **tackle** gear, i.e. ropes and sails 243 **Swell** with connotation of penile erection 244 **yarely ... office** nimbly perform the task 246 **wharfs** riverbanks/buildings

Her people out upon her, and Antony,
Enthroned i' th' market-place, did sit alone,
Whistling to th' air, which, but for vacancy,
250   Had gone to gaze on Cleopatra too,
And made a gap in nature.
AGRIPPA   Rare Egyptian!

Questions for Understanding and Reflection
Act I, scene 3
1. What "colour" does Antony give for his going back to Rome?
2. Does Cleopatra say she is getting more clever as she is getting old?
3. What is that Antony is seeking by going back to Rome according to Cleopatra?

Act II, scene 2
1. What rhetorical device is employed to describe the perfumed sails and the speed of the barge?
2. How is Cleopatra's beauty described?
3. Why is such a famous description of female beauty in Western literature put into the mouth of the unromantic Enobarbus?

IV SHAKESPEAREAN RELEVANCE

A. Shakespeare in Everyday English
Please try to understand the following Shakespearean words and expressions in the contexts designated within parentheses and give their generally used meanings in the space provided.
1. scarce-beared (1.1.22): _____
2. salad days (1.5.86): _____
3. non-pareil (3.2.12): _____
4. in the public eye (3.6.12): _____

B. Shakespeare in Literature
Read the following literary excerpts, locate the Shakespearean allusions and explain their meanings according to the contexts where they appear.
1. In a word, all Cleopatra—fierce, voluptuous, passionate, tender... and full of ... rapturous enchantment. (Nathaniel Hawthorne, *The Marble Faun*, 1860)
2. Soon he would be overtaken; but warm in the circle of Leila's arms, as if he were Antony at Actium, he could hardly bring himself to feel fear. (Lawrence Durrell, *Mountolive*, 1958)
3. Passion is destructive. It destroyed Antony and Cleopatra, Tristan and Isolde. (W. Somerset Maugham, *The Razor's Edge*, 1944)
4. Sex has left the body and entered the imagination now; that is why Arnauti suffered so much with Justine, because she preyed upon all that he might have kept separate—his artist-hood if you like. He is when all is said and done a sort of minor Antony, and she a Cleo. You can read all about it in Shakespeare. (Laurence Durrell, *Justine*, 1957)
5. 'You could have telephoned.' 'I'm very sorry that I didn't.' As indeed he was, and he knew

---

249 **but for vacancy** except that it would have created a vacuum (something nature proverbially 'abhors')   250 **Had** would have   252 **Egyptian** potentially ambiguous since the word could be a synonym for 'gipsy', and both Egyptians and gipsies were associated with magic and witchcraft

he was going to go on being sorry. 'But you forgot me.' 'Not exactly forgot, Stella. And I have apologized.' 'And I have accepted it,' Stella said with dignity, with the air of one whom to do less would be beneath her. So might Cleopatra have spoken to Antony. (Gwendoline Butler, *The Coffin Tree*, 1994)

C. Shakespeare in Music, Art and on Screen

1963: *Cleopatra*, a film directed by Joseph and starring Elizabeth Taylor as Cleopatra and Richard Burton as Antony.
1973: *Antony and Cleopatra*, a film adaptation directed by and starring Charlton Heston as Antony and Hildegarde Neil as Cleopatra.
1974: *Antony and Cleopatra*, a TV drama directed by Trevor Nunn.
1981: *Antony and Cleopatra*, a TV drama directed by Jonathan Miller.

V SHAKESPEARE QUOTES

As it is a heartbreaking to see a handsome man loose-wived, so it is a deadly sorrow to behold a foul knave uncuckolded. (1.2.58-60)
The nature of bad news infects the teller. (1.2.85)
In time we hate that which we often fear. (1.3.14)
It hath been taught us from the primal state
That he which is was wished until he were,
And the ebbed man, ne'er loved till ne'er worth love,
Comes deared by being lacked. This common body,
Like to a vagabond flag upon the stream,
Goes to and back, lackeying the varying tide,
To rot itself with motion. (1.4.44-50)
O happy horse, to bear the weight of Antony! (1.5.26)
My salad days,
When I was green in judgment, cold in blood,
To say as I said then! (1.5.86-88)
Epicurean cooks
Sharpen with cloyless sauce his appetite. (2.1.29-30)
Age cannot wither her, nor custom stale
Her infinite variety. (2.2.271-272)
Give me my robe, put on my crown: I have
Immortal longings in me. (5.2.316-317)
Husband, I come!
Now to that name my courage prove my title!
I am fire and air: my other elements
I give to baser life. (5.2.323-326)

Bibliography

(1964). *Monarch Notes*. New York: Simon and Schuster.
(1965). *Cliffs Notes*. Lincoln, Nebraska: Cliffs Notes. Inc.
(1974). *The Riverside Shakespeare*. Boston: Houghton Mifflin Co.
(1976). *Brodie's Notes*. London: Pan Books.
(1982). *The Illustrated Stratford Shakespeare*. London: Chancellor.
(1982) *York Notes*. Essex, England: Longman Group Ltd.
(1994). *Complete Works of William Shakespeare*. Glasgow: HarperCollins Publishers.
Bate, J., etc. (eds.) (2008). *William Shakespeare Complete Works*. Beijing: Foreign Language Teaching and Research Press.
Bloom, H. (1994). *The Western Canon: The Books and School of the Ages*. Orlando, Florida: Harcourt Brace & Company.
Bunton-Downer, L. & A. Riding. (2009). *Essential Shakespeare Handbook*. Liu Hao (transl.). Beijing: Foreign Language Teaching and Research Press.
Esptein, N. (1990). *The Friendly Shakespeare*. New York: Penguin Group.
Griffs, R. T. & T. A. Joscelyne. (1985). *Longman Guide to Shakespeare Quotations*. Essex, England: Longman Group Ltd.
Noble, R. (1935). *Shakespeare's Biblical Knowledge and the Use of the Book of Common Prayer*. London: Society for Promoting Christian Biblical Knowledge.
Root, R. K. (1965). *Classical Mythology in Shakespeare*. New York: Gordian Press, Inc.
Shaheen, N. (1999). *Biblical References in Shakespeare's Plays*. Newark: University of Delaware Press.
Shewmaker, E. F. (1996/2008). *Shakespeare's Language: A Glossary of Unfamiliar Words in His Plays and Poems*. New York: Checkmark Books.
Wright, W. A. (ed.) (1936). *The Complete Works of William Shakespeare*. New York: Doubleday & Company, Inc.
Zesmer, D. M. (1976). *Guide to Shakespeare*. New York: Barnes & Noble Books.
黄兆杰,《莎士比亚戏剧精选一百段》,中国对外翻译出版公司、商务印书馆(香港)有限公司,1989。
朱生豪,《莎士比亚全集》(1-11)人民文学出版社,1978。
厦门大学外语系(编译),《英语成语词典》,商务印书馆,1980。
支荩忠,《第十二夜》(莎士比亚注释丛书),商务印书馆,1987。

Appendices

A List of Works of William Shakespeare

Comedies 喜剧
1. The Tempest 暴风雨①
2. The Two Gentlemen of Verona 维洛那二绅士
3. The Merry Wives of Windsor 温莎的风流娘儿们
4. Measure for Measure 一报还一报
5. The Comedy of Errors 错误的喜剧
6. Much Ado about Nothing 无事生非
7. Love's Labour's Lost 爱的徒劳
8. A Midsummer Night's Dream 仲夏夜之梦
9. The Merchant of Venice 威尼斯商人
10. As You Like It 皆大欢喜
11. The Taming of the Shrew 驯悍记
12. All's Well That Ends Well 终成眷属
13. Twelfth Night 第十二夜
14. The Winter's Tale 冬天的故事
15. Pericles, Prince of Tyre 泰尔亲王配力克里斯
16. The Two Noble Kinsmen 两个贵亲戚

Histories 历史剧
17. King John 约翰王
18. Richard Ⅱ 理查二世
19. Henry Ⅳ, Part 1 亨利四世上篇
20. Henry Ⅳ, Part 2 亨利四世下篇
21. Henry Ⅴ 亨利五世
22. Henry Ⅵ, Part 1 亨利六世上篇
23. Henry Ⅵ, Part 2 亨利六世中篇
24. Henry Ⅵ, Part 3 亨利六世下篇
25. Richard Ⅲ 理查三世
26. Henry Ⅷ 亨利八世

Tragedies 悲剧
27. Troilus and Cressida 特洛伊罗斯与克瑞西达
28. Coriolanus 科利奥兰纳斯
29. Titus Andronicus 泰特斯·安德洛尼克斯

---

① 剧名及引文汉译均据朱生豪(1978,人民文学出版社。)

30. The Tragedy of Romeo and Juliet 罗密欧与朱丽叶
31. Timon of Athens 雅典的泰门
32. The Tragedy of Julius Caesar 裘力斯·凯撒
33. The Tragedy of Macbeth 麦克白
34. The Tragedy of Hamlet 哈姆雷特
35. The Tragedy of King Lear 李尔王
36. The Tragedy of Othello 奥赛罗
37. The Tragedy of Antony and Cleopatra 安东尼与克莉奥佩特拉
38. Cymbeline 辛白林

A List of Works of Art and *Beyond the Play* Topics in this Book

Works of Art
1. *The Quarrel of Oberon and Titania*, 1850, Joseph Noel Paton   2
2. *Titania and Bottom*, 1793—1794, Johann Heinrich Füssli   3
3. *The Merchant of Venice*, a bas relief for Folger Shakespeare Library by John Gregory   10
4. *The Wrestling Scene from "As You Like it"*, 1855, Daniel Maclise   20
5. *The Seven Ages of Man*, 1838, William Mulready   22
6. *Christopher Sly*, 1867, William Quiller Orchardson   28
7. *The Shrew Katherina*, 1898, Edward Robert Hughes   29
8. *Olivia*, 1888, Edmund Blair Leighton   39
9. *Viola and the Countess*, 1859, Frederick Richard Pickersgill   39
10. *Malvolio and the Countess*, 1859, Daniel Maclise   40
11. *Miranda*, 1888, Frederick Goodall   48
12. *The Enchanted Island: Before the Cell of Prospero*, 1797, Henry Fuseli   48
13. *The Tempest*, Act V, Scene 1, c. 1795, Francis Wheatley   49
14. *The Tempest*, Act V, 1735, William Hogarth   50
15. *Falstaff with Big Wine Jar and Cup*, 1896, Edward Grützner   59
16. *Falstaff at the Boar's Head Tavern*, before 1909, Edward Grützner   60
17. The "Darnley Portrait" of Elizabeth I (ca. 1575)   61
18. *The Banishment of Falstaff*, 1846, Moritz Retzsch   69
19. Poster for *Falstaff* (*Chimes at Midnight*), 1966   70
20. *Bardolph*, 1853, Henry Stacy Marks   75
21. *Katherine Learns English from her Gentlewoman Alice*, 1888, Laura Alma-Tadema   75
22. Winston Churchill and his Famous V Sign in 1943 (photo)   76
23. Richard III (1452—1485)   84
24. *Richard, Duke of Gloucester, and the Lady Anne*, 1896, Edwin Austin Abbey   85
25. *The Princes in the Tower*, 1878, John Everett Millais   85
26. *David Garrick as Richard III*, 1745, William Hogarth   86
27. Laurence Olivier (1907—1989) as Richard III   86
28. Anthony Sher as Richard III   86
29. *Romeo and Juliet*, 1884, Frank Dicksee   95
30. *Romeo and Juliet with Friar Laurence*, 1792-96, William Bunbury   95

31. *A Monument Belonging to the Capulets*, 1789, James Northcote   96
32. *Romeo and Juliet*, 1936   96
33. *Romeo and Juliet*, 1968   96
34. *The Ides of March*, 1883, Edward John Poynter   104
35. *Death of Julius Caesar*, Vincenzo Camuccini (1773—1844)   105
36. *Brutus and the Ghost of Caesar*, 1802, Richard Westall   105
37. Assassination of President Lincoln   106
38. *Macbeth*, 1768, Johann Zoffany   116
39. *The Three Witches*, after 1783, Henry Fuseli   117
40. Astor Place Opera-House riots   118
41. *The Play Scene in "Hamlet"*, Daniel Maclise (1806—1870)   127
42. *Ophelia*, 1851—1852, John Everett Millais   128
43. Laurence Olivier's *Hamlet*, 1948   128
44. "Two Beer Or Not Two Beer"   129
45. *Prince Charles*, 1981, Mark Boxer   129
46. *Cordelia's Portion*, 1843—1844, Ford Madox   138
47. *King Lear and the Fool in the Storm*, 1851, William Dyce   139
48. *Lear and Cordelia*, 1874, Marcus Stone   139
49. *King Lear Weeping over the Dead Body of Cordelia*, 1786-88, James Barry   140
50. Advertisement for 1819 edition of *The Family Shakespeare*   141
51. *Desdemona*, ca. 1888, Frederic Leighton   147
52. *Desdemona's Death Song*, Dante Gabriel Rossetti (1828—1882)   148
53. *Othello with Desdemona in Bed Asleep*, 1859, Christian Köhler   149
54. Paul Robeson with Uta Hagen in the Theatre Guild production of *Othello* (1943—1944)   150
55. *Antony and Cleopatra*, 1883, Sir Laurence Alma-Tadema   160
56. *The Battle of Actium*, 1672, Lorenzo A. Castro   161
57. *The Death of Cleopatra*, 1892, Reginald Arthur   161
58. Arkins, B., *What Shakespeare Stole from Rome*, 2012   162

Beyond the Play Topics
1. Mendelssohn's "Wedding March"   3
2. Anti-Semitism in Shakespeare's Time   11
3. Unraveling the Bard's Comedies: The Green World Structure   21
4. Husband and Wife On and Off Screen   30
5. Twelfth Night   41
6. "Our Revels Now Are Ended"   51
7. Whose History Is It?   61
8. Falstaff—a "Misleader of Youth"?   70

9. English Patriotism and the V Sign   76
10. The Real Richard III   86
11. "[S]he is not Fourteen."   96
12. Tidbits about *Julius Caesar*   106
13. The Curse of "the Scottish Play"   118
14. *Hamlet*, the Most Quoted Play   129
15. No-Holds Bard   140
16. Should Othello Be Black?   149
17. Shakespeare—a Plagiarist!   162

A Partial List of Phrases and Sayings Attributed to William Shakespeare

Age cannot wither her, nor custom stale her infinite variety. (*Antony and Cleopatra*, 2.2. 271-272) 年龄无法使她枯萎,习俗也不能减损她的千姿百态。
ENOBARBUS
  Never! He will not.
  Age cannot wither her, nor custom stale
  Her infinite variety: other women cloy
  The appetites they feed, but she makes hungry
  Where most she satisfies. For vilest things
  Become themselves in her, that the holy priests
  Bless her when she is riggish.

Alas, poor Yorick! I knew him, Horatio. (*Hamlet*, 5.1.141) 生命是脆弱的。
E.g. Alas, poor iPod! We knew him, Horatio: A lament for Apple's music player. (http://www.imore.com/alas-poor-ipod-we-knew-him-horatio-lament-apples-music-player? utm_source = tuicool)

All corners of the world (*Cymbeline*, 3.4.35)/**four corners of the earth, The** (*The Merchant of Venice*, 2.7.39)/ **three corners of the world, The** (*King John*, 5.7.120) 世界各地。
  PISANIO (*Cymbeline*, 3.4.35)
    What shall I need to draw my sword? The paper
    Hath cut her throat already. No, 'tis slander,
    Whose edge is sharper than the sword, whose tongue
    Outvenoms all the worms of Nile, whose breath
    Rides on the posting winds, and doth belie
    All corners of the world. Kings, queens and states,
    Maids, matrons, nay, the secrets of the grave
    This viperous slander enters.

All's well that ends well. (*All's Well That Ends Well*, 4.4.39)　结果好一切都好。
ELENA
　　Yet, I pray you:
　　But with the word the time will bring on summer,
　　When briers shall have leaves as well as thorns,
　　And be as sweet as sharp. We must away.
　　Our wagon is prepared, and time revives us:
　　All's well that ends well, still the fine's the crown;
　　Whate'er the course, the end is the renown.

All that glitters is not gold. (*The Merchant of Venice*, 2.7.66) 闪光的未必都是金子;金玉其外败絮其中。
MOROCCO
　　O hell! What have we here?
　　A carrion Death, within whose empty eye
　　There is a written scroll; I'll read the writing.
　　'All that glitters is not gold,
　　Often have you heard that told:
　　Many a man his life hath sold
　　But my outside to behold.
　　Gilded tombs do worms enfold.
　　Had you been as wise as bold,
　　Young in limbs, in judgment old,
　　Your answer had not been inscrolled:
　　Fare you well; your suit is cold.'
　　Cold, indeed, and labour lost.
　　Then farewell, heat, and welcome, frost!
　　Portia, adieu. I have too grieved a heart
　　To take a tedious leave. Thus losers part.

All one to me (*Troilus and Cressida*, 1.1.69) 对我来说都一样;怎么都行。
PANDARUS
　　Because she's kin to me, therefore she's not so fair as Helen: an she were
　　not kin to me, she would be as fair on Friday as Helen is on Sunday. But what
　　care I? I care not an she were a black-a-moor: 'tis all one to me.
E. g. It's all one to him whether he wins this match or not: he has already been
　　qualified for the next round.

All the world's a stage, and all the men and women merely players. (*As You Like It*, 2.7. 142-143) 整个世界是个舞台,所有的男人和女人只不过是演员。

An ill-favoured thing sir, but mine own (*As You Like It*, 5.4.49-50) 虽差强人意,但我也只能做到这个程度。
TOUCHSTONE
　　God 'ild you, sir, I desire you of the like. I press in here, sir, amongst the
　　rest of the country copulatives, to swear and to forswear, according as
　　marriage binds and blood breaks. A poor virgin, sir, an ill-favoured thing, sir,
　　but mine own, a poor humour of mine, sir, to take that that no man else will.

Rich honesty dwells like a miser, sir, in a poor house, as your pearl in your foul oyster.

apple of her eye, the (*Love's Labour's Lost*, 5.2.502) 被视作宝贝的人。
BEROWNE [*To BOYET*]
    Forestall our sport, to make us thus untrue?
    Do not you know my lady's foot by th'squier,
    And laugh upon the apple of her eye?
    And stand between her back, sir, and the fire,
    Holding a trencher, jesting merrily?
    You put our page out: go, you are allowed;
    Die when you will, a smock shall be your shroud.
    You leer upon me, do you? There's an eye
    Wounds like a leaden sword.
E. g. The girl is the apple of her father's eye.

As cold as stone (*Henry V*, 2.3.16) 冷若坚石。
Hostess
    Nay, sure, he's not in hell: he's in Arthur's bosom, if ever man went to Arthur's bosom. A made a finer end and went away an it had been any christom child; a' parted even just between twelve and one, e'en at the turning o' the tide. For after I saw him fumble with the sheets and play with flowers and smile upon his fingers' ends, I knew there was but one way; for his nose was as sharp as a pen, and a table of green fields. 'How now, sir John!' quoth I. 'What, man! be o' good cheer.' So a cried out, 'God, God, God!' three or four times. Now I, to comfort him, bid him a' should not think of God: I hoped there was no need to trouble himself with any such thoughts yet. So a bade me lay more clothes on his feet: I put my hand into the bed and felt them, and they were as cold as any stone. Then I felt to his knees, and they were as cold as any stone, and so upward and upward, and all was as cold as any stone.

As flies to wanton boys are we to the gods (*King Lear*, 4.1.41) 天神掌握着我们的命运,正像顽童捉到飞虫一样。

As good luck would have it (*The Merry Wives of Windsor*, 3.5.58) 幸而/不幸;碰巧/不巧。
FALSTAFF
    You shall hear. As good luck would have it, comes in one Mistress Page, gives intelligence of Ford's approach: and, in her invention and Ford's wife's distraction, they conveyed me into a buck-basket.

As merry as the day is long (*Much Ado about Nothing*, 2.1.32-33) 非常快活。
BEATRICE
    No, but to the gate, and there will the devil meet me like an old cuckold with horns on his head, and say 'Get you to heaven, Beatrice, get you to heaven, here's no place for you maids.' So deliver I up my apes, and away to Saint Peter, for the heavens. He shows me where the bachelors sit, and there live we as merry as the day is long.

As white as driven snow (*The Winter's Tale*, 4.4.234) 像雪一样洁白。
Autolycus
　　Lawn as white as driven snow,
　　Cypress black as e'er was crow,
　　Gloves as sweet as damask roses,
　　Masks for faces and for noses,
　　Bugle bracelet, necklace amber,
　　Perfume for a lady's chamber,
　　Golden quoifs and stomachers,
　　For my lads to give their dears,
　　Pins and poking-sticks of steel,
　　What maids lack from head to heel.
　　Come buy of me, come; come buy, come buy.
　　Buy lads, or else your lasses cry. Come buy!

Ay, there's the rub (*Hamlet*, 3.1.71) 唉,问题就在这。
E. g. I've always wanted to read that page-turner. But there's the rub, I just can't afford the time for it, given my tight work schedule.

Bag and baggage (*As You Like It*, 3.2.128) 连同行李地,完全地。
TOUCHSTONE
　　Come, shepherd, let us make an honourable retreat; though not with
　　bag and baggage, yet with scrip and scrippage.
E. g. He was thrown out by his boss bag and baggage.

be-all and the end-all, The (*Macbeth*, 1.7.5) 要义;终极目的;要点。
MACBETH
　　If it were done, when 'tis done, then 'twere well
　　It were done quickly: If th' assassination
　　Could trammel up the consequence and catch
　　With his surcease success: that but this blow
　　Might be the be-all and the end-all—here,
　　But here, upon this bank and shoal of time,
　　We'd jump the life to come.
E. g. Money should not become the be-all and end-all of life, to be attained by whatever means necessary.

Beast with two backs (*Othello*, 1.1.122-123) 交媾。
IAGO
　　I am one, sir, that comes to tell you your daughter and the Moor are now
　　making the beast with two backs.

Benedick, the married man (*Much Ado about Nothing*, 5.4.100) 结了婚的培尼狄克;新婚者;有妻室者。
DON PEDRO
　　How dost thou, Benedick, the married man?

better part of valour is discretion, The (*Henry IV*, *Part 1*, 5.3.117) 谨慎为勇敢之本。
FALSTAFF
[*Rising up*] Embowelled! If thou embowel me today, I'll give you leave to
  powder me and eat me too tomorrow. 'Twas time to counterfeit, or that
  hot termagant Scot had paid me scot and lot too. Counterfeit? I lie, I am no
  counterfeit; to die, is to be a counterfeit, for he is but the counterfeit of a man
  who hath not the life of a man. But to counterfeit dying, when a man thereby liveth, is to be no
  counterfeit, but the true and perfect image of life indeed. The better part of valour is discretion,
  in the which better part I have saved my life. I am afraid of this gunpowder Percy, though he be
  dead. How, if he should counterfeit too and rise? By my faith, I am afraid he would prove the
  better counterfeit: therefore I'll make him sure, yea, and I'll swear I killed him. Why may not
  he rise as well as I? Nothing confutes me but eyes, and nobody sees me. Therefore, sirrah,
  [*Stabbing him*] with a new wound in your thigh, come you along with me.

bowels of the earth, The (*King Henry IV*, *Part 1*, 1.3.62) 地底下。
HOTSPUR
  That villanous saltpetre should be digged
  Out of the bowels of the harmless earth,
  Which many a good tall fellow had destroyed
  So cowardly, and but for these vile guns,
  He would himself have been a soldier.
E. g. Miners labour in the bowels of earth.

Breathe one's last (*Henry VI*, *Part 3*, 5.2.40) 咽下最后一口气；死掉。
SOMERSET
  Ah, Warwick! Montague hath breathed his last,
  And to the latest gasp cried out for Warwick
  And said 'Commend me to my valiant brother.'
E. g. With one final lingering glance at his wife and children, the old man breathed
  his last.

Brevity is the soul of wit. (*Hamlet*, 2.2.95) 简洁是智慧的灵魂。
LORD POLONIUS
  [S]ince brevity is the soul of wit,
  And tediousness the limbs and outward flourishes,
  I will be brief: your noble son is mad:
  Mad call I it, for, to define true madness,
  What is't but to be nothing else but mad?
  But let that go—

Budge an inch (*The Taming of the Shrew*, Induction 1.8-9) 毫不退让。
E. g. Even at the cost of his life, he would not budge an inch before the enemy.

But, for my own part, it was Greek to me. (*Julius Caesar*, 1.2.274) 至于讲到我自己，那我可一点都不懂；完全无法理解。
CASSIUS Did Cicero say any thing?
CASCA Ay, he spoke Greek.
CASSIUS To what effect?

CASCA　Nay, an I tell you that, Ill ne'er look you i' the face again. But those thatunderstood him smiled at one another and shook their heads; but, for mine own part, it was Greek to me. I could tell you more news too: Marullus and Flavius, for pulling scarfs off Caesar's images, are put to silence. Fare you well. There was more foolery yet, if I could remember it. s

E. g. My son chose to major in chemical material, which is all Greek to me, a teacher of language and culture.

But screw your courage to the sticking-place (*Macbeth*, 1.7.66) 只要你鼓足你的全副勇气,我们绝不会失败;要坚定、要有勇气。
LADY MACBETH
　We fail!
　But screw your courage to the sticking-place
　And we'll not fail. When Duncan is asleep—
　Whereto the rather shall his day's hard journey
　Soundly invite him—his two chamberlains
　Will I with wine and wassail so convince,
　That memory, the warder of the brain,
　Shall be a fume, and the receipt of reason
　A limbeck only: when in swinish sleep
　Their drenchèd natures lie as in a death,
　What cannot you and I perform upon
　The 'unguarded Duncan? What not put upon
　His spongy officers, who shall bear the guilt
　Of our great quell?

Caviar to the general (*Hamlet*, 2.2.383-384) 一般人享受不到的鱼子酱;高雅但不合大众口味的东西;阳春白雪。
HAMLET
　I heard thee speak me a speech once, but it was never acted, or if it was, not above once, for the play, I remember, pleased not the million: 'twas caviar to the general. But it was—as I received? it, and others, whose judgments in such matters cried in the top of mine—an excellent play, well digested in the scenes, set down with as much modesty as cunning.

E. g. Many of the philosopher's ideas are so far-fetched as to be considered caviar to the general public.

charmèd life, A (*Macbeth*, 5.7.49) 似有魔法保护/令人陶醉的人生。
MACBETH
　Thou losest labour.
　As easy mayst thou the intrenchant air
　With thy keen sword impress as make me bleed.
　Let fall thy blade on vulnerable crests:
　I bear a charmèd life, which must not yield
　To one of woman born.
E. g. During my holiday on that island, I felt I was having a charmèd life.

Come what (come) may (*Macbeth*, 1.3.159) 不管怎样。
MACBETH　[*Aside*] Come what come may,

Time and the hour runs through the roughest day.
E. g. ... and should Parliament endorse that sentiment, come what come may, the might of England shall be put forth with a vigour and earnestness worthy of her old fame. (the *New York Times*, Jan. 4, 1878)

countenance more in sorrow than in anger, A (*Hamlet*, 1.2.240) 他的脸上悲哀多于愤怒。
HAMLET   What, look'd he frowningly?
HORATIO   A countenance more in sorrow than in anger.

course of true love never did run smooth, The (*A Midsummer Night's Dream*, 1.1.136) 真正的爱情从没有一帆风顺的。
LYSANDER?
   Ay me! for aught that I could ever read,? Could ever hear by tale or history, The course of true love never did run smooth;? But, either it was different in blood,—

crack of doom, The (*Macbeth*, 4.1.126) 世界末日。
MACBETH
   Thou art too like the spirit of Banquo: down!
   Thy crown does sear mine eye-balls: and thy hair,
   Thou other gold-bound brow, is like the first:
   A third is like the former. —Filthy hags,
   Why do you show me this? — A fourth? Start, eyes!
   What, will the line stretch out to the crack of doom
E. g. He is so stubborn and egotistic that you will have to wait till the crack of doom before he apologizes for what is his fault.

Cry havoc and let slip the dogs of war (*Julius Caesar*, 3.1.292) 发出屠杀的号令，让战争的猛犬四处蹂躏。→ **Dogs of war**
ANTONY
   Blood and destruction shall be so in use
   And dreadful objects so familiar,
   That mothers shall but smile when they behold
   Their infants quartered with the hands of war:
   All pity choked with custom of fell deeds,
   And Caesar's spirit, ranging for revenge,
   With Ate by his side come hot from hell,
   Shall in these confines with a monarch's voice
   Cry 'Havoc!', and let slip the dogs of war,
   That this foul deed shall smell above the earth
   With carrion men, groaning for burial. —

Daniel come to judgement, A (*The Merchant of Venice*, 4.1.223) 一个但尼尔来做法官了；睿智的判定。
SHYLOCK
   A Daniel come to judgment! Yea, a Daniel!
   O wise young judge, how I do honour thee!

Dead as a doornail (*Henry VI*, *Part 2*, 4.10.31)
死得像门上的钉子；完全死掉。
CADE
　　Brave thee! Ay, by the best blood that ever was broached, and beard thee too. Look on me well: I have eat no meat these five days; yet, come thou and thy five men, and if I do not leave you all as dead as a doornail, I pray God I may never eat grass more.
E. g. In the economic recession, the market was dead as a doornail

Devil incarnate, The (*King Henry V*, 2.3.23) 魔鬼的化身。
BOY Yes, that a did, and said they were devils incarnate.
E. g. That brute of a husband is a devil incarnate, who habitually gets drunk and beats his wife.

Dickeus, the (*The Merry Wives of Windsor*, 3.2.13) 表示强调。
MISTRESS PAGE
　　I cannot tell what the dickens his name is my husband had him of. What do you call your knight's name, sirrah?
E. g. What the dickens is going on?

dish fit for the gods, A (*Julius Caesar*, 2.1.180) 一盘祭神的牺牲；珍味佳肴。
BRUTUS
　　Our course will seem too bloody, Caius Cassius,
　　To cut the head off and then hack the limbs—
　　Like wrath in death and envy afterwards—
　　For Antony is but a limb of Caesar.
　　Let us be sacrificers, but not butchers, Caius.
　　We all stand up against the spirit of Caesar,
　　And in the spirit of men there is no blood.
　　O, that we then could come by Caesar's spirit
　　And not dismember Caesar! But, alas,
　　Caesar must bleed for it! And, gentle friends,
　　Let's kill him boldly, but not wrathfully:
　　Let's carve him as a dish fit for the gods,
　　Not hew him as a carcass fit for hounds.

Dogs of war (*Julius Caesar*, 3.1.292) 战乱；战祸。→ **Cry havoc and let slip the dogs of war**
E. g. Death, disease and famine are the dogs of war.

Double, double, toil and trouble (*Macbeth*, 4.1.35) 不惮辛劳,不惮烦。

Eaten me out of house and home (*Henry IV*, *Part 2*, 2.1.52) 吃光了家产；把……吃穷。
MISTRESS QUICKLY
　　It is more than for some, my lord, it is for all, all I have. He hath eaten me out of house and home; he hath put all my substance into that fat belly of his. But I will have some of it out again, or I will ride thee o' nights like the mare.
E. g. Those friends of Timon's are eating him out of house and home, but he still enjoys their company and "friendship".

Et tu, Brute? (*Julius Caesar*, 3.1.84) 博鲁托斯,你也在内吗;背叛;你也总有这一天。
CAESA   Doth not Brutus bootless kneel?
CASCA   Speak hands for me! [*They stab Caesar.*]
CAESAR *Et tu, Brute?* —Then fall, Caesar! [*Dies.*]
CINNA   Liberty! Freedom! Tyranny is dead!

Even at the turning of the tide (*Henry V*, 2.3.9-10) 正是在落潮的那一阵儿;变化。
HOSTESS
  Nay, sure, he's not in hell: he's in Arthur's bosom, if ever man went to Arthur's bosom. A made a finer end and went away an it had been any christom child. A parted even just between twelve and one, e'en at the turning o' th' tide. For after I saw him fumble with the sheets and play with flowers and smile upon his fingers' ends, I knew there was but one way, for his nose was as sharp as a pen, and a table of green fields.

Exceedingly well read (*Henry IV, Part 1*, 3.1.156) 博览群书;博学。
MORTIMER
  In faith, he is a worthy gentleman,
  Exceedingly well read, and profited
  In strange concealments, valiant as a lion
  And as wondrous affable and as bountiful
  As mines of India.
E. g. He is a lady's man—tall, handsome, clever, exceedingly well-read, and, above all, unbelievably rich.

Eye of newt and toe of frog, wool of bat and tongue of dog (*Macbeth*, 4.1.14-15) 蝾螈之目青蛙趾,蝙蝠之毛犬之齿;魔法药水配方。
ALL   Double, double toil and trouble;
  Fire burn, and cauldron bubble.
SECOND WITCH   Fillet of a fenny snake,
  In the cauldron boil and bake:
  Eye of newt, and toe of frog,
  Wool of bat, and tongue of dog,
  Adder's fork, and blind-worm's sting,
  Lizard's leg, and howlet's wing,
  For a charm of powerful trouble,
  Like a hell-broth boil and bubble.

eye-sore, An (*The Taming of the Shrew*, 3.2.88) 刺眼的东西;丑陋的东西。
BAPTISTA
  Why, sir, you know this is your wedding-day.
  First were we sad, fearing you would not come,
  Now sadder, that you come so unprovided.
  Fie, doff this habit, shame to your estate,
  An eye-sore to our solemn festival!
E. g. That pajamas-like post-modernist building is an eye-sore in the ancient part of the city.

Fair is foul, and foul is fair(*Macbeth*, 1.1.12)美即丑恶、丑即美。
All   Fair is foul, and foul is fair:
   Hover through the fog and filthy air.

Fair play(*The Tempest*, 5.1.193)公正的游戏;公平对待,条件均等;光明磊落。
MIRANDA
   Yes, for a score of kingdoms you should wrangle,
   And I would call it fair play.
E.g. A sound legal system should be characterized by justice and fair play.

Fancy-free(*A Midsummer Night's Dream*, 2.1.167)安然无恙;不受约束地想象;没有恋爱对象的;未婚的。
OBERON   That very time I saw, but thou couldst not,
   Flying between the cold moon and the earth,
   Cupid all armed; a certain aim he took
   At a fair vestal thronèd by the west,
   And loosed his love-shaft smartly from his bow,
   As it should pierce a hundred thousand hearts.
   But I might see young Cupid's fiery shaft
   Quenched in the chaste beams of the wat'ry moon;
   And the imperial votaress passèd on,
   In maiden meditation, fancy-free.
E.g. Those who are not married or emotionally involved in any way tend to be footloose and fancy-free.

Fight fire with fire(*King John*, 5.1.49)他燃起熊熊烈火,您就该还他个烈火熊熊;以火攻火,以毒攻毒。
BASTARD   So, on my soul, he did, for aught he knew:?
   But wherefore do you droop? Why look you sad?
   Be great in act, as you have been in thought:?
   Let not the world see fear and sad distrust?
   Govern the motion of a kingly eye:?
   Be stirring as the time, be fire with fire,
   Threaten the threat'ner and outface the brow?
   Of bragging horror. ?
E.g. The only way to curb crime is to fight fire with fire.

Fool's paradise, A(*Romeo and Juliet*, 2.3.124)一场春梦;虚幻的幸福。
NURSE
   Now, afore God, I am so vexed, that every part about me quivers. Scurvy knave! Pray you, sir, a word: and as I told you, my young lady bade me inquire you out; what she bade me say, I will keep to myself: but first let me tell ye, if ye should lead her into a fool's paradise, as they say, it were a very gross kind of behavior, as they say: for the gentlewoman is young; and, therefore, if you should deal double with her, truly it were an ill thing to be offered to any gentlewoman, and very weak dealing.
E.g. They were living in a fool's paradise, turning a blind eye to the cruel reality.

For goodness' sake(*Henry VIII*, pro.23)看在上帝的份上。

Foregone conclusion, A (*Othello*, 3.3.471) 意料之中的结局。
OTHELLO
  But this denoted a foregone conclusion:
  'Tis a shrewd doubt, though it be but a dream.
E. g. Given his ill preparation, the result of his exams seems a foregone conclusion.

Forever and a day (*As You Like It*, 4.1.102) 永久再加上一天; 极长久地, 永久地。
ROSALIND
  Now tell me how long you would have her after you have possessed her.
ORLANDO
  Forever and a day.

Fortune's fool (*Romeo and Juliet*, 3.1.123) 受命运玩弄的人。
ROMEO O, I am fortune's fool!

Foul play (*Love's Labours Lost*, 5.2.752) 奸诈; 不合道德行为。
BEROWNE
  Honest plain words best pierce the ear of grief,
  And by these badges understand the king.
  For your fair sakes have we neglected time,
  Played foul play with our oaths.

Frailty, thy name is woman! (*Hamlet*, 1.2.146) 脆弱啊, 你的名字就是女人。
HAMLET
  Must I remember? Why, she would hang on him
  As if increase of appetite had grown
  By what it fed on, and yet within a month—
  Let me not think on't: frailty, thy name is woman! —
  A little month, or ere those shoes were old
  With which she followed my poor father's body,
  Like Niobe, all tears: why she, even she—
  O, heaven! A beast that wants discourse of reason
  Would have mourned longer—married with mine uncle,
  My father's brother but no more like my father
  Than I to Hercules.

Full of sound and fury (*Macbeth*, 5.5.27) 充满了喧哗和骚动; 大吵大闹。
MACBETH She should have died hereafter:?
  There would have been a time for such a word.
  Tomorrow, and tomorrow, and tomorrow,
  Creeps in this petty pace from day to day?
  To the last syllable of recorded time:?
  And all our yesterdays have lighted fools?
  The way to dusty death. Out, out, brief candle.
  Life's but a walking shadow, a poor player

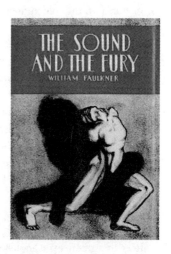

That struts and frets his hour upon the stage
  And then is heard no more. It is a tale?
  Told by an idiot, full of sound and fury,
  Signifying nothing.
NB. 美国著名作家威廉·福克纳(William Faulkner)的小说《喧哗与骚动》(*The Sound and the Fury*, 1962)即以此命名。

game is afoot, The (*Henry IV*, *Part 1*, 1.3.285) 事情在计划中。
NORTHUMBERLAND
Before the game's afoot, thou still let'st slip.
E. g. The teams are in the court— the whistle toots—the game is afoot.

game is up, The (*Cymbeline*, 3.3.112) 打猎已经完毕;阴谋已经败露;一切都完了。
BELARIUS Euriphile,
  Thou wast their nurse; they took thee for their mother.
  And every day do honour to her grave:
  Myself, Belarius, that am Morgan called,
  They take for natural father. The game is up.
E. g. The game was up; he now realized that his girl had been fooling him all along.

Get thee to a nunnery (*Hamlet*, 3.1.125) 进女修道院吧。
HAMLET
  Get thee to a nunnery. Why wouldst thou be a breeder of sinners?

Gild/paint the lily (*King John*, 4.2.11) 给睡莲镀金/涂粉;画蛇添足,多此一举。
SALISBURY ? Therefore, to be possessed with double pomp,?
  To guard a title that was rich before,
  To gild refined gold, to paint the lily,
  To throw a perfume on the violet,?
  To smooth the ice, or add another hue
  Unto the rainbow, or with taper-light
  To seek the beauteous eye of heaven to garnish,
  Is wasteful and ridiculous excess.
E. g. For a young and innocent-looking pretty girl to use makeup would be painting the lily.

Good men and true (*Much Ado about Nothing*, 3.3.1) 老老实实的好人;正直人士,陪审员。
DOGBERRY   Are you good men and true?
VERGES   Yea, or else it were pity but they should suffer salvation, body and soul.

Good riddance (*Troilus and Cressida*, 2.1.97) 总算摆脱(讨厌的人或事)。
THERSITES I will see you hanged, like clotpoles, ere I come any more to your
  tents: I will keep where there is wit stirring and leave the faction of fools.
PATROCLUS A good riddance.
E. g. He finally managed to be rid of that parasitic and selfish girlfriend of his—good riddance.

green-eyed monster, The (*Othello*, 3.3.188) 绿眼魔怪;嫉妒。→ **green with envy**
IAGO   O, beware, my lord, of jealousy:
  It is the green-eyed monster which doth mock

The meat it feeds on. That cuckold lives in bliss
   Who, certain of his fate, loves not his wronger:
   But, O, what damnèd minutes tells he o'er
   Who dotes, yet doubts, suspects, yet strongly loves!

Have seen better days (*As You Like it*, 2.7.121) 曾过过好日子;曾一度繁荣过。
DUKE SENIOR
   True is it that we have seen better days,
   And have with holy bell been knolled to church
   And sat at good men's feasts, and wiped our eyes
   Of drops that sacred pity hath engendered:
   And therefore sit you down in gentleness,
   And take upon command what help we have
   That to your wanting may be ministered.
E. g. That ghost town has seen better days./Though retired and coming down in the world, the man had seen better days once.

He will give the Devil his due. (*Henry IV Part 1*, 1.2.80) 魔鬼也有魔鬼的长处。
CONSTABLE I will cap that proverb with 'There is flattery in friendship.'
ORLEANS   And I will take up that with 'Give the devil his due.'

Heart's content (*Henry VI, Part 2*, 1.1.35) 喜悦,满意;尽情地。
KING HENRY VI
   Her sight did ravish, but her grace in speech,
   Her words yclad with wisdom's majesty,
   Makes me from wond'ring fall to weeping joys,
   Such is the fulness of my heart's content.
   Lords, with one cheerful voice welcome my love.
E. g. My memory remains as fresh as ever of my father and me sitting in our backyard, gazing into the infinite summer evening sky while listening to insects whispering to their heart's content.

High time (*The Comedy of Errors*, 3.2.140) 正是……时候;早该。
ANTIPHOLUS OF SYRACUSE
   There's none but witches do inhabit here;
   And therefore 'tis high time that I were hence.

Hoist with his own petard (*Hamlet*, 3.4.208) 开炮的给炮轰了;害人反害己;搬起石头砸自己的脚。
HAMLET
   There's letters sealed: and my two schoolfellows,
   Whom I will trust as I will adders fanged,
   They bear the mandate; they must sweep my way,
   And marshal me to knavery. Let it work:
   For 'tis the sport to have the engineer
   Hoist with his own petard: and't shall go hard
   But I will delve one yard below their mines
   And blow them at the moon. O, 'tis most sweet
   When in one line two crafts directly meet.

E. g. It was indeed a cunning move, but finally he was hoist with his own petard.

Hoodwinked (*All's Well That Ends Well*, 4.1.60) 被蒙着眼睛的;被蒙骗的。
INTERPRETER
    The general is content to spare thee yet,
    And, hoodwinked as thou art, will lead thee on
    To gather from thee. Haply thou mayst inform
    Something to save thy life.
E. g. Customers are often hoodwinked by dubious advertisements into buying commodities that they don't actually need.

horse, a horse, my kingdom for a horse, A (*Richard III*, 5.3.361) 一匹马!一匹马!我的王位换一匹马!;(喻)无足轻重之物
KING RICHARD III
    A horse! A horse! My kingdom for a horse!
CATESBY
    Withdraw, my lord: I'll help you to a horse.

Household words (*Henry V*, 4.3.54) 家喻户晓的名字。
E. g. The actress was a household word ten years ago, but nobody mentions her now.

How sharper than a serpent's tooth it is to have a thankless child (*King Lear*, 1.4.236-237) 不知感谢的孩子比毒蛇的牙齿还要尖利。
LEAR
    It may be so, my lord. —
    Hear, nature, hear; dear goddess, hear!
    Suspend thy purpose, if thou didst intend
    To make this creature fruitful:
    Into her womb convey sterility,
    Dry up in her the organs of increase,
    And from her derogate body never spring
    A babe to honour her: if she must teem,
    Create her child of spleen; that it may live
    And be a thwart disnatured torment to her:
    Let it stamp wrinkles in her brow of youth,
    With cadent tears fret channels in her cheeks,
    Turn all her mother's pains and benefits
    To laughter and contempt, that she may feel
    How sharper than a serpent's tooth it is
    To have a thankless child! —Away, away!

I have immortal longings in me. (*Antony and Cleopatra*, 5.2.316-317) 我心里怀着永生的渴望。
CLEOPATRA
    Give me my robe, put on my crown; I have
    Immortal longings in me. Now no more
    The juice of Egypt's grape shall moist this lip.

> Yare, yare, good Iras! Quick! Methinks I hear
> Antony call: I see him rouse himself
> To praise my noble act. I hear him mock
> The luck of Caesar, which the gods give men
> To excuse their after wrath. Husband, I come!
> Now to that name my courage prove my title!
> I am fire and air: My other elements
> I give to baser life. —So; have you done
> Come then, and take the last warmth of my lips.
> Farewell, kind Charmian. Iras, long farewell.

I have not slept one wink (*Cymbeline*, 3.4.102) 我还不曾有过片刻的安睡。
PISANIO
> O gracious lady:
> Since I received command to do this business
> I have not slept one wink.

E. g. The couple never slept a wink that night, anticipating fondly the advent of their first child.

I see you stand like greyhounds in the slips. (*Henry V*, 3.1. 31) 我看得出你们站在这里，就像被皮带勒住的猎犬；迫不及待。
KING HENRY V
> For there is none of you so mean and base,
> That hath not noble lustre in your eyes.
> I see you stand like greyhounds in the slips,
> Straining upon the start. The game's afoot:
> Follow your spirit, and upon this charge
> Cry 'God for Harry, England, and Saint George!'

I will tell you my drift. (*Much Ado about Nothing*, 2.1.265) 我要把我的计划告诉你们。
E. g. He didn't understand much French, but he got her drift from the anxious look on her face.

I will wear my heart upon my sleeve. (*Othello*, 1.1.66) 我就要掏出我的心来；流露感情；心直口快。
IAGO
> It is as sure as you are Roderigo,
> Were I the Moor, I would not be Iago:
> In following him, I follow but myself.
> Heaven is my judge, not I for love and duty,
> But seeming so, for my peculiar end,
> For when my outward action doth demonstrate
> The native act and figure of my heart
> In compliment extern, 'tis not long after
> But I will wear my heart upon my sleeve
> For daws to peck at: I am not what I am.

E. g. He is the kind of man who wears his heart on his sleeve.

If music be the food of love, play on. (*Twelfth Night*, 1.1.1) 假如音乐是爱情的食粮,那么奏下去吧。
DUKE ORSINO
 If music be the food of love, play on;
 Give me excess of it, that, surfeiting,
 The appetite may sicken, and so die.
 That strain again! it had a dying fall.

In a pickle (*The Tempest*, 5.1.316) 麻烦,窘境
ALONSO And Trinculo is reeling ripe: where should they
 Find this grand liquor that hath gilded 'em
 How cam'st thou in this pickle
TRINCULO I have been in such a pickle since I saw you last that, I fear me, will
 never out of my bones: I shall not fear fly-blowing.
E.g. He is in a pickle.

In my heart of heart(s) (*Hamlet*, 3.2.58) 在我的内心深处。
HAMLET
 Give me that man
 That is not passion's slave, and I will wear him
 In my heart's core, ay, in my heart of heart,
 As I do thee.
E.g. Though I was not willing to agree with her on that, but in my heart of hearts, I knew she was right.

Into thin air (*The Tempest*, 4.1.163) 化作空气;消失。
PROSPERO
 You do look, my son, in a movèd sort,
 As if you were dismayed: be cheerful, sir.
 Our revels now are ended. These our actors,
 As I foretold you, were all spirits and
 Are melted into air, into thin air.
E.g. With all the embezzled money in his pocket, the manager just vanished into thin air.

In stitches (*Twelfth Night*, 3.2.45) 笑得前仰后合,大笑不止。
MARIA
 If you desire the spleen, and will laugh yourself into stitches, follow me. Yond
 gull Malvolio is turned heathen, a very renegado; for there is no Christian that
 means to be saved by believing rightly, can ever believe such impossible
 passages of grossness. He's in yellow stockings.
E.g. That natural-born comedian seems to have no difficulty whatever in keeping his audience in stitches of laughter and glee.

In the twinkling of an eye (*The Merchant Of Venice*, 2.2.116) 瞬间。
LAUNCELOT
 Well, if Fortune be a woman, she's a good wench for this gear. Father, come; I'll take my
 leave of the Jew in the twinkling of an eye.
E.g. The cowboy whipped out his pistol and fired in the twinkling of an eye.

It is meat and drink to me (*As You Like It*, 5.1.7) 无上的乐趣,精神寄托;日常事务。
TOUCHSTONE
   It is meat and drink to me to see a clown. By my troth, we that have good wits have much to answer for. We shall be flouting: we cannot hold.
E. g. Scandal and gossip are meat and drink to the paparazzi.

It smells to heaven (*Hamlet*, 3.3.39) 臭气熏天。
KING CLAUDIUS
   Thanks, dear my lord. —
   O, my offence is rank it smells to heaven:
   It hath the primal eldest curse upon't,
   A brother's murder.

Knock, knock! Who's there? (*Macbeth*, 2.3.3) 敲！敲！敲！谁在那儿？
PORTER
   Here's a knocking indeed! If a man were porter of hell-gate, he should have old turning the key.
[*Knocking within*]
   Knock, knock, knock! Who's there, I' the name of Beelzebub? Here's a farmer, that hanged himself on the expectation of plenty: come in time; have napkins enough about you: here you'll sweat for't.

Laid on with a trowel (*As You Like it*, 1.2.74) 用泥铲儿涂抹;大事渲染;竭力阿谀,拍马屁。
CELIA
   Well said, that was laid on with a trowel.
E. g. Whenever he praises my work, I will chuckle to myself that he is once again laying it on with a trowel.

Laughing-stock (*The Merry Wives of Windsor*, 3.1.64) 笑柄,嘲笑的对象。
EVANS
   Pray you let us not be laughing-stocks to other men's humours. I desire you
   in friendship, and I will one way or other make you amends.
E. g. Bushisms, verbal blunders made by former American President George W. Bush, made him an international laughing stock.

lean and hungry look, A (*Julius Caesar*, 1.2.200) 饥饿之色;急欲得到某物的神色。
CAESAR
   Let me have men about me that are fat,
   Sleek-headed men and such as sleep a-nights.
   Yond Cassius has a lean and hungry look:
   He thinks too much: such men are dangerous.

Let's kill all the lawyers. (*Henry Ⅵ, Part 2*, 4.2.57) 把所有的律师全部杀光。
DICK   The first thing we do, let's kill all the lawyers.

Lie low (*Much Ado About Nothing*, 5.1.55) 躲藏起来;等待时机

ANTONIO
>If he could right himself with quarreling,
>Some of us would lie low.

E. g. The spy had to lie low for a month before hunger drove him out of his lair.

make a virtue of necessity（*The Two Gentlemen of Verona*, 4.1.61）甘愿做非做不可的事情。
SECOND OUTLAW
>Indeed, because you are a banish'd man,
>Therefore, above the rest, we parley to you:
>Are you content to be our general?
>To make a virtue of necessity
>And live, as we do, in this wilderness?

E. g. While taking the company bus to work, he observed what was passing by outside the window to make a virtue of necessity.

Makes your hair stand on end（*Hamlet*, 1.5.23）使人毛骨悚然。
GHOST
>I could a tale unfold, whose lightest word
>Would harrow up thy soul, freeze thy young blood,
>Make thy two eyes, like stars, start from their spheres,
>Thy knotted and combinèd locks to part
>And each particular hair to stand an end
>Like quills upon the fretful porpentine.

E. g. Watching the horror movie made our hair stand on end.

Milk of human-kindness（*Macbeth*, 1.5.12）人间的恻忍之心；人情。
LADY MACBETH
>What thou art promised: yet do I fear thy nature:
>It is too full o' the milk of human kindness
>To catch the nearest way.

E. g. That old lady was a generous woman, overflowing with the milk of human kindness.

ministering angel shall my sister be, A（*Hamlet*, 5.1.191）救死扶伤的天使；提供帮助与安慰的好心人。
LAERTES
>Lay her i' the earth:
>And from her fair and unpolluted flesh
>May violets spring! I tell thee, churlish priest,
>A ministering angel shall my sister be,
>When thou liest howling.

Misery acquaints men with strange bedfellows.（*The Tempest*, 2.2.32）难中共相济,陌路也相知。
TRINCULO
>Here's neither bush nor shrub, to bear off any weather at all, and another storm brewing; I hear it sing i' the wind: yond same black cloud, yond huge one, looks like a foul bombard that would shed his liquor. If it should thunder as it did before, I know not where to hide my head: yond same cloud cannot choose but fall by pailfuls. What have we here? A man or a fish? Dead

or alive? A fish, he smells like a fish: a very ancient and fishlike smell: a kind of not-of-the newest poor-John. A strange fish! Were I in England now—as once I was—and had but this fish painted, not a holiday fool there but would give a piece of silver: there would this monster make a man: any strange beast there makes a man: when they will not give a doit to relieve a lame beggar, they will lay out ten to see a dead Indian. Legged like a man and his fins like arms! Warm o' my troth! I do now let loose my opinion, hold it no longer: this is no fish, but an islander that hath lately suffered by a thunderbolt. Alas, the storm is come again! My best way is to creep under his gabardine: there is no other shelter hereabout. Misery acquaints a man with strange bedfellows: I will here shroud till the dregs of the storm be past.
E. g. Business and politics make strange bedfellows.

More fool you. (*The Taming of the Shrew*, 5.1.141) 你那样真傻。
BIANCA
  Fie! What a foolish duty call you this?
LUCENTIO
  I would your duty were as foolish too:
  The wisdom of your duty, fair Bianca,
  Hath cost me an hundred crowns since suppertime.
BIANCA
  The more fool you, for laying on my duty.
E. g. More fool you—don't you ever know he never shows up on time at parties!

More honoured in the breach than in the observance (*Hamlet*, 1.4.18) 遵守不如不遵守好。
HAMLET
  Ay, marry, is't:
  And to my mind, though I am native here
  And to the manner born, it is a custom
  More honoured in the breach than the observance.

More in sorrow than in anger (*Hamlet*, 1.2.240) 悲哀多于愤怒。
HORATIO   A countenance more in sorrow than in anger.

More sinned against than sinning (*King Lear*, 3.2.57) 没有犯太多的罪,却遭罪很大;受到过于严厉的惩罚。
KING LEAR
  I am a man
  More sinned against than sinning.
E. g. Once the verdict was announced, the man protested that he was more sinned against than sinning.

Much ado about nothing (*Much Ado About Nothing*) 无是生非。
E. g. Don't be fooled by that bluffing official; he was only making much ado about nothing.

Mum's the word (*Henry VI, Part 2*, 1.2.89) 保持缄默。
HUME   Seal up your lips and give no words but mum.
E. g. Please don't tell anyone I'm leaving for a new job. Mum's the word!

Murder most foul（*Hamlet*, 1.5.31）杀人是重大的罪恶。
GHOST
　　Revenge his foul and most unnatural murder.
HAMLET
　　Murder most foul, as in the best it is,
　　But this most foul, strange and unnatural.

My mind's eye（*Hamlet*, 1.2.186）我心目中，我记忆中。
HAMLET
　　Thrift, thrift, Horatio! The funeral baked meats
　　Did coldly furnish forth the marriage tables.
　　Would I had met my dearest foe in heaven?
　　Or ever I had seen that day, Horatio.
　　My father, methinks I see my father.
HORATIO
　　O, where, my lord?
HAMLET
　　In my mind's eye, Horatio.
E. g. In my mind's eye, I can still recall going to the countryside with my brother and spending so many care-free summer days there.

naked truth, the（*Love's Labour's Lost*, 5.2.708）明明白白的事实。
ADRIANO　The naked truth of it is, I have no shirt: I go woolward for penance.
E. g. That porn star is nicknamed "Truth", since the truth is said to be naked.

Neither a borrower nor a lender be（*Hamlet*, 1.3.78）既不当债户，又不当债主。
POLONIUS
　　Neither a borrower nor a lender be,
　　For loan oft loses both itself and friend,
　　And borrowing dulls the edge of husbandry.

Neither rhyme nor reason（*The Comedy of Errors*, 2.2.47）既无音韵又无情节；毫无道理，莫名其妙。
DROMIO OF SYRACUSE
　　Was there ever any man thus beaten out of season,
　　When in the why and the wherefore is neither rhyme nor reason?
E. g. There is neither rhyme nor reason to his actions.

Night owl（*Twelfth Night*, 2.3.44）夜猫子。
SIR TOBY BELCH
　　To hear by the nose, it is dulcet in contagion. But shall we make the welkin
　　dance indeed? Shall we rouse the night owl in a catch that will draw three souls
　　out of one weaver? Shall we do that?
E. g. Over the years, given the nature of his profession as a writer, he has led the life of a night owl.

No more cakes and ale (*Twelfth Night*, 2.3.89) 不再吃喝玩乐,不再享受生活
SIR TOBY BELCH
  Out o' tune, sir, ye lie. Art any more than a steward? Dost thou
  think, because thou art virtuous, there shall be no more cakes and ale?
E. g. Life is not about cakes and ale alone.

Not a mouse stirring (*Hamlet*, 1.1.11) 一只老鼠也不见走动;非常安静。
BERNARDO
  Have you had quiet guard?
FRANCISCO
  Not a mouse stirring.

Now gods stand up for bastards! (*King Lear*, 1.2.22) 神啊,帮助帮助私生子吧!

Now is the winter of our discontent. (*Richard III*, 1.1.1) 不愉快的时光。
E. g. Widespread strikes by public sector workers undermined James Callaghan's Labour government in Britian's "winter of discontent" in 1978-19.

O, brave new world. (*The Tempest*, 5.1.205) 啊,新奇的世界。
NB. 英国作家奥尔德斯·赫胥黎(Aldous Leonard Huxley, 1894-1963)的《美丽新世界》(*Brave New World*)深受该剧的影响。
E. g. Shaking off its feudal shackles in ideology and social systems, Europe created a brave new world for itself.

O, my prophetic soul! (*Hamlet*, 1.5.46) 啊!我的预感果然是真的。
HAMLET O, my prophetic soul! Mine uncle!

Of comfort no man speak! (*Richard II*, 3.2.139) 谁也不准讲安慰的话。
KING RICHARD
  No matter where; of comfort no man speak.

Off with his head (*Henry VI*, Part 3, 1.4.179) 砍他的头(表示责备某人)。
QUEEN MARGARET
  Off with his head and set it on York gates;
  So York may overlook the town of York.

Once more unto the breach, dear friends, once more. (*Henry V*, 3.1.1) 亲爱的朋友,让我们再试一次。
KING HENRY V
  Once more unto the breach, dear friends, once more,
  Or close the wall up with our English dead.
  In peace there's nothing so becomes a man
  As modest stillness and humility,
  But when the blast of war blows in our ears,

Then imitate the action of the tiger:
Stiffen the sinews, summon up the blood,
Disguise fair nature with hard-favoured rage,
Then lend the eye a terrible aspect.

One fell swoop (*Macbeth*, 4.3.252) 一下子,一举。
MACDUFF
  All my pretty ones?
  Did you say all? O hell-kite! All?
  What, all my pretty chickens and their dam
  At one fell swoop?
E. g. It was such a page-turner that I finished reading it at one fell swoop.

One that loved not wisely but too well (*Othello*, 5.2.387) 在恋爱上不智而过于深情。
OTHELLO Soft you; a word or two before you go.
  I have done the state some service, and they know't—
  No more of that. I pray you, in your letters,
  When you shall these unlucky deeds relate,
  Speak of me as I am: nothing extenuate,
  Nor set down aught in malice. Then must you speak
  Of one that loved not wisely but too well:
  Of one not easily jealous, but being wrought,
  Perplexed in the extreme: of one whose hand,
  Like the base Judean, threw a pearl away
  Richer than all his tribe: of one whose subdued eyes,
  Albeit unusèd to the melting mood,
  Drops tears as fast as the Arabian trees?
  Their medicinable gum. Set you down this,
  And say besides, that in Aleppo once,
  Where a malignant and a turbaned Turk
  Beat a Venetian and traduced the state,
  I took by th' throat the circumcisèd dog
  And smote him, thus. [*Stabs himself*]

Out of the jaws of death (*Twelfth Night*, 3.4.281) 走出虎口,脱离险境(鬼门关)。
ANTONIO Let me speak a little. This youth that you see here
  I snatched one half out of the jaws of death,
  Relieved him with such sanctity of love,
  And to his image, which methought did promise
  Most venerable worth, did I devotion.
E. g. When the family had lost any hope, firefighters came to their rescue and snatched them from the jaws of death.

Out, out, brief candle! (*Macbeth*, 5.5.23) 熄灭了,熄灭了,短促的烛光。

plague on both your houses, A (*Romeo and Juliet*, 3.1.78) 双方都不得好报。
MERCUTIO I am hurt.

> A plague o' both your houses! I am sped.
> Is he gone and hath nothing?

play's the thing, The (*Hamlet*, 2.2.536) 靠的就是这出戏（我可以发掘国王内心的隐秘）。

Pomp and circumstance (*Othello*, 3.3.392) 正式庆典、仪式。
OTHELLO
> I had been happy, if the general camp,
> Pioners and all, had tasted her sweet body,
> So I had nothing known. O, now, for ever
> Farewell the tranquil mind; farewell content;
> Farewell the plumèd troops and the big wars
> That makes ambition virtue! O, farewell!
> Farewell the neighing steed, and the shrill trump,
> The spirit-stirring drum, th' ear-piercing fife,
> The royal banner, and all quality,
> Pride, pomp and circumstance of glorious war!
> And, O you mortal engines, whose rude throats
> Th' immortal Jove's dread clamours counterfeit,
> Farewell! Othello's occupation's gone.

NB. 英国作曲家爱德华·埃尔加（Edward Elgar, 1857—1934）受此段影响创作了《威风凛凛进行曲》（The *Pomp and Circumstance Marches*），而迪士尼公司出品的动画片《幻想曲 2000》（*Fantasia 2000*）则以诺亚方舟的《圣经》故事生动地诠释了这段经典音乐。
E. g. Opening ceremonies of international events are mired in an escalating arms race of pomp and circumstance.

primrose path, The (*Hamlet*, 1.3.52) 樱草花之路；享乐但极有可能有不好结果的道路。
OPHELIA
> I shall th' effect of this good lesson keep
> As watchman to my heart. But, good my brother,
> Do not, as some ungracious pastors do,
> Show me the steep and thorny way to heaven,
> Whiles, like a puffed and reckless libertine
> Himself the primrose path of dalliance treads,?
> And recks not his own rede.

E. g. Unaware of its dire consequences, the young man continued down his primrose path.

quality of mercy, the (*The Merchant of Venice*, 4.1.184) 慈悲的品质。

readiness is all, The (*Hamlet*, 5.2.152) 随时准备好就是了。
HAMLET Not a whit, we defy augury: there's a special providence in the fall of a sparrow. If it be now, 'tis not to come: if it be not to come, it will be now: if it be not now, yet it will come: the readiness is all. Since no man has aught of what he leaves, what is't to leave betimes?

rest is silence, The (*Hamlet*, 5.2.307) 剩下的仅有沉默了。
HAMLET O, I die, Horatio:
> The potent poison quite o'er-crows my spirit.
> I cannot live to hear the news from England,

But I do prophesy th' election lights
On Fortinbras: he has my dying voice,
So tell him, with the occurrents more and less
Which have solicited. The rest is silence. O, o, o, o!

Ripeness is all. (*King Lear*, 5.2.12) 耐心等待命运的安排就是了。
EDGAR
What, in ill thoughts again? Men must endure
Their going hence, even as their coming hither:
Ripeness is all: come on.

**rose by any other name would smell as sweet,
A** (*Romeo and Juliet*, 2.1.90-1) 我们叫做玫瑰的这一种花,要是换了个名字,它的香味还是同样的芬芳;本质比名称更重要。
NB. 此为引用率极高的莎翁名句,影响了众多文学、音乐、电影作品。意大利学者翁贝托·埃可(Umberto Eco, 1932-)的历史悬疑小说《玫瑰之名》(*The Name of the Rose*)以及据此改编的同名电影更是使之家喻户晓。语言学家也常引用此句来说明人类语言的任意性(arbitrariness)。

pound of flesh, A (*The Merchant of Venice*, 4.1.100) 一磅肉(合法但不合情理的要求)。
SHYLOCK The pound of flesh which I demand of him
Is dearly bought, 'tis mine, and I will have it.

Salad days (*Antony and Cleopatra*, 1.5.86) 少不更事时期。
CLEOPATRA
My salad days,
When I was green in judgment, cold in blood,
To say as I said then. But, come, away,
Get me ink and paper.
He shall have every day a several greeting
Or I'll unpeople Egypt!
E. g. What fools men are in their salad days.
(the *Morning Oregonian*, June 1862)

Screw your courage to the sticking place. (*Macbeth*, 1.7.66) 鼓足勇气。
LADY MACBETH
We fail?
But screw your courage to the sticking-place
And we'll not fail.

sea change, A (*The Tempest*, 1.2.464) 突变,巨变。
ARIEL [*sings*]
Full fathom five thy father lies,
Of his bones are coral made;

Those are pearls that were his eyes:
Nothing of him that doth fade,
But doth suffer a sea-change
Into something rich and strange.
Sea-nymphs hourly ring his knell:

E. g. Under the sway of Mark Anthony's skillful speech, the attitude of the Roman audience towards Julius Caesar underwent a sea change.

Send packing (*Henry IV, Part 1*, 2.4.221) 把(某人)撵走。
FALSTAFF 'Faith, and I'll send him packing.
E. g. He was sent packing by his boss for negligence of duties.

Set one's teeth on edge (*Henry IV, Part 1*, 3.1.133) 使牙齿发酸;(喻)使人恼怒、厌恶。
HOTSPUR Marry,
   And I am glad of it with all my heart.
   I had rather be a kitten and cry mew
   Than one of these same metre ballad-mongers.
   I had rather hear a brazen candlestick turned,
   Or a dry wheel grate on the axle-tree,
   And that would set my teeth nothing on edge,
   Nothing so much as mincing poetry:
   'Tis like the forced gait of a shuffling nag.
E. g. The blaring and honking of horns outside the window got on his nerves and set his teeth on edge.

Sharper than a serpent's tooth (*King Lear*, 1.4.236) 比毒蛇的牙齿还要锋利。
KING LEAR It may be so, my lord. —
   Hear, nature, hear; dear goddess, hear!
   Suspend thy purpose if thou didst intend
   To make this creature fruitful:
   Into her womb convey sterility,
   Dry up in her the organs of increase,
   And from her derogate body never spring
   A babe to honour her: if she must teem,
   Create her child of spleen, that it may live
   And be a thwart disnatured torment to her:
   Let it stamp wrinkles in her brow of youth,
   With cadent tears fret channels in her cheeks,
   Turn all her mother's pains and benefits
   To laughter and contempt, that she may feel
   How sharper than a serpent's tooth it is
   To have a thankless child! —Away, away!

Short shrift (*Richard III*, 3.4.94) 简短的忏悔;忽视,轻视。
RATCLIFF Come, come, dispatch. The duke would be at dinner.
   Make a short shrift: he longs to see your head.

Shuffle off this mortal coil (*Hamlet*, 3.1.73) 摆脱尘世烦恼。
E. g. After an eventful life of trials and tribulations, the old man shuffled off this mortal coil in the small hours on New Year's Day.

slings and arrows of outrageous fortune, The (*Hamlet*, 3.1.64) 默然忍受命运暴虐的毒箭。
E. g. Despite my relentless efforts, I have not yet learned to be immune to the slings and arrows.

smallest worm will turn, being trodden on, The (*Henry VI. Part 3*, 2.2.17) 被践踏的最小的虫子也会翻身的；咸鱼翻身。
CLIFFORD
    Who scapes the lurking serpent's mortal sting?
    Not he that sets his foot upon her back.
    The smallest worm will turn being trodden on,
    And doves will peck in safeguard of their brood.
E. g. Even a worm will turn./Tread on a worm and it will turn.

sorry sight, A (*Macbeth*, 2.2.25) 难看的样子，悲惨的景象。
MACBETH
    Hark!
    Who lies i' the second chamber?
LADY MACBETH
    Donalbain.
MACBETH
    This is a sorry sight. [*Looking on his hands*]
LADY MACBETH
    A foolish thought, to say 'a sorry sight'.

Speak the speech I pray thee trippingly on the tongue (*Hamlet*, 3.2.1-2) 请你将那段剧词在舌头上很轻快地吐出来。

Star-crossed lovers (*Romeo and Juliet*, pro. 6) 不幸的恋人。
PROLOGUE
    Two households, both alike in dignity,
    In fair Verona, where we lay our scen,
    From ancient grudge break to new mutiny,
    Where civil blood makes civil hands unclean.
    From forth the fatal loins of these two foes
    A pair of star-crossed lovers take their life,
    Whole misadventured piteous overthrows;
    Do with their death bury their parents' strife.
    The fearful passage of their death-marked love,
    And the continuance of their parents' rage,
    Which, but their children's end, nought could remove,
    Is now the two hours' traffic of our stage;
    The which if you with patient ears attend,
    What here shall miss, our toil shall strive to mend.
E. g. Liang Shanbo and Zhu Yingtai are the Chinese star-crossed lovers.

Stiffen the sinews (*Henry V*, 3.1.7) 更加坚定,目标明确。

Stony-hearted villains (*Henry IV*, *Part 1*, 2.2.18) 铁石心肠的恶人。

Stood on ceremonies (*Julius Caesar*, 2.2.13) 讲究礼节。
CALPURNIA
   Caesar, I never stood on ceremonies,
   Yet now they fright me. There is one within,
   Besides the things that we have heard and seen,
   Recounts most horrid sights seen by the watch.
   A lioness hath whelpèd in the streets;
   And graves have yawned, and yielded up their dead;
   Fierce fiery warriors fought upon the clouds
   In ranks and squadrons, and right form of war,
   Which drizzled blood upon the Capitol:
   The noise of battle hurtled in the air,
   Horses did neigh, and dying men did groan,
   And ghosts did shriek and squeal about the streets.
   O Caesar, these things are beyond all use,
   And I do fear them.
E. g. Please don't stand on ceremonies; just sit down and make yourself comfortable.

Such stuff as dreams are made on (*The Tempest*, 4.1.169-170) 用梦幻构成的材料(指人)。

Suit the action to the word (*Hamlet*, 3.2.12-13) 如何说就如何做;言行一致。
HAMLET
   Be not too tame neither, but let your own discretion be your tutor: suit the action to the word, the word to the action; with this special observance: that you o'erstep not the modesty of nature: for any thing so overdone is from the purpose of playing, whose end, both at the first and now, was and is, to hold, as 'twere, the mirror up to nature, to show virtue her own feature, scorn her own image, and the very age and body of the time his form and pressure.

Sweets to the sweet (*Hamlet*, 5.1.194) 好花是应该撒在美人身上的。
QUEEN GERTRUDE
   Sweets to the sweet. Farewell! [*Scattering flowers*]
   I hoped thou shouldst have been my Hamlet's wife:
   I thought thy bride-bed to have decked, sweet maid,
   And not t' have strewed thy grave.

Thereby hangs a tale. (*As You Like It*, 2.7.28) 这事儿有由来。
E. g. Judith and Daniel are now having a stable relationship and thereby hangs a tale.

There's a divinity that shapes our ends. (*Hamlet*, 5.2.10) 我们的结局早已被一种冥冥之中的力量所决定。

This is the short and the long of it. (*The Merry Wives of Windsor*, 2.2.43)
MISTRESS QUICKLY
   Marry, this is the short and the long of it; you have brought her into such a canaries as 'tis

wonderful. The best courtier of them all—when the court lay at Windsor—could never have brought her to such a canary.

E. g. The long and short of it is that he was dumped by his girlfriend.

This is very midsummer madness. (*Twelfth Night*, 3.4.45) 这是愚蠢的想法；热昏头的行为。
OLIVIA Why, this is very midsummer madness.
E. g. The young lovers decided to marry just after their first date, a symptom of midsummer madness.

This was the noblest Roman of them all. (*Julius Caesar*, 5.5.73) 这是位高尚的罗马人。

Though this be madness, yet there is method in it. (*Hamlet*, 2.2.207) 病态中却显条理；这虽是疯话，却有深意在内。
POLONIUS [*Aside*] Though this be madness, yet there is method in 't. —Will you walk out of the air, my lord?
E. g. The woman asked her neighbours to give her their discarded cartons; but there was method in her madness because she sold them to raise money for the education of her kids.

Thus conscience does make cowards of us all. (*Hamlet*, 3.1.89) 重重的顾虑使我们全变成了懦夫。

time is out of joint, The (*Hamlet*, 1.5.205) 这是个颠倒混乱的时代。

To be, or not to be, that is the question. (*Hamlet*, 3.1.62) 生存还是毁灭？这是个要考虑的问题。

To the manner born (*Hamlet*, 1.4.17) 天生就适合。
HAMLET Ay, marry, is't:
　　But to my mind, though I am native here
　　And to the manner born, it is a custom
　　More honoured in the breach than the observance.
E. g. His newly-wed wife played the role of hostess as if to the manner born.

To thine own self be true. (*Hamlet*, 1.3.81) 对自己要忠实。

Too much of a good thing (*As You Like it*, 4.1.85) 好事过头，反成坏事。
ROSALIND Why then, can one desire too much of a good thing? Come, sister, you shall be the priest and marry us. Give me your hand, Orlando. What do you say, sister?
E. g. I don't mind burning the midnight oil once in a while, but if I have to stay up every night, it is too much of a good thing.

tower of strength, A (*Richard III*, 5.3.13) 力量的堡垒；可信赖的人；支柱。
RICHARD Why, our battalion trebles that account:
　　Besides, the king's name is a tower of strength,
　　Which they upon the adverse party want.
E. g. Charismatic, resolute and far-sighted, Mr. Johnson is a tower of strength to his party.

Trueborn Englishman（*Richard II*, 1.3.273）纯正的英国人。
BOLINGBROOK   Then, England's ground, farewell. Sweet soil, adieu.
  My mother, and my nurse, that bears me yet!
  Where'er I wander, boast of this I can,
  Though banished, yet a trueborn Englishman.

Truth will out.（The *Merchant of Venice*, 2.2.51）真相终将大白。
LAUNCELOT   Nay, indeed, if you had your eyes, you might fail of the knowing me: it is a wise father that knows his own child. Well, old man, I will tell you news of your son. Give me your blessing. Truth will come to light, murder cannot be hid long, a man's son may, but at the length truth will out.

Uneasy lies the head that wears a crown.（*Henry IV*, Part 2, 3.1.31）戴王冠的头不自在；王者无安宁。

Unsex me here.（*Macbeth*, 1.5.39）解除我的女性的柔弱。
LADY MACBETH   The raven himself is hoarse
  That croaks the fatal entrance of Duncan
  Under my battlements. Come, you spirits
  That tend on mortal thoughts, unsex me here,
  And fill me from the crown to the toe top-full
  Of direst cruelty!

What a piece of work is a man!（*Hamlet*, 2.2.284）人是一件了不起的杰作。
HAMLET
  What a piece of work is a man! How noble in reason! How infinite in faculty, In form and moving how express and admirable, in action how like an angel, in apprehension how like a god! The beauty of the world, the paragon of animals!

What fools these mortals be!（*A Midsummer Night's Dream*, 3.2.115）人真是蠢得不行。
PUCK   Lord, what fools these mortals be!

What's past is prologue.（*The Tempest*. 2.1.255）过去的一切都只是开场。

What's done is done.（*Macbeth*, 3.2.14）事情干了就算了。

When shall we three meet again?（*Macbeth*, 1.1.1）何时我仨再相遇?

When sorrows come, they come not single spies, but in battalions.（*Hamlet*, 4.4.73-74）祸不单行。
CLAUDIUS
  O, this is the poison of deep grief: it springs
  All from her father's death. O Gertrude, Gertrude,
  When sorrows come, they come not single spies
  But in battalions.

Wild goose chase (*Romeo and Juliet*, 2.3.54) 无望的探求。
ROMEO
 Switch and spurs, switch and spurs; or I'll cry a match.
MERCUTIO
 Nay, if thy wits run the wild-goose chase, I are done, for thou hast
 more of the wild-goose in one of thy wits than I am sure I have in my whole five.
E. g. The police were sent on a wild goose chase after the suspect who was as slippery as an eel.

While you live, tell truth and shame the Devil! (*Henry* IV, *Part* I, 3.1.58) 人活着要说实话, 鬼都会无地自容。
HOTSPUR
 And I can teach thee, cousin, to shame the devil
 By telling truth: tell truth and shame the devil.
 If thou have power to raise him, bring him hither,
 And I'll be sworn I have power to shame him hence.
 O, while you live, tell truth and shame the devil!
E. g. To keep your conscience, tell her the truth and shame the devil.

Who wooed in haste, and means to wed at leisure. (The *Taming of the Shrew*, 3.2.11) 草率结婚, 后悔莫及。
KATHARINA
 No shame but mine: I must, forsooth be forced
 To give my hand opposed against my heart
 Unto a mad-brain rudes by full of spleen,
 Who wooed in haste and means to wed at leisure.

With bated breath (*The Merchant of Venice*, 1.3.115) 屏息静气。
E. g. The football fans waited for the result of the penalty shoot-outs with bated breath.

Woe is me. (*Henry* VI, *Part* 2, 3.2.73) 我真伤心, 我真不幸。
KING HENRY VI Ah, woe is me for Gloucester, wretched man!
E. g. Woe is me! Everyone else has got the day off and I've got to work!